The Corporate Raider

by
D. Virtue

Any similarity to any person
living or dead is entirely coincidence.

Copyright © 1999 by D.Virtue

All rights reserved. No part of this book shall be reproduced or transmitted in any form or by any means, electronic, mechanical, magnetic, photographic including photocopying, recording or by any information storage and retrieval system, without prior written permission of the publisher. No patent liability is assumed with respect to the use of the information contained herein. Although every precaution has been taken in the preparation of this book, the publisher and author assume no responsibility for errors or omissions. Neither is any liability assumed for damages resulting from the use of the information contained herein.

This is a work of fiction. Names, characters, places, and incidents either are the product of the author's imagination or are used fictitiously. Any resemblance to actual events or locales or persons, living or dead, is entirely coincidental.

ISBN 0-7414-02328-6

Published by:

Infinity Publishing.com
519 West Lancaster Avenue
Haverford, PA 19041-1413
Info@buybooksontheweb.com
www.buybooksontheweb.com
Toll-free (877) BUY BOOK
Local Phone (610) 520-2500
Fax (610) 519-0261

Printed in the United States of America

Printed on Recycled Paper

Published November-2000

I would like to thank many people for their encouragement of me in writing this story. First God for giving me the gift, and my family and friends for their love. Thanks to Linda and Kathy (Lynka) for posting my stories in the first place. Also thank you to the fans of D. Virtue for all of the e-mail praising my writing, they were motivators. I must also say thank you to two women for their input and loving critiques that helped the story come out as well as it did. Thank you to Jennifer Mamula for her valuable feedback, and also thanks to Agatha Tutko for her feedback and honest observations. This story has come together beautifully as a result of those inputs.

A special thanks to a special woman for the inspiration that I received from her, thank you to "M" my friend, for her love and encouragement. It really meant a lot to me. Also a special thank you from me--BBS, to my dear friend "C".

Special Acknowledgement:
Thank you to the creators of Xena, for creating a wonderful character of a woman with strength and courage. Also, an appreciation to Lucy herself for showing it's possible to remain humble, despite one's success.

CHAPTER 1

"Salina what are you doing?" An amused sounding woman's voice asked of the 5'9", athletically built, and moderately attractive brunette. Salina's brown eyes always seem to be watching her boss, even now as she was bending over her bosses desk, pretending she was just reaching for a pen, when in fact, she was providing a not to subtle view down her blouse, just in case her 6ft tall, raven-haired, boss with the clear blue eyes which seem to sparkle like sapphires when leveled on her or anyone, was interested.

"Excuse me ma'am?" She asked innocently.

"Nothing, finish what you're doing and get me the reports for my meeting today." The amused woman's hand reached to pick up her cup and take a sip of the herbal-flavored tea.

"Yes Ma'am," The younger woman said, grinning to herself at the thought of having been successful in her attempt at catching the woman's attention.

Alex, however, thought the young woman was just being obvious. She knew Salina wanted to get a recommendation from her to get into the Junior Executive Program, a program that Alex had setup with one of the local universities, to train already employed personnel who showed interest and talent in the duties of an executive. While working as an Administrative assistant. Once the nominee was near finishing the 2 year training, which would give them their undergraduate degree in business management, yet special attention was also paid to what the Chief Executive Officer of Madison Inc. wanted and needed from each nominee in order for them to actually function in the high standards, fast-paced environment that was part of Madison Inc., a Progressive Technology Company. To graduate with their undergraduate degrees, they would have to make a presentation based on an imaginary project, to one of the actual Executives of Madison Inc. If they were successful in impressing the Executive, they would be given their final grade and once they graduated, they would immediately begin an orientation into their new duties and responsibilities. However, Salina didn't seem to realize she first had to have at least an associate's degree or five years of work experience as an Admin.

Salina had come to work for Alexandra Madison about 2 years ago after Alex had reprimanded and demoted her last Administrative assistant for misplacing an important acquisition report. This mistake led to Alex, the CEO of the company, having to forgo a takeover, which let one of the rival companies get their hands on it. She had lost millions as a result of that. The ex-Admin couldn't find any of the backup files and Alex blew her top at the incompetence. The ex-Admin swore she had at least one of the file stored in her computer, but when she went in to locate it, she could not find any trace of it. The file somehow just disappeared. That was the sixth Admin that the CEO had gone through in one year. It was at that time that Salina was referred to her by a senior VP in her company. Alex had her suspicions as to how the girl had made it up to an Admin Assistant so fast, but she didn't realize at the time just how few scruples Salina had when it came to getting exactly what she wanted.

Salina had done many things to let Alex know that she was willing to do whatever was necessary to achieve her goal. She had already slept her way up through her previous bosses, she had discreetly watched other Admins enter their codes, and then she would use those Admins codes to sabotage important files, and she would do it to those files that the Admins would talk about when they all gathered for lunch, and specified how important they were. Salina didn't care what she had to do or what it entailed. Alex, however, had no interest in the young woman. She found some things that Salina did amusing such as the flirting and quick peeks at different parts of her body, whether it was bending over the desk allowing a view down her blouse, or the bending over just enough to show the French-cut panties she was wearing. The clients also found the peek-a-boo shows entertaining. This was a good distraction for some of the businessmen and women Alex dealt with, especially if they happened to belong to a company Alex was thinking about taking over. Alex also saw how territorial the young woman was when it came to others catching her eye. It didn't matter to Salina whether they were male or female. She would do whatever was necessary to ensure that whoever it was did not last long around Alexandra. There had been an incident where Alex was having lunch with a young man whom Salina knew wanted Alex, and it seemed as though Alex had some interest in the man. Salina waited until they had left the office and she grabbed her purse and went to the parking garage and located the man's car. It was a very hot day and when Salina saw that the window was down, and sitting in the direct line of the sunlight, she used a mirror in her purse to cause a small spark to ignite a stack of scattered papers within the car. She then left the area and, fortunately for her, she knew the car would not be in the line of the camera's. A few minutes later, someone came running into the building and told the security to call the fire department because a car with personalized tags that said "Made it" on it, was on fire. Then Security looked up the tag in their files and saw whom the car belonged to, then located the man and told him what had happened with his new car. Alex found out that the fire had started because of carelessness. When she heard the details, she decided that was the end of lunches with the young man.

Salina continued to do things to people that she new would make them look foolish or incompetent in Alex's eyes. The younger woman assumed that Alex did not know about some of her activities. Alex had once reprimanded a man so cruelly, and then demoted him and cut his pay that he broke down. He begun drinking and one day while he was inebriated, he walked out of the bar he had gone to everyday, and just kept walking, right into a busy intersection, where he was struck and killed by an oncoming delivery truck. The police later discovered a suicide note that showed that the man was distraught over having lost his position, and he had nothing left since losing his wife a month before the demotion. The note even stated the date the man would die, which happen to be the same day he was hit and killed. That was the first time someone had killed himself, and, as a result of that incident, everyone was even more intimidated by Alex, especially in meetings.

During one of Alex's weekly Friday meetings, Alex was in her usual form.

"So, Mr. Dosman," A Vice President in Azur Industries. One of the premier International companies, that dealt in trade and development, both nationally as well as internationally. "What do you want to do? You can either be put out to pasture with the rest of your fellow executives, or you can stay and keep your position in MY new company."

"I...," The sandy-blond, muscularly built man started to answer as he looked around at the other 15 executives who were now out of a job, due to the takeover by Alex's powerful conglomerate. "I'd like to stay on."

"Very good, you've made the right choice. Ladies and gentlemen, this meeting is now over. I wish you all well in whatever your new endeavors are, but be warned...I'm always looking, so if any of you decide to start your own company, well...just know I'll come to the party. Mr. Dosman, you will remain. The rest of you...are no longer needed, so...you're excused." Alex stated dryly, then taking a sip of her water, she waited for all of the ex-executives to filter out.

After they all left the room, she turned her attention to the man at the other end of the long table.

"Charles...a superb job as always. Here's to my secret agent weapon," Alex purred, as she raised her glass in toast to the man.

"Well, with what you pay me, I have no problems with going through a little surgery to achieve such prize acquisitions. I mean LOOK AT THIS??!! You are now the CEO of one of the premier Fortune Five Hundred companies that deals in international and national trade and development. Do you realize all the companies that have tried, and failed to acquire this company? Bravo... Alex!" Charles saluted back, with a raise of his own glass.

"So, how goes it with the others? When can I close on them?"

"There are 70 more of the 500 top companies that have your agents either in place, or will be completing their assignments within the next two years. I think you should continue what you've been doing. Let them get settled in their positions comfortably enough to learn the company's inner workings thoroughly. Then, do what you do so well."

"Alright, I'll wait for a while, but not too long. You know I have no patience. Anyway, you take your usual vacation after you get our executives up to speed on my new company."

"Alright. Then I'll return to introduce the new me to you" The agent was referring to one of the unique things he and the other agents did for Alex to which they were paid handsomely for, it involved them undergoing plastic surgery to change their appearances so that they could go from company to company and not have to worry about being recognized by some ex-employee of one of the companies they helped takeover by the filtering of information to Alex. "Then I'll be off to start on the next job. What do you think this time? Thick brows, maybe dark, with matching hair color, fuller lips, slightly broader nose, cheek implants? What?"

"Whatever you do, make sure it compliments you. Remember that the C.E.O. of the company you're hired into will have to be attracted to you in someway, it will determine how effective you are within the company.

"I hear you Alex...I hear you. As long as the C.E.O. is a woman."

"Good. Well, I hear the others coming, so I will leave you to fill them in on everything about the company, and then I'll see you in a few years. Here's your bonus. Take care of yourself, Dosman," Alex said, laying a manila envelope on the table where she was sitting.

"Thank you Alex, I will."

Alexandra stood and strode out the door just as her senior executives arrived to be brought up to speed on the new acquisition. Dosman rose, and walked to the other end of the table pick up the envelope, then walked back to where he had been sitting.

Alex gave a slight nod to one of the people arriving. Her name was Kiara and she was a tall, brown-skinned woman, who was striking in looks as well, she was a detective who had an agency of other detectives working for her under Alex's direction. Alex used this department to watch the resurfacing agents after they had completed their particular jobs with the taken over companies, but she was there as just a security person, at the moment, just to see what the agent looked like now, so she could put a tail on him when he left. That way Alex would know what he looked like after his surgery. She also used the detectives for other things.

Alex didn't trust anyone when it came to anything having to do with her companies.

"Yesss...Maurice," Alex purred into the phone talking to one of her many admirers, who was at work at the moment in one of the companies Alex had takeover years ago. He was the Chief Operating Officer of the company, only answerable to Alex. "It was a prize acquisition. But you know me. I plan on having as many of the national, as well as international companies under MY thumb. Dinner at Travia's, 8pm, don't be late."

Click!! Then a dial tone was all that was left for Maurice to listen to until he hung up the phone.

Alex was use to ordering people; she had no time or patience to ask.

"I want those requisitions on my desk in ten minutes Torrence! Or you can watch how quickly you fall down this ladder! Do I make myself clear?!" Her sapphire colored eyes appeared to flash along with the slightly bared white teeth.

"Ye.. ye...yes ma'am, right away." Torrence stammered and jumped out of the leather chair he was sitting in. He ran out the door of the conservatively, yet elegantly decorated boardroom, to go to his office and get the required information. He knew he was in for a reprimand for holding up the meeting, he just hoped he made it back in enough time to not cause Alex to get pissed more than she already was. He also hoped he still held his position as one of the senior VP's in the most powerful firm anywhere, but he wouldn't know until he made it back.

Alex held these board meetings every week, which meant that all of the members were overly stressed at least once a week. They never knew what to expect, and that's the way the CEO liked it. She found that she was able to run a tight ship, and everyone, despite their dislike of her, wanted to get in good with her, or stay in good with her. Those whom she was pleased with received wonderful incentives, those who displeased her would receive demotions and drastic cuts in their checks. The worse part was that no one could just up and quit. They had signed contracts that they were bonded by to see through. Several had tried to use legal action to break their contracts, but found the contracts were upheld. The contracts, in essence, said that any employee with over five years continuous employment could not, upon leaving the company, go to work for any competitor. Due to the magnitude and diversity of Alex's holdings, this basically covered a lot of different industries. This left the former executives with few options, and this didn't appeal to any of them, especially after years of training and numerous degrees as well as the pay they were receiving at the company. The thought kept most of the employees in line. The people had to stay for at least 10 years before they could leave, unless Alex said it was okay, which was rare. Alexandra Madison, was a no nonsense corporate raider and she knew the business inside and out.

"Jonson, go!" she commanded of the next man who was head of one of the medical divisions in one of her many holdings. He was relatively new to the company, he wore square-shaped glasses that did not flatter his face at all, and he was thin framed, almost to the point of appearing underweight. He was smart, yet seemed at times to not have any common sense. His department was relatively productive, but Alex wanted the division to elevate to a level of excellence, and she gauged that as being productive.

"Yes Ma'am. Well, the research that my division has done has come up with some excellent prospects for possible research, development, and improvement, that I'm sure you will be very impressed with," Jonson boasted.

"Is that right, Mr. Jonson, I'm going to be impressed? How about a little wager Jonson?" The woman said bating the man.

"What sort of wager ma'am?"

"If your idea..."impresses me," I believe was the word you used?"

"Yes."

"Well, if it is, and I'm impressed, you, Jonson, will receive a bonus."

"Thank you ma'am!" Jonson said all to quickly.

"Then you're willing to wager me, I take it?"

"Yes ma'am."

"Aww...Jonson???" Came the groans from his peers, as they made various gestures and sounds indicating their disbelief in what he had just agreed to. They knew Alex, and they knew she loved to challenge people. Especially those she thought were too cocky. She was good at making people think one thing, when her intentions were just the opposite, and in this case, it was a simple matter of her not tolerating anyone making assumptions as to what she would like or dislike, and this was her way of making that point.

Jonson looked around at the shaking heads and then back at the predatory glint in Alexandra's eyes.

"Wh...what happens if it's not ma'am?" Jonson finally thought to ask.

"Then you, dear man, will take a pay cut of fifty percent until you DO impress me."

"Ma'am?! But, I have a mortgage, kids. How will I pay my bills?!?" Jonson whined.

Alex flashed a bright smile that did not reach her eyes, and said in a matter-of-fact tone, "Impress me, it's that simple. Now Go." Those words now had the man shaking as he looked around at his peers. They were trying to remain as invisible as possible now until it was their turn.

"Well..." Jonson started again. When he finished, he left the boardroom a broken man.

The meeting went on for what seemed like forever, with one after the other being taken down a notch or two. When the meeting finally ended, Alex strode out of the boardroom and headed to her office. Along the way, staff members greeted her, although no one dared to look her in the eyes. There was something about those eyes that intimidated people. Alex's eyes alone were capable of cutting a person down just by the intensity of them. Not to mention that the woman was considered by PR Jet, one of the premier magazines in the country, as one of the "Most Beautiful People in the World." She had been on every magazine that was known, nationally and internationally, with the exception of those that dealt in the business for the purpose of titillating people. She was firm in that way. Despite her having a beautiful body, she did not show it casually. She was a very passionate woman in many ways and in many things. She knew how to keep people guessing, despite her face appearing everywhere. People had to respect her savvy, despite her ferocious appetite to have it all.

Alex did not speak to anyone as she walked down the carpeted hallways. The walls were decorated with paintings from all over the world, but having seen them many times before, she just looked straight ahead as she went to her next destination. It was another meeting with one of her vice presidents in charge of one of her international companies. He was a bear in his own way, but a pussycat compared to Alex. He had only been with the company a year and a half, but during that time he had proven himself many times over. He was an extremely competent executive...at least he seemed so to Alex.

What she didn't realize was that he was getting some of his ideas from someone else. This person, Taylor Young, was a friend of his who had originally told him of the job opportunity at the company. She was not one to want to be in the spotlight, but she loved helping her friend succeed in the company. She didn't mind him taking the credit as she had no desire to be anywhere near the CEO of the company, in spite of her almost insatiable interest and fascination in Alexandra. Taylor was happy with her position in the company as an Admin Assist to one of her friend's subordinates. She was a nice boss who liked to teach the younger woman about the business. They had also become friends. Taylor would allow her to explain things to her, even though she was very intelligent and well versed in the way the company was run, as well as in business.

She spent many hours reading anything and everything that Alex had written. She spent long hours in the company library, after others had gone home, researching more about the woman and her companies and how she did business. Taylor had a knack for understanding the dynamics of the business world. She had gone to college and graduated with an Associates degree in business, but her knowledge base was that of someone who had nearly a decade, in the business community. The young woman went from one company to the next, trying to find one that she could learn from without being obvious, or having things given to her because she happened to be a friend of the owner.

This had been the case with her first job out of school. A friend of hers owned her own relatively successful company. It dealt in fashion and was known to be one of the places to go if you wanted to get the best, made by the best.

Her friend offered her a vice presidency on her first day at the company. She, of course, turned it down, and was somewhat offended by the offer. Taylor knew her skills didn't warrant such a position at that time and she thought it was unfair of her friend to offer it to her just because they were friends. The young woman knew there were others who had been loyal to the company long before she arrived and who were probably hoping for the position for themselves. It was because of this that she turned down the position and told her friend she couldn't work for her. The woman was shocked because she didn't understand why, even if she couldn't accept the one position, she could just work in any position she wanted within the company. Taylor explained that if she were to take any position in the company now, she would always feel that any raise or promotion she got was a result of their friendship and not necessarily because of knowledge or skills. That was the start of many moves, until she found the company she now worked for "Madison Inc". This was the company that she had told another of her friends about when he graduated with his masters in international and National Business Management and Technology. She had been working at the company for almost a year when she first told him about the position she saw opening as a result of one of the senior management having committed suicide. This was due to a wager that left him demoted to that of middle management. The loss of income and status was too much for the man to bear, so he took his own life.

It was that day that Taylor decided she didn't want to ever meet this "Raider" as they called her. She had never seen the woman in person in the nearly two years she'd been with the company. She knew exactly what Alex looked like from magazines at the grocery store, those in the library, and of course, on the covers of the books Alex wrote herself. The woman scared her as much as she scared everyone else. One day while Taylor was typing a letter for her boss, she heard a commotion outside of the door which sounded like people running.

"What's going on out there?" She wondered as she went to tell her boss of the commotion. Just in case it was an emergency, they could both get out if necessary.

"What is it?" the older woman asked hearing the commotion for herself now.

"There's something going on out in the hallway. I think we should check it out, just in case."

"You're right, let's go."

The two of them headed to the door and just as the older lady went to open it, a group of people ran inside and slammed the door shut.

"What's going on?!" Yasmeia Sains exclaimed, startled by the sudden appearance of people in her office, and their obvious excitement about something.

"It's Karlsen Evans, he's lost his mind. He has a knife, a big one, and he's heading up to the top floor to go and TALK with Ms. Madison." A woman shouted, as she peeked out the door along with everyone else.

"Okay, so why are you all running? It's only a knife, it's not like he has a gun." The older woman stated, perplexed by all of the people's behavior to one man with a knife.

"Well, we didn't know, and we didn't want to take a chance."

"Well someone has to warn Ms. Madison of what's happening." Taylor said, as she went to go and call the Admin Assistant to the CEO.

"Why?! " Came many voices from behind her.

"What do you mean why? He has a knife and he's going to try to use it against her." She said, as an obvious and accepted reason.

"No! We won't let you. If he takes that bitch out, then so be it. She deserves it, she is as cold as ice. The no heart witch! Let her get what's coming to her. She's been sticking it to everyone else, so now let her feel what it is like to have it STUCK to her!" One man shouted as the group raised their voices in agreement.

"Well you're not the one making the phone call, I am, so if you don't mind?!" Taylor said as she tried to remove his hand from her phone.

"Fine, I'll just go use another phone." She then turned to go use the phone in her boss's office, only to have the group split up and block her path.

"You're not going to warn her." The man said, as he crossed his arms over his broad chest and sat on the edge of the desk.

"You people can't be serious about this! You're talking about someone committing murder and you're not going to do anything about it, and what's worse is you would prevent anyone else from doing what is right? You know this is wrong!"

"Wrong or not, I won't lose a minute of sleep over it." Another woman said, as the rest followed with their own affirmations of comfort in what they were doing. Taylor looked at the people in amazement, then she turned concerned eyes to her boss.

"I agree with you. This is wrong, but what can we do?"

"Well, I don't know about the rest of you, but I will not allow my soul to be marked because of something that I know in my heart to be wrong. Two wrongs do not make a right and this is wrong, and I will not be a part of it. I'm leaving and going home." She said, as tears came to her light brown eyes.

The leader of the group studied her for a moment, and after judging her to be sincere, he allowed her to walk out the door of the office, but he sent one of the men to watch her. He watched her get on the elevator and he pushed the down button and then jumped off and watched it go down. Taylor wiped her eyes of her crocodile tears and with a wry grin, jumped off the elevator when the doors opened in the main lobby. She then ran to tell the guards what was happening. She then turned and ran up the stairwell past the floor she had just left and pushed the button to take the elevator to the top floor unbeknownst to those down below. The guards in the lobby had called the police who were on their way, along with an ambulance, just in case. Taylor thought it was a prudent thing to do. They then headed up in the elevator. She arrived on the top floor to see the same chaos, only this time she heard it as well.

"You're a wicked, cruel, bitch who doesn't deserve to breathe the same air as the rest of us!" The angry, 250 plus pound, unkempt man shouted at the strangely calm woman.

"Is that right, Evans? It seems to me that you're mad because I outsmarted you. You didn't seem to have a problem with me when I did others the way I did you. In fact, you laughed at them when they left the meeting, leaving only you and a few others in the boardroom with me. You even said how right I had been when I showed them their errors, so why is it any different now? Just because it's you? Did you think you were special to me or something? Is that it Evans?" Alex taunted, knowing she had the truth on her side.

Evans was still flushed from his anger and now embarrassment. Now his peers were looking at him as if he had the plague or something, especially those who had been in the meetings with him.

"You're lying! You're just trying to turn everyone's attention off of you."

The irate man screamed at the woman who had not moved from the edge of her desk as she rested her hands on her lap, just watching the man brandishing the large knife.

"Am I? Jackson! Am I lying?" The Raider asked one of the men who had heard Evans's comments, without ever taking her eyes off of the man, who stood just a short distances away from her.

Jackson was a Hispanic young man who was known for his honesty, he looked at the Raider, then at the man, and then said to Evans's chagrin,

"No, you're not Ma'am. It's true. Evans did agree with what you were doing in those meetings when others had been outwitted. Sorry man, but it's true." Jackson offered, as he then shook his head when he saw the satisfied gaze flash across the Raider's face.

Evans lost his bravado at that moment, and the group that had gathered now started shaking their heads in disgust. Just as everyone was about to turn away and head back to what they were doing, the Raider, who Evans figured had stopped worrying about him and his knife, as well charged her and lunged.

"DIE BITCH!!" Evans shouted as he charged at the woman, knife raised, ready to impale his target. But to his and everyone's surprise, the woman turned and caught hold of the man's descending arm and with a vice grip, she twisted it behind his back. She plucked the knife from his hand and threw him towards one of the wood paneled walls in her office. The man hit hard and was dazed, but he eventually got back to his feet, and once again went to charging the woman. Again, she caught him unexpectedly, this time with a solid punch to his jaw. The man fell bonelessly to the floor. He didn't move and there was a trickle of blood flowing from the corner of his mouth. The Raider then turned, picked up the knife, and threw it down to where it landed right next to the man's head, embedded in the floor on it's point. The crowd was awestruck by what they had just witnessed. The Raider had taken one of the biggest men in the company down as if he weighed only a few pounds, versus his massive size and weight of at least 250.

The police arrived and asked where the trouble was and Taylor, still flushed with excitement at what she had just witnessed, directed them towards the office.

"There, in there." The young girl pointed out, and one of the officers went to check things out, while the other stayed and began collecting information.

Finally he arrived at questioning Taylor, who now was standing in the middle of the room and The Raider in her office. The other officer and the paramedics had just taken the unconscious man down to the ambulance.

"So, do you work on this floor, and can you tell me what you saw?"

"I work on the 3rd floor, I...I heard a commotion in the hallway on my floor, and then, when my boss and I went to go and check it out, these people ran into our office to hide from Mr. Evans. They said he had a knife and didn't know if he had a gun or not, but they didn't want to be around if he did."

"What then?"

"We were told that he was on his way up here to kill The Raider. I mean The CEO... her." Taylor said, pointing towards the tall woman.

"And, what did you do?"

"I told them we had to warn her."

"And did you?"

"No."

"Why?"

"Because they wouldn't let me. They said she deserved to die and that they would not lose any sleep over her death. She's not very well liked, although everyone respects her abilities in running all of her companies." Taylor stated, as an aside.

"So how is it that you ended up here?"

"I pretended that I was overwhelmed and scared and I told them that I was going home, but instead I went to the main lobby and told the guards to call you guys. Then, I took the stairs to the fourth floor and caught the elevator up to this one, where I heard and saw Mr. Evans yelling at her."

"What was she doing all this time?"

"Sitting on the edge of her desk with her hands in her lap listening to him rant and rave about how unfair she had been with him."

"Did she say anything to him?"

"Yes. She asked him why was anything different just because he was now on the receiving end of a quick thinking mind? She pointed out to him that he didn't think it was so bad when it was happening to others. Then she went on to remind him of how he had laughed at some of the others who had been on the other end."

"Was it true?"

"Yes."

"How do you know?"

"Another employee said it was true."

"Then what happened?"

"That's when they, all started to turn and leave, and I noticed he had become even more enraged. The moment she turned her back to go and sit in her chair behind her desk, he charged her with the knife raised to stab her in the back."

"What happened then?"

"It was incredible. I have never seen anything like it! She caught his hand in mid-descent and stopped him in his tracks. Then, she whipped his arm behind his back, plucked the knife from his hands as if he had just handed it to her, and then THREW him up against that wall, and still she was calm. He finally made it back to his feet after a moment, and once again she had her back to him when he charged. This time her fist shot out like a flash of light and caught him square in the jaw and he just FELL...hard. Wham! He hit the floor. Man, what a sight. She was awesome. I don't think many men could do what she did, and not get a scratch on them." The young girl said, somewhat flushed with both excitement and the adrenaline that caused it. The police officers looked at each other and then at Taylor, who was now showing some embarrassment at her gushing. Little did she realize, she had an attentive ear locked on her every word and it's inflections. Despite the Raider appearing to show no obvious attention.

Taylor was told she could leave by the officer, and she turned to go, sparing a quick glance at the woman who was now talking to Salina, her admin assistant, about the next meeting.

"Wow." Was the final comment from Taylor as she walked out of the now nearly empty waiting area and went to catch the elevator to go back to the third floor.

The Raider heard the exclamation and a predatory smile came to her face. She found herself intrigued by the young girl who risked acceptance by her peers to come and warn her of the danger.

"Ms. Lacy! Call detective Kiara and transfer the call in here and close the door!" She ordered.

"Yes Ma'am, right away." The Administrative Assistant called back as she located and then dialed the number. When connected, she transferred the call to the Raider and then went and closed the office door, as she had been told.

"Detective Kiara, I want you to get over here NOW. Be here in 15 minutes!" The Raider commanded, then hung up the phone. Fourteen minutes later, the detective arrived at the office and was sent in immediately.

"You barely made it. Now, sit down. I have a job for you. There is a young girl who works here, that I want you to find out everything about. I want to know absolutely everything, including her medical and dental history. I want to know about her professional life, as well as personal, with emphasis on her personal life. I want information about any relationships she may be involved in. I want to know who her friends are, and whom her enemies are if there are any, which I don't believe she has any, but you never know. Have I made myself clear?"

"Yes Ma'am, but can you tell me why you want the information? I mean, is it because she has done something?"

"That's my business, yours is just to get the information to me. You have one month, thirty days from today to do so. If you fail, well, you know what that means, right?"

"Yes ma'am."

"Good, now go." Alex said, dismissing the detective without another word or glance.

"Ms. Lacy, get in here!"

The Admin Assistant and the detective crossed in passing and both rolled their eyes.

"What's her problem?" The detective asked.

"Never mind what my problem is, just go and do your job! Ms. Lacy NOW!"

"Yes Ma'am." They both replied and hurried to carry out their orders.

"So...what happened", Yasmeia Sains, Taylor's immediate supervisor, asked when she returned.

"It was awesome! The Raider took Evans down with a shot to the jaw. He fell like a sack of potatoes! It was amazing...she was amazing. Did anyone know she could do that?"

"She took HIM down?! Wow, that must have been something to see!"

"Yasmeia, it was! He charged at her, and before any of us knew it, he was lying unconscious on the floor with blood coming out of his mouth along with the loss of a few of his teeth. Man, she was incredible!" The young girl once again gushed.

"Okay, okay, I think you need to calm down." The woman chuckled and then led Taylor to her desk and sat her down. Yasmeia handed her a few documents so that she would have something to focus all her excessive energy on.

"Yes, you're right. It was just so exciting!"

"I know, I can see that...but you have to calm down. You're as flushed as a school girl."

"Hmmm...I guess I am. Okay, I'll get to work on these right now."

"Alright." Yasmeia then started to turn and head into her office, but something crossed her mind making her stop in the doorway and turn back around.

"Oh, you know that you will probably come to the Raider's attention now." Yasmeia said reflectively, as she then looked at her with both concern and amusement.

"What?! Really? You think she noticed me?" Taylor now asked, as she came to her feet to stand in front of her boss. She was unnerved by the very idea.

"I don't know about whether she noticed you or not, but you realize word will get back to her by rumor that you were trying to warn her."

"Then I have to make myself as invisible as possible. I would just die if she called me to her office." The girl said, now flustered by the thought. Taylor Young was a very shy 26-year-old who dressed conservatively and wore her hair in the fashion of a tight bun positioned in the back of her head. Her usual manner was reserved and quiet, shying away from any and all spotlights. But with all of the events of the day, she was behaving quite differently from her normal behavior and manner. It was for this reason that Yasmeia was concerned.

"Well, if you want, you can work from home for awhile. We can talk via conference calls, or I can fax the things I need for you to work on, or send a messenger to your house to bring you what I need, and send back anything that you have finished."

"Yes, I think that's a great idea. That's what I will do, I'll work from home for a while."

"Well, I didn't mean today. It's going to take some time for the rumors to make it up there...maybe."

"See, I was just about to agree with you until you said maybe. I think I would like to start working from home tomorrow."

"Okay, in that case, let me get some things together that I want you to start working on, then you can call or e-mail me and let me know how things are going."

"Alright, I'll get to work on these things right now, then I'll take lunch AWAY from the building." The girl emphasized.

"Hahahaha, okay." Yasmeia chuckled in amusement as she turned and this time she did go into her moderate sized, light colored office, which allowed the light that came through the windows to make the office appear brighter than it already was. She closed the door and made a few phone calls.

Meanwhile, the phone on Taylor's desk rung and she was startled as a result of it.

"He...hello, Ms. Sains office, Ms. Young speaking, may I help you?"

"Yes, this is Salina Lacy, the Admin Assistant to Ms. Madison...Hello? Hello?" The assistant called, due to having heard a sharp intake of breath and not knowing if something had happened to the person on the other end. " H.e.l.l.o...?" The assistant called, now exasperated.

"Hello? Hello? I'm sorry, I...anyway, what can I do for you?" Taylor finally managed to stammer out.

"The CEO would like to see...Hello? Hello?! Goodness." Again she heard the sharp intake of air and silence.

"What's the problem?!" Alex snapped, hearing the Admin repeatedly calling to the person on the other end.

"Oh, it's just that the assistant keeps gasping or something."

"Really? Well hurry up." The Raider ordered although her eyes showed some amused interest at the fact that she was the cause of the other assistant's loss of composure.

"Yes ma'am. Hello? Hello?"

"Yes, yes, I'm here. I'm sorry, I thought you were about to tell me that the CEO wanted to see someone from this office." Taylor said, completely rattled.

"If I answer you, you won't pass out, will you?"

"No, no, I'm fine." She said, as the phone shook like a leaf in her hands.

"Okay, the CEO wants to see...you okay?"

"Yes, yes, I'm fine, go on."

"Alright, she wants to see the reports from your department." The Admin said in a rush, only to hear not only the gasping sound again, but also the woman on the other end of the phone was now celebrating her relief about something that the other admin had no idea as to what it could be.

"What's going on?!" The Raider asked, as she strode over to take the phone from her assistant, who held it away from her ear due to the screaming.

"She's screaming." The assistant said, as the phone was yanked from her hand.

"Screaming about what?!"

"I don't know."

The Raider put the phone to her ear and listened.

"Thank you GOD! Thank You God! She doesn't want me! God I can hardly stand it!"

"What's going on?!" Yasmeia asked, as she rushed out of her office at the sound of the screams.

"Yasmeia, she doesn't want me! Goodness! Thank you Lord! Thank you Lord! Thank you Lord!"

"Who doesn't want you?!"

"The RAIDER!! She doesn't want me; she only wants the reports from the department! Yes! Yes! Yes! Whew!! She didn't notice me after all. Soon I'll be at home working, man!" Taylor finally gasped, as she finally sat heavily in the chair, having completely forgotten the phone, which was now hanging down the side of the desk, and she was almost out of breath.

"Excuse me, but is there someone still on the phone?!" Yasmeia asked, as she glanced down at the phone to make her point.

"Oh my God, I completely forgot about it. You think she's still there?"

"I don't know, but I think you should check, don't you?"

"Yes, of course, I'm a professional. I'm just so relieved she doesn't know I'm alive."

She sighed, as she reached down and picked up the phone. "He...hello? Hello?"

"Hello. It's about time you picked up the phone." Came a smooth voice from the other end that was different sounding than the previous voice that the girl had been speaking with.

"Excuse me, but who am I speaking with?"

"The Raider." Came the simple, yet sarcastic answer.

"Haa...Ohhhh...My...God...excuse me, I'm going to be sick!" Taylor said, gagging as she nearly threw the phone to Yasmeia, covering her mouth, at the same time as she ran out the office down the hall to the restroom where she proceeded to get sick.

Meanwhile, Yasmeia brought the phone to her ear and with a smile both amused and perplexed lighting her face, she spoke to the person on the other end.

"Hello, this is Yasmeia Sains, who am I speaking with?"

"Alexandra, Yasmeia. Who is that young girl, and where did she learn her phone matters?"

"Oh, ma'am, I didn't realize it was you."

"Obviously. Is your assistant always so unprofessional?"

"Oh, ma'am please don't judge her by her actions at this moment. My assistant is actually a very professional person, she's just a little shaken at the moment. She's been my right hand in this department and she's very smart. I just think you shook her up with being on the phone and possibly overhearing her a moment ago."

"Really, she didn't sound very smart."

"Oh, but she is."

"How smart is she Yasmeia?"

"Well...for instance, she did these particular reports with no help from me. She doesn't know that I know this, but V.P Shearer in Acquisitions comes to her for all kinds of advice and assistance because she knows the business. She's just a very shy person. Please ma'am, don't punish her for this one loss of composure. She's really a very sweet, young girl and an excellent employee. Besides, I'm sure you'll hear about it sooner or later, but she risked herself to come and warn you about Evans. By the way, bravo on laying him out with one punch. She couldn't stop talking about that."

"Is that right?" Alex now asked, intrigued by the girl's reaction to her.

"Yes Ma'am."

"How old is she?" The woman asked. At the same moment, her own Admin's ears perked up and she began to listen to the rest of the conversation discreetly.

"Twenty six."

"Are you and she close?"

"I'd like to think so ma'am, why?"

"Never mind why. I'll let it go this time, but I expect you to tell her to get her act together, and I mean ASAP! Also, have those reports sent to my office within the next ten minutes."

"Yes Ma'am."

"Oh, and a couple of other things, she is not to work from home, and I want HER to personally deliver the reports to me. In fact, from now on I expect her to deliver any and all correspondence from your office directly into my hands personally."

"But Ma'am...?"

Click!!

The phone hung up, and Yasmeia stood listening to the dial tone for a few moments, feeling like she had just been shell shocked. Just then, Taylor walked into the office, wiping her mouth with a paper towel, then stopping by the water dispenser. She poured herself a cupful and drank it down, then filled her cup again, this time she carried it towards her desk.

"I can't believe that the Raider was on the phone and heard me screaming that I was glad I still hadn't come to her attention. I can't believe I dropped that phone on her. She had to be pissed. Are you still talking to her?"

"Oh, no, she hung up." Yasmeia answered, now remembering that she was still holding the phone. She placed it back on the holder, then turned to look back at Taylor.

"So what's my punishment? I've been demoted? Docked? Written up? Suspended...I hope." She added.

Yasmeia had not answered any of her questions as of yet, and finally after a few minutes Taylor noticed.

"Yasmeia? What is it? Oh...she fired me?!! Oh my god, out of all people to drop the phone on, gods, I can be so...."

"No, no, she didn't fire you, or anything like that. In fact, she's not even punishing you for it, although she did say for you to get your act together, she added ASAP, which were her exact words." Yasmeia informed the young, panicked girl, hoping it would calm her.

"Oh, thank goodness! I have to go to church and give thanks. Whew! So...why are you looking at me like that?"

"Like what?"

"Like you have something to say, but you're not sure as to how to say it."

"Oh, I was just thinking about a movie I saw."

"Oh, what?"

"Oh, it was about some prisoner taking her last walk before being executed, or something like that." Yasmeia added as a result of seeing the perplexed look in Taylor's eyes.

"Oh, I didn't see that one, but I heard about it. It sounded like a good movie, but what does that have to do with anything?"

"Just a moment, I have to get something." Yasmeia then turned and went to her desk and pulled out the reports that the Raider had asked for.

"Here."

"What? Oh, you want me to send for the runner to take them to the Raider? Okay, no problem. I'm just relieved it's not me. Man, I don't envy anyone who has to go to her office for any reason, raise or otherwise." Taylor stated as she went to dial the number for the runner.

"No, don't call a runner. She wants you to deliver them to her within the next..." Yasmeia looked down at her wristwatch and saw how much time was left, then she continued. "Four minutes, to her hands, she also wants you to deliver any and all correspondence from this office to hers, to her hands personally, not to her Admin. Dead Woman walking." Yasmeia finished and then she flinched at the reaction she thought she was going to get from the young girl. Instead, Taylor had a blank expression on her face and her mouth was agape while she still held the phone.

Yasmeia took the phone, hung it up, then turned the young girl, who had not said a word, and guided her to the elevator where she pushed the up button, and then once it had arrived, she put Taylor in the elevator and turned her around, then pushed the express button to the top floor. She jumped off and watched the girl as she started to come out of her shock just as the doors were closing.

The next sound Yasmeia heard were those of Taylor screaming to be let out, and that she couldn't go there and for Yasmeia to help her. She began pushing all of the buttons in the elevator hoping to stop the ascent to the top, but it stopped for a moment, and then after a minute it restarted. Once the express button was pressed, it overrode all of the others, except the stop, but even that one was temporary. Therefore, she was on her way to the top, whether she wanted to be or not.

"It'll be alright, just take her the reports and leave!" Yasmeia called up to her.

While the elevator was going up, Taylor paced inside, and then she leaned heavily against the wall of the elevator and covered her face with her hands as she tried to soothe herself.

"It's okay, I can do this, I can do this. All I have to do is just walk out of this elevator, into the office, hand the reports to the Admin and turn around and leave. Yes, I can do that. Okay, okay, just breathe, she thought to herself.

By the time the elevator made it to the top floor, Taylor was a bit calmer. She took a few quick breaths, and tried to calm herself more. She knew her face was flushed, but hoped her skin tone would not allow it show. But she couldn't do anything about it if it did, but at least she could straighten herself up.

Little did she know, she was being watched the whole time. With every push of the express button, a camera activated inside, so that The Raider could see who was coming to the top floor. That was how she knew about Evans before he arrived.

No one knew about the camera except for the installers who put it in when the building was initially being built. All of the Raider's companies had the feature, and only she and the builders knew about it.

Alex watched the young girl the whole time she was in the elevator, hysterical at having to come and see her in person, especially when all she wanted was to remain invisible to Alex. Now she was killing any hope of Taylor's to remain anonymous.

She watched the girl straighten her clothes, then her hair, which was pulled back into a bun, which Alex thought did nothing for the young woman's looks.

The doors finally opened, and the girl clasped the reports to her body, against her chest, and went rigid, waiting for the door to open fully before she moved.

"Okay, you can do this, SHOOT! I have no choice!" She argued with herself, as she came out of the elevator and walked the long track to the open door of the outer office, then walked to the desk of the Raider's Admin.

The Admin saw her coming and just waited for her, and The Raider also saw her coming, although it wasn't obvious, considering she was reprimanding someone from her Projects development department. Taylor made it to the desk. Her eyes locked on the office behind the Admin and everything that was going on within the office. The Raider pounded her fist on the desk and the man startled and the young girl watching flinched. Alex was now pointing an angry finger at the man, as she sat sideways in her large chair, looking sideways at the flushed man, who was now gripping his own chair hard, as he vigorously nodded his head, obviously expressing his understanding of what he had just been told. At least that's what she reasoned was going on until Salina's voice cut through her line of thought.

"May I help you?!" The woman asked irritated. Obviously she had been calling to her for a few moments, but because she was so intrigued with what was going on in the office, Taylor did not hear her.

"Oh, I'm sorry. I'm from Ms. Sains office. I came to bring the CEO these reports."

"Ohhh...you're that one? Hahahahaha, well, you certainly made an impression on The Raider." The woman said dubiously. "Have a seat, I will let her know you're here. Have you read those reports?"

"Yes."

"Oh, well good. She sometimes likes to test the Admins'." Salina said, somewhat disappointed that the young girl had read the reports. She was hoping she hadn't, and therefore, if the woman gave one of her impromptu tests, then the girl would be embarrassed.

"Tests?"

"Yes, but not like school or anything, hers have a way of making even the most practical efficient person breakdown and cry."

"I thought all I was here to do was bring these to her and leave them with you to give to her. I thought the presentations were done by the department heads, not the Admins."

"They're done by whomever she chooses for them to be done by. And she specifically wants you to hand them to her. Have a seat and I'll let her know you're here."

Taylor gave a slight nod of her head, again in shock. She then went and sat in one of the many brown leather chairs that lined the outer office wall around the room. Her nerves were now raw, as she thought about what would happen to her when she went into that office to give the supposedly benign reports.

"Why did I come up here in the first place?!" She scolded herself for coming to the attention of the Raider. But she knew the answer to that question, she knew she would probably, no, definitely do it again. To her, all life was precious, even a tough as nails person like The Raider. "My luck, I have to have morals." She finally said in disgust.

"Hey?!"

"Yes?! Yes?! I'm sorry." Taylor said, as she jumped to her feet.

"Do you always daydream?"

"No. I mean, not normally. I'm just very nervous right now."

"Hmm...well, you had better pay attention in there, otherwise she'll eat you alive and spit your bones out and use them as toothpicks."

"I will."

"GET IN HERE!! I DON'T HAVE ALL DAY!!" The Raider shouted out to the young girl.

"GOODNESS! She sounds pissed!"

"She is, but it's not when she yells that you should be worried, but it's when her voice lowers and it takes on that calm tone that belies her true feelings, but she'll only get worse if you don't get in there right now."

"Oh, yes, okay, I'm going." She said, now flushed in her cheeks once again from the fear racing through her.

"Good luck." Salina said as she closed the door behind the young girl, and A conspirator's glint lit her eyes.

"Well?" The Raider asked as she held out her hand.

Taylor's brows knitted as she tried to break the hypnotic trance the woman seemed to have captured her with. The Raider's eyes glanced down at the report in her hands that were being crushed against her breast, while at the same time her fingers were blanching, due to the grip she had on it.

"OH! God yes, the reports, here you go ma'am." She said, snapping out of the trance and quickly handing the reports to the outstretched hand that now receded back, along with the reports.

She stood where she was, shifting nervously from foot to foot as if she was too restless to stand still. The Raider pulled out the reports and read over all of them, taking her time, as if she were alone in the office.

"Maybe I..."

Alex looked over her brows at the girl and then raising one, she cocked her head and said in an unnerving tone of voice.

"Did I ask you a question?"

"Nn...nnn...no ma'am." Taylor stammered out.

"I didn't think so." The woman said, as she narrowed her gaze, and then went back to reading the reports.

Taylor now stood shaking as her hands were nervously playing with the material of her dress.

"Stop doing that!" The Raider chided, annoyed by the fidgeting.

The hands instantly stopped all movement, although Taylor was now shaking like a leaf. She felt like crying, but then she thought that would only make herself look foolish. Especially considering The Raider had not done anything to her, except to call her on her manners and tell her to stop doing something she had been trying to break herself of for a while now anyway. But she was also feeling nauseated.

"Who wrote these?"

"I...I did ma'am." The girl answered all too quickly, but then realized that she had now given herself away.

"Do you always stutter?"

"Nn...no, I mean, not usually, except for when I'm really nervous."

"What are you nervous about?" Alex asked, although she knew exactly why she was so nervous. Everyone who walked in to her office was nervous, and most of them were regulars. That's what made it worse for the young girl. She hadn't wanted to come to the Raider's attention, yet here she was, standing before the very person she had been whooping it up about not having to be the one that was called for earlier.

"I...I..." Taylor tried, but once again the Raider had her gaze leveled on her.

Alex's eyes narrowed when she saw the moisture coming to the girl's eyes, despite her valiant efforts.

"Sit down."

"Oh, thank you." Taylor gasped as she immediately sat down on her hands to prevent them from annoying Alex. The gesture didn't go unnoticed by the woman.

"Well that's one way." She said, with less sternness in her voice.

"So...how is it that someone on the third floor, working as an Admin, can write such a thorough report by herself?"

"Oh, I had lots and lots of help. As a matter of fact, I pretty much just wrote what others had suggested. I barely had anything to do with that." Taylor blurted, hoping that she could convince the Raider that she was not worth a second thought.

Alex put the reports down on the desk and turning her chair, she came to her feet as gracefully as a cat. She walked around the large, polished cherry wood desk and sat on the edge of it, crossing her arms over her chest as she glared at Taylor. The girl swallowed hard as her heart nearly beat out of her chest. She lowered her eyes as she slightly rocked forward and back on her hands, trying to steady herself against the rising apprehension that was rising rapidly within her.

"Look at me." The voice said calmly.

Taylor's eyes lifted up to meet those of The Raider and once again, the sapphires held her captive until the woman decided to release her.

"The one thing that I will not tolerate is a liar. I can handle a cheater and a thief, but I have absolutely NO patience for a liar. Get out of my office." She commanded. The Raider's gaze broke and Taylor felt as though she had been stabbed in the heart.

"I..."

"Did I say anything else to you?"

"Nn...no ma'am!"

"Then I suggest you get out. NOW!"

"Yes Ma'am." She startled, as she jumped out of the chair and practically ran for the door.

She stopped just as she was about to open it. Taylor didn't want the Raider to think of her as a liar. That was worse than being recognized unwillingly and she wanted to apologize. She started to turn around, but when her eyes fell on the disgusted look on the woman's face, she swallowed hard and began to chew her lips. She turned back around and ran out the door and out the area of the office. She pushed the down button and impatiently stood counting the numbers as she tried to stay her tears from falling, but it was taking too long and it was unnerving to her, especially considering that The Raider watched her while still sitting on her desk.

Taylor nervously shifted from foot to foot, and then, not being able to take it any longer, decided to take the stairs back to her floor. She turned and ran for the stairwell and then ran down them. She ran all the way until she was back on her floor where she flew out the stairwell door and ran breathlessly back to her own office area, straight to her desk where she fell into the chair and buried her head in her arms and cried.

Yasmeia, her boss, was on the phone and had just hung up, when she saw Taylor come back into the office. She walked out to the desk and for a moment she just stood debating whether to tell the young girl what the Raider had just told her.

"I'm sorry, it must have been awful for you, especially considering how you had tried to help her. But I have to tell you this, she just called down and told me that you were to report to the mailroom for your new job. She said that she's going to let you keep the pay you earn from this position, but from now on you will report to work in the mailroom starting tomorrow. I tried to talk her out of it, but she was very angry. She said she has NO patience for a liar. What happened?" Yasmeia asked, as she caressed the sobbing woman's hair. Confused by how her Admin and friend was being labeled a liar.

Taylor raised her head slightly and let her mind go back to that moment as she told her friend what happened.

"She asked me if I wrote the reports and I told her I did."

"Okay, that wasn't a lie, you did write them, all by yourself." The woman said, sure that there was no lie to be found within that statement.

"That's just it, I told her I had lots of help on it and I barely did anything. That's when she told me to get out of her office. I saw the disgust in her eyes for me. She thinks I'm a liar. That's worse than trying to stay obscure." The girl lamented.

"Well, look at it this way, at least you can slide back into obscurity from her gaze." Yasmeia said, trying to find a positive.

"It's not the same! Now she knows me, and she knows me as a liar. How can I ever live this down? My Boss sees me as a liar. I can't stay here; it's too much. My desire to remain unseen now has me shining as brightly as a neon light on a darkened street. It's just blinking "Liar, Liar, Liar", Gods!" She exclaimed, and then buried her head in her arms once again.

"You don't have to leave. You can get past this."

"No. If it was anyone else then yes, I would try, but how can I get past this? She's the boss! I blew this. All I wanted to do was just work and grow quietly within the company, now I'll be known as the liar of the company. I'm going to lunch and then after this day is over with, I'm putting in my resignation."

"You don't have to do that, besides, who will help me with things.

And what about Shearer, what is he going to do?"

"I know you're trying to make me feel better, but I just want to go and sit some place where I can think about why I did what I did. Besides, it's not like I'm leaving your lives, I'm just going to leave the company, and we're still friends. I'll see you in a little while."

"Alright. You want me to go with you?"

"No, I'll be fine." Taylor then stood up and hugged her friend and boss, then walked out of the office and went to the elevator to go down to the restaurant to eat, or rather to see if she could eat something.

While she was waiting for the elevator she thought about what she was going to do after she quit the job. The elevator came and there were a few people on from some of the above floors, but she stepped in and didn't speak to any of them.

"Aren't you the woman who was talking to the police about your intentions to warn The Raider?"

She simply nodded her head, but before the person could ask her another question, the elevator doors opened and she quickly walked out and down the corridor and went into the restaurant.

It was quite a restaurant, made for entertaining clients as well as for the employees. It was a top-notch restaurant. Alex had master chefs working in the kitchen so the food was always the best. Taylor was led to a table and a waitress came over within moments with a glass of water and asked if she could take the girl's order. She gave her order, and then the waitress asked her if there was anything else, just to make sure. The girl answered "no", and the waitress turned and left. After the waitress was gone, Taylor picked up her glass of water and sipped from it. She sat just looking blankly out towards the center of the restaurant, feeling down over what had happened just because of her desire to remain in the shadows. Her food soon arrived, it was just a Caesar salad, but there was no guarantee that it would be eaten. She picked at it for a few minutes and then went back to thinking how one little mistake had changed her life.

She was sitting just thinking, when a group of people's voices caught her attention.

"I think that if we can accumulate enough of Akiro's stocks, we have a chance to take it over. What do you think ma'am?"

"Do it!" Came the commanding, yet smooth voice of The Raider herself. Heading in the direction of the young girl.

"No, no, this cannot be happening. I can't seem to get away from her. Man!" She cursed to herself.

Just then the group stopped and then they went on, all except one of them. Taylor looked up and to her utter chagrin, it was the Raider standing at her table looking down at her with one brow raised. The girl lowered her eyes and shook her head slightly from side to side in disbelief at her unfortunate luck to once again be face to face with the woman. Alex pulled out a chair and sat down. The girl was now flushed with embarrassment, and she couldn't bring herself to look at the woman, and once again, she felt on the verge of tears. Alex knew the girl was intimidated, and that's exactly what she wanted her to feel, that way she would learn not to ever lie to her again.

"May I get you anything Ma'am?" The same waitress asked.

"Yes, tea. Decaf."

"Yes ma'am."

The Raider then cut her eyes over at the young girl who was still trying to avoid eye contact with her.

"So...I'm told that you're quitting?" She said with a raised brow.

"Gods! She called YOU?!! Man, I can't win for losing."

"Is it true?"

"Yes."

"Hmmm...typical." The Raider said, with disgust in her voice.

"Excuse me?" Taylor managed to gasp out.

"I said typical. You're not only a liar, but you're a quitter. What? What is it? Are you too good to work in the mailroom after working as an Admin? Or is it just that you don't think it's worth the effort to regain my respect?"

"It's neither, it's just that..." Taylor said, trying to keep herself from tearing up, but she was failing. She knew this was probably going to be her only chance to make it right with The Raider, so she let the tears roll as they pleased, still determined to tell the woman how sorry she was. "It's just that I can't handle being looked upon as a liar by anyone, but especially by you."

"Then you shouldn't have lied to me."

"You're right! You're absolutely right, and I was so...wrong. I am so very sorry. But please... I promise you, if you give me another chance I will never lie to you again...about anything!" She said, in a contrite voice.

"Why should your apology mean anything to me? I mean, you are quitting. So quit!" The Raider said, as she started to stand up and leave.

Taylor caught the woman's hand and held her midway between standing and leaning.

"What?!" The Raider sneered, as she looked down at her hand that was covered by the young girl's hands.

"I won't quit. I'll work in the mailroom, or anywhere else you say, but please give me a chance? I do want to earn your respect. It means more to me than you realize." Taylor said, as her vision blurred from the tears that were filling her eyes.

Alex moved her hand slightly, and the young girl quickly removed her hand from over top of hers.

"Sorry." She apologized.

The Raider stood to her full height as she regarded the young girl who was staring up at her with remorseful eyes.

"Okay." She started, but paused for a moment when she heard the breath that Taylor let out suddenly.

Alex crossed her arms and with an assessing gaze she found herself thinking how pretty the girl actually was, despite the harsh bun and the simple clothes. "Alright, I'll give you a chance to earn my respect. You work in the mailroom part-time, and the other part you will continue assisting Ms. Sains in her department, until I say differently. Your duties in the mailroom will be for you to handle any and all of MY mail. You will deliver my mail directly to my hands, no one else's. You will clear my outbox of all mail to be sent out. I will leave notes for you on each item as to how it is to be sent. If you handle this without messing up, then I will return you to full time duty as Ms. Sains Admin. If I catch you in one lie, of any sort, then I will not only fire your little ass, but I will blackball you in this and every town from here to Japan, and the only job you'll ever have will be as a fisherman's assistant. Do I make myself PERFECTLY CLEAR?"

"Yes! I won't disappoint you. I promise."

"For some reason, I believe you. Tell me one more thing."

"Anything."

The woman smiled at the thought that flashed through her mind, and then shook herself out of it.

"Are you the one who's writing Shearer's reports for him?"

"Yes." Taylor answered without hesitation, for fear that to hesitate would cause the Raider to doubt her. She did not realize that Alex used the eyes to tell her if someone was lying to her, not necessarily their words.

"Hmmm...interesting, a little genius, hiding in the shadows."

The girl smiled a small, shy, smile at the dubious compliment.

"Enjoy your meal." Alex said, as she started to leave, but then she stopped and turned back, causing Taylor to sit up straight once again.

"Yes?"

"One other thing, I don't like the way you look, change it. Here...go and see this lady, she'll take care of you. I'll call her and tell her what I expect."

"But I..." She started to protest, but then stopped, due to the look she was receiving from Alex. "Okay."

"Good girl." The woman turned and strode out the door without a second glance.

Taylor, in the meantime, sat at the table now unsure about why The Raider had any concern about her looks, then she put it off to being that the woman just wanted her to look more professional. Although she thought she did already.

She returned to the office and Yasmeia was waiting for her, and called her into the office.

"I'm sorry, but I didn't want you to quit, you're so good at what you do, it would be a complete waste. I hope I didn't make things worse for you."

"It's okay Yasmeia, we worked it out."

"Really, so you don't have to go to the mail room to work?"

"No, I still have to work there, but I will only be there part-time, the other part I will be here working with you."

"That's good, right?"

"It was the best offer. Besides, all I will be doing in the mailroom will be delivering incoming and picking up outgoing mail only from her office and her desk. I'm to handle all of HER mail. She also asked me about Shearer. I hope he doesn't get in trouble with her."

"I hope not either. Anyway, is that all she wants you to do?"

"No."

"What else?"

"Let me ask you something. What do you think of the way I dress?"

"Um...well..." Yasmeia tried to answer, but only managed to stumbled over her words, as she did not want to hurt her friend's feelings.

"Oh, I see. Well, it's okay, I know I dress a little conservatively..."

"Like librarians of old." Yasmeia added, before she even knew the words were out of her mouth.

"Yasmeia! I don't think I look that antiquated. Do I?"

Yasmeia circled around Taylor giving her a once over, and then came back to stand in front of her.

"Yes...but...but it fits you, I mean you're just so..."

"Okay, I get it, I have to do something about the way I dress."

"You're not mad are you?"

"No. Besides, you're not the only one who thinks I look dowdy."

"Really?"

"Like it's a surprise? She didn't like the way I dress either."

"Hahahahaha, okay, well I'll leave that alone. Let's get back to work, okay?"

"Well that's fine, but I was sort of hoping I could leave a little early today so that I could go and check out the mail room and see what I will need to do come tomorrow. I like to be ahead on things, that way I'm not stumbling through my first day, but instead, look like a professional, especially going up there."

"Okay, I think that is a wonderful idea. Well then, I will see you sometime next week?"

"Well, I'm not sure, but I'll let you know. In the meantime, you might want to call personnel and have them send a temporary assistant for a few days. Just until I get used to the mail room thing."

"That's a great idea. So are you going to start work today?"

"No, I don't dare show up in her office before tomorrow!" Taylor exclaimed.

"Okay, you're right. She may not appreciate it."

"You're telling me! You know she had me begging her to give me another chance? I would never have thought to do that with anyone, but for some reason, I couldn't let her think of me as a liar or a quitter. Thanks for looking out for me."

"You're welcome. You're my friend, as well as my employee you know."

"And you're my friend. Well, I'm going to head out. I'll see you later Yasmeia."

"Alright, take care."

Taylor hugged Yasmeia and went out the door of the office. She got on the elevator and went down to the basement where the mail center was located. She went inside the uncommonly quiet and clean room, looking around to locate someone who could help her.

"Excuse me?"

"Oh, yes ma'am, may I help you?" The man asked, assuming she was from one of the management personnel.

"Hi, I'm here to get oriented to the mail room and my new duties."

"Oh, you're the girl who was demoted. Well, it's alright, we've all felt the icy hand of our supreme leader on our backs, but just do your job and you won't have any problems."

"Alright, just show me what to do and how to do it and I will."

"Okay, but you don't have to orient until tomorrow. You know that right?"

"Yes, but by tomorrow I plan on being a consummate professional when I make my first delivery and pickup." Taylor said with conviction.

"Well, if anyone can, it'll be you." The man said, assessing the woman's style of dress.

She sighed and then said, "Okay, let's get on with it."

By the end of the workday, she had perfected handling the mail, without getting cut by the paper. The head mail handler was impressed with her aptitude for picking things up so quickly. He let her handle Alex's mail that was to be sent to Italy to one of her companies over there. She quickly located the correct country code, placed the two day air express label on it, and then called for the driver to get it on it's way.

CHAPTER 2

When Taylor left the mailroom, rather than going to the library to read for a while like she usually did, she decided she wanted to go and see the lady that had been recommended to her by Alexandra Madison. She pulled into a large parking lot that had cameras in every lane. The lot was pretty much empty, except for a few cars, but looking at the building and seeing the people inside, she got out of her car.

It was a practical car for its uses. Taylor was not poor or anything, she was just not materialistic. She had some expensive things, but she didn't have a need to buy anything useless. She walked in the door of the building and saw the upscale beauty parlor and spa, but she didn't see any clothes in the area where she was, so she wondered what the woman was going to do for her, and then debated if she was even up for a change.

"Hello. May I help you?" A stylishly dressed woman asked the girl as she came and stood in front of her and regarded Taylor, who was now thoroughly embarrassed by the attention that was coming her way.

"Hello, I...I was told to come here and talk to a Mrs. Chambers, by Ms. Madison." Taylor said quietly, not wanting to draw anymore attention than she already had.

"Aha!! Yes, she did call about you. Wow, she said you had a style that needed to be updated. Come with me and we'll get started." The woman said, as she led Taylor into one of the private areas of the salon.

"Okay, let's see...how old are you? No, let me guess. Hmmm...by the way you're dressed, without looking at your face, I would say you were about 45. But looking at your face, and seeing no lines, and all of that innocence shining so brightly in your eyes, I would say you're about 26, 27 maybe?"

"Yes. Do my clothes really make me look that old?"

"Yes. But I'm going to make you look like a new woman."

The first thing she did was have Taylor take off all her clothes and put on a robe. The girl did as she was told, and after that, everything became a blur. The next morning Taylor woke up in her condominium. And after showering, she brought out the outfit that she had been given. She had wanted to pay for it, but the woman had told her it had already been taken care of.

Taylor dressed herself the way she had been dressed up yesterday. Then, rather than putting her hair in the bun she usually wore, she let it hang loosely over her shoulders and having naturally wavy hair that was thick and full, the cut that was done to it made it wave ever so gently. She then picked up a lipliner and lined her lips the way the woman had shown her. Then she used the lipstick. When she finished putting them on, she stepped back to look in the full mirrors of her closet doors.

"Wow!" She gasped at her reflection in the mirror. A young lady who now looked stylish and professional in her deep lavender colored, two piece, cocktail length, silk skirt suit. She regarded herself for a bit and then she realized something. "Sexy, wow, I actually look...sexy." Then she looked down at her cleavage showing and thought it was maybe a little too much. She went to her drawer and dug around in it until she came up with what she was looking for. Taylor put the silk scarf around her neck and then tucked it into the jacket of the outfit to thoroughly cover her exposed cleavage. "There. That works okay." She said to herself as she turned, and then picking up her purse, she headed out of the house. She got into her bronze colored Saab and headed off to work.

Taylor arrived a few hours before everyone was to head in to the office to start the day. She wanted to get a head start on her day, so she went straight to the mail center. After punching in, she went and picked up an apron of sorts to cover her clothing from any dust that may be present, although she didn't see any, but she wanted to be safe. She then went and located all of the CEO's mail. She quickly sorted it, putting the important things on top and the general and junk mail on the bottom. She arranged them in a specific way so as to quickly identify what was what when she went to put them in the inboxes. She had not been trained by the head mail handler to do it that way, it just sort of made sense to her, and besides, it was how she always had done Yasmeia's mail. That way she would be able to answer the most important things first, and then deal with the other less important things when she felt like it, if at all.

After she had everything of Alex's, including the boxes and packages, she took off her apron and headed out to go and make her delivery. She got in the elevator designated for service personnel, rather than the general public elevators, and hit the express button that would take her straight to the top floor. The building was still dark due to the time of morning, the sun had not even risen yet, so when she got off the elevator, she found it a little unnerving to be going into an unfamiliar, empty office. She unlocked the outer door with the key that the head of security had given to her yesterday when she was introduced to him as Alex's new mail deliverer. Alex had left it for her so that if both she and her assistant had to step out of the office at the same time, the girl would still be able to do her job. Taylor unlocked the door and went inside, pulling her cart in behind her. Then she went to pushing it again as she headed for the CEO's office. She started to unlock the inner door, but was surprised to find it already unlocked.

"Oh, that's interesting...oh well, maybe she just forgot to lock it." Taylor thought to herself. Then, setting concerns aside, she went inside and went to putting the new mail in its proper slots as outlined on the sides.

"Requisitions, reports, budgets, prospectus, hmm...where is personal?" Taylor asked, as she came to those personal, yet important envelopes. "Aha, here you are." She put many envelopes into that holder, including a large picture size, stiff manila envelope. She finished with all of the delivering and started collecting all of the outgoing. She began humming to herself as she sorted through the types of mail and placed them in their respective bins on her cart. Taylor made sure that none of the notes came off so that she would be able to send them the way they were meant to be delivered. While she was sorting, someone came into the office and stood behind her just watching the efficient way she was handling the mail.

"Well...?" The voice called, breaking the silence, except for the young girl's humming.

"Oh!! Ms. Madison! I mean, Ma'am, you startled me. I didn't realize anyone else was here. I just thought that I would get an early start on things. That way you could get your correspondence done as soon as possible and get on to other things. I hope that was okay?"

"It's fine. Actually, I think it shows initiative. But I have a question for you." Alex said, as she casually looked the girl over while speaking to her, her nose wrinkled when she saw the scarf. "What's this?" She asked, as she unwrapped the scarf from around Taylor's neck and threw it into the girl's hand. "That's better."

She then continued in her line of thought, as Taylor stood blushing, and her hands nervously playing with the scarf that was now in them, rather than around her neck and covering her cleavage.

"How is it that you are so efficient at handling the mail? Have you ever worked in a postal service before?"

"Nn...no ma'am..." Taylor said, still distracted by the scarf and her partially exposed cleavage.

"Give me that!!" The CEO demanded, as she snatched the distracting scarf from the girl's hands. "Now answer me!"

"Yes ma'am. I...I had gone down to the mailroom yesterday and had Mr. Olsen orient me in how to handle and process the mail. I didn't even get a paper cut either." Taylor said, proud of herself that she was able to master something that he, himself, had not been able to do without years of practice.

Alex smirked, and then said with a lighter tone of voice.

"Well, for someone who wanted to remain anonymous to me, you sure are showing me things that I will admit impress me. " She walked around Taylor again, her eyes taking in the 5'7, petite, yet softly curved body. She then went and sat down in her chair as the girl slowly turned around to face her.

"Well, I thought since you know who I am now, and I have to earn your respect, then the best way to do that is to show who I really am. Although, the clothes are very different for me, they are very nice. I am still quite nervous around you."

"Good, it'll keep you humble, as well as keep you from thinking about lying to me again."

"I won't. I've learned my lesson."

"Good." Alex acknowledged, as she took out one of the newly delivered pieces of mail from the report holder and opened it with a letter opener. She then looked it over for a moment, then sat back in her chair to regard Taylor once again. "Do you know why I didn't allow you to remain obscure to me?"

"Sort of...well no."

"Because anyone who works so hard to stay in the shadows is usually up to something she shouldn't be. I don't like feeling uncomfortable about anyone working in my companies. It causes me to wonder what they are up to. Anyway, you made me feel uncomfortable and I couldn't let it go. So here you are, in my full view. And I must say, I'm pleased with the view." She said quietly.

Taylor blushed fiercely for some unknown reason.

"Do you always come in early to work?"

"Yes." The girl answered as Alex began going through her mail once again, and gestured for Taylor to continue gathering the outgoing mail.

"Do you stay late?"

"Yes." The girl answered again as she started collecting and sorting the mail at the same speed she had done before the other woman came in.

Alex watched the girl's efficiency as she answered correspondence after correspondence.

"I'll go and get these taken care of, and bring back any new mail." Taylor said, expecting something, but not knowing why."

"Go." The woman said simply."

"Oh, yes, okay." The girl answered as she turned and went and opened the door of the office. She pushed her cart out, then turned back around and slowly closed the door, trying not to disturb the woman inside. As Taylor was closing the door, watching the woman as she did, Alex looked up from her correspondence and saw the girl watching her. She raised a brow at her, and the curious thought that came into her mind. The girl blushed from embarrassment, at being caught looking at the woman, then quickly lowered her eyes, and as the woman went back to reading. Taylor quickly closed the door and headed back to the mailroom.

She went to work immediately sorting the mail. She read each of the notes as to how each of the pieces was to be handled for delivery. She also made sure to take matching, empty envelopes and, after writing the destination of each of the originals on the copies, she then placed the quick informational notes from the Raider onto them. She taped them in place on the empty envelopes, so as to remember the way the certain envelopes from the office were to be sent. It would also allow her to determine if all of the mail was sent the way she had them labeled. By the time she had all of the mail ready, everyone had made it to work, and the mailroom was now bustling with activity. People were collecting mail to be delivered, and the drivers were arriving with incoming mail that needed to be sorted and delivered to the floors.

"How long have you been here?" Mr. Olsen asked Taylor.

"I came in a little early and made my run to the top floor. I've already finished sorting and sending all of that mail. I am now waiting for the newly arriving mail to be sorted for the different floors. Then I was going to make another run to Ms. Madison's office with any mail she may have received in this shipment, and get any outgoing mail. After that, I'll make my hourly runs."

"Well, I see you have your day all planned out. If you need anything let me know."

"I will, but right now I'm pretty much on top of things."

"I can see that. You're not only on top of the mail, but you look great! Big difference from yesterday."

Taylor smiled and subconsciously straightened her jacket sleeve.

"Thank you." Taylor said, and looked over and saw someone coming towards them.

"Here you go." Came one of the sorter's voices, as he laid almost a table full of letters and packages in front of her. He then stood, staring at her, looking up and down her shapely body. He was looking so hard that she had to say something.

"Is there something else you want, or do you just have a condition that makes you a rude person?"

Olsen laughed out loud at the clever put down of the rude man. The man huffed and, then turned and stalked away. Olsen then looked at Taylor and put his hand on her shoulder and said in a friendly voice.

"You know you should expect that type of response now. I mean yesterday you were...well you know? Now look at you. You're a fine young lady, and the men are going to stare and respond. Especially with THAT showing." He said, gesturing towards her exposed cleavage.

"Oh, well I'll have to think of something to do about that."

"It's not necessary that you do anything about it. I was just telling you how some men will respond, but I don't expect any of them to get out of line, just display some bad manners at times."

"I know, but I'll pin it anyway."

"Okay, well...you'd better get started with your mail, seems like you have a lot of mail for Ms. Madison."

"Okay, and thanks."

"You're welcome." Olsen said, as he went about checking on everyone else.

Taylor put her apron back on and sorted the mail the same way she had earlier. Then she put it all in her cart and headed out to make another run. She made it up to the top floor, but this time she was nervous, because she knew the boss was in her office working. Taylor pushed her cart through the door and then let it close behind her. She went to Salina's desk and the woman looked up, ready to ask if she could help her, then realized it was the Admin from the other day.

"Wow! What happened to you?" The young woman asked, more out of curiosity than interest.

"What do you mean?" Taylor asked, subconsciously straightening her clothes once again.

"That... You? You look totally different. Like night and day from yesterday."

"Oh, it was a gift."

"Oh. Well anyway, I see you're here to deliver the mail."

"Yes."

"Well, leave it with me and I will give it to her." Salina said, as she proceeded to go about some of her other duties, expecting Taylor to do what she had been told to do.

"I'm...I'm afraid that I can't."

"What do you mean you can't?"

"I was told to deliver her mail to HER hands personally."

"Right, but you know that means to her Admin. You're an Admin, at least part time. Anyway, when mail comes for your immediate boss, does it go straight to her, or do you receive it for her and then you take it in to her? I am her right hand. Besides, you can see she's in a meeting. The way she's pounding her fist on the table, I don't think you really want to go in there and deliver mail, do you?"

"Well...no, but...okay, I'll just leave it with you and you can go in and take it to her, and bring the outgoing mail."

"Okay, you go ahead and start unloading the mail and I'll go in and get the other." Salina said, as she turned her chair around and came to her feet, heading for the door with a wicked grin on her face. She knew The Raider would be pissed that her orders were not followed to the letter. Salina then went and knocked on the door.

"What?!" Came the sharp tone of voice. Obviously annoyed by the interruption.

"Ma'am, I'm sorry to interrupt, it's just that I need to get the outgoing mail from your desk for the mail carrier, if that's alright."

"NO! It's not alright! Where is the new girl who is supposed to do this?"

"She's waiting in the outer office."

"GET IN HERE!!" Alex yelled out the door as she glared at Taylor, who was now standing board straight, looking back at her.

Taylor put the mail she had in her hand back in her cart and ran into the office once again, flustered in her cheeks.

"Ye...yes ma'am?"

"What are you doing?!"

"I...I... "

"Didn't I make myself clear when I told you what your duties were to be?!" Alex asked angrily, reprimanding her in front of the people she had been meeting with, and Salina the Admin.

"Yes Ma'am." Taylor answered, even more embarrassed.

"Then what the hell is Salina doing in here asking for the mail?!"

"I...she...it won't happen again." The girl said, not having an answer that would meet with Alex's approval, trying not to sound like she was making excuses.

"We'll talk about it later. Get the mail and do your job!" Alex demanded, as she leveled a hard look at her.

Taylor had moisture forming in her eyes but she tried to fight it off.

"Yes ma'am." She said quickly, as she glanced at the others and then went to get her cart to do her job as she had been told.

Salina moved out of her way and eased out the office without ever saying anything about her part in what had happened. Taylor quickly retrieved her cart and went to work placing the mail where it went. She was desperately trying not to let her tears roll down her face while also trying not to look at the eyes she knew were burning into her. She couldn't help herself, but chance a glance up at Alex as she was putting the pieces of mail into their respective places. To her utter chagrin, Alex was still glaring at her. The others in the room were waiting for her to continue, but they didn't dare say a word. They were just happy for a reprieve from their own reprimands. Taylor's breathing increased as she now was shaken by the piercing gaze, which showed the woman's obvious disapproval in her actions.

After Taylor finished placing the incoming mail, she began collecting the outgoing mail. She was trying to do the job and not scream from the stress she was feeling as those piercing sapphires bored into her. She looked up again at Alex, who had not taken her eyes off of her the whole time. This time Alex was looking at Taylor's altered top and her eyes narrowed and shot back up to look at the girl's face. Taylor once again, without realizing it, brought her hand to her top where she had pinned it closed. Her hand dropped down and picked up another letter, as she now felt completely ashamed. Despite her skin tone, her face became more flushed than before. She was now wiping her eyes as she sped up her efforts at getting all the mail. Finally, she finished and turned to leave. Alex, who had sat there the whole time without saying a word, now spoke.

"I expect you back here at 5 PM. It's obvious I have to re-instruct you in some things."

"Yes Ma'am." Taylor said quietly as she once again glanced at the others, who were all feeling badly for her.

Taylor then turned, and with shaky hands, went to open the door. One of the men jumped up and opened it for her. Taylor said a whispered, "Thank you" and rapidly left the office. She went to the elevator and continued to wipe her eyes as she waited for it to come. Alex, in the meantime, had returned her attention back to the men in the office. She could be seen pointing at them, tapping her fingers impatiently on the table, or employing some other intimidation tactic.

The elevator finally came and Taylor got on. The minute the doors closed, she pushed the down button, then went and leaned against the wall of the elevator as she covered her face and cried for a moment. When she heard the elevator slowing down, she quickly wiped her eyes and straightened herself up. As the doors opened, she exhaled and pushed her cart out to go and take care of the mail. Taylor took her time sorting the mail, even though the run had a lot less mail than the first one, she just wanted to stretch the time. Anything to keep her mind on something other than the meeting she was extemporaneously scheduled for. She finished sorting and sending the outgoing mail and was nearly finished with the incoming when she looked at her watch. Her heart sank at the thought of having to go back up there, but it was that time again and she knew she had to go.

She got into the elevator, but just stood there for a few minutes looking at the button that would take her to the top floor. Finally, taking a deep breath, she hit the express button. Taylor stood in the corner of the elevator with her head down and angrily wiped the tears out of her eyes. The elevator stopped and the doors began to open. Taking one more deep breath, she pushed her cart out and headed for the office.

Salina was not at her desk, which made her feel a little better. She had been surprised that the woman did not say anything during the whole encounter, she just eased out like a weasel. Taylor was disgusted with the behavior of the Admin. She looked past the desk into the main office and was relieved to see that Ms. Madison wasn't in either.

"Thank goodness for a little luck." She exclaimed to herself. She pushed her cart into the office and began sorting the mail.

Taylor had almost finished when she heard the door to the main office open and close behind her. She put the letter she still had in her hand in the appropriate box, then turned around to find Ms. Madison standing behind her. The girl exhaled a breath of air from her lungs, as she now stood locked in her boss's gaze once again.

"Finish up and then leave." The woman said evenly, and then walked around to her desk and sat down.

"Yes ma'am." Taylor said quickly, then turned to put the last few pieces of mail in the boxes.

After she finished, she turned her cart and headed for the door. She had just gotten to it when she stopped. She wondered whether she should say something to the woman. But for some reason, she had a feeling it was NOT the time, so she decided to just leave. Taylor pushed her cart out the door, and rather than closing the door with her back to it, she chanced a glance back at Alex, curious about what she was so distracted by. Taylor's eyes looked upon the desk at first, but seeing really only a few forms upon it, and the woman's chair turned sideways, Taylor figured it was not anything on the desk that had the woman distracted. Taylor's curiosity had the better of her and so looking past the desk and onto the red, tailor-made jacket of the woman's, her eyes traveled up the well fitted suit jacket, up until her eyes meant those of The Raider's. Alex's eyes were leveled on her, with one brow raised. Taylor quickly closed the door and nearly ran to the elevators with her cart, almost running down the Admin.

"Hey! Watch it!" Salina yelped, as she nearly had to jump out of the way to avoid being run down.

Taylor ran inside of the open elevator, happy that she didn't have to wait for it. Alex, in the meantime, pursed her lips as she thought about what the girl was thinking about. She then turned her attention to Salina, who had now come into the office to go over her boss's afternoon schedule with her. Salina wore a short skirt, blue rayon suit with a scoop neck and tank top. She had taken her matching jacket off once she was back in the office. Alex would glance at the young woman's exposed cleavage at times, while she ran down her appointments.

"The Sackens Group will be here at 2pm. You have a 3:30 with Mr. Li, from the International Development Group, who's working in the newly acquired Mariah Building in Sendai. Then at 4:45, you have an appointment with Mr. Marcus Shearer."

"Alright. Call my planner and have her arrange my spring annual as usual."

"Yes ma'am."

"Good." Alex said simply, and dismissed the Admin.

"So, how is your first day going working as the personal mail handler to Ms. Madison?"

"Alright. It would be better if I could just stop pissing her off. But outside of that...Great!" Taylor stated with irony in her tone, to Yasmeia, who had come down to check on her.

"Hahahaha, well, I'm sure that things will be fine."

"I hope so. I mean, every time she looks at me, I feel like she's looking into my very soul. I get so flustered around her. I've never had that problem before."

"Well I don't know about that Taylor. I remember when you first came to work for me, you were very flustered. But you're not the most socially active person I know. So of course, when someone with such a large persona whisks into your life, it only makes sense that you or anyone else would be flustered."

"Hmm...I guess that makes sense. But I was only flustered with you because I didn't know you. You were so nice that I didn't want to make your department look bad by messing up."

"I know. So do you want to have lunch together?"

"Hmm...let me think about that for a moment...lunch with a friend, or sit here and worry about my 5 p.m. meeting with Ms. Madison. Hmmm, whatever shall I do? Let's go!" She said with a wry smile.

"Great! It's sort of a late lunch, but lunch none the less."

"Okay, let me tell Mr. Olsen?"

"Alright."

"Mr. Olsen?"

"Yes?"

"I'm going to lunch, but I will be back in an hour."

"Ok, enjoy."

Taylor then went back to join Yasmeia. "Okay, let's go." Taylor said, as she walked towards the door. Yasmeia headed for the door with her and they went to the restaurant within the building to eat.

"So will you be back in the office next week with me?"

"Yes, but I have arranged to pick up Ms. Madison's mail when I pick up yours."

"That's fine."

"Do you have anything that you need done, that I can help you with when I'm at home?"

"Yes, lots of things, but I didn't want to take up your free time."

"Oh, it may take me a few hours to get them done, but not enough to rob me of time to myself, plus you're my friend also, I don't mind helping."

"You're wonderful, thank you."

"You're welcome Yasmeia, but you know it's not necessary to thank me."

"Yes it is, because I know how hard a compliment is to come by from some people. You know me, I like for people to know that I appreciate what they do for me, especially friends. Besides, you should stock up on the praise where ever you can get it, because they will be hard to come by with Ms. Madison."

"I know, and I do appreciate the kind words, really." The girl said with a bright smile.

Taylor was very comfortable with Yasmeia. She had known her for almost the whole time she had been with the company. They met by way of one of the women in the temporary staffing pool, who knew the girl from another company. She told Yasmeia how good Taylor was and after working as a secretary for one of the lesser supervisors, Yasmeia personally asked for her. Taylor was transferred from the first floor, to the third floor, and she had been there ever since. The two ate their lunch while talking about her duties and how things were going. When Taylor returned to the mailroom, she was shocked to find that there was a table full of mail for Alex.

"What's this? I was only gone one hour?" She asked, stunned by the volume that accumulated after such a short period of time.

"It is amazing isn't it? Well, you better get to work, didn't you say you had a 5pm meeting with her?"

"Yes, but it's only 2:30."

"It's going to take you at least a hour and a half to get through all of this, then deliver it, and then get back down here."

"At least?!! Oh no it's not, I am not going to be late for any reason, even if that means me grabbing you to help me?"

"Well I don't mind helping you, but I need to get something done of my own first, and then I'll come back and help, if you need me too."

"Okay, hopefully I won't need you too, but just in case." Taylor then took off her jacket and put her apron on and dove into her task.

By the time it was 3:30, she was three quarters of the way done with her sorting and placing. She put the mail directly in the cart, rather than stacking it on the table, which would have taken more time to then, put in the slots. By 4:15, she was on her way up to the top floor to make her delivery. She got off the elevator and quickly went into the office. She looked at her watch and saw the time ticking away. Alex was in her office meeting with Mr. Li still, although it looked like it was about to end. Taylor saw the woman sitting sideways once again, she was tapping on her cheek as she listened to the man, and so when Taylor knocked on the door, she motioned for her to come in with that same finger. Mr. Li was winding up, when Taylor entered. She entered quietly, and went immediately over to the desk area where the in and outgoing mail slots were sitting. She immediately went to putting the incoming mail in the slots.

Mr. Li finally left, and Alex's attention switched from him to the girl. She looked at her watch and then up at Taylor, who had noticed, and she raised a brow at her.

"I won't be late." The girl said quickly as she looked at her own watch, and went back to sorting. While she was doing that, Salina led Mr. Shearer in the office.

"Mr. Shearer." Alex said with a certain tone in her voice.

Taylor looked over her shoulder and smiled at him. He looked up and saw his friend and smiled back, then greeted Alex, who had watched the whole exchange.

"So Mr. Shearer, do you know why I sent for you?"

"Not really, I've learned not to try and second guess you."

"Hmm, well I sent for you to talk to you about your reports." Alex said, then stopped when she noticed that Taylor had stopped what she was supposed to be doing.

"You're running out of time. I suggest you mind your business. I'm not very pleasant to be around when someone is late for a meeting with me."

"Yes Ma'am!" The girl said nervously as she returned to her work.

The man looked at the young girl's nervous behavior, and he saw how wide her eyes had gotten with the mention of the reports. The hairs on the back of his neck now started to stand up.

"Okay, what would you like to know about them?" He asked, trying to maintain his air of calmness.

Taylor was hoping against hope that the woman would not ask who did them. If she did, Taylor hoped he would answer truthfully. The girl looked at her watch and saw that she had seven minutes. She wanted to stay and hear what the conversation was, but she had to get the cart back to the mailroom before her meeting with Alex. Taylor put the last piece of mail into the slot, then turned her cart and headed out of the office quickly. Alex glanced at her watch as she watched the girl nearly run for the elevator. She had five minutes. The elevator took one minute to come up, if it started from the bottom floor, which meant another to go down. Taylor calculated her time as she made it down and into the mailroom. It took one minute to give Mr. Olsen the priority mail to send out. The others she would get to when she came in the morning. Olsen looked at the clock. She had one minute and a half to make it back.

"Better get going!"

"Yes. Bye. Thanks!" Taylor called, as she ran out the door to get the elevator. She hit the up button, and thought she was going to have to wait, but as luck would have it someone was coming down to the mail room. She jumped on and hit the express button and was on her way. She checked her watch again. It was just passing the minute mark. The elevator doors opened and the girl shot out. Her time was down to ten seconds. She ran into the outer office and then to the door, quickly straightening herself as she knocked. Alex casually looked up at her and motioned for her to come in. Taylor darted in the door, breathless and flushed. But on time. Alex stopped her stop watch just as the girl entered the office and then she held it up to her.

"One second. You like living dangerously. Sit down!"

"Yes Ma'am." She said, happy to be able to sit down and catch her breath.

Alex then stood up and went to sit on the edge of her desk as she once again regarded the girl sitting before her. Taylor's breathing was labored and it caused the woman to notice her heaving chest.

"So, what do you have to say for yourself?"

"I am so sorry, I knew I should have done what I thought to do. I should have done exactly what you said: your hands and no one else's. I was so wrong to be talked astray, please forgive me, it will not happen again. I know I've made mistakes, but I learn fast. I usually don't make the same ones twice. I know I caused an interruption in your meeting by you having to address my mistake. It won't happen again, I promise." Taylor rattled off in one long exhaled breath.

Alex raised a brow at her and then said in a tone of warning.

"Next time I tell you to do something, I expect for you to do only as I say. You tell me you're a quick learner, well I'm going to call you on that. If you make this mistake again, I will see to it that every time you see me you will want to run the other way. Am I making myself clear?"

"Yes Ma'am." Taylor said through her tight throat.

"Alright, go home."

"Thank you ma'am." Taylor then stood up to leave, but just as she was about to turn to the door, Alex saw the top once again.

"Wait! Turn around!" She ordered, as the girl turned back to face her.

"Yes Ma'am, is there something else?"

"Yes!" Came the answer through clenched teeth. "Why haven't you removed that pin from that top?!"

"Oh, I...I forgot about it."

"Listen to me, when I do things for people, I don't like being slapped in the face by them. Now if you don't want to offend me anymore, I suggest you get rid of that pin...and now!"

"Yes Ma'am! I'm sorry, I didn't realize..."

"You didn't realize what? That it shows no appreciation to me for what I tried to do for you?"

"I'm sorry, it won't happen again."

"It doesn't matter! The top is ruined, look at it!! Pin holes... from a safety pin no less!"

"I'm sorry, I can cover them with...."

"When you get home, I want you to throw the whole outfit in the trash. I don't ever want to see you wearing it again! You don't appreciate it!" Alex accused, as she turned and walked back to her chair.

"But I do appreciate it, and everything else you've done for me. Please don't make me throw it away?"

"Better than throwing it away, I want you to bring it back to me tomorrow morning, and I'll throw it away, that way I will be sure it is taken care of."

"But Ma'am, I was not trying to be rude or anything, I'm just uncomfortable with my breasts showing."

"Your damn breasts were not showing! Just your cleavage, and not much of that! You're 27 years old, and you dress like you're an old woman! I try to help you and that's how you repay me, by putting a scarf over the outfit, or pinning it with a damn pin! You know, I would make you strip out of it right now, if there was something else for you to wear out of here. But seeing that there isn't, I'll have to settle for having you bring it to me in the morning. Be here at 4. Now get out!! Damn it, so ungrateful!" The woman hissed, as she turned her back to the shocked girl, who still had not moved from the chair.

"I...."

"Get the Hell Out Of My Office!!" Alex growled.

Taylor jumped from the chair, and this time she opened the door, and ran out crying. She didn't even go to the elevator, she immediately headed for the stairs, without waiting for the elevator. She ran down them to the mailroom, where she grabbed her things. She then ran back up the stairs and out of the building to her car, where she sat and cried.

There were only a few cars on the level she was on, so she sat there and let her tears roll as they would. After a bit she decided she needed to get home. She drove to the exit of the parking garage and as she was waiting for the light to change, she saw Alex in her silver Porsche. Taylor was a little surprised to see this considering how she left the woman still sitting in her office. But then she figured the woman had left right after she did, and while she was in the mailroom crying, the woman obviously made it to her car.

The girl's distressed eyes locked on Alex's studying gaze, and then she looked away completely mortified by the look reflecting back at her. The light changed and the girl took off out of the lot driving fast. Alex watched the girl's driving and became concerned about her state of mind. She decided to follow Taylor to make sure she made it home alright.

Alex watched Taylor weaving in and out of traffic trying to get as far away from the building as fast as she could. The older woman cursed, during most of the drive, at the girl for driving so wildly. After 20 minutes of heart stopping driving for most people, Taylor pulled into a driveway and Alex could see her leaning over her steering wheel obviously crying once again. Alex had come to a stop, under a lamp post that was on due to the time of evening it was. She was parked across a narrow street where similar townhouses stood. She then just sat and watched the girl. Finally, Taylor got out of the car, and slamming the door of the car, she pulled out her house key and opened the door to go inside. Alex saw when she turned on the lights of the townhouse. She saw Taylor, through the glass door. The girl slammed her keys down on a counter and then wiped her eyes again. She disappeared into another room. After a few minutes she saw the girl come out, pick up the phone and call someone. Alex would soon find out who it was, but in the meantime, she saw her go into a further room.

After a few minutes the girl came out and went upstairs, once again the lights showed what floor she had arrived on. Taylor was now in a room that Alex figured to be a bedroom, facing the side of the street where she was sitting in her car. The woman sat there for a while just watching the girl's silhouette as she took off the outfit. Her brow raised as a result of the outline and a smirk came to her face despite her irritation and concern about the girl.

While she was watching Taylor, a dry cleaner's van drove up into the driveway, and the driver got out and went to the door of the townhouse. The woman saw when the girl left the bedroom, and then the next time she saw her was when she was opening the door. Taylor handed the outfit to the man, as she spoke to him. She then paid him and sent him on his way. Alex then saw the girl go back into the room at the furthest end of the hallway and stay for a while. Alex decided she would give Taylor an ear full tomorrow about her driving, but as far as tonight was concerned she would not let the girl see her. She pulled out of the spot she had parked in and headed home.

The next morning Taylor showed up at the office at 2 am. She went to the mailroom and sorted the mail that had arrived after she left, then got the mail that was left from yesterday and made it ready to deliver when the business day begun. Taylor then went to Alex's office and did all of her required tasks, including laying the outfit on top of the desk now back inside of the original garment bag that had been given to her. She then returned to the mailroom and dealt with the mail she had just picked up from the office. After she finished, she looked at the time and saw it was almost four. Taylor sat down on the stool she was standing near and just watched the clock tick until it hit four. She wondered what Alex was doing at that moment.

Alex had arrived at the office a few minutes before four. She went into her office and saw that both the doors were locked, yet when she was inside, she saw that Taylor had indeed been there. She wondered what time the girl had come in, but then thought it didn't matter. She walked over to her desk and saw the outfit, with a note taped on it.

"I'm sorry."

The woman looked at her watch and saw it was a few minutes before four, so she picked the outfit up off of her desk, and hung it on the coat rack that stood in the corner. Then she sat in her chair and waited for Taylor to come. Passing the time by reading over some of her mail. When the Cherrywood finished, pendulum clock, that sat on a mantel off to the side of where the woman sat at her desk, struck four and the girl was not on the floor in her office, Alex slammed her fist on the table and picked up the note. Alex then stormed to the elevator and took it to the basement. Taylor was sitting on the stool with her head in her hands as she just tried to buy herself some quiet time before everyone came in at 7, and wondering what the woman was doing. She was startled out of her moment when a sharp voice cut through her thoughts.

"TO THE LETTER!!" Alex seethed.

"Ma'am?!" Taylor gasped, as she was startled off of the stool.

Alex stormed towards the girl who backed away to the other side of the table, looking like a deer facing a panther.

"Didn't I tell you to be in my office at 4:00?!"

"Yes. But I thought it was just to give you back the outfit, I didn't know you meant for me to actually be there?"

"When I say something, I mean for it to be carried out to the letter! I don't remember leaving any room for assumptions."

"I misunderstood, I'm sorry."

"You certainly are!" Alex said as she turned to leave. Disgusted by the girl's behavior.

Taylor felt hurt for some reason by the sharp words.

"What do you want from me?! She called out after the woman.

"I don't want anything from you! Not even your cowardly apology!" The Raider sneered, as she balled the note up in her hand and threw it to the ground.

Taylor was now beside herself with hurt and confusion. She ran out the door after Alex to try to explain her actions. The woman was waiting for the elevator with her arms crossed over her chest, looking all the more intimidating.

Taylor slowed down and then walked over to where Alex stood, glaring at her.

"I couldn't face you. You had done something very nice for me, and I unintentionally offended you with my lack of taste. I'm not used to having such things, and therefore I didn't know it was inappropriate to do certain things. But I don't understand why you're so angry with me about an outfit? I can understand you being upset with my job performance. Since I've come to your attention, I have made mistakes, and I'm sure I will make more, but I give you my word I am trying to do what I need to in order to please you. I'm just very intimidated by you, and therefore, every time I have to be near you I get all flustered. I am not the type of person who is used to strong personalities. I did not mean to offend you. I have and will continue to do what I have to, in order to show you that I am completely focused on pleasing you with my performance. Should you decide to do something else nice for me, I will look for your opinion on what's proper."

Alex stood looking at the elevator as she listened to the young girl. She gave a sidelong glance, and then turned around and faced her squarely. Taylor looked up at her with tension in her brows.

"Okay, I'll accept your apologies, but I'm not going to let you off that easy. It seems to me, that because you are so distracted with trying to avoid me, you can't show ME your real skills, which I know you have in spades. I've seen your abilities through others. I want to see them without being hidden under the guise of someone else's work. So, I am going to make you MY Personal Assistant."

"Your Personal Assistant?"

"Yes."

"But what about my job here, and in Ms. Sain's department?"

"Don't worry about them, I will have the staffing agency send over one of the Admins I use when Salina goes on vacation. Don't worry, she won't have any problems. Starting tomorrow you will begin your work as my Personal Assistant."

"Okay. But may I ask a question?"

"What?"

"What exactly does a Personal Assistant do?"

"I'll explain it tonight at dinner."

"Dinner?"

"Yes, your place. 7 PM sharp. "

"But..?"

"No fish, no pork. I'll bring the wine." Alex then stepped into the elevator. Just before the doors closed she caught them and held them open as she said one last thing to the open-mouthed girl. "And we'll talk about your driving yesterday." She then raised a brow and her eyes showed disapproval of those driving skills.

Taylor blushed, then stood watching the doors close as Alex stood watching her. The day went by quickly, and she managed to only get scolded by Alex once. Taylor left work a little early to go grocery shopping. She hadn't planned on doing it until Saturday, but now was as good a time as any. Especially now that she had a guest coming over. She planned on making a pasta dish, vegetable, and homemade bread as well. She also made apple pie from scratch. She bought French vanilla ice cream, for it just in case

Alex wanted it 'a la mode. She made sure the table was set with her best dishes. She was lucky to have two sets of real china, given to her by her grandmother. She set her stereo on an all-jazz station and turned it low enough for people to talk without having to raise their voices. Taylor checked everything to make sure things were perfect.

She had a spacious townhouse, although if someone were to look through the solarium window they would be able to see the dining room slightly, and the living room depending on which way they looked. Taylor ran into the bedroom and showered and dressed in a periwinkle colored, cocktail length, two piece skirt with accordion pleats. The pleats, if pulled outward at the hem, would spread gracefully and then fall gently back in place. The blouse was made of the same material, but it did not have any pleats on it. The gently dipping cleavage area of the blouse made the outfit really come alive. It was a mixture of softness, and subtle sexiness. Not that she was going for sexy, but that's how the woman at the department store described it, when she had tried it on. She did her hair in one long corn roll down her back and put a bow of the same color as her outfit on the end to hold it in place. After she finished dressing and cleaning the room back up, she went to go check everything one more time.

Taylor looked at the time and it was 6:30. She then remembered something else her grandmother had told her, so she immediately looked in her cabinets for her cinnamon scented candles. When she could not locate any, she went to her spice rack and took the powdered cinnamon out. She filled one of her decorative teakettles with water and brought it to a boil. Then she poured some of the cinnamon powder into it and turned the eye down so the cinnamon could simmer over very low heat. Her grandmother once told her that the smell of cinnamon after a long, hard day at work could do wonders for a person's disposition. When the cinnamon smell had made its way throughout the living room, Taylor turned it down to its lowest temperature without turning it off. This way when the door opened, it would not overpower the smell of dinner and the freshly baked bread. She had just rechecked everything and remembered to get her notepad to take notes on what a Personal Assistant's duties were, when the doorbell rang.

"Oh God! Okay, just be calm, she's not mad at you, she's just here to discuss business, okay, okay." Taylor said to herself as she went to the door to answer it.

She saw whom it was without having to ask due to the light outside the door, and the blinds providing enough detail. She opened the door with a nervous smile on her face.

"He...hello, please, come in?" Taylor said, inviting the woman into her home.

Alex stepped through the door and while she waited for the girl to close it and ask for her coat, she glanced around the entranceway of the townhouse.

"May I take your coat and purse?"

"Thank you. Oh, and this is the wine." She said, as she handed the bottle to Taylor, who shyly thanked her and went to put it on ice so that it could chill.

"Please make yourself at home, the living room is up the stairs. I'll just go put these in the bedroom. Can I bring you something to drink before dinner?"

"A glass of water with two ice cubes." The woman said, as she started up the stairs to the living room area. But then she saw the library of books the young girl had in her den. She turned and walked back down the few steps she had taken up and went to go and peruse the books. Taylor had a lot of books on business, as well as every book written by or about her. There were romance novels, Better Homes and Gardens books and many other types as well, but those were the ones she was able to peruse before the girl came back to join her.

"Oh, you're still down here."

"Yes. I was just looking around, is that alright?"

"Oh yes, fine, Um...dinner will be ready in about an hour, if that's okay?" Taylor said. Alex moved to the stairs and headed up them with the girl following after her, still holding the two glasses.

"That's fine. Is that cinnamon I'm smelling?"

"Yes Ma'am. I hope it doesn't bother you?"

"No, I like it, it's very relaxing, I have candles that I use." Alex said, noticing the difference in the simmering smell and that of candles.

"Oh, I'm glad to hear that. I usually use candles, but I didn't have any." Taylor said, as she handed the woman her water. "Would you like to sit down?"

"Thank you. I want to get right to your duties as my Personal Assistant, we can continue after dinner if we don't get everything covered beforehand. Get your pad." Alex commanded.

Taylor immediately picked up her pad and prepared herself to take extensive notes.

"I expect you to arrive at my house at 3 in the morning, for the first few months, then you will be there at 5. I want you to learn my morning routine, that way when we travel you'll know what I expect. You will be by my side throughout the day. Meetings, conference calls, whatever. You will literally be like my shadow, everywhere I go, you go. You will not be late! You will handle all of my correspondence, at my home, as well as at the office. I expect for you to learn what things are priority to me, and those that aren't. If I'm talking to someone about an important business dealing, and something else comes up more important during that time, you'll know by then what I consider to be important, anyway, if it's more important than what I'm dealing with; just hand the phone or a note to me while informing me as to who it is. If a priority letter comes in for me, I expect for you to also put it IN my hands. You have not seen any of those type letters yet, because of having only been in the mailroom for two days. I usually get them weekly. You will know them by their color. They are red with a white stripe across the front. I want that put in my hand. I don't expect to see any on my desk. They will go from your hand straight to my hands, if I see otherwise, I will show you intimidation. Do you understand me?!"

"Yes Ma'am, I won't do otherwise." Taylor said, stopping her note taking long enough to look her in the eye.

"Good. Anyway, you'll learn the types of things I like, and don't like. You'll most likely learn the dislikes first." Alex said, with a wry smile at her.

The girl gave a shy smile and then lowered her eyes back to her pad.

"Go check on dinner."

"Yes Ma'am." Taylor answered, as she stood to go and do as she was told.

Alex used the break to ask some personal questions.

"Are your parents alive? Do you have any sisters or brothers, any cousins that you're real close to?"

"No, my parents died in a car accident when I was 7. No sisters or brothers. I have some cousins, but I haven't talked to any of them since I was a child. I was pretty much raised by my maternal grandmother." Taylor answered from the kitchen area, which had a pass through which allowed for her to see the woman. She finished checking the food, then returned to her seat and picked up her pad once again.

Alex then went back into her expectations of the young girl, and by the time they sat down to dinner, Taylor had taken multiple pages of notes. Over dinner Alex once again took the opportunity to find out more of the personal things about her, for reasons only she knew.

"So...how did you get interested in business?"

"My grandmother. It was sort of a daily thing. She used to own her own business, which I used to work with her in. She would tell me about the things she had to do to get her own business. From coming up with an idea, to drawing up the plans as to what she wanted, to arranging for taking out an initial loan with the best rates. I mean she told me all the steps that she went through. Our conversations were more adult oriented than child. When I was in school, I didn't have many friends, but the ones I did have were good ones. We were together all through high school and then college. But during my junior year in high school, I heard of this woman who had been whizzing through the business community like a tornado. It was then that my grandmother gave me a book written by this woman. She told me that if I could be even a quarter like the woman in that book, I would be a force to be reckoned with. So I went to my room that evening and I read that book, and every book after it. Everything about her. But despite having read all of them, I knew I would NEVER be anything like or near such a force. I knew myself well enough to know that. I have never felt comfortable being in the spotlight. I like working in the background. My friends went on to either get their own businesses and offer me a position in them, or I helped them get positions in whatever company I was working in."

"The woman was me wasn't it?"

Taylor hesitated at first, but then she answered.

"Yes."

"I knew that. I saw your library."

"Oh."

"Anyway, you're right, you could never be like me. You're too sensitive. You don't have the killer instinct." Alex said pointedly.

Taylor looked hurt by the statement, but she tried to hide it.

"I didn't mean for that to be an insult, I was just being honest with you." Alex said, lifting the girl's chin up with her fingers, and looking her in the eyes.

"I know. I think I should get the dessert?" Taylor then stood up and nervously went to get the dessert.

"Are you involved with anyone?"

"No, not really, I mean I have a friend whom I have over sometimes."

"Hmm....I see, so you're intimate with this guy?" Alex asked, now somewhat disappointed.

"Here you go." Taylor said as she placed the apple pie in front of the woman.

"Mmmm...smells wonderful, you make it from scratch?"

"Yes Ma'am."

"I'm impressed."

She toyed with it for a moment, and then looked up at Taylor.

"So are you going to answer my question?!" She asked, somewhat sharply.

"Oh, no, we're not intimate, I mean he wants to do more than kissing, but I don't feel like he's the one I want to...you know?"

"Deflower you." Alex now said with a gleam in her eyes.

"Right." Taylor replied, as she blushed fiercely.

"So...what would this person be like, I mean the person whom you would desire to receive your gift?"

"I don't know, I haven't really thought about it."

"Well think about it!" Alex said snappishly.

Taylor picked up on the tone, but put it off to the woman having a lot on her mind and not wanting to dilly dally on the current subject for a long time.

"Well...a lot of the person's qualities would probably be almost opposite of my own. I mean..." She paused, trying to think of something that would describe exactly what she was talking about, then her gaze fell on her boss. "Like you."

Alex's brow raised in response to the statement, and a smirk came to her face.

"I mean, someone strong, confident and sure of themselves. Someone who has the ability to be as awesome as a raging fire, or as serene as a lake on a quiet evening. Someone who could teach me things, but allow me to teach them as well." Taylor now leaned back in her chair and cocking her head slightly, she let her gaze drift off. " The person would be near perfect, always seeming to have the answer, even to the most complicated questions, or circumstances. The person would constantly be amazing me with their talents. Overwhelm me with their passion, and then let me melt into them and they into me afterwards. They wouldn't show their fear on the outside, but when we were alone together they would open up to me, and let me soothe away whatever fear or concern they may have. That would be for the most part, the type of person I would give myself to, and I would do anything and everything to make that person happy." She sighed contently afterwards, and then remembering where and with whom she was talking to she blushed. " Oh goodness, man what you must think of me?" Taylor now said, averting her eyes away from the woman across from her.

Alex sat studying the young woman.

"I think you have a very passionate side to you, that can't seem to get past the introverted side of you. I think that if someone were to be able to bring out that other side of you, then it would completely take you over. I think it would scare you so badly, that it would either make you completely withdraw into yourself, or release the fire that is in your soul. I think in both your professional and personal life you could satisfy even the most demanding person with that fire and passion. " Alex picked up her glass of wine, and silently saluted Taylor, then took a sip of it as she watched the girl's reaction to her words.

"Wow! You really think that?" Taylor asked, completely amazed.

"I would not have said it if I didn't. I also think you read to many romance novels. Now shall we get back to work? Alex said seriously, but her mouth still had a bit of a curl to it.

Taylor let out a nervous giggle and then composed herself.

"Yes Ma'am."

The rest of the evening Alex explained to Taylor exactly what she wanted. At times she would catch the girl just staring at her, but then Taylor would become flustered and apologize for her behavior and return her attention to taking notes. When the Raider finally thought the girl had enough to get started with, she decided to end the evening. But before she did she brought up the driving.

"You know, I don't appreciate people making me worry about them."

"Excuse me?"

"Yesterday, when you left from the office, I saw how upset you were, but I didn't think you were stupid."

Taylor flinched at the harsh words, which were a contrast to how the evening had been going.

"Stupid?"

"Yes. Your driving yesterday." Alex said. She was now standing, the girl still sat out of surprise, looking up at her.

"Oh...that well I...." Taylor started, as she rose to her feet to explain to the woman.

"Save it! Just listen. From now on, when you're upset by something I've said, or done, or anyone else, I expect you not to go running off, jumping into your car and driving like a madwoman on the streets! You not only risk your life but everyone else's on that street. I don't want to ever see, or hear about you doing some shit like that again. If you feel overwhelmed, then go sit somewhere for a while until you feel you are more in control of yourself. Is that clear?!"

"Yes Ma'am." Taylor answered quickly, as tears of embarrassment ran down her face. She knew her driving was reckless and irresponsible yesterday, but to have it pointed out to her by the boss of the company, was almost unbearable. She lowered her eyes out of shame, but then Alex's voice caused her to raise them once again.

"I just don't want anything happening to you, because of that sensitivity of yours, Okay?"

"Okay, I won't do it again."

"I know. Now I have to go, but I expect to see you bright and early tomorrow at my house. I wrote the address and directions down for you on your pad. Don't be late." The woman then waited for her coat and purse to be brought to her. Taylor helped her with her coat and then opened the door for her.

"Thank you for giving me another chance." She said to Alex as the woman settled her purse strap over her shoulder.

"You're welcome. You realize you're the only person that has ever gotten a promotion by trying to remain anonymous? I told you I wasn't comfortable with people who tried to hide from me. Now, you are more apparent to me than most people are in my life. I'll see you tomorrow. Oh, and by the way... I'm very pleased with the outfit, it flatters you." The woman said, as an aside, although she had noticed it the moment Taylor had opened the door.

"Thank you, I tried to find something that you wouldn't think made me look like an old woman." Taylor said, with a nervous hand subconsciously smoothing the blouse.

Alex chuckled and then said in a light voice, "No, you definitely do not look like an old woman. Although, now that I think about it..." The woman said, turning back around and walking back into the house. "Your bedroom is where?" Although she already figured she knew, but this way it would be confirmed without her giving away anything.

"It's...it's the top floor, first door to the right." Taylor stammered out, as she closed the door and ran to catch up with the woman now striding effortlessly up the three flights of stairs.

Alex went into the first room to the right and looked around to locate the closet. The room was decorated in pastel colors, The curtains matched the bedset, which was made up of mauve and floral colored pillow shams and sheets, with solid colored dust ruffle, along the bottom. The comforter was also solid mauve colored, the room had a very feminine ambience to it. The carpet was an off white, and the walls were an eggshell white, with a border running along the top.

The Raider was very comfortable with the feel of the room, and smiled as a result. Taylor arrived a moment later and saw her throw her purse and coat onto the bed, and looking at three doors, two of which were on the same wall, but one obviously the closet and the other probably a bathroom, but she couldn't think of what the other was so for now, she headed for the closet.

"What...what are you doing?" She asked, completed thrown by Alex's actions.

"I'm checking your wardrobe."

"Why?" The girl asked in bewilderment.

"Because I need to see if all of your other clothes are like the others. After all, you will be in a very visual position."

Taylor went silent as a result of the explanation, not sure of what to say to it. Alex meanwhile had opened the sliding mirrored doors of the closet and literally scanned the entire contents, and then she began throwing the things she did not like at all out. She set other things off to the side, to think about.

"This has got to go, this, this, oh...definitely this, this, Hmmm...what is this supposed to be?" Alex asked, as she turned around with a blouse that had some type of fur on the cuff and collar.

"It was given to me as a gift from the guy I told you about."

"Really? Have you ever worn it?" The woman asked with wonder.

"No, well only the one time, when he first gave it to me and asked me to wear it for him." The girl said, trying not to laugh at the way the woman was looking at the hideous thing.

Alex brought the fur part to her nose, and then with a frown, she threw it to the floor, but away from all of the other things.

"Don't let him buy you anything else, he has NO taste." She said with disgust. She couldn't believe someone would give such a so-called gift to anyone, yet along to someone like Taylor. She was appalled at why he would try to pass off dog fur as real fur, to her.

"But he likes..." Taylor started to protest, when she saw it tossed to the floor.

"Did I stutter?" Alex asked, as she stopped for a moment and cut her eyes back over her shoulder to look at her.

"No Ma'am."

"Good." The woman then went back to throwing things out of the closet, by the time she was finished with the closet it was empty except for a few blouses and a few pairs of shoes.

Taylor was now sitting on the bed with her mouth open. She was looking at huge pile of clothes on the floor in front of her.

"Ma'am, I won't have anything to wear. I can't afford a whole new set of clothes." She managed to whimper out.

Alex was now in a zone, and she literally just dusted her hands of the closet things, and with a satisfied, "Okay." She moved to the drawers.

Taylor jumped to her feet intending to try to keep her from doing the same thing with her personals.

"Please?"

"Move."

"But?"

Alex cocked her head at the girl, eased her aside and opened the drawer. She took a moment to take in the contents of the drawer. It had stockings and lingerie. The next drawer had T-shirts with socks and scarves galore. She smirked and looked up at the flushed girl who was now biting her lips as she stood watching her inspect the drawers. Alex looked in every drawer, and then she began to do what she had done earlier with the closet. Once again talking as she went.

"These go. All of these, these, and these, you shouldn't wear these type of panties, they're not good for you, these go, and these." Alex cleared the top drawer of all of her underwear, except for one pair to get through tomorrow with, she was not concerned with only one pair being left, because she already had plans to replace the lingerie. A few pairs of stockings were left also.

She moved to the next drawer. She did not throw out any of the T-shirts, but she did throw out every scarf except for two.

"Were any of these scarves your grandmother's or mother's?"

"No."

"Good." She replied as she moved on to the next drawer.

"Go get some trash bags and put all of the clothing things in one bag, and all of the personal things in another. Socks in a separate bag, and shoes in their own. Also a separate one for that thing" indicating the fur trimmed outfit. "Are you catching my drift here?"

"Yes Ma'am."

"Then go."

"Yes Ma'am." Taylor said, as she moved to go and get the bags.

She came back after a few minutes to find Alex had cleared out the other drawers completely, and was now going through her jewelry box.

"Hmm...at least your jewelry is real, I'm pleased."

Taylor's heart stopped for a moment as she waited for Alex to close it without throwing anything away.

"Yes Ma'am."

"Get to work on those piles."

"Yes Ma'am." She went to her knees and began folding and putting things in the bags neatly, still not sure of what the plan was for them. Meanwhile the woman went to open the other door on that same wall, but found it locked.

"What's in here?"

"Oh...nothing, just some more clothes." Taylor said, somewhat shaken.

Alex saw the change in the girl's expression, and got suspicious.

"Open it." Came the simple statement.

"No, please, it's just a room of clothes?"

"Open it now, or I'm going to have a real hard time trusting you." She said, informing the girl of the consequences.

Taylor sat back on her heels and then after a moment she stood up and took the key out of cleavage. This caused Alex's brows to rise. The girl then walked over and after a moment or two, and a glance back at the woman, she put the key in and opened the door. Alex looked at her as she pushed the door open. A gasp escaped her lips as she turned to go inside the room. It was like a whole new world inside of that room.

"What is this?" Alex asked, as she touched one outfit after another in complete shock. But when she did not hear a response, she looked over at Taylor with suspicion now obvious in her gaze. "I asked you a question. What is this?!"

"Just clothes." She answered quietly, due to the look.

"From where? How? How could you afford such things? Why have you been pretending you knew nothing about fine clothing? Why have you been lying to me? Answer any of them and I may not get angry."

"A friend gave them to me."

"Gave?! Are they stolen?"

"No."

"Really?" Alex said, not convinced.

"I swear. She gives me some of the newly designed clothes from her company. She says that I need to start dressing better, and less like a conservative old woman or something. I've never worn any of them, I don't really know what goes with what. I didn't want to hurt her feelings so I cleared my second bedroom and made it into storage for the clothes. I could never afford any of these things, I don't think I would ever buy any of them for the simple fact of not knowing what to do with them. I didn't lie to you about my naivetes, I don't know about designer clothes, you've seen what I have. Those are what I know about, not these, so I store them. I come in here sometimes and try to see if I can match something up, but it intimidates me the same way you do, so I get flustered and I just admire them."

"Why didn't you ask Ms. Sains or your friend to show you how to put things together?"

"I was just too embarrassed."

Alex stood looking at the many rows of designer outfits. She leveled a studying glance back at Taylor. She saw in her eyes that she had told the truth, and an ironic smirk came to her lips.

"Okay, I believe you. This actually works out better than I thought. Come over here."

Taylor walked over to where the woman stood, and then Alex said with a satisfied smile.

"Okay, you are now about to be educated in how to wear the finer things. I don't expect to see anything added to them after I put the things together, clear?!"

"Yes ma'am."

"Okay. Your friend owns her own designer shop I take it?"

"Yes."

The woman then lifted a hem to look at it, and she got the answer she was looking for.

"Your friend is Zadria?"

"Ye..yes. You know her?"

"Hmm....she owns one of the top fashion houses in the country, I get a lot of my own clothes from there. I'm surprised you couldn't tell? But then again, maybe I'm not, you did say clothes were not your forte. Anyway, take those off and put this on with this and this."

"Yes Ma'am. " Taylor turned to go and change in the other room but was called back.

"Where are you going?"

"I was going to go change."

"Change here, we don't have time for you to go back and forth, it's just you and I. Now hurry up and put that on, I want to see how it looks on you." Alex commanded.

Taylor stood for a moment, still unsure, but then she finally decided to go ahead and change where she was. She didn't want to offend Alex, who was just trying to help her, at least that's what she thought the woman's only intentions were. Taylor stripped out of the outfit she had on, and while she did, Alex watched discreetly as the shapely body was revealed to her. She made sure that Taylor did not see her looking, as she knew it would make her feel uncomfortable. But during those times when Taylor's eyes were covered by a garment either going over or coming off, Alex took in her fill. After a few hours of the stimulating fashion show, Alex finally called an end to the evening.

"Okay, I think those will hold you for a while, I really must be going. We have a lot to do tomorrow, including lingerie shopping."

"Oh, okay." Taylor said, somewhat disappointed that the evening was really ending this time. She had been really enjoying herself, and she actually got Alex to laugh a few times.

The woman heard the tone and a smile curled her lips.

"I had fun too. I'll see myself out, just make sure you wear those the way I've shown you, clear?"

"Yes Ma'am, I understand."

"Good, I'll see you in a few hours, wear the blue outfit. Bye."

"Bye, and thank you!" Taylor called from the doorway of the room where the clothes were, as she watched the woman grab her purse and things, and head for the door to the bedroom. With a wave over her shoulder, Alex called back to her.

"You're welcome."

CHAPTER 3

That night when Alex arrived home, she was really worked up and needed to calm herself. She went to her personal gym and worked out for a while, until her tension was gone. When she finally made it into bed, her thoughts were of Taylor, and how enjoyable the evening had been once they had both loosened up a bit. She chuckled at the memories of how Taylor looked at her in total confusion as to what to do with certain pieces of clothing. She laughed louder to herself thinking about the look on Taylor's face when she discovered that some of the strap tops were what was to be used to cover her breasts. Alex smirked when she thought of how the girl would blush and then shake her head and say things under her breath like, "I guess that one will sit there forever." Then she would look up to see Alex looking at her with one brow raised as if in challenge. After a while the woman finally drifted off to sleep with those pleasant thoughts floating through her head.

The next morning when Taylor arrived at Alex's residence, she was amazed at the size of it. Then she thought about Alex and it made sense. Taylor knocked on the door and a woman answered it. She was dressed in a maid's dark blue and white outfit.

"May I help you?"

"Yes, I'm supposed to meet..."

"Aha, very good, you're on time with plenty of it to spare, come on it." Alex called from the staircase, as she descended down them. "That'll be all Theresa." She said, dismissing the maid.

"Wow, you have a beautiful home Ma'am." Taylor said, as she stepped inside and looked around the open foyer.

"Thank you, now come with me, I want to get you started in learning my routine. By the way, that outfit looks good on you, I'm pleased."

"Thank you, but I have a question."

"What?"

"I didn't know if this broach goes with it or not?" She asked, seeking the woman's advice.

Alex cocked her head at the girl. She approved of Taylor seeking her counsel.

"Hmm....that's very nice, but I didn't see that when I was looking through your jewelry box?"

"I know, I have a collection of them from my grandmother."

Alex's eyes narrowed slightly as she turned fully around to face Taylor, and with an inquisitive brow raised she asked evenly.

"Why didn't you tell me?"

"I...I'm a little embarrassed to say why."

"Why?"

"Because, I didn't know if you would have disliked them and therefore thrown them out."

"What would you have done if I didn't like them?"

"I would have kept them. I would have tried to appeal to your sense of family and how important anything from my grandmother is to me. Some of them are my mother's, but I don't really care which, I just love them because I have a piece of something that they themselves used to treasure." Taylor said, subconsciously caressing the broach in her hands.

"Well, first of all I am disappointed that you would think that I would throw anything of your grandmother's or your mother's away. I thought I made it clear to you that those type of things were important for you to keep." Alex said, as she turned to walk towards the gym she had in her home.

"That's why, I was embarrassed." Taylor called out after the woman.

Alex stopped, but she did not look back except to turn her head slightly, as she waited to hear the explanation.

"When you were in my drawer of scarves and things, you asked me if any of them were from my grandmother. I saw then that you did understand what I might feel if you threw anything that belonged to either of them out."

"But that was before the jewelry box, if that is true..." Alex said as she turned to once again face the blushing girl. "Why didn't you trust me with the broaches?"

"I was on overload at all of the things you were doing, I mean it's not everyday that someone comes into my home and literally throws away all of my clothes, with the expectation that I will just accept it." Taylor said, lowering her eyes. She then looked back up at Alex, then down again to regard her broach.

"Hmm....I guess not, but that is the way I work, I like to know everything about those people who are around me the most. It doesn't matter whether they are in my professional life or my personal. I've done this with other employees, mainly the senior management staff, only in a little different way."

"Oh." Taylor said, somewhat disappointed by the fact that she was just another of the employees, especially after the wonderful, yet strange dinner yesterday.

Alex heard the disappointment, but she did not let on to the girl that while she had rid the other's closets of things that she didn't like, it was a very different situation. She did it by telling them not to wear whatever they were wearing to the office again, and they then took it upon themselves to get rid of those things that Alex did not like. The men were especially easy as they all hoped that Alex would become attracted to them. Alex did give her a little something to make her feel better.

"If it makes any difference to you, I have never had dinner over at any of their homes." She then smirked at Taylor when she saw a smile playing at the girl's lips, despite her holding her head slightly down, trying to hide it.

"Come on, I need to go workout." Alex turned and headed to her gym.

When she removed her robe, she had nothing on but a one-piece body suit that was like a second skin on her. The muscles showing through it rippled along her abdomen and legs, as well as her back. Taylor stared openly at the woman's remarkable physique, and she couldn't help thinking how beautiful Alex was.

"Of course she's beautiful, she modeled and has been on every publication there is." Taylor chided herself for being naive, she couldn't help gasping at the magnificent body that was now stretching.

"Ahem." Alex said, clearing her throat to gain the girl's attention to what she was saying.

"Oh God, she caught me staring at her body, what must she think of me."

"I'm sorry ma'am, I..I.." The girl tried to explain, but nothing came to her mind. Alex cocked her head as she watched Taylor struggle to compose herself.

"It's alright, I'm not ashamed of my body, I worked hard to get it like this and I work just as hard to keep it strong and intact. It looks like you work out some?"

"I do, but I could never achieve such a physique as yours." Taylor said, praising the woman's body.

"No, you can't, because your body is not like mine. You're shorter than I am, but you can achieve just as toned a body as I have, and you will." Alex said, now doing some flexing exercises, starting with bending backwards and walking over to come to a standing position again.

Taylor's mouth dropped open as she watched the woman do it again and again. Alex looked like a piece of smooth band of steel gliding away from her. She stopped and stretched a moment, then did the same thing in a forward fashion. When Alex stopped this time she was standing right in front of the open-mouthed girl.

"Close your mouth." She ordered and Taylor's mouth snapped shut. "Go push that button on the wall over there, and then sit down right there and watch. After you learn about my morning activities, you will be joining me in working out." Alex watched the girl's mouth drop open again as she pointed to a far wall.

Taylor's eyes had a hard time leaving those of the woman's. Finally she managed to follow the direction of the indicating finger, and with a quick glance back at Alex, she went to go and do as she had been told. After she pushed it, she went to sit down and watch. Alex turned around and the wall in front of her divided up as a large video wall appeared. Taylor sat watching and was startled when a man's voice came on.

"Good Morning Alexandra, all set?"

"Morning Joe, let's get on with it shall we?"

"Alright. Let's begin."

Suddenly music started and the two video conferencing people began moving with basic aerobic movements. Taylor thought at that moment that she could do what they were doing, and a smile came to her face. Alex saw the girl's response to what they were doing in a mirror that allowed her to watch behind her.

"Okay, ready?" Came the man's voice on the screen once again.

"Go!" The woman answered simply, and suddenly the music changed and the two of them were now moving in a synchronized pattern of boxing, and Martial Arts moves. It was rapid, and powerful looking, each move sharp as a knife, precision cut.

Taylor once again sat completely amazed at all of it, especially with how powerful Alex looked. At the same time, Alex showed she was human by the perspiration that was now dripping from her brows as the workout went on for an hour. It was followed by a fifteen minute cool down. The girl managed to hold her mouth closed when Alex walked over to her after saying goodbye to her personal trainer, and stood wiping her face and neck of the moisture.

"So, what did you think?"

"WOW! That was incredible, you just never seem to stop amazing me, I mean when I think I finally think I've got you figured out to a small degree, you come along and floor me again. How did you learn that? Did it take long?" How long have you been doing it, where did you meet him?" Taylor said, asking a litany of questions as she stood up to follow Alex out of the gym.

"There is an almost endless list of things you don't know about me, but as my assistant you will learn most of them, if I feel I can trust you. I'll have to see. Anyway, I learned the martial arts first, and I used to do some boxing as exercise. Anyway, I met Joe a few years ago during a competition. He told me he had this workout that he thought I would really like. He offered to teach me the moves and let me see if I liked it or not. I did, so he's been my personal trainer ever since."

The two women ended up in the kitchen where Alex headed over to the refrigerator.

"Have you eaten breakfast yet?"

"No Ma'am."

"Good. Well, look in that cabinet and get two bowls and two glasses out, and below it in the drawer, two spoons."

Taylor got the things she was told to and put them on the table. Alex brought the milk and a box of cereal over to the table. She took two apples out of the bowl and set them on the table for them. The woman filled both bowls halfway and then the girl poured the milk for the two of them. Alex waited for Taylor to start eating before she began talking to her about what she would do when she came to the house.

"I will give you a key to the house, you are to keep it in the same place you keep your other key. I don't want to take a chance that it will get lost. Anyway, once you arrive, you will get my paper and bring it inside with you. Come straight to the gym and workout with me, unless I am still in bed, and then I expect for you to wake me up. Depending on the time, we will either skip the workout, and just eat breakfast, and continue from there. I have never been late, and I don't expect to be late. If I am late, I will blame you for it. Part of your job is to make sure that I am never late, clear?" Alex asked, as the girl swallowed the mouth full of cereal she had in her mouth.

"Yes...yes Ma'am." Taylor choked out, while still trying to get all of the cereal down.

"You're going to need a note pad with you at all times, you will take over planning my day. I'm going to be having a business party here in the spring and I will of course expect you to be there. You will speak with the coordinator about how things are progressing. Have Salina give you the notes as to types of food, music and things like that I will want.

Now, as far as appointments, you are now a straight line to me, so if people get through you then I will take that to mean that you already screened them for whatever their business is. Do you understand what I am saying?"

"Yes Ma'am. No one gets in to see you unless it's important."

"Everything is important to everyone when it comes to wanting to get in to see me. No, you will see what their business is, and then handle those things that you will have learned how to, hopefully very soon."

"Okay I understand now, but may I ask you a question?"

"What?"

"You realize it is going to take me a little time to get used to this, as well as your habits and the things you like and dislike. I feel like you're going to be getting upset with me A LOT! and that really scares me." Taylor said, looking over her brows at Alex, who just sat listening to her without indicating whether what she had just expressed was true or not.

The girl took a drink of her milk with shaky hands due to the silence. Alex finished her quick breakfast and rose to her feet.

"Come on, I need to go and get changed, I want you to take the garment bag with the silver tag out of my closet and lay the clothes out on the bed with the shoes." They arrived at the bedroom while the woman was telling the girl what she wanted her to do while she went to clean up.

Taylor looked in the room and was amazed at the size and beauty of it.

"The closet is over there, the stockings are located in there also, in the top drawer of the cabinet."

Taylor moved to go and get the requested items, while Alex went into the bathroom to get cleaned up. She spoke to the girl through the door as she did.

"Look on the dresser and get my planner out." The woman brushed her teeth while she waited for her to get it.

"Okay, I have it."

"Good. Look inside and familiarize yourself with my schedule for today. When we get to the office I expect for you to get my mail, sort it, and then watch what I do as I go through it. It'll show you what I feel is important for me to handle right away, versus those things that are less important."

"Why?" Taylor asked, as she heard the shower turned on. Alex stepped into the shower and cleaned up as she continued to talk to Taylor through the doors. Then Taylor heard the door open and Alex came out in a robe and went into her closet and pulled out a pair of panties and the matching brassiere. She put them on while she was in the closet and then came out and sat on the bed to put her stockings on.

Taylor made herself busy by writing, so as not to stare at the woman, but at times she found herself stealing quick glances at her as she dressed, out of curiosity.

Alex continued to speak to her as she finished dressing and applying the small amount of makeup she wore. This included eye drops, facial moisturizer, skin protecting sunscreen, mascara, and lipstick. The woman left her hair hanging freely over her shoulders and back.

"I want you to eventually be able to step in and handle a lot of the routine parts of my work schedule, as well as be able to handle my mail when I am busy with other things."

"Oh, okay."

"Don't worry, I'm not about to just throw you into the fire without strict training as to what I want and expect. There will be many times you will wish you never came to my attention, but I can assure you that if you are not a quitter, then you will see the change in yourself. You'll be stronger and more confident about being around and interacting with people." Alex said, turning herself around to look Taylor straight in the eyes. The young girl could see the truthfulness in those piercing eyes.

"I'll do my best."

"That's a start. Call for a driver." The woman ordered, as she turned to get her earrings. Taylor stood for a moment not sure of how to contact the driver.

"Um..."

"The numbers in the planner on the phone list page." Alex said, as she put the next earring in her ear, and then turned around to watch the girl locate the number.

"Aha, here it is!" Taylor exclaimed, as she scanned the room to locate the phone.

She found the phone and made the phone call. Alex stood listening to her call for the driver, and when Taylor hung up, she sent an approving gaze towards the girl. Picking up her purse, she motioned for the girl to follow her while reminding her to start memorizing their schedule for the week. Taylor was also told that she would be expected to have her own list of Alex's schedule so when they were apart, she could determine where to locate her. They were driven to the office in the limo, while Alex instructed Taylor on different things she wanted done. When they arrived at the building, they went inside together, but then split up.

"I'll see you in my office in 10 minutes, and make sure you get the information from Salina when you arrive."

"Yes Ma'am." Taylor said, then turned and went to go to the mailroom, while Alex headed for her office.

"Well Hello there." Olsen called to the girl, who jumped as a result of being startled.

"Oh! Mr. Olsen, you scared me, I didn't realize anyone was here yet."

"I came in early to get Ms. Madison's mail ready for you."

"For me?"

"Yes, you no longer work in the mail room so it would not be proper for you to come in and have to wait for the boss's mail."

"You know about that already?"

"Yes, but I'm the only one. She called my house to tell me to make sure her mail was sorted from the general mail, and that her new Personal Assistant would be in around 5 to pick it up."

"Oh. Well, Thank you."

"You're welcome, I'm just curious about something?"

"What's that?"

"How is it that you managed to go from Admin Assist, to mail room, to Personal Assistant to Ms. Madison herself all in a matter of days?"

"It's really a VERY strange story, one that I find hard to believe, I think it rates right up there with a D. Virtue novel, absorbing and a fast read. But in short I'll tell you this, I tried to remain anonymous, and now I've been thrown headlong into the limelight. I have to go, but thank you for getting the mail ready for me, I'll see you later."

"Okay, I hope things work out for you. It's a known fact that Ms. Madison has never had a Personal Assistant. I can only imagine what it will be like for you, hopefully not hellish. Anyway, good luck to you, and the mail will always be ready for you."

"Thank you Mr. Olsen." Taylor said, now more nervous than when she was first told about becoming Alex's assistant.

She made it up to the floor, went inside the office and saw Salina was already there.

"Hello." Taylor said in greeting to the woman sitting at her desk.

"Oh, hi, what are you doing here?"

"Um...I need you to give me the information on the Business party that's scheduled for the spring?"

"Why? That's not for mailroom personnel. I'm surprised you would even know about that, let alone have the nerve to ask about it. Anyway, I have that handled. Now you better get in there with the mail before she has to call you, you know it upsets her if she has to wait?" Salina said condescendingly.

Alex was on the phone and had her back to the open door of her office, but she was listening to the whole conversation. She had told the person on the phone that she would talk to them later, and was just holding the phone up to her ear while listening to the two women. She wanted to see how Taylor would handle an interoffice power struggle with one of the greediest and most determined, lower echelon of the company. Salina was known to be a very determined young woman who pretty much did whatever it took to get to where she now was in the company. She wanted to get a leg up so as to be offered a recommendation into the Junior Executive Program in house. That would also pay for her education. The last supervisor she had worked for told her the best way to get into that program was to either graduate from college with a degree in business, or get a position as Alex's Personal Assistant. She was told that Alex did not trust anyone enough to put them in that position. The only other way to be accepted into the program was to go to work for Alex as an Admin Assist.

"Um...Salina..."

"Ms. Young, it's very unprofessional of you to address me or any other person by their first names. You should know that, you use to be an Admin yourself...until you were demoted...ha. Now I have work to do, and so do you, I would think?"

Taylor was completely flustered by the woman's response to her request and the tongue-lashing. She was not sure as to how to handle the woman. She held the mail she had in her hands closer to her chest and with a look of humiliation on her face, she walked nervously by Salina, who now acted as if she was no longer in the office. She went into the office where Alex still had the phone to her ear but was just getting ready to hang it up.

"Aha...there you are, so...you ready?"

"Ye...ye...yes Ma'am." Taylor said, as she glanced back at the outer office while moving towards the large desk.

Taylor began handing Alex the mail in the order of priority. While Alex took the time to read some, she sorted the rest and then handed it all to her. Then Taylor picked up her pad and pen and prepared herself to go to work observing the woman. But Alex wanted her to handle things with Salina, so she brought the subject up indirectly.

"Let me see the layout for the party." She asked, sticking out her hands for the information that she knew the girl did not have.

"Um...Well.." Taylor said, looking over at the door trying to decide whether she should tell the woman that Salina had been rude to her or just accept the blame for not having it.

"Well, give it here!" Alex now demanded.

"I...I don't have it."

"What do you mean you don't have it? Didn't I tell you in the lobby you were to stop and get it from Salina?" Alex was now glaring at Taylor who was fidgeting with her notepad due to the gaze that was leveled on her. She nervously flicked at the corner of the notepad.

"Yes Ma'am."

"And didn't I tell you back at my place that you were to get the information? And STOP THAT!!"

Taylor's hands stopped their fidgeting and she gripped the pad closer to her as Alex now began to lay into her about the information. Reminding her that when she was told to do something she was expected to carry it out. She now had tears rolling down her face, as Alex continued to reprimand her.

"Now go and get them!!" The woman demanded, and Taylor moved towards the door as if she had just been whipped. She didn't know whether to keep her eyes on the woman who made her feel that way, or one who caused it.

"Yes Ma'am." She said, as she opened the door of the office and went quickly out to get the reports.

Salina was talking to someone from one of the departments, and when Taylor came out, she just looked at her and went back to talking. The girl waited for a moment for the woman to finish her conversation.

"NOW!!" Came the commanding voice from the inner office and both women jumped, as well as the man Salina was talking to.

"Salina, I'll talk to you later, bye!' He said, as he nearly ran out of the office.

Salina looked at Taylor and then back at the office.

"What?!" Salina said angrily towards Taylor.

"I need the information about the party." She stated, trembling at having to come back and ask Salina for the same information she was originally denied.

"I told you, that is not for you and if you ask me about it again, I'll report you to her, and let her deal with you. Now go away, I have to get in there." Salina turned, and picking up the information, went into the office with it.

Taylor followed after her, Salina looked at her and said sarcastically, "What are you doing?"

"I'm...."

"What? Are you slow in the head? YOU...Are...Not...Supposed...To...Be...Here, you understand that?" Salina purposely emphasized each of her words as if she were speaking to a mentally challenged person.

Alex didn't say anything, she just sat and looked at her, waiting for her to say something for herself. Taylor was now completely embarrassed. She had never had to deal with confrontations so she was totally unprepared for this. She looked at Alex, and then back at Salina and finally, she just turned to run out.

"Damn it!" Alex hissed to herself, and then she called out to Taylor. "Where do you think you're going?! Get back in here RIGHT NOW!!"

The girl dropped her head into her hands and took a deep breath, then turned back around and headed back into the office.

"Close the door, and the two of you sit down!" Alex said, as she now sat back in her chair and studied the two for a few moments. Then she finally spoke again. "Salina I want you to meet your new boss." Salina's mouth dropped open, and she came to her feet in a huff.

"What?!! HER?! YOU?!! You made her my boss Ma'am?! How, why?"

"She's my new Personal assistant, therefore she is over you as my Admin What she says goes without question, as if I had said it myself, clear?"

"Ma'am...how could you put her in such a position? She's a timid little rabbit who will be eaten alive by all of the other CEO's. Ma'am she's not the right choice for that position." Salina said, outraged but keeping her control so as not to offend Alex.

"Then who is?"

"Me! I would do anything for that position, ANYTHING." She emphasized.

"Hahahahaha, I'm sure you think so, and would, but she has her degree in business. She graduated the top of her class, and writes perfect reports, even though she was only working a lower office. She is a bit shy, but I thought she would be the perfect candidate to mold the way I want. You already have your own mindset with your goals clearly outlined. I see you want to one day be a vice president, if not a president in one of my companies. But this young woman will one day own a company, and it will be one of the elite companies, because she will have learned from the best...ME. I will mold, push, shape, and reprimand her when necessary, to get her to come out of that shell of hers. But she will be great by the time I get done with her." Alex said, directing the last part of her statement at Taylor, who was sitting on the sofa chair rubbing her forehead.

Salina looked back over at Taylor who was now looking at her.

"I can't believe you got such a position?! You must be kissing ass damn well. Maybe I need to take lessons from you on how to properly kiss ass?" The angry woman said, with venom pouring from her lips, as she stood, towering over the young girl.

"Do you mind backing up?" Taylor asked, wanting her space, and expecting the woman to do it, seeing as they were in the CEO's office and she was watching all of it.

"NO."

"Excuse me?"

"I know you heard me, I said no, I will not move, I can stand anywhere I choose to stand."

Taylor gave the young woman a look of complete amazement, and then looked towards Alex, who had her head cocked, just watching with both amusement, and anger.

"Whatever."

"I know." Salina said as she stepped back and turned around. With a shake of her head she left to go back out to her desk.

Once the door closed, Taylor covered her face with embarrassment.

"If you intend to make it as MY personal assistant, then you're going to have to develop a backbone with people. I will not waste my time with a weak person. I knew you were timid, but what I just saw borders on cowardly behavior. Are you a coward?"

"No, at least I never thought of myself as being a coward." She said, blushing with embarrassment at being considered a coward by the woman she wanted to learn the business from.

"Hmmm...I didn't think so either, until this little display." Alex said, as she steepled her fingers and sat back to look at her with curiosity and thoughtfulness.

"I'm sorry."

"Sorry won't cut it, from now on I expect for you to stand up for yourself with everyone. If I think they are beyond your handling, I will step in and handle them, until you develop more confidence."

"Yes Ma'am."

"What you seem to not realize is that you are now over everyone in the company except myself. This means what you say is as good as if I said it myself. If they give you a problem that you've tried to handle and find that they are just resistant to listening to you, then I will handle them in my own...special way." The woman smirked.

Taylor sat listening to her mentor, as she explained the facts of the position's rank in terms of her job. Alex picked up the party plans, glanced over them and then handed them to the girl to look over, as she spoke to her.

"Remember, you are the first line to me. If you allow them to walk all over you then I will be left to handle them, and that would mean that you failed. I don't tolerate failure...Are you catching my drift?"

" Yes Ma'am."

"Alright. Here, take this budget analysis to the accounting department and give it to Ms. Huston, then come back and we will get to work on all of this."

"Yes Ma'am." Taylor said quietly, as she stood to take the folder from the woman, only to have it held back from her.

"When you get back, I expect for you to be ready to get to work. You have 20 minutes, go." Alex then handed the folder to the girl, who gave a timid reply, and then turned and left the office. When Taylor had gotten onto the elevator, Alex turned her attention to her Admin.

"Salina get in here right now!" She demanded.

"Yes Ma'am." The young woman said, as she came in and closed the door.

The next 17 minutes were the longest of Salina's life. Alex read her up one side and down the other. By the time she was finished with her, Salina was crying hysterically as she ran out of the office to go and get herself composed.

When Taylor returned from her errand, she saw the desk was empty, and assumed Alex had sent the young woman to do something. She went into Alex's office and was told to call purchasing and have them deliver another file cabinet for her to store her records in. After that was taken care of, she told Taylor to come over to the desk. She began to go through her mail showing the girl those things she needed to know. She explained to her why certain things were handled in particular ways, and why with other things she made the calls necessary to handle them. She put the speakerphone on while she spoke to different people, but did not tell them about her new assistant just yet. She wanted Taylor to develop a lot more before being put out to the wolves.

After four months, Taylor was now more of a shadow to Alex than her own shadow. She was still shy, and somewhat timid, but she was handling most of the everyday correspondence. The Admin Assistant was becoming more and more resentful at how much Alex depended on the girl to handle things that she herself used to handle. Taylor was not impolite or rude, in fact, she was very nice with how she asked Salina to do something, but the woman was eaten up by jealousy.

One morning, Taylor had collected all of the mail, when she saw a red envelope with a white stripe on it. She remembered what Alex had told her about those envelopes, she had not seen one since picking up Alex's mail, despite being told she receive the envelops weekly, so she immediately grabbed the other mail and went to deliver it to her hands. Alex had left the office to go and do something, and the girl asked Salina where she was. Before Salina could answer, the phone rang and Taylor went to answer it since it was in Alex's office on her private line.

"Hello, Ms. Madison's Office may I help you?"

"It's me, meet me in the lobby, we have to take a ride over to a company that I am about to take over. The CEO wants to see if he can talk me out of taking it over."

"Yes Ma'am." Taylor said, as she put the mail into her briefcase.

She met Alex in the lobby and as they walked out to the limo, she explained to the girl what was going on.

"So why are you taking this particular company over?"

"Because I can." Was the simple response.

"But what is it going to do for you?"

"I know what you meant, but that answer is the basis of why I take over any company. In this case, they have a wonderful distribution industry, and I am always looking for faster ways to get things to my overseas companies."

"Oh, so why would The CEO think that you wouldn't take it over?"

"Because it's been in his family for such a long time, over a century, and they're hoping I will give in because of the sentimental value." Alex said, with an ironic gleam lighting her eyes.

"Well...I can understand why they would try then." Taylor said, not noticing the look of surprise that came into the woman's eyes at the very thought.

"What??"

She turned to look at Alex when she heard that tone, and flinched as a result of that look in her eyes.

"What?"

"You're not serious are you, I mean after being around me all of this time?"

"Well I...."

"You what? You think that my business success is based on other people's sentiments?" The woman asked pointedly, as she looked hard at Taylor, who was now embarrassed.

"Well..."

"You said that! Now answer me. Is that what you think?"

"No Ma'am." Taylor finally managed, as she swallowed a lump in her throat.

Alex relaxed a little, but continued to look at her with some skepticism.

"Why are you going to them, usually you make them come to you? Taylor asked, cognizant of the change in Alex's normal routine. She looked out the corner of her eyes at the woman who had not taken her eyes off of Taylor.

"Because, they'll think I'm thinking about it."

"Oh...so you have NO intention of even considering not taking the company from them?"

"None what so ever."

"Hmm..." Taylor answered, as she chewed her lips.

They arrived at the company, and Alex told her to take notes of everything.

"Welcome to Lanskey's Corporation, I'm Mr.Jessup's President in charge of export, and this is his Admin."

"Thank you, where is Mr.Jessup, and why didn't he meet us himself?" Taylor asked pointedly, as Alex scanned the corridor of the building.

"He's waiting for you..." The President started, but was cut off.

"Excuse me, but please address me." Taylor said, calling the man on his manners.

Alex just looked at him and waited for him to continue.

"Oh, pardon me, I didn't mean to offend you, you are?"

"I'm the Personal Assistant to Ms. Madison. Please take us to Mr.Jessup."

"Yes Ma'am." The President said, as he turned along with the Admin Assistant to lead them to where the meeting would take place.

The Admin kept looking back at Taylor as they walked to the elevator. Alex, in the meantime, strode to the elevator as if it were no big deal. She was actually very proud of the girl's progress in terms of handling people and it was showing in how she handled the President, and she would make sure to tell her later. They arrived at a large conference room where many of the senior staff as well as the CEO himself were sitting at the table. He stood, as did the rest of his staff.

"Welcome." He said in greeting as he watched Taylor pull out the large chair for Alex.

"Hello, and thank you for the invitation. If you don't mind, we really need to get straight down to business."

" Certainly, and you are?"

"I am Taylor Young, The Personal Assistant to Ms. Madison" Taylor said.

The man gave a conciliatory nod of his head and proceeded to go into the purpose of the meeting.

"Well, I asked you here so that we could try to come to some type of agreement."

"What type of agreement?" Alex asked, now stepping in to deal with the CEO as Taylor began taking notes.

"Well, I know you're interested in adding to the distribution abilities of your foreign based companies. I thought that if we could come to some sort of mutual, yet beneficial agreement, then maybe you will look at other options, rather than acquiring the whole company?"

"And what would these other options consist of?" Alex asked.

The man looked at her for a moment, and then he answered. He explained the options he thought would be good enough to satisfy the woman's appetite, yet maintain his family's company. The girl whispered to Alex.

"Yes, that's exactly what I want to do." Alex said to Taylor. Then she returned her attention to the CEO. "My Assistant makes a good point. Mr. Jessup, as a show of good faith, I would like to have a look around. I might change my mind about wanting any part of your company depending on what I see?" Alex said, insinuating something that she knew Taylor hoped would happen, despite having been told in no uncertain terms that she planned on taking over the company.

The man smiled at the thought, but he was still cautious. He had to allow the tour despite his concern, and Alex knew he would allow it, even with his suspicions, as to the real purpose of the tour. He was somewhat more relaxed by the Assistant's innocent looking face and polite manner.

"Alright, I'll have Mr. Johnson take you around."

Alex leaned forward in her chair and steepled her fingers under her chin as she rested her elbows on the table in a thoughtful matter. She then made a counter suggestion.

"NO. I would feel more comfortable if the woman there...showed me around, she doesn't appear to be the type to lie."

The man looked at Ms. Rainer, and then smiled.

"Very well, Vice President Rainer is one of my right hands, she'll take good care of you both. Ms. Rainer, will you escort our guest around?"

"Certainly sir, it would be my pleasure." The woman said as she came to her feet. Alex and Taylor both came to their feet to follow her.

"Thank you Mr. Jessup, we'll be in touch."

Alex was already out the door when Taylor spoke to the man. She followed the woman to the elevator and they did not speak until they were down in the shipping area.

"So how long do you think you will need before I close on this acquistion?" Alex asked the woman, as Taylor was talking to one of the managers in the shipping department.

"Another month, and then you will have all the information you need to take it to the board for their approval, although the board will do whatever you tell them."

"I know, but good work. I'm pleased with how valuable you have become to Mr. Jessup. I hope that doesn't mean anything?"

"No Ma'am! I know where my loyalties lay, it's with you Alex."

"Happy to hear it." She said, giving the other woman a sidelong glance.

"So I see you finally decided to take on a Personal Assistant. How did that happen?"

"Long story."

"I bet, she's very good, but it would be the least I would expect from any Personal Assistant you decided to take on."

"True, but she still has a lot to learn. I'm working on her, you can believe that." Alex said, as she watched the girl deal with the managers.

Some of the men loading the trucks were somewhat crass in their language towards Taylor.

Alex saw her blush a few times as a result of some of the words the men were using to describe her body.

"She's very cute. The men seem to really like her. They talk one way when they think she's out of hearing range, but when she's close to them, they seem to straighten up as if she is inspecting them. Hmmm....I wonder?"

Alex's ears rang with the tone of the woman's words, and her eyes cut to the woman standing next to her. She spoke in a warning tone of voice.

"Don't even think about it, she's already spoken for." She said with meaning.

"Oh, she has a man already, okay. I was just wondering." The woman said quickly.

"Well now you can stop." Alex said sharply.

At that moment the girl headed over to where they were standing.

"They have an excellent system here, I see why you want it." Taylor said to her.

"Yes, well let's go, I've seen all I need to. Tell Mr. Jessup I'll be in touch." Alex said in a formal tone, so as not to give the woman away to her Assistant.

"Yes Ma'am. I'll walk you out?"

"Fine."

When the woman and the girl returned to their car, and were on their way back to the office Alex spoke to her.

"I'm pleased with your performance."

"Really?" Taylor said with a bright smile.

Alex saw how happy it made her to be complimented on her work.

"Yes, Really. You were strong and confident, although I saw you blushing with the workers. What was that all about, are you interested in one of them?"

"No!" Taylor said, blushing again, this time at the way the woman was looking at her.

"Well don't let me see it again. Especially, when you're dealing with a client of sorts."

"Yes Ma'am."

"Good. So what did you find out from the workers?" Alex asked, as she sat watching the girl go through her notes, and begin telling her the benefits of having the added distribution capabilities. They arrived back at the office around 2:30 p.m.

"Go get the mail, and I will see you in the office in a few minutes. I have a meeting."

"Yes Ma'am." She said as they split off and she went to get the mail.

She picked the mail up and went to take it back to Alex's office. She arrived to find the woman in the meeting with a department head. Taylor went inside and sorted the mail and then handed it to Alex as she spoke to the man in the office. Alex would open and read through the mail as she listened or spoke to the man. He was amazed at how smoothly the two of them worked without either ever breaking their flow. As the girl would come to something the woman would want to see, she wouldn't say anything just flip it into the woman's empty hand as she made gestures that allowed her to take the mail without dropping it. They worked like an assembly line, only with two people rather than a line of them. When the day finally ended, the sun was just going down, but it was still comfortable outside. Alex told Taylor that she would see her back at her place in the morning and that they would discuss the upcoming party. They went back to Alex's place where the girl's car was left.

"Alright, I'll see you tomorrow Ma'am."

"Alright. Be on time."

"I will." Taylor got in her own car and headed out of Alex's estate to go to her own home.

When she was getting undressed to get into bed, it was around 10:30 p.m., she decided to clear out her briefcase for the evening. She had not taken it into the meeting with Mr. Jessup; she had just taken the notepad. She left the briefcase in the limo. She put her briefcase out in front of her now, and when she opened it, the first thing she saw almost caused her heart to stop.

"OH MY GOODNESS!!! OH, My Goodness, Oh, My Goodness, oh, okay, what do I do? Arrghh!! How could I forget about all of this mail?" Taylor scolded herself for forgetting such a thing. But then as she was pulling it all out, she felt like a wrecking ball had hit her.

The red envelope, with the white stripe, was like a beacon. She fell back on the bed and covered her head with a pillow, and cried into it. But she had to get the envelope to Alex and try to explain to her what happened.

"She's going to kill me." The girl sobbed into the pillow. She looked at the clock and saw how late it was, but it didn't matter, she had to get it to her.

She got out of bed and dressed in a T-shirt without her bra, and some jeans. Then she put on tennis shoes and a coat and got in her car to drive back over to Alex's residence. When she got there she thought about using her key, but decided it was too late at night, and she knew the woman would not be expecting her and may already be asleep.

Taylor stood outside for over 30 minutes debating whether to ring the doorbell or not. Finally she decided to ring it, and hoped that the maid would answer. She had been told the maid didn't live there, so she stood nervously hoping against hope. After a few minutes, she heard someone coming down the stairs, but when she looked at the height of the figure her heart dropped. The woman obviously knew it was her, from seeing her through the sheer window treatments.

"What are you doing here at this time of night?" Alex asked, as she stood in the doorway with just a nightshirt on and her arms crossed over her chest. Her long legs were bare and had no marks or blemishes on them.

Taylor didn't answer for a few moments and it was then that the woman noticed something was wrong.

"Have you been crying? Come in here." She ordered, so that she could close the door. Seeing how cool it was at that time of night.

"I...I...I messed up." Taylor finally managed to admit.

Alex's eyes narrowed at her as she tried to figure out what she was talking about.

"I forgot to give you your mail this morning."

"You forgot?! The woman said somewhat harshly, but then seeing the flinch as a result of it, she tried to find a way to keep her cool.

"Well...it was VERY irresponsible of you, but if it was the routine mail, then it'll be fine, you'll just have to call a few people and straighten things out. I'm upset with you, but I'll get over it, at least you didn't cause any real damage." The woman said, as she pinched her lips to keep from scolding her any further. She turned and headed up the stairs and Taylor followed after her.

The tears rolled down Taylor's face despite the woman's words and she was concerned by it.

"I told you it will be alright, it wasn't like it was a red envelope or anything." Alex said, trying to express to her that she was actually fine with the mistake.

Taylor then pulled out the red envelope, and the woman's eyes went wide, as did the girl's. Suddenly, Taylor's heart was racing from fear, and Alex's was racing from anger. But she held it. She needed to get to some water.

"Take off your coat, you'll be staying for a VERY long while." The woman hissed, as she turned and stormed towards her bedroom, after having stopped briefly to see why the girl was teary, now she understood why.

Taylor took off her coat and followed slowly towards the bedroom, and by the time she got there Alex was using all sorts of expletives. The girl stood in the doorway afraid to enter the room, but her arm was literally grabbed and she was pulled inside with the door slamming behind her. The woman glared at her for long moments, and then she let go of her arm and pushed her so that she was sitting on the bed.

"Do you realize what you have done?!"

"I'm sorry." Taylor gasped, as the tears ran.

"Sorry isn't good enough! I told you how important these were!" Alex shouted, as she held up the now opened envelope.

The girl dropped her head and covered her face with her hands as Alex yelled at her.

"Look at me!!" The woman shouted, and Taylor's hands immediately dropped from her face and she looked back up at the angry woman. "That does no good!"

"I don't know what to say!"

"You already said it! You screwed up, and because of it I've lost millions of dollars." Alex said evenly.

Taylor looked at her horrified, her hands came to her chest as if her heart was about to beat out of it and she had to stop it.

"Millions, Oh My God...I..." She said coming to her feet, despite how weak they felt. She went over to where Alex was now leaning on the dresser with her back to the girl, shaking her head.

Taylor went and stood behind and to the right of her. Both women were facing the mirror, but the girl had her head down as the tears and stress of what she had done felt as if it were about to consume her. Alex looked at her via the mirror, and it was then that she noticed the tee shirt without a bra. She looked at Taylor discreetly for a bit, but when the girl finally raised her head, she looked up into her eyes. They both looked at each other via the mirror.

Alex finally stood up and turned around. She sat on the edge of her dresser and studied the girl for a few minutes. She didn't want Taylor to be eaten up with guilt, but she did want her to know how badly she had screwed up. Despite the fact that millions were lost, it wasn't a lot, when compared to the woman's net worth, it was like losing 3 dollars out of a 1000. It was still a lot of money, and she usually used the money from those investments to do certain charity things with. But because of this mistake, she would have to use money from other investments, and she didn't like to do that. As a matter of fact, she had never done it, and now she may have to.

Alex sharply raised her hand with the envelope in it for the girl to take and look at. Taylor slowly took the envelope, and taking the slip of paper out, she read the note that simply said, " Call me before the end of the day, and let me know what you want me to do, otherwise the loss could be at least three million."

Her hands shook at the thought, and she wanted to crawl under a rock and die at what a huge mistake she had made.

"I'm sorry..." She gasped again as she laid the envelope on the table and once again covered her face and cried.

Alex sat and watched her for a few minutes and then with a sigh, she took a few deep breaths. She let them out slowly and spoke to Taylor in less harsh tones.

"Come here." She said, as she opened her arms to her.

Taylor looked up at her, and at first her brows knitted, but when she saw the questioning brow of the woman's raise she decided she didn't care. She went into her arms and wrapped her arms around Alex's neck and buried her head in the woman's neck and cried pitifully. She was shocked to feel the tender touch of the woman's hands on her hair, as she spoke to her and told her it would be alright. She even praised her for being responsible and honest enough to come over in the middle of the night and own up to her mistake. Taylor quieted, and then leaned back away from the woman with her head still lowered. Alex handed her a Kleenex and she dried her eyes and then blew her nose. Alex then spoke again.

"This had better not EVER...."

"It won't. I promise." Taylor interrupted, before the woman could finish her sentence.

Alex leaned back and regarded the girl for a bit, and then said understandingly. "I know."

Taylor gave a small, appreciative smile, but her brows still had concern written through them.

"May I ask you something?"

"What?"

"Actually two things?"

"What?"

"Why did you...hug me just now?"

"Because you looked like you could use it, I was hard on you, but not without good reason, right?"

"Yes."

"Anyway, does it bother you that I did that?"

"No, I actually did need it, but I was just...surprised that it would be you to give it. I mean...you're not really known for your...maternal side." Taylor said, trying not to offend her.

"Just because I don't show certain emotions of myself to others, doesn't mean I am not capable of them." Alex stated factually.

"It's just that...," The girl said, as she gave a thoughtful look at the woman, then turned to go and sit on the bed once again.

"Just what?" Alex asked, remaining on the edge of the dresser with her arms now crossed under her breasts.

Taylor noticed the difference in how the woman had her arms crossed. Normally they covered her chest, but now her chest was on top of them. She blinked her eyes to avoid staring, and looked off to one of the sides, or down at her hands as she spoke.

"Look at me when your speaking to me, you know I don't like when you do that." Alex said, having noticed the glances at her breasts by the girl, and how she blushed when she caught herself looking.

"Sorry, I'm just still shaken up about what I did."

"I know, but it's rude and it makes me suspicious when people don't look me in the eye.

"I understand. But you realize it's very hard to do that with you?"

"Why?"

"Because...your eyes are so...piercing, they seem as though they could penetrate a person's very soul, they're so...expressive, when you allow them to be."

"Really? I didn't think you've been studying me?" Alex asked, raising an inquisitive brow.

"Well...you told me I'm to watch everything you do, and how you do it, so I have to study you...right?"

"Yes, I guess so. So that's why you have a hard time looking me in the eye?"

"Well, I only have a hard time when you're upset with me. You have this way of looking that is so...disconcerting. Actually a look from you can either cut a person down, or send their spirits soaring. At least that's what I find."

"And what do my eyes do to you?"

"Both. When you're upset with me, I just want to crawl under a rock and die, because I know how busy you are. I know how hard it was for you to take on a Personal Assistant, when you have been adamant about not having one prior to now. I find myself trying to please you as I have never consciously tried to please anyone. I don't like disappointing you, and I don't know why that is so important to me, but I have for so long admired your success. I mean...I questioned your harshness, and the necessity of it, but I see how well it works for you. I do want to be successful in this business, and I know I'm learning from the best. But whenever I mess up, I feel like I'm causing you to reconsider whether this was a good idea or not, and I don't want you to question your decision. At first I didn't want this position, but now, I find I really want it, and I want to keep it...BADLY. "Taylor spoke honestly of her feelings about the woman, and her position.

Alex leaned back and continued to balance herself on the dresser, as she listened.

"So what about the other?"

"Hmm?"

"You said my eyes can make people feel one of two ways...what's the other."

"Oh...yes. Well, you have many looks that light your eyes when your either pleased, or if something is humorous to you, or when you are just tickled by something."

"Tickled? Hmm...not a word I would use to describe a part of myself." Alex said as an aside, as she listened to Taylor.

"No...I wouldn't guess you would, but it is what causes you to laugh out loud."

"Okay."

"Anyway, I know when you're pleased with something I've done. You have this way of looking at me out the corner of your eyes with a slight curve to the corners of your mouth that you don't quite let show as a smile, but I can tell that's what's hidden within it. Your brows, no matter what side of you I'm on, you seem to raise the one that is nearest me to acknowledge your approval of whatever it is that I've done to please you. You also have this look that lights your eyes when something is humorous. You get this sort of raised brow look while at the same time you're pinching your lips, and your eyes then look over your brows when they return to their normal position. It's like you're thinking about something, like you're trying to figure out the punchline before it's revealed or you've already figured it out. You're always looking as if you're thinking no matter what's going on. When you were yelling at me, you still looked like you were thinking about your next move. How to rectify the mess I've made, while at the same time wondering if you should let me off the hook or not, as long as you believed I've learned from my mistake and understand the importance of what I've done. Which by the way, I really do, and again I am so sorry, it will not happen again, I hope you believe me?"

"I do, now go on, I want to hear about these looks you say I have."

Taylor smiled as she continued.

"Well, you seem to have a depth to you that shows through your eyes when you choose for it to. When I asked you why, a moment ago. The look in your eyes was one that I had not seen in them before, one of compassion. It touched me, deeply, that I was the cause of it, very unsettling you know?"

"So you were seeing me as one dimensional?"

"Hmm...I don't think I would say one dimensional, I just didn't know whether you were capable of those soft feelings."

"Why? Do you think I am always a hard ass?"

"No, but when you're not hard you're usually still too busy to have time for those emotions."

"I relax."

"Well maybe so, but over the last several months that I've been around you, I have yet to see that. Except for the time you came over to the house to talk to me about this position, and right now, but other than that, I haven't seen you relax. I mean, what do you do when it's the weekend? Do you ever take a day off from work during the week? Do you go on vacations, if so, what type?

Where do you go? What do you like to do for entertainment? Is there a man in your life? What type of people do you like to be around, what type of games do you enjoy? What type of books do you read? Do you even have time? Where did you find the time to write your books?" Taylor was now on her feet approaching Alex, wanting to get to know her, wanting to see the other emotions that the woman possibly had.

Alex stood up, turned and sat down in the chair of her dresser vanity. She picked up the brush, not sure whether or not she wanted to open up that much to the girl.

"Are you going to answer me?" Taylor asked, as she gently took the brush from the woman's hands and began to brush the woman's hair as she admired the silky softness of it in her hands. "Wow, your hair is so soft. You must spend a fortune on your hair?"

"Why would you think that?"

"Because of how healthy and well cared for it is."

"Well I don't. I don't believe in being wasteful with my money, despite how much I make. I just take care of my hair the same way I take care of my body, and mind. Speaking of which, I understand from an acquaintance of mine that you are back in school?"

"Oh, yes, I was going to surprise you with my Bachelor's Degree." Taylor said, lowering her eyes to look at Alex's hair.

"Why is it important for you to do things to surprise me?"

"I don't know, I guess I like seeing that approving look in your eyes, especially from someone like you? I mean to me, you're like the preeminent goal and motivator of every businessperson. All striving to emulate your successes, in their own businesses."

"Well I'm pleased that you're using that brain of yours to get the papers that match the knowledge you have already. It shouldn't take you long to complete the courses. If you want I can have the instructors come to your home or send you all of your study information via your computer."

Taylor smiled a gentle smile, and Alex smiled back at her with a thoughtful look in her eyes.

"It might help, that way I will be able to study at night, and it not interfere with my work."

"Okay then, I'll call them tomorrow and set it up, I'll also have it available via my computer, that way maybe I can help you study...if you want?" Alex said, looking up at Taylor as she stopped her hand from brushing her hair.

"You would do that for me?"

"If you like, maybe I can give you the benefit of my experience with your studying?"

"If you can't, then there is no one who can." Taylor said, with a wry smile for her. To her complete delight she received a full smile in return.

"Finish brushing my hair, that feels good." Alex said, as she looked back at the mirror image of Taylor. The girl began brushing her hair again, this time in earnest.

Taylor lifted her eyes to look at the woman's eyes in the mirror, and she smiled again and then said in a quiet, shy voice.

"Thank you."

"You're welcome." Alex said, understanding the meaning without having to have her explain.

"You know you need to get used to calling me Alex."

"Yes Ma'am." Taylor replied, then blushed when Alex chuckled.

The two developed a more obvious connection from that point on, their relationship took on a deeper meaning. As the party neared, even though Taylor had made no overt overtones towards her mentor, Alex, for some reason was possessive of her, although she was never obvious about it. She found she would become upset with anyone who spent too much time with Taylor. This did not please Salina at all. One day the two were coming into the building with some clients, when Taylor looked around upon hearing a familiar voice. She caught the guy's eye, and gestured that she would be with him in a moment. She then turned and whispered to Alex.

"Where?" Alex asked, now concerned about the fact that there really was a boyfriend in the girl's life. Even after all of the time they had been around each other, Taylor had managed to avoid any conversation about him.

"Over there." Taylor smiled, as she waved at him, and he waved back.

The woman's eyes narrowed as a result. More than just her concerns about the girl being in a relationship, but who the man was..

"Come on, I want to introduce you to him?" Taylor said quietly to Alex.

"I don't..."

"Oh, please?"

"Alright, you go ahead and I will tell Mr. Halson that we will meet them in my office in a few minutes?"

"Okay." She said, as she turned and strode off to go and talk to the man.

Alex watched how they greeted each other, and it was a reserved kiss on the cheek Taylor gave to the man. Alex then turned and spoke to the men she was with, and had one of the guards show them to her office. She made a phone call to her office to tell Salina to take care of the men, but Salina was not in. She called Mr. Shearer to handle it until she arrived. The woman hung up the phone and then looked back over at the two, and Taylor was motioning for her to come over. The woman nodded her head, then strode over to meet the boyfriend. A tall Medium tone young man, with chiseled features

"Dominic, I want you to meet "The Raider" herself. Alexandra Madison, this is the man I told you I was involved with, Dominic."

"Dominic, huh?" She said, with a suspicious look in her eyes, as her brow raised questioningly.

"Yes, So...you're the Bitch who demoted, my girl?"

Taylor's face dropped; a moment she thought would be one of her happiest, had turned into a nightmare within the first few seconds.

"Dom...Dominic, you apologize." She gasped out in total shock.

"You've got to be kidding, I'm not apologizing to some...woman, no matter how fine she is, besides, why should I?" The man said, as he looked at Alex and then at the girl whom had she been any lighter would have shown just how flushed with embarrassment she was.

"Because she's my boss." Taylor said through her teeth in a loud whisper.

"Some boss, I remember how you use to cry at the very mention of her name."

"Dominic, please apologize?" She pleaded, hoping Alex was not making assumptions.

"I said I'm not apologizing, anyway, I came to take you to lunch."

"Ma'am, please don't be upset with me, I never..." She started to say, but was cut off by the woman's hand.

"Save it, we have to get to a meeting. I'll wait for you over at the elevator," Alex gave an assessing glance at the man, then with her brow raised, now in real concern about him, she looked at the girl and indicated for her to hurry up.

"Okay, I'll be right there," Taylor said to her boss.

Alex strode away towards the elevator, and the guy watched her go and with both lust and contempt in his voice he said to himself.

"Now that's a woman I wouldn't mind doing," then he turned his attention to the girl he was with. "You know you are looking too good these days. You finally took my advice to fix yourself up. Wow, I knew you had a body, but those clothes you used to wear did nothing for them, like these. By the way, where did you get the money to afford clothes like these?" He now asked with suspicion.

"Never mind my clothes! Do you realize what you've done?"

"What?"

"You humiliated me! You insulted MY Boss, to her face, about something that happened a long time ago. You've been out of town for a while taking care of some type of business. You don't even know what's happening with me lately." Taylor stated, as she kept pulling her arm away from his grasping hand.

"I can see you've learned to dress, I like it."

"I have to go," She said, sensing that she was not getting through to the man.

He grabbed her arm and she couldn't get loose this time.

"Let go, you're making a scene," Taylor said, trying to free her arm.

"No! And I Don't Care If I Cause A Scene, you're My Girl, and I don't appreciate the way you're acting. I've been gone for a few months and I come back to this attitude. What's wrong with you? I'm just trying to help you!"

"How Dominic?! How are you trying to help me?" Taylor now said, with tears rolling down her cheeks. The man let go of her arm to allow her to compose herself. "By Insulting MY Boss? By humiliating me in front of her, and the people in this lobby? By manhandling me? Dominic, tell me how you are trying to help me, because right now all I see is a man who doesn't like the idea that the girl he hasn't seen in months has changed to a more confident woman. I wanted to bring the two people to whom I felt the closest to, together. I hoped that we could all be friends, But No! You blew any hope of that. You insulted a woman who has been instrumental in the changes you see before you. I'm hurt that you would have so little regard for my feelings. I have to go, My Boss is waiting...for me, her Personal Assistant." Taylor then turned to walk away, but again her arm was caught, this time however, it was gentler.

"I'm sorry. I'm just a little caught off guard with all of this. Can I stop by tonight and we can talk?"

"Not tonight Dominic."

"Will you call me? Or can I call you?"

"I'll call you...maybe."

"Are you breaking up with me over this?"

She didn't answer, just glanced up at him. He let go of her arm and taking a deep breath, he glanced over at the woman standing by the elevator just watching them. Then he looked back at Taylor, and despite the fact he knew what she said was true, he felt jealousy rise up in him. He saw how close she was to her boss and how distant she seemed to be to him now.

"Fine!" He turned and stormed away from her and then out of the building. Alex glanced at the guards and gestured to them that they were not to let him in again.

Taylor stood and watched him leave with her arms crossed as if she were hugging herself. She let the tears roll. She looked over towards the elevator and saw Alex looking at her with compassion and concern in her eyes. Taylor smiled and at the same time more tears rolled down her face, she dropped her arms, and wiping her eyes she strode over to where the woman stood watching her.

"Are you alright?" The woman asked matter-of-factly. To which Taylor automatically assumed that she was upset with her about what the man had called her. She was afraid Alex would take his words as having come from her.

"Yes."

When they got into the elevator, Taylor pushed the regular button to the top, and once the doors had closed and they had gone up one floor, Alex pushed the stop button. Then she turned to look the girl straight in the eyes.

"I...I didn't call you that, I never would have, especially now, please don't let his words reflect on me with you, I am so sorry, I just wanted to introduce the two of you. I never dreamed that he would act like that, or say something so disrespectful to you, I'm sorry," Taylor pleaded with her.

"First of all, don't apologize for someone else's behavior or words, it's not your place. Secondly, I don't blame you for anything that he said."

"Really?"

"Yes. And finally, I don't want to see him around you again." Alex said, not expecting any disagreement.

"I know you're upset with him, but who I see is my personal business."

Alex cocked her head at the girl, and raised a disbelieving brow at her. Taylor flinched at the look and looked away for a moment. Alex then decided to just tell the girl straight.

"The man you know as Dominic is not his real name. His real name is Giovanii Macellis. He belongs to one of the most dangerous crime families in the country. I met his father, who helped me with my first takeover, years ago. He's dangerous, and I will not allow anyone to be around me who chooses to socialize with such a person. The odds are that he has his father's disposition of being very physically abusive towards his women. If you choose to be a part of such a life, then I not only want you away from me, but away from any and all of my companies. I don't need all of that drama coming into my life. So close your mouth and make your choice right now," Alex stated with a harsh and curt tone. Although she was hoping the girl was not a fool.

Taylor's mouth snapped shut, but her eyes were wide with both uncertainty and fear.

"Well, who do you choose?" Alex asked impatiently.

"You."

"Good, then we'll talk about the rest of this after our meeting with the clients in the office." She hit the start button and the elevator once again climbed. Alex noticed the girl looking at her with concern in her eyes, so when they arrived to the top, just as the doors open, she stepped out, turned and looked Taylor straight in the eyes. " And No I do not still have ANY dealings with him or his family." She saw the girl's eyes soften, and a small smile came to her face. "Let's go." She then turned and they went into their meeting.

While Alex and Taylor held their meeting, Salina, who had overheard the conversation between the girl and Dominic down in the lobby, ran and caught up with him outside the building.

CHAPTER 4

"Excuse me?"

"Yes, what do you want?" The man asked angrily.

"Hi, I'm Salina, I work with your ex-girlfriend."

"Really?" He said, turning around with an evil glint in his eyes.

"Yes, so what are you going to do? I mean considering that timid, little, rabbit just rejected you, I'm sure you want to get even."

"I take it you don't like her? That's unusual."

"This isn't about me, it's about you. You know you won't be able to get to her when she is in the building?"

"Why not?"

"Because the minute you left a signal was sent to the guards to not let you back in the building."

"But, I could get back in if someone helped me?"

"Yes, maybe."

"Okay, what do you want for your help, should I need it?"

"Just that she'll be out of the picture, one way or the other, I don't care what you do to achieve that, I just want her out of this company, and out of Ms. Madison's life."

"Well, I'm not going to kill her, as long as she doesn't force me too, but I can guarantee that she will quit. She may even sign herself into a mental hospital with a breakdown."

"That will be perfect, Alex would not want a mental case like that working for her, she wouldn't even want her around. Great! Okay, here, this is my messenger number. When and if you need my help just let me know, alright?"

"Okay, thanks, I'll be in touch, and who knows? Maybe you and I can hook some things up together?"

"Well let's just deal with one thing at a time right now. I have to go, but let me know what you need?" Salina then turned and headed back to the building. She went inside and up to her office.

The meeting had ended and Taylor was seeing the men out. Alex had picked up the phone and made a few calls, and by the time the girl returned, she was just hanging up from the last one.

"Sit down." Taylor closed the door and sat down as she had been told to do. She waited for the woman to talk.

"You can't go back to your townhouse."

"What? What are you talking about?! I have to go back to my home." She blurted out.

"Be quiet and listen. He will not just let you break up with him, his family is not the type to just go away quietly. He'll beg you to come back to him, and for about a week, he will be as sweet as pie to you. Then he'll offer you an engagement ring, thereby ensuring you will not leave him again. After that the abuse will start, and you will be stuck, because he will let you know in no uncertain terms who he really is, and what his goal is. He chose you to be his girlfriend for a specific reason, you were shy, meek, and humble, yet honest. You're very loyal, and not the type to ask a lot of questions, which is perfect for the type of business he's in. You would be the ever faithful, little housewife, while he on the other hand would be out philandering all over the place if you know what I mean?"

"He wouldn't hurt me." Taylor said, trying to hold on to some semblance of believing she knew the man, at least in that respect.

"Why wouldn't he? When he shows up at your house tomorrow, and believe me, he will if he's anything like his father. If you're there to greet him and tell him again that you two can't be together anymore, the first thing he will want to do is convince you that you're making a mistake. If you don't go for the verbal, then he will resort to physical means to convince you. If you're still capable of refusing him, well then he will just make you disappear, and it will look as if you just up and left. Are you understanding the type of man you're involved with yet?"

Taylor was trying not to cry, but it just did not work, and she buried her head in her hands.

"Do you have a place where you can go and stay?"

"My grandmother."

"Does he know anything about her other than that she's your grandmother?"

"No, I never talked to him about her. We had only been together for about four months or so, not including these last ones when he was out of town."

"Good, but I don't think you should go there to stay, plus I would worry about something happening to you and your grandmother."

"Then I could stay at a hotel or someplace like that?"

"No, he'll most likely have people out looking for you in those types of places."

"Then I don't know."

"I do, if you're willing?"

"What?"

"Come and stay with me at my place. It's well secured, plus he doesn't have any idea as to where I live. Even if he was smart enough to figure out that you're staying with me."

"I don't know, I mean you said you didn't want all of that around your business, why in the world would you risk it coming right to your front door?"

"Because I don't consider it a risk. Plus you chose the way I'd hoped you would, therefore, if you listen to me, then I will continue to help you. I can't help you if you're hard headed or stubborn, or prideful."

"Thank you. It seems like I've been doing a lot of that lately since I became visible to you, ha...." Taylor said, managing a weak chuckle.

Alex smiled at her, then picked up the phone again and called for a moving company to go and pack up the girl's things to put into storage. Everything except her clothing and personal items, which were to be delivered to her place.

The moment she hung up the phone, it rang.

"Yes?" She said, irritated by the interruption.

"I got that information you wanted, and you will not believe it." Kiara said from the other end.

"I'm sure I would, you know what to do with it. I'll talk to you later, keep up the good work." Alex said, and then hung up the phone.

"Hmmm...well it seems like my life is all turned upside down." Taylor said with sadness.

"Don't worry about it, it'll be back to normal again soon enough, you have my word." Alex said, as she let herself show her maternal side towards the girl. But only through her eyes.

That evening after work the two of them went to Alex's residence and she showed Taylor where she could sleep until things were back to normal. Her things had been brought to the house and they settled everything in the room. After everything was done, Alex left her alone to give her some time to think about things.

Meanwhile, she read the reports that Kiara had sent her about the boy, and the women who had passed through his life. Alex became very concerned about what she read and her mind instantly went to thinking about the girl. She went to go and make dinner, considering the fact that she had given the maid and cook the day off. While she was in starting dinner, Taylor came down the stairs and went to the kitchen to see what she was doing.

"You cook?" She asked in surprise, in spite of how she was feeling.

Alex knew she was trying to get her mind off of things so she went along with the attempt.

"Don't sound so surprised, I told you that there was a lot of things you didn't know about me."

"Yes, I know, but my goodness, every time I turn around, you're doing something else that I thought you couldn't do."

"Well, well aren't we the pessimistic person." Alex said with a smirk.

"Okay, since I'm always trying to prove myself to you, then I think it is only fair that you prove something to me. Considering I am staying here with you for a while, I would just like to know one thing for sure."

"Are you challenging me to something?" Alex asked, with a gleam in her eyes, as she stopped what she was cutting to look at the girl.

Taylor saw the look that showed in the woman's eyes, and at first she had second thoughts. Then she thought about the smile that was playing at the corners of the woman's mouth, and she decided she needed to see it in full. She took a deep breath, and just said what she was thinking.

"Yes."

The smile was fighting to come forth, but Alex was still controlling it.

"What?"

"Tell me ten things that you can't do as well as you run your businesses? Just ten."

"Hahahaha. " The woman laughed out loud, and then said in a light tone. "There are plenty of things I'm sure I can't do."

Taylor smiled brightly at the laughter, and felt her heart skip a beat as a result of it.

"Well...name something?"

"What do I get if I do?"

"What do you want?"

Alex held back the grin that tried to cross her face, due to the thought that flashed in her head. She thought to herself, "Maybe another day I can get her to ask me this same question, when things are a lot different, but for now, I better play it safe."

"You make breakfast and dinner for the next few months."

"Why cooking?"

"Because I don't like to."

"Aha, well...that makes sense, if I lose, can I call out for dinner?"

"Only if it's because of your studying, other than that, you have to cook."

"Okay."

"So what is it?"

"I want you to name ten things you don't do as well as you run your business."

"Ten things?"

"Yes."

"Okay." Alex said, as she went about preparing dinner.

"Well, I'm not good at being patient, I'm not good at being tolerant, I'm not good at pretending to be someone I'm not, I..."

"No, no fair."

"What isn't?"

"You're telling me all of these traits. I want to know things you're not good at, like swimming, or hang gliding or things like that."

"No, just like you get to choose about dinner, I get to choose what I want to tell you."

"But?"

"No, no buts, either it's my way, or you automatically lose due to being disqualified?"

"But..."

"One more of those and you lose."

Taylor opened her mouth, but she realized the only word that was on her lips was the wrong one, so she closed her mouth and just nodded her head.

"Good, I thought you would see it my way."

"Like I really had a choice." She said under her breath, as Alex raised a brow at her, but continued to prepare their meal.

"I'll tell you the others later." The woman said, after winning her way.

"What? You mean you're not even going to tell me?"

"No, not today."

"Aw b.." Taylor started to say, but Alex looked at her and with a smirk, caught her before she said it.

"Ah...careful."

Taylor gazed at her and then averted her eyes as she let out the air that she would have used to say the defeating word.

"Good, let's eat, or else you'll lose before we even really get started."

She blushed at the truthfulness of the words, and then they took their dinner to the dining room and sat at the dining room table and ate, while they talked.

"So do you?" Taylor asked, picking up a topic where she had left off a day or so ago.

"Do I what?"

"Have a special man in your life?"

"Where did that come from?"

"You never answered me the other day."

"Why?"

"Why what?" Taylor asked, as she cut a piece of meat and slipped it into her mouth.

"Why do you want to know?"

"I'm just curious."

"Well you know what they say about curiosity." Alex said as she took a sip of her wine.

"Yes, but I have an answer for that one." Taylor said with a confident raise of one of her brows. Yet there was an innocence in it.

"Really? And just what is that answer?" The woman asked, leaning forward in her chair while she held her fork hanging in the air, pointing downwards in her fingers, towards her food. Taylor took a drink of her wine, and then leaned forward and said in the same tone Alex had used on her earlier while dinner was being prepared.

"I'll tell you later." She then smiled, timidly at first, but as the woman's mouth twitched trying to contain the laughter that was trying to force it's way out, Taylor's smile broadened, and her eyes lit up. She was happy that she was once again going to be the cause behind the woman's more pleasant disposition. Alex managed to contain herself, and said to the girl's disappointment.

"We need to clear the table." Taylor sat back in her chair with obvious disappointment, but when the woman knitted her brows at her in wonder, the girl thought she was causing the woman to worry about her. She immediately came to her feet and said in a light tone of voice.

"You're right, the table does need to be cleared." She collected some of the dishes and headed for the kitchen. When she was around the corner and down the hall a bit the woman chuckled at the joke she had made only a moment before.

When the two went to relax, Taylor perused the collection of books that Alex had in her library, which was a far better library than her own. She picked out a mystery type story, and went to sit down on one end of a sofa while the woman sat in a sofa chair, reading over some reports. Alex looked over at her at times and just watched. She saw how Taylor would, at times, move strands of hair out of her face whenever she turned her head in a certain fashion. The woman watched the delicate movements of the girl. She found that she had not really noticed just how delicate Taylor was.

Alex closed her eyes and leaned back in her chair as if resting, but it was actually her way to avoid being caught gazing at Taylor. In her mind she continued to see and examine the delicate featured girl. Seeing the soft, yet chiseled cut of her face, and the long graceful neck that faded gently into her shoulders, and the soft curves of her body as she sat with her legs curled under herself. Taylor glanced up from the book she was reading and saw Alex with her eyes closed. She assumed she had just drifted off to sleep, but she did not want to disturb her by getting up just yet, although she had planned to go and get some water. Taylor found herself sitting there with her book in her hand, looking at the sleeping woman.

She leaned back on the sofa she was sitting on and just looked at Alex. She found herself becoming intrigued at how peaceful she seemed. How completely devoid of any stress, or concern. She was amazed at the contrast she thought she would see between anyone else who had those same stresses, and how obvious they would have been even in their sleep, showing on their brows.

Alex's brows were completely relaxed looking. She was beautiful, she was sexy, and she was powerful. Taylor had no concept of just how powerful this woman really was, but even in the small corner of the world that she was able to see, there had been glimpses of it.

She then started to think out loud without really realizing it.

"How do you do it? How are you able to be so hard and regal out there, but so capable of such softness in here? Hmmm...You're so... multi-faceted, yet capable of making it look so simple. I wouldn't be surprised to find out that there are men lined up around the corner who would love a chance to be with you. But then again, a lot of men probably would be very intimidated by you. My goodness you're incredible." Taylor said, with a note of sadness and obvious admiration in her voice, as she reluctantly returned her attention to her reading.

Alex opened her eyes and looked over at her with a slight smile curving her lips. She thought about what Taylor had just said out loud. The next morning the two were eating breakfast, and the sun was not even up yet, before they went to workout together. The girl had learned the moves. She wasn't as sharp with her moves but she was effective in them. Alex had seen the change in Taylor's body since she had been working out with her. She was more toned all over and her clothes looked even better on her.

When they had finished their workout and went to get dressed Taylor had thought she finished first, and she went to go and talk to Alex about her schedule. She found her dressed and already downstairs waiting for her.

"How do you do that?"

"What?" The woman asked, already concentrating on her expected day.

"Never mind. Do you want me to call for a car?"

"Yes, and then you can go over my schedule for the day while we're on our way to the office."

"Yes Ma'am." Taylor said, as she went and made the call for the driver. As they waited, she began going through the schedule for the woman.

"Cancel that one, I really don't feel like dealing with the whining."

Taylor chuckled, and then when she saw Alex's brow raise, she swallowed and simply acknowledged the woman's orders.

"Yes Ma'am."

Alex smirked, but kept her eyes on the planner she had in her own hands. When they arrived at the office at 5 am, Kiara met them in the lobby of the building. Alex saw the detective coming towards them and she knew what it was about, so she quickly sent Taylor to go and get the mail.

"Meet me in the office, after you get my mail."

"Yes Ma'am." She said, as she turned and headed off in the opposite direction. The detective, who saw Taylor leaving, slowed her pace toward Alex until she was gone.

"Here's the information I got on the young man, and also on some of the women he's been involved with. I think you will find it very interesting reading."

"Why do you think that?" She asked, as she opened the folder and glanced over the contents within it.

"Because it seems that our young man is a serial rapist on top of all of his other antisocial activities."

Alex's brow raised and then knitted deeply as she thought about what the information could mean to Taylor's safety.

"How did you find this out?" She asked, pointing to a specific paragraph within the report she was reading, as they went up in the elevator.

"I went to talk to each of them."

"And they told you that they were all virgins, before he raped them?"

"Yes, isn't that something? He's a rapist who defiles the innocent on purpose. They all said they either tried to get out of the relationship, or thought they had gotten out, when he showed up at their houses or other places out the blue. At first he tried to talk them into coming back to him, but when they refused, he lost it. They said that he told them he was not about to let anyone else have the pleasure of having them first. He said he would leave them a present so that they would always remember him, FONDLY, was how he put it to them."

"He's a sick puppy that needs to be neutered, and I'm just the one to do it." Alex said tightly, as she strode out of the elevator. She went into her office, turned on the light, sat down behind her desk, and picked up the phone to call a friend of hers. When she hung up the phone, the detective was shaking her head.

"What is that about?" Alex asked, sparing only a moment to glance at the woman, and then returning her attention to what she was reading.

"I'm just amazed at the people you know. Does this girl have any idea at all?"

"No, and there really is no reason for her to know either, is that clear?

"Yes. So what do you want me to do?"

"Follow him and his shadows, make sure you have enough people along to help you. That way if he sends them on an errand then you'll have someone available to follow them, while you continue to follow him."

"Actually, you'll be pleased to know that I already initiated surveillance the day you called. Oh, and by the way, he and his men were over at Ms. Young's house looking for her. He was very upset that she was gone. It seems he didn't expect to find that. There's a videodisc in there, I think you will find it interesting also. Do you plan on letting her watch it with you?"

"Yes, it is her life we're talking about, she has the right to know what's going on."

"Are you going to tell her about the rapes?"

"No, that I don't think she needs to know just yet."

"Well, I'll get going and whatever I find out, I'll send to you with the usual, "for your eyes only," on it?"

"Fine, good work."

Kiara left the office, but she took the stairs just in case Taylor arrived before she could leave. The elevator opened and the girl stepped out, just as the stairwell door closed behind Kiara. Taylor meanwhile headed into the office.

Alex loaded the videodisc and had it set when she came in.

"Anything good?"

"No, just the usual things." She answered. She sat down, handed half the stack of priority mail to Alex and she took the other half.

She was ready to open the mail, but the woman told her to wait.

"I want you to see something from last night."

"Okay." Taylor said, as she watched the woman lean back in her chair and call for it to play.

The videodisc began playing. Taylor was surprised to see her neighborhood, and her neighbor's townhouses in the images, then she saw some men heading towards her place.

"Who are they?"

"Wait." Alex ordered.

Taylor's mouth fell open when she saw who it was at her townhouse.

"What is he doing there?"

"You'll see."

After a few minutes her ex-boyfriend and some other men were seen walking up her driveway towards her door.

"What is he doing there, and who are those guys?" She asked, as her brows knitted with concern and confusion.

"Where did you get this?"

"Never mind, just watch it."

Taylor returned her attention to the images. She saw the boy knock on the door, despite being able to see straight in, due to the curtains having been removed.

"Open it!" He ordered, and one of the men took out his lock picking set and immediately went to work. "Hurry up!!"

The man soon had the lock open and they went inside and began searching for her.

"Where the hell is she?!!" The man shouted, at no one in particular.

Taylor sat riveted and shaking as she watched and listened to the man she thought she knew.

"Where are you?! How did she get moved out of here and no one know anything?! Someone helped her, and I intend to find out who."

"Well sir, if we don't find her, she'll be the mouse that got away."

"SHUT UP! I have never lost one, and I don't intend to lose one now, especially her! And, she no longer looks like a mouse, she's actually very fine, and that's even more reason why she's not going to get away. I want her found, and whoever the person, or people are who are helping her, I want them dead. Let's go, maybe one of her neighbors know something."

The man knocked over a coat rack by accident, and noticed the outfit that he had given to her, hanging on it. Taylor's eyes had left the images and immediately locked on Alex when he made the threat. Tears that were already rolling down her face now came faster at the thought that she had now truly endangered this woman.

"God! God, oh God, he's looking to hurt you, God..." She groaned in distress. "Maybe I can go talk to him?." Taylor now cried, as she tried to figure out how to get the woman out of danger.

Alex was touched by Taylor's concern for her, especially considering it was the girl herself who was really in danger. Taylor came to her feet and was breathing hard. She stood still for a moment, then she made a decision. Turning she headed for the door to go and act on it. Alex was on her feet and standing in front of her before she reached the door. Taylor startled as a result, but she looked up at the woman with eyes widened by fear.

"You're not going to talk to him, he's not interested in talking." Alex stated matter-of-factly, as she crossed her arms under her chest and stood looking down at the teary eyed girl.

"But he wants you dead. I couldn't live with myself if something happened to you because of me, if I can just get him to understand...."

"Understand what? That you're terrified of him, so that he can use that and keep you from speaking up, or defending yourself? Is that what you want him to understand?"

"No but..."

"No buts. I'm not worried about him, and you shouldn't either, he's just a wanna be who is nothing more than an annoying fly. One which I will have no problems swatting. Now sit down."

"But?"

"S.i.t....d.o.w.n." The Raider emphasized through her teeth.

Taylor felt for the chair and eased back down in it. She watched Alex walk around to sit on the edge of her desk. Once again she studied the shaking girl.

"Why are you so worried about me? I mean he's after you?"

"Because you're an innocent person in all of this. I should have never let you talk me into moving in with you. Goodness, he wants to kill you. I can't believe I dated this man! I thought I knew him, and I find out I didn't know anything. How stupid is that?!!" Taylor cried, as she continued to beat up on herself.

"Stop it!! There was no way for you to have known about him or his family. That's what they do, now stop beating up on yourself, that's what stupid!" Alex scolded, but not the same way she would scold her or anyone else if they had screwed up in their duties. This was different, it had a tone to it that rang with concern for the girl.

Taylor quieted down. The woman smiled at her, then leaned forward and whispered.

"It's going to be alright."

She looked in the woman's eyes, and for some unknown reason, she believed her. She gave a weak smile. Alex brought her hand under Taylor's chin to cup it, and gave it a little squeeze. The girl blushed despite everything. The woman once again controlled a grin that wanted to show. Instead of letting it out, she stood up and said in a firm voice.

"We have a lot of work to do, let's get to it." She then walked around the desk and sat back down in her chair.

She picked up a piece of mail and opening it, she went to reading it, and then had the girl make the necessary calls. Taylor watched the woman. She thought it was discreetly, but of course, Alex saw her every time. She didn't say anything, she just smiled to herself, and stored the information to think about it later.

The next few days were quiet enough, with the return of Alex's strong hand on everyone. Taylor thought things were back to normal, but Alex knew that while things at the office may be back to normal, everything outside of the office wasn't. The man was still out there, and still looking for Taylor, so parts of her thoughts were always on that.

One morning, a week or so later, around 1 a.m. in the morning, Salina received a message on her messenger. She picked up the phone and called the number that was showing.

"Hello?"

"Yeah, it's me, I need your help finding out where Taylor is. Do you know where she is staying?"

"No, I have no idea, I don't even see when she leaves."

"Shit!"

"But I know when she gets in pretty well." She informed the man.

"Really? When?"

"She usually arrives at the office around four or five so that she can get the boss her mail from the mailroom, which, by the way is in the basement." Salina said, conspiratorially.

"Excellent! I can meet her in the basement." He said.

"Yes, but first you have to get into the building, and I can assure you, you are not welcomed there."

"Okay, well that's where you come in."

"What do I get out of this?" Salina asked, wanting to make sure their deal still stood.

"What you asked for, for Taylor to leave the company. I can assure you, when I get done with her, she will be under tremendous stress. She won't want to have anything to do with that place or "The Raider" when I'm done."

"Okay, then here's how you get in. I will call one of the geeks who has been begging me to go out with him, and ask him to do me a favor. I will have to return the favor to him at some point."

"But won't he ask questions?"

"No, not if I tell him not to."

"Alright then, when can you get me in?"

"How about this morning?"

"Can you arrange it?"

"Be there at three and you'll be let in. Once you get off the elevator the mailroom is off to the right. It does a circular type thing that comes out at the top, right across from the office I work in, which is the same floor Taylor works on."

"I'll be there at three sharp." He replied, then hung up the phone and rubbed his hands together as he jumped up to get dressed.

That same morning, Alex had gotten a phone call in the middle of the night from one of her VPs calling to ask her if he could see her before the start of day. She told him she would meet him at the office at four in the morning, and for him not to be late. Whatever it was that he wanted to talk to her about had better be worth her coming in early. The man promised that it would be. She hung up the phone and went to dress. She wrote a note for Taylor that she would see her at the office. She put the note on the dresser in the girl's room as she slept. Alex noticed that she had come uncovered and went to cover her back up, albeit slowly, as she let her gaze rake over Taylor's barely covered body. The woman breathed out slowly through her mouth as she finally covered the girl. With a look of desire in her eyes, she shook her head and stood up, composing herself. She turned and walked out of the room, as quietly as she had come in.

"Whew! Can't do that again, not good!" She said to herself as she looked back at the closed door. She primped her hair, and went down the stairs and left the house.

When Taylor woke up and dressed, she saw the note on the dresser and she picked it up to read it. She saw that Alex had already left and would see her at the office. She smiled at the thoughtfulness of the woman, and picked up her briefcase. She took out the day planner and looked over Alex's schedule. She put it back in her briefcase and getting her things together, she went to get in the waiting car. Alex had told her that she didn't want her driving anywhere alone for a while. During the ride, Taylor went over some notes she had typed up for Alex last night while they were doing some work at the house. When she got to the building, she stepped out of the limo and headed in while still reading over the notes. She headed for the mailroom to get the mail. Afterwards, she headed to the elevator to go to Alex's office. Taylor did not see where the man came from when he jumped on just as the elevator doors closed and it began going upwards.

"Dominic?!!" She gasped in alarm, when she saw him jump in.

"Hi, how's my girl? I've missed you?" He said, as he moved closer to Taylor and she moved away from him.

"What are you doing here?"

"What do you think? I'm here to see you."

"Why?"

"Because, I don't like the way things were left between us. You know?"

"Dominic, please just leave?"

"Is that any way to talk to the man you said you were happy to be with?"

She wanted to tell him she knew who he really was, but she didn't dare, just in case he thought she was still in the dark about it.

"It's just that I'm trying to focus on school and things." She said, giving a plausible excuse as to why she didn't have time to see him anymore. While at the same time glancing up at the numbers as the elevator expressed past the floors.

Dominic saw her eyes and knew she was hoping to make it to the top before he did anything, but he just smiled and then hit the stop button.

CHAPTER 5

"There! That way we don't have to worry about being interrupted with the door opening."

At the same moment that the stop button was hit, Alex's video alarmed. She hit the switch and the image of Taylor and the man in the elevator immediately showed.

"Damn it!!" She cursed, as she hit the speed dialer and called the police. She told them what was happening, then hung up and hit another button that alerted the guards of the building that something was happening on the top floor. The final call was to the in-house medical clinic. She told the Doctor to bring her rape collection kit to collect possible specimens, and get to the top floor immediately. She then hit a switch on the video panel to have it continue to record as it always did, but without the images showing. "Damn it! Damn it! Damn it!" She cursed, as she raced to the elevator to wait for it to automatically restart and come on up the last few floors.

Meanwhile, Taylor was screaming for Dominic to stop, and she was saying "no" every way she knew how. He cursed at her in Italian, and then in English.

"If you think I'm going to let someone else have the pleasure of popping your cherry, then you are obviously a fool. I've invested months with you, I even planned on having you become my wife, but no, you up and try to break up with me. Well...I'll leave a very real reminder of our special time together right now. You'll never forget me, no matter who comes and goes in your life." He laughed evilly, as he reached for her. She knocked his hands away. He decided to just overpower her in the corner and have his way with her.

He caught one hand, but couldn't catch the other before she laid a staggering blow to his head. When she went to try to get away, he hit her across the face with his hand and she fell back against the wall of the elevator. He then pinned her up against the wall, and while she had her hands pinned behind her back he slipped one of his hands under her dress. It went into her pantyhose and then into her underwear. Taylor was going wild as she tried to fight him off of her. Several times she managed to keep his hand from going further by sliding down the wall, but he would pull her back up, pin her firmer, and then try again. Finally, just as he was about to end her innocence, the elevator began moving again, and it startled him. He tried to reach the stop button from where he was, but he could not reach it, so his hand came out, and he went to hit the stop button again, but found that it did not work this time.

"Shit!" He hissed, as he turned to confront Taylor again. She was wild-eyed, and when he turned, she caught him across the face with her fist. He staggered again, this time far enough away from her for the elevator to make it to the top floor. Just as he was about to charge the girl to lay her out for striking him, and take her, he caught a figure out the corner of his eye and turned to see who it was.

He never got a chance. He was rendered unconscious by a powerful blow to his face. It sounded like it had broken some bones in the man's face. Taylor was now shaking violently in the corner of the elevator, and was going into shock. She barely heard the familiar voice calling to her.

"Come here." Alex had been calling her to come out of the elevator, so that she would not have to go in after her and mess up the evidence scene.

"I...I...can't." Taylor managed, as she stared at the unconscious man who was bleeding from his nose and mouth.

"Come here, now!" Alex commanded with purpose.

Taylor was startled by it, but it got the effect the woman wanted. The girl's eyes locked on Alex's as she once again told her to come out of the elevator. Taylor hesitated for a moment, then she rose from the corner she was cowered in, and cautiously eased around the downed man and reached for the reaching hand. She ran into Alex's arms.

Alex felt her shaking and it radiated through her own body as a result. The police and crime lab people all arrived at the same time the medical personnel from Alex's in house clinic had. The woman had gotten enough information from Taylor to be able to tell them where to collect the specimens, specifically those that would be the most crucial evidence. One of the medical personnel happens to work part time at the hospital as a rape specialist. The specimens were taken and then the MD turned to Alex.

"I need to take her to the hospital to take some samples from her as well." She said, as she saw the reaction from the girl.

"No!, No! I don't want to go to the hospital!!" Taylor said, almost hysterical at the thought.

"It's alright, calm down, shhh...she needs to get the samples so that we can get this piece of scum sent to prison for as long as possible. You know she has to do this. I know you're scared...look at me!" Alex scolded gently, seeing how the girl's eyes would widen every time she looked over at the man. She knew that only hindered Taylor's understanding further, especially considering she was on overload.

"Go with her, it'll be alright, I promise, nothing will happen to you."

"I don't want to go to the hospital!!"

Alex sighed at Taylor's pleading, fear filled eyes.

"Okay, okay. Clarissa, is there any way you can do your test in the clinic here? I mean it is fully stocked with pretty much the latest equipment."

"Yes, I guess I can, but I can't run the labs here, they have to be run at the hospital."

"That's not a problem, You can have one of your staff take them over to the lab at the hospital, it's only five minutes away."

"That's fine, but the police would have to have one of their people go along to insure the security and integrity of the specimen, to make sure it has not been tampered with."

"That's fine, whatever, just do it!" The woman said impatiently.

Alex then looked back down at the girl in her arms and asked her if that would work for now.

"Will you come with me?" Taylor asked, scared to leave the protective arms.

"I'll come down as soon as I know he is in custody, okay?"

"Promise?" She asked, tears streaming down her face as she was being gently taken by the Dr. and the female police officers out of Alex's arms and guided towards the stairs.

"I promise, oh Dr. come here a moment, I want to tell you something."

The Dr. left the shaking girl with the female officers and walked back over to where Alex stood watching everything.

"Yes."

"She was a virgin, I think she may still be since I didn't see any blood on the man's hands. Be careful that you don't accidentally change that if she managed to preserve it." She said, warning the woman.

"Don't worry, I'll be very careful, I've had a few who managed to keep it long enough to be rescued before it happened. I have to go, but I will let you know what I find."

"Good. I'll be there as soon as I can."

Alex watched the woman and female police officers escort Taylor to the stairs. Just before she went through the door the girl looked back and asked with her eyes one more time whether the woman would indeed come. Alex nodded her head and Taylor let out a relieved sounding gasp. She turned back to the other women who spoke softly to her as they now guided the trembling girl. Once they were gone down the stairs Alex turned her attention back to what was happening in the elevator. She stood and watched, taking mental notes on everything. Once the police had the man restrained on the stretcher, they told her that one of the officers would stay and get any information she may have about what had happened.

The physical evidence was already taken care of, so she could again use all of the elevators.

"I want him locked up until his trial." She stated.

"That'll be up to the Judge. But I'm sure even if he did have the chance to get out, it would take a large bond to do it."

She realized that the man's father could easily raise whatever amount of money was necessary, and that he would probably have his men sent out to take care of Taylor. Her mind went to darker thoughts and she knew what she had to do.

"Fine, but don't let it be known who is in custody right away, and why?"

"We know who he is, and you can be sure that we have no intentions of letting the information out. Here's my card, if you need anything please just give me a call?"

An officer took information from her, and then went to leave. He too left a card.

"Thank you." She took one last look at the unconscious man, then turned and headed into her office to make a few phone calls.

"I want you in my office in the next few minutes, and if I'm not here you had better wait!"

CLICK!!

She slammed down the phone and then after taking a few moments to calm herself, she picked it up again. She called her friend, the Attorney General, and told him what just happened. She told him to go forward with the cases against the man, and to put the new rape charge on the top. He was to present the case the way they had talked about before, and she would testify if she was needed for Taylor.

"You know by having such a powerful witness, I'm sure we can get a conviction." The man on the other end of the phone said.

"I want him to remain behind bars until his trial date. I want the case brought forth within the next week. I want the trial within a few days after that, am I making myself clear? I don't want this guy on the street with the chance to disappear and then reappear and do something worse to her." Alex said adamantly.

The man knew the woman meant what she said, and he told her he would start the process right away. They hung up and she put her head in her hands for a moment as she thought about Taylor. Although she did not have time to think long, one thought played over and over in her mind.

"What is it about...this...girl...that I feel so protective of her? When did she go from being just another employee, to someone that I care about, someone I like having around? Or was she ever just another employee? Since that first day she came to my attention there was something about her; qualities that I admire. Her kindness, and her devotion to her friends. But she's also naive and shy. Hmm...I have to get down to the clinic to check on her." Alex said, shaking her head of the thought and refocusing on her next move.

She arrived in the clinic a few minutes later.

"How is she doing?"

"Fine, now. At first she fought us when we were trying to examine her, but then I remembered seeing how much of a calming effect you had on her. I used that to get her to allow us to take the specimens we needed. We also took pictures of her face and fist. Luckily her light caramel skin tone allowed the bruises to show up. She's going to have a bruise around her eye for a bit, but it'll heal fine. I also dressed the cut to her eyebrow on that same side, after the pictures were taken.

"Cut?" Alex asked, not remembering seeing a cut.

"Yes, but it's just a small one. His ring evidently caught her, but it was not the stone part, it was the band part. So it wasn't a gash, just a cut. It will heal without scarring as well."

"Well good. It would be a shame for such a pretty girl to be scarred physically by such a violent act. It's already horrible enough she'll carry the scars of this day in her mind." Alex said tightly through her teeth.

"Well, with time and help, even those can heal." The Dr. pointed out to the angry woman.

"Well that won't be a problem." She said, as she glanced over at the Dr. now with a more determined look.

"I'm glad you said that." The Dr. replied.

"You said the mention of me had a calming effect on her?"

"Yes, she seems to calm at the mention of you, or even the thought of you. I figure it was because you were the first one to get to her, and you actually saved her from him."

"Hmm...speaking of saving?" Alex quickly jumped to the other important issue.

"Oh...yes, he didn't get a chance, she's still very much intact."

Alex let out an audible sigh of relief, and the doctor looked up at her.

"Are you okay?"

"Fine." She said briskly.

"Well that seemed to get the same response from the girl. I had to sedate her a little right after I told her. I think the reality of how close she had come to losing that, really shook her up again."

"Which door?"

"That one." The Dr. replied, pointing to the closed door of the room Taylor was in.

Alex headed over to the door and opened it slowly to look in. The officer motioned for her to come on in. The officer then whispered to the girl and told her that the woman was there. Taylor slowly and groggily turned her head over to look towards the door. When she saw the woman, a weak hearted smile came to her face, as tears rolled slowly down her cheeks. Their eyes locked on each other, and Alex found herself trying to maintain her composure. She felt herself about to lose it, so she motioned for the officer to leave them. The officer nodded and told Taylor she would come back later. The officer then walked over to where Alex stood and leaning over she whispered to her.

"She's been asking for you the whole time."

After the woman had left the room and Alex stepped nearer to the bed Taylor was laying on. She spoke to the girl.

"You okay?"

"I'm glad you're here." Taylor said, as her tears rolled unhindered down her cheeks, and her eyes showed the effects of the sedation.

She tried to reach for the woman's hand, but the sedation kept her from controlling her arm enough. Alex saw what she was trying to do and took Taylor's hand in her own and held it.

The girl managed to squeeze the warm hand a bit as the tears rolled faster. The woman sat on the bed and was determined to maintain her composure.

"I told you I would come."

She smiled slightly, at least it looked like an attempt at a smile, but the effects of the sedative, kept her from using her muscles well enough.

"Are you okay?" Taylor asked, causing an ironic chuckle to escape the woman's lips.

"Look at you? Asking me if I'm alright, and it's you who were attacked? Aren't you just the one?" Alex said, as she used her other hand to move stray strands of hair out of Taylor's face. It also gave her something to do with her free hand, seeing how completely off balance she now felt.

"I'm sorry this happened at the company. I know you didn't want it to come anywhere near...." The girl started to ramble off.

"Stop. This was not your fault, you know that right?"

"But If I...."

"No! You listen to me, this was NOT your fault! This guy is a jerk he wanted to hurt you for his own purpose. There is absolutely nothing to blame yourself for. NOTHING! Is that clear?"

"Yes."

"Why don't I believe you?"

"I just think if I could have gone and talked to him, then maybe he would not have done this?"

"Did you talk to him in the elevator?"

"Yes."

"Did you say any of the things you think you would have said to him if you had spoken to him before this?"

"Yes, a lot."

"Then if you said a lot of those things in the elevator, and he still tried to rape you, what do you think he would have done if you two were alone. Do you think you would still be a virgin?"

"Well?"

"I know you're smarter than this, I'm assuming that you're hesitating in your responses due to overload and being sedated? Because it can't be for any other reason. Especially after I've told you that you were not to blame? Unless you think I'm lying?"

"Oh, no, I wasn't thinking that at all." Taylor said, fearful that she had offended the woman.

"Good. Now you try to rest...."

"You're not leaving are you?!" She asked, with rising panic at being left alone, despite the sedative.

Although Alex had planned to return to her office to make a few more phone calls, she gave Taylor an answer she could handle.

"I'll be back in one hour, I'm just going to my office to TALK to someone. I will be back, and if the medicine has worn off some, then I'll take you home."

"One hour?"

"Yes, maybe sooner, but no longer."

Taylor held the woman's hand tightly, but then with a final squeeze she let go. Alex caressed her cheek, and with a reassuring look she told her, " I'll help you get past this if you want me too?"

"Thank you." The girl said, as she tried to smile again, but instead tears rolled down her cheeks.

Alex gave her a sympathetic smile, then with a final pat to Taylor's cheek, she stood to her full height and turned to walk out of the room. She was controlling her breathing as she motioned for the officer to return to the room. She also told the Dr. that if the girl needed anything to let her know. She would be in her office and would return in one hour.

She left and when she was in the elevator once again the questions ran through her mind. When she arrived on the top floor she stepped out of the elevator and strode into the outer office. Salina was now at her desk talking to some of the other people who had seen the police going up to the top floor. They all took the next elevator up as soon as they had been restarted.

"Good morning Ma'am." They all said, greeting the woman.

"I KNOW YOU ALL HAVE WORK TO DO. I suggest you get to it!" Alex warned.

The outer office cleared and Salina turned on her computer to start work. She did not even spare a second glance at Salina, but now focused on the pacing woman in her office. Salina let out a sigh of relief.

"Whew! She doesn't even know about my involvement, and I hope that jackass can keep his mouth shut." Salina thought to herself, disgusted with the man's failure.

Meanwhile Alex went into her office and slammed the door behind her as she then laid into the woman who had been waiting for her.

"What the hell happened?! How is it that, THAT boy was able to get to her?! And on top of that, inside of the elevator's in MY building?! Especially, if you were supposed to have him under surveillance?!!" Alex shouted, as she stood within inches of the woman looking slightly downward into her wide eyes.

"We were following him from a discreet distant. He was just a few cars ahead of us when suddenly...this 4x4 truck came skipping out in front of us and the police was right behind in pursuit. We had to get out of the way, which meant that we lost him. I'm sorry, I hope the girl is alright?!"

"Sorry?! That is no where near good enough!! The woman hissed, as she turned away from Kiara. She stormed over to sit in her chair and glare at the woman who now had obvious signs that she wanted to cry, but instead kept them balanced on her lids.

"Those aren't helpful either!" She sneered. "That child was raped, and almost lost her innocence because you failed in your job!!"

"What could I have done?! We had to let the police by." The woman said, trying to defend her position. She probably would have been able to do that with anyone else, but Alex always saw alternatives, and was not buying it.

"Have you ever heard of a DAMN PHONE?!!" She shot back, and the young detective now stood thoroughly chastised.

"Who...who would I have called?"

Alex's eyes narrowed as she now looked at Kiara with disbelief.

"Who do you work for?" She asked calmly, belying the rage that was running through her, and not necessarily at the detective.

"You." The detective said, as she realized that she could have done that and then the woman would have been able to do something to protect the girl.

"I didn't think of that, I jeopardized the girl." She admitted, as she now lowered her eyes.

After a long moment of silence she raised them back up to look at the woman. Alex was still glaring at her.

"Get out, and next time you tell me you have something handled and don't, you and I are going to have another MEETING! Do I make myself clear Kiara?"

"Yes Ma'am."

"Good, now leave!" She turned her chair and the young detective dropped her hands in frustration and guilt as she turned and walked out, closing the door behind her.

Alex sat looking out the window of her office, out over the skyline of the city. The sunlight reflecting off of the steel and glass of the buildings. Thoughts of Taylor came to her, and what had happened to her. Then, an unexpected thing happened. While she was sitting there, she felt tears on her cheeks. Alex had not allowed herself to feel anything emotional for anyone in a very long time...sadness, rage and joy all were washing over her. She felt sadness for the stark fear Taylor must have felt doing the whole ordeal. Rage at the rapist, who almost succeeded in his assault. Joy that the girl escaped the full savagery of the attack and was left intact. She gave herself over to these emotions for just a moment before she put her wall back up and was in control once again...but she could feel the walls had cracked just a bit.

Alex returned to the clinic one hour later and took Taylor home. Once they were back at her home, she told the girl to go and get cleaned up. She would go and get them something to eat, and bring it to her room. Taylor didn't want to stay in the room, and she didn't want to go to sleep, so she came up with an excuse not to.

"I'd rather get cleaned up and then come and help you make dinner?"

"You need to rest."

"Please, it'll give me something to do?"

Alex wanted her to rest, but she also realized that Taylor was still scared.

"Alright, but when you come, bring your hair brush with you and after dinner I'll brush your hair for you, okay?"

"Okay." The girl said with a grateful smile, but the tears were never far away in her eyes. She started to turn and go to shower, but then turned back around and wrapped her arms around the woman's waist and hugged her. "Thank you." She said, as she let go just as abruptly as she had taken hold of the surprised woman. She ran up the stairs and into the bathroom to get cleaned up not wanting to see the possible disgust in Alex's eyes at her emotional reaction.

- Alex again felt tears on her cheeks and wiped them away, determined not to allow Taylor to see how much she hurt for her. She knew the girl needed someone strong to be there for her, and if anyone was capable of it, she knew she was. She was determined not to fail. Wiping her eyes once again she turned and went to go and start dinner. Taylor came down after a while wearing pajama's and a terry robe and slippers. Her hair was wrapped in a towel hanging down behind her back. The woman looked at her and smiled. The girl moved over to the counter where she was just getting ready to cut up some vegetables.

"Here, you can do this I think?" Alex said evenly, giving her something to do.

"Yes." Taylor said quietly, as she took the knife, positioned the first vegetable and began chopping it up.

Alex watched her discreetly as she moved around the kitchen, to get one thing or another for their dinner. She saw the tremble in the girl's hands whenever she let her mind drift back to what happened in that elevator.

"If you want to talk, I am a very good listener." Alex offered, as they went about setting the table to eat.

"Thank you, maybe later?"

"Alright."

The two sat down to eat and the woman kept the conversation light. She asked about Taylor's studies and how they were coming along. By the time they had finished eating and cleaned up the dishes, she thought the girl was ready to go to bed to rest, but Taylor had other ideas.

"I brought the brush."

Alex smirked at Taylor's attempt, but wanted her to get some rest, so she made her own suggestion.

"Okay, I will brush your hair for you, but only if you'll get in bed?"

"I'm fine, really."

"You need to be honest with yourself. That's the only way you're going to get past this. I'll make you a deal, if you are honest with yourself and your feelings about what has happened to you, then I won't make you talk, and I'll stay in the room with you until you fall asleep, alright?"

"Alright." Taylor agreed, as they went to the room she was using. She climbed into the bed and was told to lay on her belly. Alex sat beside her on the bed and began to brush her hair. Not because it needed to be brushed, but more as a therapy. She knew that the sensation of having one's hair brushed was very relaxing, and if one was not careful, they could easily wind up asleep. That was Alex's plan. Taylor slowly relaxed, but she had things on her mind, and she knew she needed to talk to someone she could trust. Someone who was not out to use her for their own benefit.

"Have you ever known anyone who was raped?" She suddenly asked Alex.

"Yes, but it was slightly different."

"What was different about it?"

"She was dating a guy, and they had been intimate before, so she was not...a virgin. Unlike you, but it was still a violent crime committed against her."

"Did she file charges against him?"

"She wasn't going to at first, but I told her she was going to, and she did. He was sent to prison for 10 years without possibility of parole."

"Have you heard from her since?"

"Yes, she works in one of my companies overseas. She's now happily married."

"You mean you helped her the same way you're helping me?"

"No, it's a lot different. She was just an employee who was new to the company. I just happened to see her crying one day in one of the hallways as I was heading to my office. I asked her what was wrong and at first she was too shocked to talk to me because of who I was, but then I told her maybe I could help if she told me what had happened."

"And she did?"

"Yes, and I had to scold her the same way I did you to get her to understand that what happened was not her fault. Despite the fact that she had slept with him before, the fact that she had said no, made it rape when he forced himself on her. Eventually it went to trial and the jury saw it the same way we all did, so he was convicted. She was able, with help, to get past it and she's doing very well in the company now. She has a wonderful attentive husband, and their looking at having children."

"So there's another quality that you're good at." Taylor said, still resting her chin on her folded arms."

"What's that?"

"You have this maternal side to you that seems to be as natural to you as it is to most mothers. Only you keep it hidden, why?"

"Hmm...when did this conversation change to being about me? And I wish you would STOP referring to me as a mother figure. I'm only a few years older than you are."

"Oh, I'm sorry, I didn't mean anything by it, it's just a softness I see in you, that's all I meant." The girl said, as she turned to look Alex in the eyes with her meek one's.

"Well that's different." The woman said, with a playful smile lighting her eyes.

Taylor smiled back and then slowly turned her head back around when she was sure that Alex was not mad. Then she went on.

"It's just something I noticed. You know you still owe me seven more things that you're not good at?" She said through a yawn.

"Yes, I know."

"Well?"

"Well what?"

"Tell me?"

"Okay, let's see, what am I not good at? Hmmm...Well I can't paint."

"Can you draw?"

"Yes."

"Okay, I guess painting is a little different, why can't you paint if you can draw?"

"I don't have the patience to wait for the paint to dry."

"Hahaha." Taylor laughed into her arms, and Alex caught a bit of her hair and gave a slight tug on it to quiet her back down.

"What's so funny?"

"It's just funny as to how much that fits your personality. You don't even have the patience to wait for art paint to dry, hahaha, sorry." She said through her laughter.

"If you laugh again at that, then I am going to stop brushing your hair." Alex warned with humor in her eyes. She was actually happy to see Taylor laughing so soon after everything that had happened. It gave her hope that the girl would indeed be able to get past this with her help.

"No! I mean I won't laugh at it again, or at least I'll try not to, okay?" The girl said, stifling the rest of her laughter.

"Alright I won't stop then. Now close your eyes and relax."

Taylor did as she was told and then Alex spoke.

"You have very beautiful hair yourself, it's soft, thick, and...mmm...smells very nice, like...honey dew?"

"Oh, well I use a natural shampoo and conditioner. But my hair is nothing like yours. Yours is so silky soft, and it has that spring fresh scent." Taylor yawned again and this time she mumbled something else. Before long, her breathing had lightened, and became regular. Alex brushed a few more strokes and then stopped and set the brush on the bedside table.

She stood up and tucked the girl in and then she leaned over and was debating on whether to kiss Taylor's forehead or not. She decided not to and leaned back, stood up and took a deep breath. She looked at the dressing over the girl's eyebrow, then the swelling and light discoloration to her eye. Anger came washing over her at what the man did to her. She turned and eased out of the room. She finished cleaning up from the day, and had gotten into bed to try to rest, but her mind was on Taylor in the next room. Alex laid in her bed wondering why she felt the way she did. She knew there were qualities in Taylor that she admired, but she herself was practical about things. She did not have time for a long-term relationship, she didn't even know if she wanted a relationship with anyone. For some reason, this girl had burrowed a hole straight to her heart, without her even realizing it.

She thought long into the night, and just as she closed her eyes to finally go to sleep, she heard Taylor screaming. She flew from her bed, grabbing a heavy silver candlestick holder along the way, as she ran to the girl's room to see what was going on. The door flew open and she scanned the room instantly looking for the danger. Her eyes fell on the girl, who was still screaming "NO!" Taylor was in her bed still asleep, having a nightmare. Alex put the candlestick on the dresser next to the door, and then went over to the bed and shook her to wake her up. Taylor's eyes flew open, wild, fearful and unfocused.

"It's okay! You were just dreaming, it's okay!"

The girl fought for a moment, but because of Alex's strength and determination to wake her, she finally calmed the girl. Taylor soon realized where and with whom she was with. She wrapped her arms around Alex's neck and held her tightly as she trembled with relief and fear from the realistic dream. The woman sat on the bed holding the trembling girl, all the while whispering words of comfort to her. Eventually she was able to calm her down. Once she had, she laid her back down on the bed and covered her back up, then she pulled up a chair to sit by the bed.

"I don't want to stay in here alone, I know I'm asking a lot, and I feel like a child asking it but..."

"I'll stay in here with you if you like."

"Yes please?"

"Alright. I'll sit here."

"No, I wouldn't feel right you sitting in a chair all night in your own home. I don't mind if you lay in the bed, please?" Taylor asked, with sincere gratitude and pure intentions.

Alex, on the other hand, had to remember why she was being asked to stay in the room with the girl. Not that she had forgotten, but there were many things going on with her that Taylor had no idea about.

"I don't think that's a good idea, I'll be fine sitting up, besides, I can read a little. I've stayed up many nights, working on things."

"Yes, but we have to go to work tomorrow."

"NO. You are not going to work tomorrow, matter of fact not for a few days. Until you're feeling better about things, work will only remind you of what happened. Besides, when we do go back, it's going to be hard for you to get on the elevators. I won't allow you to NOT get on that proverbial horse again. Anyway we have time to think about that later. I want you to close your eyes and go to sleep, and I'll be right here."

Taylor had a nervous yet appreciative gaze in her eyes, but she slowly relaxed and soon was closing her eyes as she fell asleep. Alex eased out of the room, went and got her briefcase and went back to the room. She sat back down on the chair and began to go through the paperwork in her briefcase. Over the next few days, Alex stayed in the room with Taylor, sitting in the chair or taking brief naps in it. Whenever she had other episodes of nightmares, the woman was there to calm her, and eventually the nights would come to an end. Taylor woke one day to find the woman had cleaned up and dressed. She was making phone calls on the phone that was in the room the girl stayed in. Alex heard Taylor stir and looking back at her, saw her eyes opening. The woman covered the speaker part of the phone and whispered.

"Good morning."

"Good morning, you're going to work?"

"Just for a few hours, but I will be right back. You won't have any problems. If you need to talk to me, you can either call me on the regular phone, or use the video conferencing line, that way you will be able to see me."

"I'll get dressed and go with you." Taylor said, as she started to move to get out of the bed.

"No you won't. You will stay here and rest. I'll be back real soon, and if you need me just call, and I'll come back alright?" Alex said, as she caught the girl's legs and moved them back into the bed.

Taylor looked like an abandoned kitten, and Alex had to strengthen her resolve not to just hug and protect her.

"If I call you every hour that I am out there, will that make you feel better?"

Taylor wanted to say, "NO, I'll feel better if you stay here with me." But she couldn't ask such a thing of a woman in Alex's position. It was bad enough she was intruding into the woman's home, but to be a needy house guest was something she did not want to be seen as, despite her fear of being left alone.

"No, you don't have to do that, I'll be fine, plus the maid is here right?"

"Right, and the cook."

"No, you go ahead to work, if I need something, I'll call, if that's alright?"

"It's fine, I'll see you in a little while and I'll call to check on you." Alex said, as she noticed how tightly Taylor was holding the covers in her hands.

Reaching down, she tentatively caressed the girl's hair, then cheek. Catching herself before she got carried away, she said in a strong, yet gentle voice.

"I'll see you in a while."

Taylor's hand caught her warm, yet strangely stimulating hand and held it to her cheek.

Alex smiled at her, and then gently caressed her cheek again, and then removed her hand from within Taylor's.

"Lay back down for a while. I'll have the cook make you something to eat and bring it up here for you."

The girl laid back down, and the woman tucked her in. Taylor smiled a truly lost, doe eyed smile at her. Alex inhaled quietly, and slowly. Then she stood to her full height and with a light wave of her fingers, she turned and left. Taylor laid in the bed. Her mind was racing with all sorts of thoughts; from those of what happened to her to what would happen when the trial came about. Mostly she thought about what was going on with herself. She was confused about the feelings she had towards the woman. Feelings she didn't understand and therefore did not recognize for what they were. Alex, in the meantime was barely able to keep her mind off of Taylor the whole time she was at the office. When she was not in a meeting, and just sitting in her office, she found her mind drifting. Wondering how she would have handled laying in the bed with the young woman. Her mind teased her, presenting images to her that allowed her heart to skip beats at the very thought.

"Ma'am? Ma'am?"

Alex suddenly heard Salina's voice cut through her thoughts and she felt both irritation and surprise. But her voice betrayed neither feeling.

"Yes Salina?"

"Ma'am, your next appointment is here, Mr. Yodash."

"Aha, send him in and then close the door." She ordered, and prepared herself for another meeting.

Taylor was now up walking around the house, and found herself in Alex's bedroom. She had been walking around in a contemplative state, and couldn't figure out why she was feeling so restless and unsettled. She figured part of the reason was because of what had happened to her a few days ago, but there was something else. Something was missing and for the life of her, she couldn't figure out what it was.

The phone rang, and she waited to see if the maid would get it, but when she didn't the girl went to go and answer it.

"Hello, this is the clerk at the district courthouse, may I speak with Alexandra Madison please?"

"She's not here, but this is Taylor Young her Personal Assistant, may I help you?"

"Ms. Young, yes, I am calling to inform you that Mr. Giovanii Macellis' trial date is set for the 25th of the month."

"The 25th?" She asked, suddenly nervous again.

"Yes Ma'am, have a nice evening."

Taylor didn't think to say goodbye, she just hung up the phone, and before she removed her hand from it, she looked down at it thoughtfully. Just when she was about to pick up the phone again to call Alex, it rang again, startling her.

"He...hello."

"Hello, it's me, I was calling to see how you were doing, everything alright?"

Taylor exhaled in relief at the sound of the woman's voice. Alex heard the fear and her heart tightened at the thought something had happened.

"What's wrong? Are you okay?"

"The clerk at the courthouse called..." Taylor managed to say before she lost her voice due to the fear of soon having to face the man who raped her.

The woman heard the crack in her voice and the fear in her tone.

"What did the person say?"

"The trial date is the 25th." She said, with a tremble to her voice.

"I see, well good, this'll soon be over. How are you doing?"

"Um...I...I'm alright..." Taylor said, leaving the words hanging.

Alex heard more need in those words than the girl wanted to admit to.

"Hmm...did you eat breakfast and lunch?"

"Yes. Thank you."

"Good. What have you been doing today?"

"I just read some, but I was feeling a little restless."

"Restless?"

"Yes, it's like something was or is missing, something just doesn't seem quite right."

"Missing from where?" Alex asked, then changed her mind about wanting the answer at that moment. "Never mind, don't answer that, you can tell me when I get home. I have one more meeting scheduled and then I will come home and we can talk."

A smile came to Taylor's face despite the previous news.

"Alright."

"Alright, I'll see you soon." Alex then hung up the phone.

The girl looked at the time and seeing that it was almost dinnertime, she decided to make dinner for them. Taylor had prepared dinner, set the table, then went and cleaned up and put on a sundress. She heard Alex's car, and going to the window to look out discreetly, she smiled when she saw her. She did not know why she was feeling both giddy, and nervous, upon seeing the woman, but for some reason she was happy just to see her. The disturbing news of earlier was now on the back burner of her mind. She hurried into the kitchen to check the food one last time, and then when she heard the front door open and close she came out of the kitchen.

"Hi." She said, greeting Alex with a shy but bright smile.

"Hi yourself. So...what's up with you?"

"I'll tell you after you go and change into something more comfortable."

Alex cocked her head at her and a curious smirk came to her mouth. With a raise of her brow and a slight nod of her head she turned to go and change. She noticed the blush come to Taylor's face, along with a brighter smile. Alex's heart leaped at the sight. She was relieved that Taylor could smile despite knowing the trial was starting in two weeks. She also entertained wishful thoughts that maybe the girl had some feelings for her. The woman then turned and headed upstairs with the image of the girl's smile imprinted in her mind. By the time she had changed, and come back down, light jazz was on the stereo, and a glass of her favorite wine was already poured and waiting for her.

"Here you go." Taylor said, offering the glass of wine to her.

"Thank you. Something smells good, did you cook?" Alex asked, walking over to her favorite lounging chair and sitting down in it. Taylor moved to sit on the sofa, closest to the chair.

"You're welcome, and yes I did. Have you eaten?" She asked, hoping that Alex hadn't.

"No." She answered, as she watched the girl.

"Good, because I made a wonderful dinner. I figure you didn't eat very well while you were at the office, if at all, and that you would probably be famished by the time you made it home."

"Well, aren't you the studious little one?" She said, with a teasing voice, but there was something else in her tone.

"Well I've been around you for a long time now, I sort of know some of your habits."

"Hmm..." She replied, as she took a sip of her wine, and continued to consider what was going on between the two of them.

"What?"

"I was just thinking how nice it was of you to make dinner, that was very thoughtful. I mean you didn't have to do it, especially considering everything?"

"It was no big deal, it's the least I can do. Plus it gave me something better to think about, rather than worrying about the upcoming trial. So are you ready to eat?" Taylor asked, changing the subject.

"Sure." Alex answered with a smooth tone.

Taylor jumped up from the sofa and waited for her to stand up, and the two headed out of the den.

"You go ahead and have a seat at the table, I'll bring everything out."

The woman once again didn't say much but instead, gave a considering gaze, and raised a brow. She nodded at Taylor, who smiled at her. Alex narrowed her eyes in a thoughtful fashion as she turned and headed into the dining room. Taylor brought out the food and they sat down to eat. Alex praised her for her cooking abilities, then said in a tone of teasing and seriousness.

"Once I win our little wager, I'll expect such delicious meals." Her eyes never leaving the girl's face. She wanted to see Taylor's reaction to her words. She did not disappoint Alex with her reaction.

"If you ever tell me the ten things then maybe you'll get your wish?"

"I'll tell you, but not right now. I want to know what you meant earlier. Something about feeling like something was missing, do you still feel that way?"

"No I don't feel that way now, it was just earlier. I felt it all day. I was restless and anxious, but now I don't feel like that."

"How long had you been feeling like that?"

"I'm not sure, but whenever I'm alone I feel like that. It's like I have a hard time concentrating on anything. For instance when I was trying to read today, I had to reread over parts that I normally would not have had to, because I wasn't concentrating on what I was reading. Therefore I didn't remember what I had read, it's really strange." Taylor said thoughtfully, as she took a bite of the filet mignon she had made.

Alex sat cutting a piece of hers as she thought about what the girl had told her. Her mind had a million thoughts running through it, and her heart was pounding, at some of the possible causes of Taylor's restlessness. But she didn't dare hope it was for the reasons she was thinking, that maybe, just maybe, the girl had missed her. "No..." She thought to herself. "It probably has to do with this boy mess." Her mind continued to search for a more plausible reason.

"How long have you been having these feelings? Were they before or after what happened at work?"

"I'm not sure, but I think...it was before, yes, it was before."

"Are you sure?" Alex asked without emotion.

"Yes. But it seemed to become more apparent to me after, I don't know why I feel like that, but I can tell you that it started when I first came to stay here with you. Hahaha, maybe I miss you when you're not here?" Taylor said innocently, not realizing what she had just said to the woman and the truth and meaning of her words.

Alex's heart now pounded wildly in her chest and her palms were damp from the inadvertent revelation made by Taylor. But the only reaction she showed was that of simply raising one of her eyebrows.

For the next few days the two women pretty much dealt with going over her testimony with the Attorney General who was handling the case personally, because of the people involved. One day while Alex was at the office, she received a call from Kiara, the detective.

"Yes Kiara, what is it?!" Alex said sharply, still angry with her for failing.

"I sent you a video, I think you need to watch it alone because of what it contains. It's the guy's father and some of his people talking, and the conversation is very ominous, you should get it in the next hour. When you're done watching it, let me know what you want me to do?"

"Fine."

Alex hung up without further conversation. Almost 40 minutes later Salina brought a large envelope to her.

"Close the door and I don't want to be disturbed, until I tell you differently, unless Ms. Young calls, is that clear?"

"Yes Ma'am."

Salina left the office, closing the door behind her. Alex hit the button to close the blinds to the office so that no one could see what she was doing. She then put the videodisc in and sat watching to see what would come up.

"Mr. Macellis, we haven't found the girl yet. No one seems to know where she is. It's like she just disappeared off the face of the earth sir."

"Well I know the police don't have her in protective custody. J. Tylan would have informed me, and then I could have had him take care of the girl. No, she's out there somewhere, but she hasn't disappeared from the earth...YET. Have J.T get some of the men at the police station that have worked with us before to be on the lookout for her. Have some flyers and posters printed up with her picture."

"What do you want us to put on them?"

Alex saw the devious smile flash across the man's face but it did not reach the gray eyes of the salt and pepper colored head of the distinguished middle age man.

"Have the printers put something sweet on them, like...

"Please help us find our granddaughter, she has been missing from our lives for far to long and we are willing to give a big reward to anyone who can tell us where we can find her. We pray she's alive, but if that should not be the case, please let us know where her remains are so that we can collect her and give her a proper burial." Anyway, you get the point, now go. We'll wait for a few days and if we don't hear anything back at that time, then I plan on having a talk with my guy on the inside on Thursday. We can meet with them and see what we can come up with. We'll meet them at midnight on Thursday, at the restaurant on 3rd street."

Alex sat, her nostrils flaring, her eyes boring into the image of the father of the boy who raped Taylor.

"We'll see who gets to who first Angelo." She said, as the image faded from view and the disc player stopped playing. She sat and thought for a while, then picked up the phone and made a few calls, one of which was to Kiara.

"It's me, I want all of Macellis' people talked to about the errors of their ways. Before the police arrive at the restaurant, make it a conversation between families, if you know what I mean?"

"I understand. They'll be spoken to, you can be sure."

"Fine, let me know how the conversation goes."

"I will Ma'am."

"Also, when the first group of police arrive, they will be the one's who work for Mr. Macellis. See that you get their pictures and send them along with an anonymous letter to the chief at the police station. Send a copy to the Attorney General also, clear?"

"Yes Ma'am."

"Good. Oh, and Kiara, don't mess up again." She warned.

"I won't Ma'am."

Click!

Again she hung up without so much as a goodbye. Alex swore an oath to herself that she would not allow anything to happen to Taylor again if she could help it. This was one of the ways she planned on assuring that oath.

"Ma'am, the girl is on line 1 for you." Salina's voice chimed in over the intercom.

"Okay. Hello."

"Hi, I know you're probably very busy, but I was feeling very restless again, and since I couldn't concentrate, I thought maybe..."

"Maybe what?"

"Um...never mind, it was stupid of me to call you at work about my petty problem, I'll see you when you get home, I'll make dinner?"

"A.l.r.i.g.h.t. I'll see you when I get home." Alex said, with satisfaction in her tone.

She arrived home and once again Taylor's restlessness ended as they enjoyed a nice evening.

"I want you to go to the office with me tomorrow." The woman stated, as she sipped her tea and looked over her cup at the same time.

"I...I, I don't..."

"You'll be fine, I'll be right there with you. Besides, I want my Personal Assistant back there with me in those meetings." Alex said in a firm voice.

"But isn't Salina handling things for you, I mean she is your Admin. I'm sure she's doing fine."

"Don't question me about things like this, it bothers me. Now I told you what I want, if you don't think you can handle my help, let me know and I'll hire a therapist for you. We can always go back to a working relationship." Alex stated, somewhat annoyed by her assumption.

"I'm sorry, I...I didn't mean to offend you, I really am grateful for all of your help, I will never be able to repay you for it." Taylor said solemnly, as she covered the woman's hand with her smaller hand.

Alex looked into her eyes, but when the girl covered her hand she lowered her gaze to look at the smaller hand on top of her own.

"Alright, I forgive, just don't let it happen again. Now, answer my question, and then go and get the brush and I will brush your hair for you."

"I'll go in with you tomorrow, but I really don't think I can go to the mail room by myself and..."

"I'll send one of the guards with you, and she'll stay with you until you have the mail and come to the office."

Taylor smiled a relieved smile at her, and she felt and saw the girl's gratitude in her eyes. She quickly patted her hand and then said in a firm voice, trying to cover what she was feeling.

"Now go and get the brush."

"Okay, I'll be back in a moment." Taylor said, as she jumped from the chair she was sitting in and went to go get the brush.

Taylor returned with the brush and the two went to the den where Alex sat on the sofa near the warm fireplace, and Taylor sat down on the floor in front of her. Alex then took the brush from Taylor and began brushing her hair as Taylor talked to her about her day and the woman spoke about hers.

CHAPTER 6

The next morning they were sitting in the kitchen listening to the morning news. They were talking in between the different reports, and then when one report came up, there was a picture of Angelo on the screen.

"Wait!" Alex said, shushing Taylor in mid-sentence when she saw the picture.

"Good morning, I'm Georgia Lasher coming to you with breaking news. This morning around 4am in the morning, the bodies of Organized Crime Boss Angelo Macellis was discovered with 20 other men, four of which were his sons, dead of multiple gunshots wounds. The police are saying Angelo and his men were meeting at this restaurant which happens to be one of Mr. Macellis' restaurants, when a rival family surprised them and a rain of bullets sprayed the interior, leaving all inside dead. Mr. Macellis is survived by one son. Mr. Giovanii Macellis, who ironically enough is in jail, being held on rape charges. His trial date is set for the 25th of the month, and when it takes place we'll be there covering it for you. We will bring you the updates to this and all the news throughout the day. For now, I am Georgia Lasher, have a good morning."

"Wow, can you believe that, his whole family wiped out in one fell swoop, wow." Taylor said, completely astonished by the news.

"Hmm...well if one has evil in their hearts, then evil seems to find them." Alex said without emotion, as if it were just another day for her, the elimination of just another problem.

The next few days before the trial was to begin, Taylor was more anxious than usual, and she found it hard to be alone. So she accompanied Alex everywhere she went including those places that had nothing to do with business.

"Okay, today's the day you go to trial, I would be there if I could, but you know why I can't, just in case I'm called to testify on your behalf. Don't worry, I'll be at the office when you're done."

"I don't want to go by myself."

"You won't be by yourself. Yasmeia will be there with you, although she won't be able to be inside until after she has testified for you as one of your character witnesses."

"I know, but..." Taylor said, not sure of what she was trying to say, but she knew she wanted Alex with her in the courtroom.

"It'll be fine, besides, I'm sure he's still grieving the loss of his father and brothers. He's in just as vulnerable state as you are, actually more." Alex pointed out to her.

"Yes, you're right, I have to do this, he can't be allowed to rape anyone else." Taylor said, putting on a brave front, although her heart shook with fear at the thought of exposing herself to strangers.

"That's right, now go with Yasmeia. Ms. Sains, I expect for you to watch out for her." Alex warned in a protective tone.

"That is my plan Ma'am. She's like a little sister to me, and I wouldn't want anything to happen to her, just like you don't."

"Good, you better get going."

"Yes Ma'am." Yasmeia turned and headed for the waiting car that would take them to the courthouse and bring them back.

Taylor turned to look at Alex for a moment and then with a timid smile she turned and headed for the car also.

The opening arguments took place. The first witness was a man that Taylor had never seen or met before.

"Mr. Carrey can you tell us why you're here?"

"Yes, I heard about what that woman was trying to do, making a claim that she was raped by Mr. Macellis."

"Why is that a problem?"

"Because, she's a slut!" The young man spat, as he shook his head in feigned disgust.

"A slut? Okay, why do you say that?"

"Because she use to give many of us...well you know, B.J.'s."

Taylor sat there listening to the man, but because she was not experienced, she did not know what he meant by the term, so she leaned over and asked her attorney.

"What's a B.J.?"

Her attorney looked at her and then whispered in her ear what it was.

"THAT"S A LIE!! She yelled to her attorney.

"I know, I know, but this is what I was telling you was going to happen." He whispered back to her to calm her.

The defending attorney continued to call man after man to all defame Taylor and all she could do was sit there and endure all of the lies. Her very soul felt as though it were being ripped apart. Luckily whenever her attorney cross-examined the men, he was able to show them for the liars they were. The day ended after the defending attorney had called twelve witnesses and all of them had been crossed.

When they finally left, Taylor was an emotional wreck. Yasmeia saw her home to Alex's house. She was unable to get her key in the lock due to her shaking hands, so Yasmeia had to do it for her. Alex was told by the maid that Taylor was home and she immediately left her study to see how she was doing. When she came around the corner of the wall she saw her crying with her head on the armrest of the sofa. Alex's eyes cut to Yasmeia in an accusing glare. Yasmeia whispered to Taylor, then immediately went to go and talk to the fuming woman. Yasmeia started to speak, but Alex caught her by the arm and pulled her out of the den and into the hallway.

"What happened, why is she crying like that?!"

"Ma'am, it was a rough day in court."

"What happened?!"

"I heard a conversation in the bathroom by some women who were in the courtroom, that the guy's attorney called a bunch of men to slander her reputation."

"And?"

"They were saying things about her that she didn't even know what the terminology meant, much less the actual deed."

"She's naive in that way."

"I know. I know just like those women in that bathroom knew, that the girl those men were talking about, was not sitting in that courtroom."

"But it still hurt her none the less."

"Yes, they said that every time she would ask the attorney what something meant, she would yell out that it was a lie and then sit back stunned by the accusation. It was a very emotional day for her."

"I can see that, well I'll take care of her, I'll expect you here tomorrow to go with her."

"Yes, Ma'am, I plan on being there through this whole thing. Tomorrow, I think his attorney will be calling him to the stand."

"Hmm...it's moving fast. How did the Attorney General handle all of the men? He showed them for the liars they were right?"

"Yes, the jury just shook their heads at the very nerve of them to come to court and lie the way they did."

"Good, I look forward to hearing what he has to say."

"Ma'am you know you can't go to the courthouse?"

"Of course I know that! I'm just hoping this all will be over soon. Taylor's been through so much with this jerk, he's lucky I can't get to him myself." Alex said through her teeth, as she turned to go back to where the girl was. Just before she left Yasmeia to see herself out, she looked over her shoulder and said in a sincere tone of voice. "Sains, thanks for being there with her, I know it means a lot to her, and me. I won't forget this."

Yasmeia gave a bewildered smile, and then a nod of her head and turned to leave. When she was outside, she stood by the car that had brought her to the house, for a moment. She thought about Alex's comments and the statement of her caring for Taylor, who meant a lot to her and how she wouldn't forget it. Yasmeia's eyes narrowed at the thought that came to her mind, but now was not the time to make waves. She would talk with Alex when all of this was over with. In the meantime, Yasmeia saw how much Taylor, her friend, depended on Alex.

"Alex you better not be taking advantage of my friend, especially during all of this." She said to herself, as she finally got inside of the car and was taken away from the property. She was disturbed by what she thought might be happening.

Meanwhile, Alex went into the den where Taylor still sat crying into her arms over top of the armrest of the sofa. She walked over and poured some water from a pitcher into a glass, then walked over to where the girl was. She sat down beside her and after taking a few deep breaths to maintain her own control, she spoke to the hurting girl.

"I heard it was rough in the courtroom today." Taylor cried more, and Alex inhaled and let it out slowly, determined to help her. "I know it was hard to sit through people purposefully lying about you, but you know that that's all they were doing. You shouldn't let things you know to not be true, get to you like this, otherwise you will always be vulnerable to being hurt. Here, sit up and drink this. Come on, sit up." Alex said, noticing she was listening, but not knowing how to respond, or what to do.

Taylor sat up and looking like a punished child, she took the glass in her shaking hands and drank deeply. She coughed when some of the water went down the wrong pipe. She handed the glass back to Alex and dried her mouth of the water that had sprinkled her lips as a result of her coughing.

"I...I don't see how people can just lie so blatantly. I didn't even know what they were talking about until I asked what a lot of things meant. I felt like such a child in there, I mean I consider myself to be intelligent, but I didn't even know...' Her words choked off as she dissolved into tears.

"Come here." Alex said, as she pulled Taylor into her arms and held the shaking and distraught girl.

After a while Alex told her to go to her room and she would bring her something to eat. Taylor reluctantly did as she was told, and the woman watched her go, and then watched her go up the stairs. Despite putting on a brave front, she could see the heaviness on Taylor's narrow shoulders. She swore under her breath and then turned sharply on her heels, and headed for the kitchen to get some much-needed food. When Alex brought the food, she found Taylor crying once again. She set the tray of food down on the table next to the bed and sat down next to the crying girl. She caressed her hair with her hand and Taylor quieted once again. Then after a moment, she rolled over onto her back to look up at Alex.

"I'm sorry, I'm acting like such a baby." Taylor said forlornly.

"You're acting like a young girl who is naive about some things, and like a woman who has been deeply hurt. Sit up, I brought you some soup to start with."

"You didn't have to do this." Taylor said, with some distress in her voice at having this woman wait on her, just because of her behaving like a child.

"Open up." Alex ordered and began feeding her, despite the fact that she was perfectly able to feed herself. Alex found herself enjoying the role of taking care of Taylor, and deep within herself she admitted she could probably get used to it.

Taylor didn't think to tell the woman that she could feed herself. She just found herself comparing the compassion Alex was bestowing on her, with that of her grandmother's, and she found it comforting. She was reminisced when her grandmother used to sit with her at night, and feed her soup. Alex fed the girl her whole meal. Afterwards Taylor laid down and once again Alex pulled up a chair to sit next to the bed until she fell asleep. Then she leaned over and placed a soft kiss to the girl's forehead. She let her lips linger on her forehead, just enjoying the smoothness of the skin against her lips. She leaned back and stood up to her full height. Looking down at the sleeping girl she thought to herself.

"This will be all over soon little one."

The next day the two ate breakfast and listened to the news together about the trial. This became a daily routine. The trial was wearing on Taylor, especially seeing how the defending attorney had called more people to lie about her.

Finally, it was the prosecuting attorney's turn. He called a few character witnesses to testify about the girl, and then because of a phone call Alex had made to him to speed things up, he called Taylor to the stand.

"Now, I just want you to tell the people of the jury what happened."

"Alright." She said to the attorney, and then looking over at the jury, she lowered her eyes at first, trying to find the courage to just tell her side of things.

She raised her eyes and looked over at the table the boy sat behind, glaring at her, then her eyes went to her own attorney who was nodding his head for her to go ahead. Finally her eyes fell on her friend, who now was allowed in since she had testified. Yasmeia flashed her a smile and she gave a sad smile back to her, then returned her attention to the jury.

"It started when I broke up with Dominic....I mean Giovanii."

"Is Dominic the name Mr. Macellis told you when you two first met?"

"Yes, he told me that, and the fact that he worked for his father in his restaurant business."

"Is that the only business he is involved in?"

"I object, Mr. Macellis' line of work has nothing to do with this case."

"I'll withdraw the question Your Honor. Okay, jump to the days before the rape happened."

"I object, Mr. Macellis has not been convicted of rape."

"Objection sustained, rephrase your question."

"Certainly your honor. Tell us what happened between the two of you before the incident in the elevator."

"Four days before I was RAPED..." Taylor said, emphasizing the term. "Mr. Macellis had shown up at my job unexpectedly, to take me to lunch. I was with my boss and some clients when I saw him. I was happy to see him and I wanted him to meet my boss. I told my boss that he was the man I had told her about and she told me she would be right over to meet him after she sent the clients to her office to wait for her. Meanwhile, I went over to greet him and I kissed him on the cheek. Although he tried to kiss me on the lips, I'm not much for public displays. Anyway, I told him I wanted him to meet my boss. When she came over, I introduced the two and the first words out of his mouth were disrespectful to me, my boss and my career."

"What were they?"

"He called my boss a Bitch."

"In what context?"

"His exact words were, "So you're the bitch that demoted my girl." I was shocked, humiliated and embarrassed, that someone who I cared about could ever do such a thing. Even if it had been true, it was not his place to say anything like that to her."

"Do you consider her to be a bitch?"

"NO. She's a very focused woman, who knows what she wants and how to get it. She's hard on people, but she only wants the best working for her, she has no patience for liars or slackers."

"Were you one of those liars when you were demoted?"

"It was really a matter of my timidity. Like I said before, I am not one who likes to be in the spotlight. This trial is so overwhelming to me, but I know I have to do this, so that he doesn't do to others what he did to me. Anyway, my boss asked me if I had written some reports that she had been given by one of her vice presidents, who also is a friend of mine. I had done the research and written them. Then I gave them to him and let him take the credit for the work."

"Wasn't he able to do the work himself?"

"Yes, but he had so many things to get done, that I offered and he accepted the offer."

"Okay, continue."

"Okay, anyway, she...my boss had asked me if I had done the reports. I told her that I had, but I played down my role. I didn't know she knew I had done them, and therefore she considered me to be a liar. That's when she demoted me to the mailroom. I was only responsible for her mail, it was her way of bringing me into her full view considering she overheard me on the phone shouting how happy I was that I was still anonymous to her."

The jury chuckled at Taylor's inadvertent joke, and she gave a small smile with knitted brows at the jury. Then she continued.

"Anyway, I only worked in the mailroom for a short time before she promoted me to be her Personal Assistant."

"Aha, so she obviously didn't think of you as a liar anymore once she found out why you said what you did?"

"Right, and I've been her assistant ever since. Anyway, I told Mr. Macellis that I didn't want to see him anymore. Four days later he showed up at the building and when I had went and gotten the mail and had gotten in the elevator to go up, that's when he jumped into it just before the doors closed. He startled me at first, but then he started talking and telling me what he was not about to let happen..."

"What was it that he was not going to let happen?"

"His exact words were, "If you think I am going to let someone else pop that cherry then you are more of a fool than I thought."

"Did you know what that meant?"

"Not exactly, but because of the way he said it and the look in his eyes, I guessed what he meant, and I was right."

"What did it mean?"

"Do I have to say it?"

"No, but it would help the jury understand more about you."

"Okay, He meant that he was going to take my virginity, that way I would always remember him, because I would never forget who took it." Taylor's eyes watered at the memory, and she dropped her head for a moment and looked at her hands.

Her attorney let her have a moment to compose herself, and after asking her if she was ready to continue, she nodded her head.

"Okay. Was he successful?"

"No, thank God! The elevator had started moving again and it distracted him long enough for me to hit him. He staggered backwards, and then just as he was about to come back after me, I can only assume he was going to beat me, anyway, the elevator doors open and he turned and was taken down by a punch thrown by my boss...She broke his nose and a few bones in his jaw." She smiled slightly at the jury when they chuckled again.

"So what happened from there?"

"I don't remember all of it, because I must have gone into shock once he was down. I just remember waking up at the company clinic with my boss asking me if I was okay. I'm sorry, I don't remember anything else before that."

"Thank you that'll be all."

"Counsel you may cross examine the witness if you like?"

"Thank you Your Honor. Okay Ms. Young, you said that he wasn't successful in this attempted rape?"

"No I said he wasn't successful in taking my virginity. He was successful in raping me."

"You called it rape, but was it really rape?"

"Yes!"

"I beg to differ with you, did my client ever try to put his penis inside of you?"

"N..no, but..."

"But what? Either he tried to rape you or he didn't?"

"He did."

"But you just said he never tried to put his penis in you. How is it considered rape if he never put his penis inside of you?"

"Well..." Taylor didn't have the answer to the man's distracting question, and her attorney decided he would not object but let her answer as best she could. He would call Alex to answer the questions that Taylor was unable to answer.

"Did he ever pull his pants down?"

"No." The stress on Taylor's face was evident.

"Did he pull his penis out of the front of his pants?"

"No." She said, as she noticed the man grinning at her. He was gaining confidence from her lack of answers.

"So in other words, it wasn't rape."

"It was!" Taylor argued, but she felt as though the case maybe lost as a result of her testimony.

"No further questions of this witness Your Honor."

Taylor looked at her attorney to see what she should do, but the Judge's words to her to step down cut through the tears. She stepped down and walked back over to her table and put her head in her hand and quietly sobbed. Her attorney tried to comfort her. The Judge called a break, and when court resumed she still had no idea what her attorney was going to do next, considering how her testimony had ended. She didn't know who he had went to call during the break, but she would soon find out.

"Mr. Henassey are you ready to call your next witness?"

"Yes Your Honor."

"Who are you going to call?" Taylor asked, surprised that there was anyone else to call.

"We call...Alexandra Madison, "THE RAIDER."

Taylor's eyes went wide, although she thought Alex would possibly be a witness, she hadn't heard anything about her being called since the day she and the woman had talked about why she couldn't come to court. Now here she was, striding into the courtroom. She was wearing a luminescent white, tailored, double-breasted, coat length, silk pantsuit, carrying a leather briefcase. Taylor's mouth dropped open and there were whispers all around the courtroom. Even the Judge himself didn't seem to notice how loud the mass of people in the courtroom was whispering. Alex didn't look left or right, not even at Taylor, she just headed straight for the witness stand, and people's eyes followed her. No one noticed the other women who had come in behind her, and taken seats at the back of the courtroom. Alex sat in the chair and was sworn in and stated her name for the court. The man then went into his examination.

"Ms Madison, you're here on behalf of Taylor Young?"

"Yes."

"Can you tell us how you came to meet her?"

"Yes. I met Ms. Young as a result of an attempt on my life."

"Someone tried to kill you?!" The attorney asked, surprised by the information and even more surprised that she did not tell him about it.

"Yes." She answered nonchalantly. "Anyway, she came to the top floor where my office is located, in an attempt to warn me of the man's intentions. By the time she arrived he was already there threatening me, but I overheard her talking to one of the police officers about what she was doing on the top floor. She told him she had come to warn me."

"What did you think about that?"

"I thought it was suspicious."

"Why?"

"Because as the nickname "THE RAIDER" implies, I am not a very likable person, mainly because of the very nature of what I do."

"And what is it that you do?"

"I acquire other companies. In other words, I'm a Corporate Raider, thus the nickname."

"Aha, alright, let me ask you this, was there ever a time that you considered this young woman to be a liar?"

"Yes."

"And what made you think of her as such?"

"She tried to lead me to believe that she did not write some reports, that I knew she had."

"Were the reports any good?"

"They were excellent, and I wanted to tell her that I was very pleased with them, but I wanted to see what type of person she was first. Because I was going to keep my eye on her and possibly give her a promotion that befitted her talents."

"But what happened?"

"She lied, or at least that's how I saw it at the time."

"As a result of the supposed lie, what did you do?"

"I told her to get out of my office, and I demoted her to work in the mailroom, where her only duty was to handle my mail, and hand deliver it to me."

"Why did you feel it was important to have her deliver it to you in person, why not let her give it to your Admin?"

"Because I was suspicious of her, but I also thought maybe she just made a mistake and I would give her a chance to get back in my good graces."

"So did she?"

"Eventually. There was a conversation she had with her immediate supervisor, about her quitting because she couldn't handle the idea that I didn't trust her and I thought of her as a liar."

"How did you hear about this conversation?"

"Ms. Sains called my office to plead her case. She told me she did not want to lose Taylor because of all of her potential, as well as her being a sweet and loving person. She also brought up the fact that she was the only one who tried to warn me about Mr. Evans, the man who attempted to kill me."

"So you felt like you owed her?"

"No. At the time all I saw and heard was that she was not only a liar but a quitter, so I told Ms. Sains I would talk with her."

"You went to find her?"

"No, there is no need for me to GO and find anyone, I was just going to have her come to my office when she returned. In the meantime I went to a meeting in the dining hall with some of my upper management personnel, and when we came out of the private area of that same dining area, I saw her sitting at a table."

"What was she doing?"

"She was just sitting looking out into the distance, as if in thought."

"What did you do?"

"I dismissed the management people I was with and went to go and talk with her."

"What happened?"

"She went wide eyed at seeing me standing in front of her."

"Is that a common reaction you get from people?"

"Yes. Anyway, I sat down and I told her that I had heard she planned on quitting."

"What did she say to that?"

"She said she didn't have any other choice, she could not handle the idea that I thought of her as a liar. I asked her if she thought I would think any better of her if she quit? She said she hadn't thought about that. Eventually she saw it was worse for her to quit, rather than just go work in the mailroom and earn my trust again."

"Okay, so eventually you made her your Personal Assistant?"

"Yes."

"Is she any good at it?"

"The best. She learns quickly, she doesn't make the same mistakes twice, and she listens."

"Have you ever had to reprimand her since she became your Personal Assistant?"

"Yes, and I still do when she messes up. I haven't had to for a while, and then when all of this happened I didn't want to overwhelm her anymore than she already was."

"Overwhelm her more? How?"

"Well, she's very intimidated by me, as are a lot of people."

"Does your opinion hold any weight with her?"

"Yes, she seems to value it, and seeks it when she is having a problem."

"Do you consider her to be just another employee?"

"I used to."

"But you don't now?"

Alex finally looked over at Taylor, who sat there teary eyed, and a slightly sympathetic smile came to the woman's mouth.

"No, I don't."

"What do you consider her to be?"

"I'm not sure, but if I had to put a word to it, I would say...a friend."

"Hmm...a friend? That's unusual for you isn't it?"

"What, having friends, or her being a friend?"

"Her becoming your friend."

"Yes, it is, I usually don't mix business with my personal life."

"So why do it now?"

"At first I did it because I saw a young girl who was trying to do what was right, and was trying to please me all at the same time. I thought it was only right that I didn't make it too hard on her. Now, it's different, I began to see a young girl who needed to be protected, not that she asked for it, but I saw it. I saw that with her naiveté, and sweet innocence, she was being used by people, I began to feel very protective of her."

"So you're here as a protector and friend?"

"No, I'm here because a woman was violently assaulted and the person who did it must be punished for it. I would do it for any of my employee's if I were a witness to a crime committed against them, as well as any stranger."

"Okay, so tell us how you met Mr. Macellis."

"I had heard about him, but I had not met him until months after Taylor became my Personal Assistant. He came to the company to take her to lunch, a surprise lunch date. We had just come into the building and were heading to my office for a meeting with some clients. When she saw him, she told me she wanted to step over to him and say hello and see what he wanted and that she wanted me to meet him. I told her I would meet him, but I needed to send the clients to the office."

"And?"

"And that's what I did, I had one of the guards show the clients to my office and I went over to meet the young man."

"How did she introduce him to you?"

"She introduced him as Dominic."

"Was that his name?"

"No, I knew him the moment I saw him, so when she said Dominic, I repeated the name to him in a questioning matter, but he didn't pick up on it."

"What name did you know him as?"

"Giovanii Macellis."

"Where did you know him from?"

"He's the son of the late Angelo Macellis, the head of a crime family."

"Did Ms. Young know this?"

"No. I was the one who told her who he was."

"How did that come about?"

"After she had introduced us, he proceeded to try to insult me by referring to me as a bitch."

"Were you angry by that?"

"No, I was just irritated by his presence, I was angry at Ms. Young."

"Why?"

"Because I couldn't believe she was with such a person. I figured he may have lied about his name, but she had to have seen what type of life he led."

"And did she?"

"No, she was completely in the dark about him and his real identity. Anyway, after I told her we had a meeting, I told her I would wait for her at the elevators. She went back to talking to the man, completely mortified by his actions towards me."

"Why?"

"Because she was afraid that I thought she had used the term to speak of me. Anyway, while she was talking to him there was a point where he had grabbed her by her arm and was manhandling her."

"What did you do?"

"I kept myself from going back over and laying him out for it. I wanted to see how she was going to handle herself with him. I wanted to see if she was in an abusive relationship with this man. Eventually she talked him into letting go of her and they spoke for a few more moments before she came to the elevators. She had a hard time looking me in the eyes, but I made her. That's when she blurted out that she was sorry for what he had said, and that she would have never said anything like that, and things to that effect."

"What did you say?"

"I told her first of all not to apologize for someone else's actions or behavior, that was not her place, and then I told her I didn't want to see her with him anymore."

"You inserted yourself into her personal life?"

"Yes."

"Why?"

"Because she worked for me, and I didn't want that type of element anywhere near any of my companies."

"What did she say?"

"Pretty much the same thing you just did, that her personal life was her business, and that only upset me more. I decided the only way she would understand why I felt so strongly about it, was to tell her who he was. That's what I did. She stood there with her mouth agape, staring at me as if I had four heads or something."

"Did she believe you?"

"For a brief moment, no, she didn't want to believe me, but she knew me to be a no nonsense person, and an honest one, so she eventually accepted it, despite the bitterness of the pill."

"What happened then?"

"We went to our meeting, and then I made some phone calls.

In the meantime, Taylor sat down and was talking about how she couldn't believe she didn't know him, and that maybe she could talk to him."

"What did you think about that?"

"I thought she was being foolish, and I told her so. I also told her she had to get moved out of her place that day, and of course she balked at that at first, but she did it."

"Why?"

"Because I told her to."

"Aha, okay so you made her move out of her place, why?"

"Because I knew he would show up there to try to smooth talk her into going back with him, and then if she refused he would hurt her."

"This is because of your knowing his father?"

"Yes. Anyway, I had a detective watch the empty place and sure enough that night he and some of his associates showed up at her place. When he found her gone, along with all of her stuff except for some tacky suit with dog fur on the cuff and collar, hanging on a rack, he was outraged. He began cursing and he told his hitmen that he wanted her found, and whoever was helping her, he wanted them dead."

"Do you have proof of all of these threats?"

"Of course I do! I told you I had a detective staking out her place to see if HE in particular would show up."

"Where is this proof?"

Alex placed her briefcase on the counter of the witness stand, opened it and handed a disc to the attorney. He took it and presented it as evidence to the Judge. The Judge asked if there were any objections and none were rendered, mainly because the young man didn't believe she really had anything. The disc was then played for the entire courtroom. The young man saw that he had indeed been caught on disc making the threats. After the tape was finished playing, the attorney went back to his examination.

"So you showed this to Ms. Young?"

"Yes, but only when she brought up the idea of going to talk to him again. After she saw it, she was once again stunned by it."

"Did she give up the idea about going to talk to him?"

"No, in fact it made her want to go and talk to him more."

"Why, I mean you had just shown her this disc, she saw for herself that he meant to do her harm. Why would she want to risk herself to go and talk to him?"

"She was scared for me."

"You? Why?"

"Because I was the one helping her, and with the threat she thought that if she could just talk to him he would back off and not come after me."

"Were you worried about your own safety."

"Worried, no, he is just a pesky fly of a nuisance to me. I had no worries about him, my concern was for Taylor."

The man sat up with a huff at the description that was just made about him.

"So Ms. Young was willing to risk herself to protect you once again?"

"Yes."

"Why?"

"What do you mean why?"

"Why would an employee even think to do such a thing? I mean you said she was a friend and things, but as a friend she should have realized that there was no way you would allow her to do such a thing?"

"True, but that was her intention."

"Is she in love with you?"

Alex was caught off guard by the question, but when she spoke her voice gave no indication.

"I don't believe that is what I would call it."

"What would you call it?"

Alex looked over at Taylor and saw she had a bright smile on her face, that too caught her off guard, but again she didn't falter.

"I would probably call it hero worship."

"Hmm...okay, that makes sense, I mean after all, you've done so much to help her, but that wouldn't be the end of your helping her, right?"

"Right, a few days later he showed up at the company again, only this time he stole his way inside and he waited for her in the basement. He waited for her to get the mail and get on the elevator, then he jumped on just after she had pushed the express button and the doors were about to close."

"Express?"

"Yes, it is used to come directly to the top floor without stopping on any of the floors between."

"Oh, alright, continue."

"Anyhow, when it had gotten 3/4s of the way up he pushed the stop button, and that's when he began to really make his intentions known to her. She tried to fight him off, but he was bigger and stronger and was able to pin her in the corner with her arms behind her back. He lifted her skirt and proceeded to slip his fingers inside of her with the intention of raping her."

"I object your honor!" The opposing counsel's voice chimed in.

"On what grounds?"

"There is nothing proven yet to the claim of rape Your Honor."

"Sustained."

"Can you rephrase your statement?" Taylor's attorney asked of Alex.

"Certainly, the man has a pattern of repeatedly violating his ex-women for the sole purpose of despoiling them so that he will be remembered. So you can call it whatever you like, Rape, pattern, repeat offender, it doesn't matter, a flower is a flower and a DOG, is a Dog and there is no changing that, so there's your rephrasing." She said impatiently.

There was no objection to the rephrased statement, although she was still able to slip the word rape in.

"Okay, how do you know that's what happened, or is that what she told you?"

"No. When the stop button is depressed, it automatically activates a camera that records everything that is going on." Alex was resolved not to give away any information that was not absolutely necessary. So she didn't mention about the express button feature.

"Alright, anyway, what happened then?"

"The elevator restarted. It's an automatic thing, anytime the express button is hit, if for some reason the stop button is hit in the meantime, the elevator restarts after one minute and proceeds on to the top floor without being able to stop it again. Although he tried, and was angry that it did not stop, eventually it arrived and I was there to greet him."

"What did you do?"

"I knocked him out."

"Were you angry?"

"Of course."

"Why?"

"Because he would dare to do that to anyone who worked for me, yet alone a friend."

"What happened then?"

"Well that's when the police, medical personnel and the other investigators all showed up."

"What of Ms. Young?"

"She was cowering in the corner going into shock over everything that had happened. I got her to come out, and I began asking her if he entered her and things like that. She told me, and eventually she was needed by the MD, who was also a rape specialist, working at the company clinic that day. She took her to the clinic to take samples and specimens and do an examination on her."

"Why not take her to the hospital, it was only five minutes away?"

"Because she was too shaken up and scared to go anywhere without me being close by."

"Why?"

"Because she obviously felt safe around me."

"Okay. Was there anything special that you needed to infer to the MD?"

"Yes, I told her that Taylor was a virgin prior to the attack and that I thought she still was, considering I did not see any gross amount of blood on his fingers or hand from the breaking of her hymen. I told her to be careful, that way if he was not able to succeed in completely violating her, I didn't want her to mess up and end up doing it with her examination. I thought it was important that Ms. Young be spared as much as possible, in the way of remembering that day."

"So you believed that if he was not successful then she would have a better chance of getting past all of this?"

"Yes. Her deflowering should not be remembered as a violent act, but as a gentle and loving one." Alex did not look at Taylor, she knew that if she did, she would not be able to maintain her regal persona. She knew the girl would probably be teary eyed and even crying, she heard the soft sobbing, but she kept her eyes and attention focused on the Attorney General.

"No more questions. Thank you Ms. Madison."

"Your witness."

"Thank you Your Honor. Ma'am, you said that my client raped the young girl?" The defending attorney asked, trying to use the same technique to trip up the woman.

"Yes."

"Are you sure?"

"Yes, all of the tests confirmed that."

"Yes...the tests, well I'll get back to that, right now I want to know what you consider rape to be?"

"It's a violent sex act committed usually against women, but men are also susceptible to it, as well as children."

"Okay, yes that is one of the definitions of it, but what makes it rape? What act particularly."

"Ask your client, he would know, he did it." Alex said, with some irritation in her tone at the man's attempt to blur the issue.

The jury chuckled at the statement, and the defending attorney smirked at her, then pinched his lips to prevent himself from chuckling.

"Well, we've already had our conversation. I would like to have you answer it for me."

"Very well, there are two ways that I know of that are considered ways of raping."

"Two?"

"Yes."

"Oh, please tell us what these two ways are, I'm sure we all would love to hear your wisdom and insight on what two ways there are to rape a person."

Alex raised a studying brow at the man, and sat back in the chair, and casually crossed her arms, studying him for long silent moments. The man was uncomfortable with the steady gaze; so much so that he dropped a pen he had in his hands. She had made her point with the man, and he blushed a deep red and stood waiting for her with more respect.

"That's better." She said to him, letting him know she recognized his contriteness, although the jury and the rest of the people in the courtroom didn't understand the silent communication between the two. At least everyone else except for Yasmeia, and Taylor, they both had seen that look and even though it was not leveled on them, they felt it none the less.

"If you wouldn't mind continuing Ms. Madison?" The attorney asked, with more respect.

"Certainly. One of the ways of rape is that of what all of us know, the act of penetration of the vagina with the penis. The other way has come about due to the society we live in today, therefore the use of digital penetration is also considered a way of rape."

"Digital?"

"Yes, it is a new law you know."

"How is fingering someone considered rape?"

"The law says it is, but even outside of that, how do you think two women have sex?"

"Um...well...um." The attorney said, at a loss for words at the moment.

With Alex looking at him through those piercing sapphires, he was unsteadied. "Well, okay, I guess that is a matter of interpretation for the jury."

"What's to interpret?" She asked, looking over at the jury, who now was receiving a once over by "The Raider." They all look like intelligent people who recognize that the law says it is rape. Therefore, what is there to interpret, the law has already done that, they only need to determine how many years or lifetimes without parole he should get?" Alex said, and again looked over at the jury.

"Well, it's not that simple, first it must be proven that a rape occurred."

"I thought that's what I just said, he crossed the line between assault and rape, when he violently entered her vagina. If he had rubbed against her clitoris without entering her, then I would agree with you that it was not rape. But he PENETRATED HER VAGINA with his fingers to deflower her so that he would be remembered forever as the man who took her virginity. He's a serial rapist who needs to be castrated and imprisoned for the rest of his natural life."

"I object Your Honor! This woman..." The man started to say. But seeing her eyes narrow at him, he changed his tone. "Ms. Madison is defaming my client in front of the jury, biasing them based on no evidence to support such an outrageous claim. I demand that she be made to prove these claims or I ask for a mistrial."

"Ma'am, do you have any proof to back up your claim?"

"Well if he will stop whining maybe I'll present some, but if I don't then what will you do?"

"Hahaha, I will declare a mistrial." The judge chuckled despite himself, at the fact that he agreed with the woman.

"Hmm..."

The defending attorney now had a smug look on his face, and Taylor's eyes were filled with fear, yet her attorney sat calmly waiting for Alex.

"Well?"

"Well Your Honor, I have to say...it's a good thing I do, wouldn't you say?" Alex said, with a smirk at the judge, who smiled and then turned his attention back to the stunned attorney.

"You do?"

"Yes. He has not only raped my employee, for the purpose of being the first to have a virgin, but he has done it to at least ten others and their cases are still pending due to the back log of cases."

"Have those cases brought to me." The Judge ordered of his bailiff, but the Attorney General interjected at that moment.

"Your Honor if we may approach the bench?"

The Judge motioned for them to approach.

"Your Honor I have all of those cases with me. I was told about them, but I didn't think I would need them due to the open and shut nature of this case. If you would like, I can either give you all of those and we continue on with this trial and spend more money, or I can offer the defending attorney a final deal of 50 years without possibility of parole. I can always present all of the women and go for life imprisonment?"

"Your Honor, I knew nothing of these possible witnesses."

"Sure you did, I told you that I had some women who claimed they had been raped by him, but you refused to believe it and said "Bring them on." Well...Alex has brought them, and I WILL bring them on if you like?"

"I need to talk to my client, may I ask for a continuation?"

"What do you say?"

"No Your Honor, Ms. Young and all of these women have been through enough without having to wait for him. It's time he is made to take responsibility for his actions. I want a decision now, today."

"Fine." The attorney left to go and speak with his client. Giovanii was heard cursing and bitterly refusing, but eventually his attorney got him to see the wisdom in the decision. The young man sat down heavily, with rage in his eyes as well as defeat.

His lawyer walked back over to the bench where the Attorney General and the Judge had continued to wait.

"We'll take the deal Your Honor."

The Prosecuting attorney smiled, then said with a satisfied tone.

"Accepted."

"Step back Gentlemen." The two attorney's stepped back and Taylor was trying to find out what was happening, but her attorney shushed her. She sat looking between the Judge, the defending attorney, the Attorney General, and her boss.

"Mr. Macellis please stand."

The man came to his feet along with his attorney.

"A deal has been made by your attorney, do you accept it?"

"Yes."

"Do you understand that you are now giving up your right to a trial, and your civil rights, and will be considered from this day forth as a Rapist? Do you still wish to accept the agreement?"

The man looked at his attorney, and then over at the jury, then at Alex and finally at Taylor. He then looked back at the judge.

"Yes." He decided the odds were more against him than would be for him.

"So be it. People of the jury, seeing that Mr. Macellis has agreed to waive his right to a trial, I will now thank you for serving and performing your civic duty, and I will dismiss you all."

The jury then thanked the Judge and they were led out of the jury box and out of the courtroom via the jury exit. The Judge then turned back to the man.

"Mr. Macellis, you will be returned here in one week to be sentenced. Court dismissed."

Taylor was both happy and dismayed at the thought of having to return to the court in a week for the sentencing, but she was happy that it was going to happen. After court was dismissed Alex stood up and stepped out of the witness box. She watched as Taylor hugged her attorney, then her friend Yasmeia, and then with tears rolling down her face, she turned and saw Alex with tears balancing to fall from her own eyes. She lost it, and rapidly walked over to the woman where she wrapped her arms around Alex's waist and sobbed with gratitude. Alex wrapped her arms around Taylor and buried her head in the girl's mass of ebony hair, so that her own tears were not seen by anyone else. Yasmeia saw the encounter and her initial thoughts about talking to Alex about the girl, were now a far memory, as she saw how tender the woman was with her. She actually felt own tears fall from the scene she was witnessing.

"Okay Alex, you have shown me you really do care about her." She said to herself as she watched them.

"Let's go home okay?" Alex finally managed in a composed voice.

"Okay!" Taylor said, breathless from the adrenaline that was racing through her, as she gazed up into the woman's moisture filled eyes.

They headed for the door and Yasmeia stepped in line with them and Taylor wrapped one arm around her and continued to hold Alex with the other arm around her waist. Alex had her arm over the girl's shoulder and the three of them went out of the courtroom. After the woman had thanked her friend for his fine work, he then thanked Alex for hers.

CHAPTER 7

They dropped Yasmeia off at her house and then they headed home. Once they had arrived, Taylor was in an upbeat mood. She was relieved that the trial was over, only the sentencing remained, and that the man had gotten so many years.

"I'm hungry, you hungry? I'll make you the biggest and best meal you ever tasted, and whatever you want it's yours for the asking, I don't care what it is, my first born, anything you want, you just name it. I can not tell you... The girl's words were choked off from the large lump that had formed in her throat, at the very thought of all that Alex had done for her.

"I know, I can see it in your eyes. You're welcome." Alex said, reading her thoughts correctly.

Taylor once again wrapped her arms around the woman. Alex found herself really enjoying times like these, when the girl would embrace her. She realized it was a guilty pleasure, but she knew she would never do anything to hurt Taylor, so she allowed herself to revel in it. She held the girl tightly to her as she comforted her. After a bit, the woman decided it was time for the girl to get on with her life and put all of this stuff behind her.

"Okay, that's enough, you owe me a dinner. I suggest you go and get cleaned up, changed and start cooking. I am very hungry and I can be a bear, I think you know that, so go, now." Alex said, as she swatted the girl on the behind as a parent would. Taylor chuckled and allowed herself to be turned and slightly pushed in the direction of the stairs. She went up them, but before she was out of sight of the woman she stopped and turned back around to look at her. Alex saw her stop.

"You okay?"

"Yes, now, thanks entirely to you. Thank you for being there for me. I couldn't have asked for a better friend." Taylor said as tears ran. She broke the eye contact, suddenly confused by what she was feeling. She looked away slowly, not sure if she should go on upstairs or say something else. She finally decided to go on up the stairs.

She was not bouncing as she had started, but more of a confused stagger. Alex watched her, and her brows knitted with concern and wonder.

The next week was stressful and relieving. Finally the day came for them to return to court for the man's sentencing.

"Are you ready to go?"

"Yes, I just want this to be over." Taylor said, as they stood by the door to the courtroom.

"Okay, let's get it over with." Alex replied, as an officer opened the door and they entered the courtroom.

"Mr. Macellis, do you have anything to say before I pass sentence?"

"NO!" The man said, then turned and sneered at Taylor. She started to look away, but Alex caught her chin and turned her back to look right back at the man.

"You don't let him intimidate you." She then let go of Taylor's cheeks and the girl's eyes remained locked on his. Eventually, he scoffed and looked away. Taylor smiled to herself at her success, and Alex looked down at her and gave a slight nod. The girl grinned and interlocked their arms, albeit discretely.

Alex looked down at the embrace, and her heart leapt at the possibilities of what she had been seeing in her mind for months now, but she said and did nothing about it, except to casually cover Taylor's hands with one of her own, and gave a pat to them.

"Alright Mr. Macellis, I will now pass sentence. I hereby sentence you, Mr. Giovanii Macellis based on the agreed upon time by both counsels, and yourself, to...fifty years without possibility of parole. Bailiff, take Mr. Macellis to be processed." The bailiff took custody of the man, as he cursed at Taylor on his way out of the courtroom.

"Ms. Madison, it has been an absolute pleasure to have met you in person." The Judge called from the bench he sat on, to the woman as she sat in the front row of benches with Taylor and Yasmeia.

"Thank you, your Honor." She returned, with a teasing wink at the elderly man.

He blushed and said "Court dismissed." Then struck his gavel, thereby ending the trial. The next two weeks things were returning to normal, although Taylor was quieter than usual. She had not thought about the things that had happened two weeks ago, her mind was constantly on Alex.

One day while she was at Alex's house looking through a book of homes, which Alex didn't know anything about, the phone rang. The maid came and told her that she had a phone call. Taylor excused herself from the woman and went to go answer the phone.

"Hello, Grammy?! How are you? I'm fine, yes Grammy, I really am. Yes, I would love to. It's been a while I know, but I'll come to visit for a week. I don't know if I can come next week? Okay Grammy, I'll see what I can do. Yes she's right here. Grammy no, you don't even know her, she's a very busy woman!"

Alex was now looking at her with inquisitive eyes. Taylor told her grandmother to hold on for a moment and she covered the speaking part of the phone to whisper to Alex.

"My grandmother wants to know if I can come and see her next week for a week?"

"Yes, that's fine, a lot of the things that are scheduled can be rescheduled. Plus it would be nice for you to get away from this town for a while. Tell her yes."

"Great, but..."

"What?"

"She wants to know if you will come also. She wants to meet the person who has been so "sweet." to her granddaughter, so she can give her a hug." Taylor finished, with a fierce blush coming to her cheeks as she tried to avoid looking the woman in the eyes.

Alex knew that's what she was trying not to do, and she thought the blush was absolutely adorable. She sat silently waiting for the girl to look at her. Finally Taylor chanced a glance to see why it was taking the woman so long to answer.

Alex had not taken her eyes off of her and in fact had one brow raised.

"Good, now I'll give you your answer."

Taylor seemed to stop breathing at that moment, not knowing if the offer would be rejected, but assuming it would be due to who was being asked.

"I would love to go, it's been a while since I've gone on any type of vacation."

"Really?" She said, uncovering the phone due to her amazement at the woman.

"Yes, now tell her." The woman, ordered as she looked at the phone and then back at the girl.

"Oh, hello, Grammy, yes, you heard that? Well I guess you would, okay, we'll see you next week. I love you Grammy. Okay, bye." Taylor hung up the phone and at first wasn't sure if she should turn around, or just stand there by the phone.

"Are you going to stand there all day, or are you going to come back over here and finish this game of chess?" Taylor turned, still flushed but grinning, and went back over and sat down. She took her move, then looked up at the woman who was concentrating on her move, the girl smiled to herself.

"What are you thinking about?"

Taylor's eyes widened at the unexpected question, then those deep sapphires of Alex's captured her eyes.

"Um...I..."

The woman cocked her head, but did not allow the girl to break eye contact with her.

"I...um...was just thinking about us."

"What about us?" The woman asked calmly, which was in total contrast to her heart, which was now racing wildly in her chest.

"Just...how ironic things are. I mean, less than nine months ago I was doing anything and everything to stay away from you, trying to remain completely faceless and nameless to you. Now when I think about everything that would have happened had that fateful day not happened..."

The woman didn't say anything, she just listened to the girl.

"I mean have you ever thought about it, how if Mr. Evans had not tried what he did, how I would have never been put in the position to try and warn you. Therefore you would have never known about me, and I would have ended up marrying a rapist and a mobster, WOW! That really blows me away." The girl narrowed her eyes slightly, trying to break the eye contact, but not being able to, due to the radiance of the stars that were shining at her. "You realize I owe you for not only saving my virginity...?" Taylor blushed, but managed to continue. "But also my very life, the quality, if not the actual. I would have been involved with a family that has no concept for the value of life, and I would have died a thousand deaths due to my very soul being torn apart. I probably would have had to have children and subject them to whatever abuse I would have been going through. Man, I owe you, and I thank the Lord every day and night for you..... Hmmm...I better stop talking before I get all emotional again." She said, as she felt the tears forming in her eyes.

Alex brought her hand up to the girl's face and caressed her cheek.

"I will gladly accept anything you want to give me, other than money." She said quietly.

Taylor caught the woman's hand, and without thinking about it, she brought it to her lips and kissed her palm, and tears fell into the open palm. Alex wiped her eyes with her other hand, then inhaling deeply to compose herself, she lifted her hand back to Taylor's cheek to caress it again before she slipped it out of the girl's grasp.

"It's your move." Alex said, changing the subject.

"Oh, right." The girl said, returning her attention to the game, as the woman now looked at her with pure love.

The two played many matches throughout the night, and then during the day they went to work, still having not admitted anything to themselves or one another. Although the woman knew what her feelings were, Taylor still was confused by her own feelings. She loved the woman, and knew it was something more than just a friend type of love, but she couldn't put her finger on it. The next week came quickly and everything was turned over to Mr. Shearer to handle.

Alex and Taylor arrived at the girl's grandmother's house late in the day. It was out in the country in a small town in Georgia. It was a misfit in the environment, with the surrounding area being more subdued. The house itself sat in the middle of a large, well manicured lawn with multicolored flowers encircling the whole thing. The house was white brick, with bay windows sticking out from different areas. It was a modern day house in a quaint environment.

"Hmm...I take it this is your grandmother's home?"

"Yes. I know. I told her when she first was having it built that it would stick out like a sore thumb. But she said "why settle for anything less, when she's worked hard all of her life to have the things she wanted for us". She's not a flashy woman or anything like that, but she does believe in living comfortably, especially at her age. She likes the quietness of country living, but she couldn't live without some modern elegance and conveniences."

"Who helps her take care of it, and the lawn?"

"Oh, a few men like her and they take turns maintaining things for her. She sees them as nice gentlemen, but she has no interest in them any further than that. She said she was too in love with my grandfather to think of marrying anyone else, and she doesn't want to miss the chance to be with him when she passes on. I love her so much, I wish she could live forever, but I know one day the Lord will call her home, and I will miss her terribly" Taylor said, stopping at the door, and composing herself so that she didn't greet her grandmother with puffy eyes.

Alex smiled down at the girl and once again she found herself caressing her cheeks. Taylor smiled up at her, then rang the doorbell. After a few minutes the girl's grandmother opened the door.

"Little one."

"Grammy!" Taylor exclaimed, as she hugged her grandmother tightly. It's so good to see you." She whispered as she continued to hug her.

Alex stood patiently waiting for the two to break their embrace, finally the grandmother was the one to do it.

"I'm sorry, forgive us, please come in and make yourself at home."

"Thank you." The woman walked in and stopped, as the older woman closed the door behind them.

"Grammy, I want you to meet my dearest friend, Alexandra Madison. She's also known as "The Raider"." The girl whispered conspiratorially to her grandmother.

Alex cocked her head and looked at the girl with a question in her eyes. Taylor did not see the look, but her grandmother did.

"Well Ms. Madison, welcome to my home, I am very grateful to you for watching after my granddaughter. I was heartsick when I heard what had happened to her, but thank the Lord she had a friend like you to guide her." The elderly woman said, as she opened her arms to embrace the slightly taller woman. Alex allowed the embrace and even returned it. Taylor stood looking at the two, and her heart leapt with joy at the connection.

"Okay you two, I want you both to march up those stairs and pick any rooms you like. Get cleaned up and then we can sit in the living room by the fireplace and get to know each other better." The elderly woman said, directing the last part of her conversation to Alex.

They did as they were told and chose rooms that were right next to each other. Taylor gave the bigger room to Alex and she took the other. The two quickly cleaned up, changed and went downstairs to the living room where the girl's grandmother had tea and finger food waiting for them.

"Have a seat. Would you like some tea Ms. Madison?"

"Alex, please, and thank you."

The woman poured the tea and handed the cup to the woman. Then she poured some for her granddaughter, who sat closest to the fireplace.

"So...Tell me about yourself Alex?"

"What would you like to know?"

"Well let's start from the beginning, are your parents alive?"

"No, they're both deceased."

"Any siblings?"

"A half sister."

Taylor sat listening intently. She had not thought to ask Alex about her family or anything that personal, but her grandmother was not one to bite her tongue.

"What's her name?"

"Francina."

"Nice name." The older woman said, as she noticed the subtle glances the woman sent at Taylor when the girl was not looking.

The elderly woman also noticed the slight smile that seemed to form during those times on Alex's lips. "So, are you from here?"

"No Ma'am, I'm from overseas."

Taylor's brows knitted at the sound of Alex calling anyone else "Ma'am", out of all of the time she had known Alexandra, she had never heard her talk to anyone in such a respectful tone. Taylor smiled at the thought.

"Oh?" The grandmother replied.

"Really?" The girl asked, surprised by the news."

"Yes."

"But I thought you were born and raised here in the states? I mean your English is perfect."

"How did you come to that conclusion when I never told you where I was from? We were taught English in grade school." Alex asked, focusing her gaze on the girl.

"I...I..."

"You assumed. What have I told you about assuming anything about me?" She chided teasingly, but with a serious undertone.

The elderly woman watched the exchange and found herself wondering. She decided to observe the two interacting more before she said anything.

"Sorry."

"It's okay, just don't do it again." Alex said meaningfully.

The girl chewed her lips, but nodded her head in understanding.

"So, are you a legal resident of the U.S?"

"Yes."

"Where are you from?" Taylor asked, curiosity getting the best of her.

"Does it matter?"

"Hmmm...not really, I was just curious." She said disappointedly.

"I'll tell you one day, but it will depend on how good you are." Alex ended the dubious statement with a smile, and the girl beamed and blushed.

The elderly woman was now really intrigued by her granddaughter's reaction to this woman.

"Hmm...I see, Alex, do you mind helping me with these dishes?"

"Of course not."

"I'll help also." Taylor volunteered.

"No darling, you stay here and tend the fire, we'll be back in a few minutes."

"Oh, but Grammy?"

"Ah...stay here and wait, or I'll show your friend the photo albums of you as a child."

"Grammy, you wouldn't?!"

"You know I would dear, now take care of the fire, and we'll be right back."

"Yes Ma'am...I can't believe you would threaten me like that." The girl said, as she pouted.

Alex was speechless at how absolutely adorable the girl was, sitting there pouting, while poking at the logs in the large fireplace. A bright smile actually lit her face and eyes.

"Come along you." The elderly woman said sternly, so much so that Alex blinked at her boldness, but she followed her without a word. "Put them there." The elderly woman said, pointing to the counter near the sink. Then she went to a back door and motioned for the woman to join her out on the patio.

The woman looked back at the door they had come through and then back at the elderly woman.

"Don't worry, she'll be fine, we won't be gone long, I just want to talk to you about something."

"Oh, alright." Alex said, as she stepped outside onto the patio.

The elderly woman went to sit on the swinging bench, while Alex went and sat on the steps, right near the swing.

"So what is it that you want to talk to me about away from your granddaughter's hearing?"

"Well first let me ask you this, what do you think of me?"

"Hm..well..." Alex said, licking her lips slightly at the unexpected question." I think you're a very intelligent woman, a lot like myself in knowing yourself and the things you want in life and knowing how to get them. I also think you're a funny old bird, who obviously has a suspicion about me but wants to be sure before she comments?" Alex said, as she looked over at the elderly woman with a smirk.

The elderly woman returned the smirk and gave a nod of her head to indicate that Alex had indeed read her correctly.

"So, what is it that you're suspicious about?"

"Well first I'll tell you that you are completely right on track with who I am. I'm not the type to bite my tongue, and I make no apologies for being true to whom I am. I also have been around for a long time, and just because my body has aged, my mind is still as sharp as a razor. I've seen a lot of things in my 80 years, and God has blessed me to remember all, while still in my right mind. I believe I will pass from this life with my mind still intact one day, and therefore I don't have time to beat around the bush."

"So, what is it you want to ask me?"

"How long have you been in love with my granddaughter?"

Alex exhaled the air she had just inhaled in a gasp, and then looked over at the woman. She saw her looking at her the same way she looked at others when she already knew the answer, but was just waiting to hear the response.

"Hmm...is that what you see?" Alex asked, without admitting or denying anything."

"Yes."

"How?" She asked, wanting to know what weakness in her defenses the woman had seen.

"By the way you look at her. You steal glances at her when she's not looking, and your mouth curls into a slight smile with whatever thought is going through your mind at the moment you are looking at her. It seems to me you're either afraid to confront your feelings, or you don't know what her reaction will be to you if you admitted your feelings to her?"

"I'm not afraid of my feelings, I have no problems being in a relationship with either a man or woman. The only thing that matters to me is whether they will love me as I will love them."

"I believe you." Alex looked over at the woman with a thoughtful gaze, but she continued to just listen. "So, the problem is that you're not sure how she feels about you, why?"

"I don't know, sometimes I feel as though she is just waiting for a sign from me, then there are those times when I feel as though all she sees me as is just a mentor and or friend."

"I noticed you looked a little surprised by how she introduced you to me, it was as if it were the first time you heard those words."

"It was."

"Hmm...I thought so. Do you know why I asked you to come with her?"

"She told me that you wanted to thank the "sweet" person who took care of your granddaughter, which by the way was not necessary, I adore her."

The elderly woman smiled and then looked up towards the heavens as if in thought. She turned back to look at the woman who was now watching her.

"You're a very beautiful woman, and I can tell that you are not the type to

take any relationship lightly. I see by how she reacts to your touch, or a gaze by you, that she's in love."

"Love?" Alex gasped, coming to her feet to go and stand in front of the woman.

"Yes, she is in love with you."

"Did she tell you that?

"No, but I know my granddaughter, like I know myself. She used to tell me all the time what type of person she would love to fall in love with and spend the rest of her life pleasing that person, learning, and growing, and sharing her deepest thoughts with, without fear of being judged. She is a sweet, innocent child, and I am so proud of her for succeeding in her life, but most of all..." The elderly woman came to her feet and placed a hand on the woman's cheek and said in a gentle voice. "I am so very thankful and proud of her for having a friend like you in her life. You're caring for and protecting her without asking for anything in return, your selflessness has not gone unnoticed by her, or me."

"Love? She's in love with me? You don't know how much I want to believe that."

"Yes I do, I see it in your eyes. But I have to tell you, I am not the least bit comfortable about that aspect of your relationship with my granddaughter."

Alex blinked, then removed her cheek from the woman's hands when she realized she had tears on her cheeks.

"Funny, I never remember being so...."

"Out of control?" The elderly woman offered.

"Yes, I think your granddaughter has put a spell on me or something."

"She has, the most powerful spell in this world."

Alex knitted her brows at the fact that the woman didn't seem to catch on to her little joke.

"I know you meant it as a joke, but I am serious. She has put the spell of LOVE on you, and you're not used to the feelings."

"You're scary." Alex said dubiously.

"And you dear child I will consider the biggest fool, if you say you didn't know that." The woman said factually.

The two women stood regarding each other, as if they were different sides of the same coin. One elderly and wise, the other young and intelligent, full of energy. Both strong and passionate women.

"I think we should go back now, she'll be pouting something fierce." The elderly woman said, and opened the door to allow the younger woman to go in, but instead Alex reached above the other woman's hold on the door and held it for her.

"After you."

"Thank you."

They walked through the kitchen, to the kitchen door that would lead them back into the main house, but just before the elderly woman went out, she stopped and turned back to look at the woman walking behind her.

"I know you have more questions as to what I said about my discomfort, but we will talk again later about that." The woman then turned back and went on into the main house.

Alex looked after the receding figure, as she thought about the woman's statement. Then she too continued on into the main house, and back to the family room.

"Oh, there you are."

"Did you miss me?" Alex asked, now more confident in her dealings with Taylor.

"Well...yes, I mean...you two were gone so long."

"So you missed your Grammy also?"

"Hmm...well...no, I mean not the same way, I mean..."

"Um, ladies if you will excuse me for a moment, I need to go check on some things upstairs, and make a few phone calls, but I will be back in a while."

"Oh, alright Grammy, if you need anything let me know?"

"I will little one, relax and enjoy yourselves, I'll make dinner in a while, if you two are hungry."

"Alright. But I'm not hungry right now." Taylor called after her grandmother, as she tried to avoid looking back at Alex.

"You know I'm waiting for you to look at me, so you might as well do it now." She said knowingly.

The girl nervously looked back at the woman, who had now moved over to where she was sitting on the floor in front of the fireplace, still poking at the logs.

"I think they will be alright." Alex said, taking the poker.

"So tell me what the difference is in the way you missed me, versus your Grammy?"

"I...I..." The girl said flustered.

"You what? Did you feel restless, and anxious again?"

"YES, that's it!" The girl exclaimed.

"Did you feel that way when your grandmother came back into the room?"

"Well yes, but not as much."

"Do you still feel restless or anxious at all?"

"Hmmm...no. I don't, isn't that something?" Taylor said without realizing.

"Have you thought about why you don't feel that way right now?"

"Hmm...not really, I just put it off to the things that were happening."

"Do you think it could be because of me?"

"You? What do you mean?"

"The fact that you felt so restless and things when I'm not with you and how calm and relaxed you become when I am?"

The girl looked at her with both confusion, and thoughtfulness.

"Maybe, or it's just a coincidence?"

"Maybe. Anyway, you told me that whatever I wanted you would be more than happy to give me, did you mean that?"

"Yes, of course I did."

"Really why? Out of gratitude or out of deep feelings?"

"Both. Whatever you want, if it's mine to give I will."

"Well it's nothing that grand, but I will hold you to it. Right now why don't you go and get some sleep and I will see you in the morning. I'll check on you before I turn in okay?"

"But what about dinner? Grammy said she would cook if we were hungry."

" I'm not hungry, are you?"

" No, I'm fine,

"Okay then, and besides it is rather late to be eating anyway. I'll tell her not to worry about dinner tonight, because I'm sure she was only cooking for us, thinking we would be hungry."

"Okay, I am a little tired." Taylor admitted.

"Alright, then you go ahead and get some sleep."

"Okay." Taylor said, rising to her feet. She said goodnight to Alex, then turned and went to say goodnight to her grandmother.

That night after Taylor had turned in Alex and Taylor's Grandmother talked more about the girl for a while. Then they moved on to other topics. They spent a few hours just getting to know one another better. When Alex was ready to turn in she said goodnight to the grandmother, and then headed up the stairs to go and check on the girl before she, herself, turned in for the night. Taylor had been sleep for a few hours, so when Alex arrived at the door and heard her moaning, she was concerned that Taylor might be dreaming about her attack and it was just the start of the dream. The woman went into the room and looking down at the girl. She saw the girl was flushed and moaning and squirming slightly in the bed, as if she were in the throes of passion. This made her wonder whom the girl could possibly be dreaming about in such a matter. Her heart could only wish, but her mind told her impossible. She caressed the girl's face and cheeks to soothe and calm her. Taylor's squirming and moaning eased and then she quieted down. After a few minutes Alex thought the girl had gone back to a calm state and bent over to kiss her on the forehead. She was completely caught off guard when Taylor's arms wrapped around her neck and she began kissing her with the passion she had just been dreaming about.

At first Alex thought to try to free herself, but then she thought better of it, figuring this could be the start. Obviously the girl was dreaming about her and that made the woman's heart swell, and she allowed herself to be kissed by the girl.

After a few moments, something touched the conscious side of the sleeping girl, and her eyes flew open. Fear, confusion, and horror lit her eyes as tears welled up in them. Her arms dropped like a stone from around the woman's neck, as she couldn't break the gaze. She was horrified and Alex saw it.

"It's okay."

"NO IT'S NOT!! GODS What You must think of me!!" Taylor shrieked in complete horror.

The woman sat on the bed and the girl immediately sat up with her knees pulled to her chin, and her eyes now averted from Alex's.

"I said it was. It's perfectly natural for you to have these feelings."

"How could it be natural?! I'm a girl and you're a girl?! Gods I could just curl up and die!" She sobbed, as she thought about what Alex was probably feeling about her.

"You obviously have feelings for me, and I see nothing wrong with that, at all. Do you think people should limit themselves when it comes to love? Or do you think love between two people is all that really matters when you're looking for happiness?"

"I...I'm not sure." Taylor said honestly, still unable to look at her.

"Well, I'll tell you what, in the morning I want you to talk to your grandmother, alright?"

"No I couldn't!" She said, even more horrified.

"You can, and you will." The woman said sternly. Sounding more like The Raider.

"No. I can't."

"Did I sound like I was asking you to? I'll make it clearer.

You...Will...Talk...To...Her...Otherwise I'm going to get VERY upset, and we don't want that...do we?"

"No Ma'am. But she's going to be so disappointed with me." Taylor said, more composed by the tone of Alex's voice. Although it was still low and compassionate, she definitely heard the warning.

"Well that's okay, you need to talk to her. Now lay back down and get some sleep, and I'll see you after you've spoken with your grandmother."

"Are you mad at me?" Taylor asked, needing to know.

Alex's eyes narrowed at the thought that the girl would assume she would be angry with her.

"No. I'll see you tomorrow." She said, and leaned in to kiss Taylor on the forehead, then made sure she was settled in. She smiled, then turned and left the room. She hurried to her own room and immediately stripped out of her clothes, grabbed a robe and went to take a cold shower.

"Ahh..." was the only sound she could manage from all of the sensations that were bombarding her body. The cold water steamed off of her, due to the contrast in temperatures with the cold water hitting her hot body.

It was hours before she was able to finally clear her mind enough to drift off. The next morning she made herself scarce. She went into town to look around leaving Taylor and her grandmother alone so they could talk.

"Good morning Grammy."

"Good morning child, how did you sleep?"

"Hmm....not well."

"Oh, why, was the bed to firm?"

"No, the bed was fine, it was because of something that happened last night."

"Last night?"

"Yes. By the way where is...."

"Oh, she went to town to look around, she said she would see you in a few hours. I really like her, she reminds me of me, in my heyday." The grandmother smiled nodding her head in fond memory. " You have a great friend there, you realize that right?"

"Yes, she's the best. It's about her that I need to talk to you."

"Okay, have a seat, I'll get you some breakfast and you can tell me while you eat."

"Okay." Taylor said, sitting down at the kitchen table and removing stray strands of hair off of her face.

"Here you go. Okay, so what about your friend Alex?"

She looked at her grandmother for a long time, before she decided to just tell her what had happened.

"Last night I was having a dream."

"What type of dream, and was your friend in it?"

"An erotic dream, and yes she was." The girl said, and stopped to gauge her grandmother's reaction.

"I see. Go on." The older woman said, not showing any reaction.

"I was dreaming that the two..." She couldn't bring herself to say it out loud.

"The two of you were making love?" The grandmother asked knowingly.

Taylor's eyes teared up at the fact that her grandmother obviously saw something going on with her.

"Yes."

"Hmm?" The grandmother said.

The girl's brows knitted not sure of how her Grammy was taking her news.

"Grammy I'm so confused." She said honestly." I know you're shocked to hear me talking like this, or even thinking like this, especially with the way I was brought up by you?"

"I'll admit, I am surprised by this, and bothered by it.

"It does bother you that I was dreaming something like that." Taylor stated, not surprised by her grandmother's reaction.

"Why wouldn't I be? Although I shouldn't be, I mean just because I'm old, and live out in the country in nowhere land, does not mean I don't have access to what's going on out there in the world. I've seen and done most things, so nothing should shock or surprise me. But this does. What I want to know is, are you in love with her?"

"Grammy?!" The girl gasped, spraying the orange juice she had just taken in her mouth, out on the table. She was stunned by the question.

"No, no, don't act like you're shocked that I would ask that. Child, I have seen just from the brief time that you two have been together since coming here yesterday, that you have very strong feelings for her. I tried to put them off to hero worship, but now I see it's not."

"But Grammy, I was brought up to believe that a relationship consisted of a man and a woman."

"True you were, but times have changed, and sometimes people have to change. You have to make whatever choice is right for you. That means also accepting everything about whatever decision you make, the good, the bad, and the ugly."

"Have you ever thought of a woman like this?"

"Yes. In fact I can remember one time when I looked at a woman in that way, she was a Commander in the military, at a training camp. She was so fine, I thought she was made out of the stars in the night sky. She was a hard ass too. She didn't put up with petty behavior, or trivial conversation. She had a purpose to everything she did and said."

"Did you use to dream about her?"

"Yes, all of the time, during my whole time there."

"Did she know how you felt?"

"No, and I'm glad she didn't. I found out sometime later that she liked me but she would never tell me because she didn't want anyone in the unit to feel like she was pressuring them or me. So I never knew it. I was just as confused as you are right now about my feelings and why I was having them. I wondered what must be wrong with me to be thinking about another woman in such a way, I must be the vilest person alive." The grandmother said, sharing the feelings she had felt then and the feelings she knew her granddaughter must be feeling now.

"Yes, that's how I feel, as if she will look at me in disgust."

"Did you tell her the dream?"

"Yes, but only after..."

"After what?"

"After I woke up with my arms around her neck, kissing her."

"Aha!! Now I understand. You were dreaming about her and she just happened to come in to check on you last night. She was probably looking to give you a goodnight kiss on your cheek or forehead and you somewhere inside knew she was there and reacted to the feelings you were having for her, right?"

"Yes." The girl said, looking as though she was not breathing.

"Honey I would like to tell you to follow your heart, but I can't. Although your feelings are perfectly natural for a person in love. Especially when it's your tender heart we're talking about.

"You really think I'm in love with her??"

"Yes. Honey, I overheard a conversation the two of you were having just before you turned in last night, do you remember it?"

"Yes."

"Well if you think about that conversation and what happened and this conversation and you put them all together, you'll see that what I am telling you is true. You are in love with her and probably have been for a while. I think you came here to try to figure things out.

"I came here because you asked me Grammy."

"Yes I did ask you to come, but I think you're happy I did, this way it gives you a safe place to explore your feelings without fear of ridicule?"

"Maybe? But what about the fact that she's a woman?"

"Yes there are problems associated with that fact. But the question you should be asking yourself is how does she make you feel? Are you uncomfortable when she's near, or is it only when she isn't that you feel anxious? Do you ever have those times where you feel something is missing, yet it seems like everything is right there, so what could it be that you're missing?"

"Yes."

"Well think about whether it's her that's missing when you have that feeling, and then when she's near whether you still feel like that. Or does she make you feel complete?"

"Yes." The girl's eyes widened with disbelief and joy.

"You're in love child. Does she feel the same way?"

"God! I wouldn't know, I doubt it! Taylor said, sure that the woman had never had thoughts like that about her. She completely missed her grandmother's concerned brows knitting deeply.

"Hmm...well, as far as I'm concerned, it's up to you what you choose to do with your life." The grandmother said vaguely, not really letting on how she felt about it one way or the other. She decided she would talk with Alex when she returned.

Taylor jumped out of her chair and hugged her grandmother tightly.

"I love you Grammy, thank you, thank you for loving me."

"Always child, always."

Later that day, Alex returned with a few packages of things she liked enough that she bought. Most of it was for Taylor, but she would give them to her later, maybe when they returned home.

"So...you've made it back, how was your trip to town?" The elderly woman inquired, as she took the woman's packages and coat.

"Fine, thank you. How is everything here?"

"Enlightening." The older woman said, leaving the meaning floating vaguely in the air. "I'll take these to your room, she's in the den."

"Aha...okay, thank you, I think." The woman, said with knitted brows, as the older woman took the packages and started to walk away, but then stopped and turned back around to look at the woman.

"We need to talk later."

"Of course." Alex replied, seeing the look of deep concern on the older woman's face.

The older woman then smiled and looked towards the den as she headed towards the stairs, leaving the woman to her thoughts.

CHAPTER 8

Alex turned and walked to the den, not sure of what she would find. She walked in and Taylor was once again poking at the fire. Since the entrance to the room was from the back, Taylor did not see or hear Alex come in. The woman walked over and sat down behind her on the floor before Taylor realized she was there. When Taylor went to sit back she felt the body and she started.

"OH!! My Goodness! You scared me!" She said in a teasing, yet nervous voice.

"I can see that. So what were you so deep in thought about?"

"Um...nothing, we can talk about it later, how was your trip?"

"We'll talk about it now, and it was fine." Alex said sternly, although she didn't mean to sound sharp with the girl, her need to know was just too much.

Taylor looked back at the fire, as if she were waiting for it to tell her how to tell the woman.

"I know you spoke with your grandmother, do you have any questions, for me?"

"Yes."

"What?"

"Have you ever been with a woman?" The girl asked pointedly, and then waited anxiously for the answer.

Alex's brows went up in amusement and surprise for a very brief moment, and then she narrowed her eyes in thought as she searched the girl's eyes.

"No."

"Oh. Have you ever thought about it?"

"Yes recently I have."

"Really? Who? I mean if I'm not getting too personal?"

"You're getting very personal, so before I answer you, I'll ask you a question and then I will answer yours, okay?"

"Okay." Taylor said uncertainly.

"Are you in love with me Taylor?"

The girl's mouth started to fall open, but she covered it with her hand to hold back the gasp that was about to escape. The woman cocked her head and waited.

"I...what made you ask me that?"

"Answer me." The woman said impatiently.

Taylor swallowed hard and started to look away, but her chin was caught by Alex's strong fingers, and turned back to look at her.

"No, look at me. Now answer me."

"Yes." She said, with tears forming at the thought of the rejection she was about to receive.

But, the woman instead smiled at her and let her chin go. The girl's brows knitted deeply at the meaning of the smile. Feeling a little braver, she ventured on to ask her question again.

"Now are you going to answer my question?"

"Yes. You."

"Huh? Wait a minute..." The girl said, completely missing the conversation. She went back over in her mind as to what she had asked Alex, and then Alex's response to her question.

The woman saw the instant Taylor realized that she had answered her question. Her eyes locked on those of Alex's, and a slow smile begun to form on the woman's mouth.

Taylor's heart seemed to skip a beat, and then many beats as she stared into the endlessly, clear pools of the woman's eyes. Alex purposely licked her lips, and the girl became unsteadied by it.

"What do you want to do right now?" Alex asked the enraptured girl.

"I..."

"What do you want me to do right now?"

Taylor blushed fiercely and came out of her trance like state. She turned and picked up the poker once again and began poking at the fire. Alex grinned at her nervous reaction, but now her heart was leaping with joy at the knowledge that Taylor was in love with her, and obviously wanted to show it, but didn't know how. Alex then thought about how she could help.

"You know, I was just thinking about something you told me."

"What?" She asked, without looking back.

"You said you would do anything for me because of all that I had done for you? Not that I expect anything for what I've done, but I would be curious to see what you would offer?"

"Okay."

"Did you mean it?"

"Yes, of course. I told you I did." Taylor said, sparing a glance back at Alex, but then looking back at the fire.

"Better yet, I dare you to do what you were just thinking about."

The girl looked back at the woman and saw her smiling. Taylor's eyes narrowed, unsure if Alex was just teasing her or what.

"And what do I get if I do?"

"A lesson."

"A lesson??"

"Yes."

"What does that mean?"

"You'll see."

"Will this...lesson hurt?"

A wicked smile came to Alex's face and Taylor suddenly felt like she was the fly in the spider's den.

"Only if you want it to." The woman said cagey. The hairs on the girl's arms and back of her neck seemed to stand on end.

"I..."

"Can you do it?"

"Of course I can, I have no problem showing my gratitude to you." Taylor said, trying to be brave, in spite of the sheer terror she was feeling inside.

"Shhh...I don't want you doing anything for me out of just gratitude. You understand?"

"Yes, but that's how I feel."

"You just feel grateful towards me?" Alex asked, with concern in her eyes.

"Well...no, it's not just out of gratitude, I do love you, and you are my dearest friend."

The woman smiled, and let out the breath she was holding in relief. She then thought to herself,

"I can change that, I'm just happy it's not just about being grateful."

"Does that make sense?" Taylor asked.

"Yes it does. Now show me you are brave enough to meet my challenge." Alex said, returning to her original plan.

Taylor smiled and came to her knees to face Alex, determined to show she was brave. But once she was facing her, Taylor's face took on a shy quality as if she suddenly felt embarrassed. She leaned in with the intention of kissing the woman on the cheek, but when she closed her eyes, Alex leaned forward slightly and their lips met. The electricity that raced through both of them was jolting. Taylor sat back on her heels and blushed a deep wine, her eyes lowered, her body trembled, and her breathing became rapid. Alex on the other hand blushed slightly, her own breathing increased, but quietly, and she watched the girl, waiting to see what her eyes looked like when she finally lifted her head. Taylor sat there unsure of everything that was going on within her. She sat stiff as a board with only the slightest tremble moving her. She was afraid to look up at Alex, she was sure she would see complete and total disgust. The woman didn't say a word she just sat waiting and remembering the feel of Taylor's lips on her own.

Finally the girl lifted her eyes with tears in them.

"What is it?" Alex asked quietly.

"You're not mad at me??"

"Why would I be mad at you?"

"For...kissing you like that? Again?!."

"Did you like the way you kissed me?"

"Haa...I don't think I should answer that?

"I think you should, if you don't want me to get upset with you."

"But you'll hate me."

"Why would I hate you?"

"Because, a woman kissing another woman like that?"

"Well it wasn't really a kiss, more like a peck, and it was not like the kiss you laid on me the other night."

"But, our lips touched."

"Let me show you something." Alex said, as she pulled Taylor back to her and kissed her the same way she had done only a moment before.

"That's not a kiss, so let me give you your lesson." The woman then intertwined her fingers in the girl's hair and pulled her head to her.

Alex started the kiss with a slow, tender, meaningful embrace, and when Taylor moaned into her throat she increased the kiss, in both pressure and passion. The girl was now leaning against the woman, her arms and hands supporting her weight on the woman's thighs, albeit they were shaking from the dizziness she was feeling. Finally Alex allowed the two of them to breathe and Taylor gasped and struggled to raise herself up off of the woman. She tried to go back to sitting on her heels, but just as she thought about it, Alex's voice cut into her thoughts.

"That's a kiss." Taylor looked her in the eye and although the woman was obviously turned on by the experience, the girl being new to such passion, didn't recognize Alex's passionate glow, or her gaze. All she saw was a woman teaching her the difference between a kiss and a peck.

"O.k.a.y...I won't forget it." She said, as she finally managed to sit back on her heels. Breathing hard. She changed her mind and sat on her behind because she didn't feel steady enough to stay on her heels.

"Okay, so what are you doing?"

"I beg your pardon?" Taylor asked, confused again.

"You were going to give me a kiss, well...I'm waiting?"

"But I thought?"

"What? You made another assumption?"

"Um...well...never mind." Taylor said, and hurriedly went back to her knees once again.

But Alex moved from the floor to the sofa, and the girl watched her settle at the end furthest from the fire. Her back was resting against the armrest of the sofa.

"Well?"

"Oh...yes, sorry, I just...never mind." Taylor said, catching herself.

Alex smiled at the self-control. The girl came to sit facing her and again she blushed. Alex's eyes narrowed in thought at the sight and then she smirked.

"I'm waiting."

Taylor shook her hands as if they were wet and she was trying to air dry them.

"Okay." She said to herself, both excitement and anticipation, showing in her eyes.

She leaned forward, but this time Alex waited for her to make the contact. Once again when their lips met, a surge of energy raced through both of them. Taylor instantly moaned in response, but the woman gathered her close and turning her body slightly, the girl ended up laying across her thighs. Her back was against the sofa and Alex was now leaning over delighting in the sweetness of Taylor's soft mouth. Alex took a chance and pushed her tongue slightly between Taylor's teeth. She waited to see if the girl would allow her to proceed. After a moment or so, Taylor's teeth parted more, and Alex's heart leaped as she buried her tongue deep inside the young woman's receptive mouth.

Alex moaned herself this time, and she delighted in every part of the girl's mouth. Finally, when she thought Taylor could use some air, she broke the passionate kiss. She continued to hold the girl over her, as she waited for her to open her eyes. Eventually, after Taylor had taken in several large gasps of air, she slowly opened her passion filled eyes.

"Are you okay?" Alex asked tenderly, as she gazed into the young woman's eyes.

Taylor searched the woman's eyes, and she wasn't sure, but it didn't matter.

"I love you. I'm in love with you. I've loved you since the first time you sat by my bed. I've had these feelings since the day you told me to choose. I didn't understand them, or maybe I was just afraid of them, but whatever it was, it doesn't matter now. I am so in love with you, and I will do whatever you want me to do if it will make you happy." Taylor said, confessing her deep feelings for the woman, who now had tears rolling down her own face.

"You don't know what that means to me. I have loved you for a while, but I didn't know how you felt, and I couldn't risk opening myself up to you until I was sure of your feelings. I love you, oh...that feels so wonderful to say, I love you, I love you, Gods...I feel like I'm about to be overwhelmed by a great flood." Alex said, in a dazed and shaky voice.

Taylor lifted up and wrapped her arms around the woman's neck and the two of them held each other, just enjoying the feel of each other, and their hearts on the verge of discovery. The rest of the evening the two were inseparable. Of course Alex was the dominant figure in the blossoming relationship, but Taylor didn't seem to mind. Her grandmother watched the two learning about each other. She amused herself at how her granddaughter would blush at the slightest meaningful glance from the woman. At times she became so flustered that she would have to grab hold of the nearest solid object to steady herself. She also saw how Alex would hold back a grin that obviously wanted to show whenever she saw Taylor respond in that way. But at the same time, the grandmother was deeply concerned for her granddaughter. She knew the girl didn't really know what she wanted, although it appeared on the outside that she did. The older woman knew her granddaughter, and knew she was reacting to all of the new feelings that she was experiencing. The two went for a walk out back of the house towards a large field of wildflowers, talking as they went.

"Can I ask you something?" Taylor said, looking up at the tall woman as they walked hand in hand towards the wildflowers.

"Anything."

"Do you have any doubts?"

Alex stopped walking and turned to look Taylor straight in the eye.

"Are you having doubts about this?"

"No. I just wanted to see if I was the only one, or if we both felt the same way?"

"Well rest assured, I have no doubts."

The girl smiled and then the woman squeezed her hand and they continued their walk. When they were in the middle of the field Alex sat down and pulled Taylor down to the ground with her.

"Are you scared?" Taylor suddenly asked.

The woman gave her a thoughtful look and then said honestly.

"A little, I've never given my heart to anyone, like this before, and it does concern me."

"You think I would hurt you?"

"Not on purpose. But you are young."

"I would never do anything to cause you such pain."

"I know, because if you do, it would be worse for you." Alex said with a smile, but her tone was serious.

"You're serious?"

"Yes, I am. It's too hard for me to open up to someone, only to have them hurt me for whatever reason."

"Would you hit me?"

Alex looked at her, and with concern and honesty both playing in her eyes and tone of voice, she said.

"I honestly don't know. I honestly wouldn't think so. But I do know this relationship will not be based on any abuse, physical or mental. I am in love with you, and the only feeling I want you to ever have towards me is love. The only touch I want you to feel from these hands, is gentleness, care, tenderness compassion, and pleasure."

"Does this mean you won't scold me anymore when it comes to work?"

"I don't scold you, I reprimand you." The woman corrected.

"Well they mean the same thing, so will you?"

"Will I what?" Alex asked, giving her a sidelong glance.

"Will you continue to reprimand me?"

"Yes. If you mess up, one thing has nothing to do with the other, and I expect for you to remember that."

"But aren't we supposed to be equals?"

"We will be when it comes to our personal lives, but when it comes to our professional lives, I am still your boss, AND I HAVE NO EQUALS."

"Hmm...." Taylor replied, as she fought to control a grin that was pulling at the corners of her mouth. Then she went on to ask another question. "But we're perfectly equal in our personal right?"

"To a point. I do know more than you do when it comes to the ways of the world, so you have to have respect for that, right?"

"Okay, I can accept that."

"Good." Alex said, as she gave a gentle pat to Taylor's cheek and then lay back with her hands and arms behind her head. The girl positioned herself so that she was laying on her back at a right angle to Alex. Both their heads were touching, side to top. The two looked up into the evening sky and sent a silent prayer of thanks.

"So are you going to tell me?"

"Tell you what?"

"Tell me the ten things that you're not good at?"

"You're still on that?"

"Yes, I have to make sure that I haven't gotten involved with MS. Perfect."

"Why? Scared of the expectations that may follow?"

"Yes! To be frankly honest."

"Hahahahaha, well, I'm not perfect. Hey that's one."

"No, no fair, no traits, no character things, just tangible physical things."

"Well I would be naming all day, if I did it that way."

"So, we have four more days." Taylor countered.

"Okay, let's see, I'm no good at basketball."

"Have you ever played it?"

"No, but what does that matter?"

"Well you can't name it if you've never done it before. Besides, you're one of those people who could pickup things easily."

"Hmm...I don't remember all of these rules when we first made this deal, but...since you see fit to change the rules, I too will make a change."

"To what?"

"Our little wager."

"Okay, so what? You're going to make me serve you the meals in bed?"

"Hmm...that's an idea, maybe later, but no that's not it."

"Okay, what?"

"I don't want to make you feel like I'm rushing you or anything. I've decided that when you are ready for us to consummate this relationship, then you will come to me, that way there's no pressure and you don't feel rushed. When you're absolutely sure you're ready, you come to me and show me? Deal?"

Taylor looked at the many stars that were now gracing the sky, as she thought about what the woman was asking her.

"Okay."

Alex turned onto her belly to look at the girl.

"No! Don't agree to something that you really don't want to, that's worse than lying to me, tell me what you're thinking." She demanded.

Taylor looked up into the intense sapphires that were now staring down at her.

"I...I was just wondering if I would ever be ready for that?"

"Are you saying you couldn't see yourself giving your complete self to me, as I would be doing with you?"

"It's just that I don't know if I would want.."

"You don't know if you would want to?" Alex asked, shocked and hurt.

"I..."

"Never mind. I'm going back to the house, I'll be heading back tomorrow, and you can stay the rest of the time. I'll see you at the house." Alex said, and then rolled to her feet and strode back towards the house with catlike grace. She did not look back at all.

Taylor rolled onto her side and watched the woman, shocked at what had just happened. Alex went into the house and headed for her room, The girl's grandmother saw her and caught up with her.

"Everything alright?"

"No."

"Can I help?"

"I don't think so."

"Okay, well how about if we have our talk now?"

"Now?"

"Yes."

"Fine."

The two of them went into the house to the kitchen, where the woman told Alex to have a seat. Alex sat down and the woman brought over a teapot, two cups and saucers. Pouring the tea, she then sat back in her chair to regard the woman for a moment. Alex's mind was obviously on the girl.

I see how much my granddaughter loves you, and I can see that you care about her as well.

"Yes, but," Alex said, jumping past all of the small talk.

"Okay Alex, you want me to get to my point, I will. I don't condone this, I didn't tell my granddaughter this, I figured it's her life and she has the right to make up her own mind."

"So why tell me then?"

"Because you're older and you have been around enough to know that she is confused, especially about such a relationship. It goes against everything she has been taught, and I don't just mean spiritually, I mean, you know the drawbacks to this type of relationship?"

"I know the obvious problems with it, but I'm willing to deal with them."

"But is she? What happens when one day she comes to you and says, I wish we could have children, it would be so nice to have little ones running around? What then?"

"Well, for one thing, when I'm sure about her feelings and her conviction at being in this relationship, I plan on talking to her about that and the other problems that I know are on your mind."

"But why not talk to her about them now...before she gets so wrapped up in this, so that she can make an informed decision? I don't think you're being fair with her, and I won't let you use her. I may be old, but I know how to deal with people like you. Don't get me wrong, I like you and I'm glad you're in my granddaughter's life. I am indebted to you for helping her. But I can and will bring you down so fast woman it will make your head spin. Are we understanding each other?"

"Yes ma'am, very well. But I don't agree with you about talking to her about the problems of a relationship before she even knows if she wants to be around me. I want her to get to know me first. Once that is done, we will deal with the issues of children, society, church, and whatever else comes up, together."

"So, is that why you were going to leave just now? Is that what you call together?"

"I was leaving because of something I asked your granddaughter to do when she felt she was ready. That way it would not appear that I was pushing myself on her, or pressuring her in anyway. I was going to leave to give her a chance to think about things. Now, if you'll excuse me, I need to go pack." Alex stood up, turned and walked out of the kitchen leaving the woman feeling a little better about things. She still had her doubts, and she would not encourage or discourage her granddaughter, but she would tell her the truth if she asked.

The older woman stood up and headed into the other room. She didn't know her granddaughter had heard her conversation with the woman. The older woman made it to the stairs just in time to see Alex come down the stairs without her bags.

"I thought you were leaving?"

"I am, I just came back down to tell you something, just

to make sure you understand me before I leave."

"So you want to tell me why you're actually leaving, specifically?"

"Yes."

"Alright."

"I just asked your granddaughter to come to me when she was ready for us to consummate our relationship, but not until she was ready."

"Okay, that's a reasonable request within a relationship. I do think one should be married first, or in this case been together for a while, but you kids are ahead of my time with your impatience."

"Well, I thought it was a reasonable request also, but evidently your granddaughter doesn't WANT to give me the gift of herself, as I would to her. I love your granddaughter, but I am a woman who expects complete intimacy, not half ass. I have no inclination to deal with that."

"So you're leaving?"

"Yes."

"Then what?"

"What do you mean?"

"What happens when she returns to work? What will you do, how will you act? Are you going to pretend you have no feelings for her? Do you expect for her to pretend the same?"

Alex licked her lips at the truth in the woman's statement. She looked at the woman with some frustration, and then asked.

"No, but what am I supposed to do? I don't even know why I'm asking you, you would love for this to all end here and now."

"True, but it would hurt her. I think you should tell her what you expect. You have the right to have your needs catered to just as she has the right to expect the same. If she cannot or does not want to handle it, then you will be right in ending things before you both go too far and then find out that one is not willing."

"I don't want her to feel like I am pressuring her in anyway, I'm not about that when it comes to something so intimate. I would want her to come to me willingly."

"Expecting what?"

"Expecting me to be gentle, loving, tender, and touched by the gift that she would be giving to me of her free will."

"No one could expect anything more, could they child?" The woman said louder than what was necessary for Alex to hear her, since she was standing right in front of her.

Alex's brow knitted at first, and then she understood. She looked at the woman's eyes, followed the gaze over towards one of the doors. Taylor then stepped out from behind it and stood with her hands behind her back. Both women looked at the girl. Alex leveled her gaze and then spoke to the girl.

"Come over here." She said in her authoritative voice. Taylor moved to where Alex and her grandmother stood, and then she waited for the woman to speak to her again. " Are you going to answer your grandmother?"

Taylor looked at her grandmother with the gentle, yet concerned smile on her face, and then she looked back at Alex. At first, she looked at a design in Alex's top, but then Alex spoke to her again.

"Look at me!" Taylor looked up with tears balancing. " That does not answer the question."

"I... "

"Did you lie to me when you said you loved me?"

"NO!"

"Did you lie to me when you said you would do whatever it took to make me happy?"

"No."

"Did you lie to me when you said I could have whatever I wanted from you as long as it was yours to give?"

"No."

"Then you must have lied to me about this lasting."

"No."

"Then what is it? Why can't you see us together completely? Is it because I am a woman?"

"No, I mean yes, I mean...I don't know." Taylor said completely flustered and embarrassed, especially with her grandmother standing there listening to the whole conversation.

"I see. Were you hoping that I wouldn't expect that of you?"

"I don't know."

Alex stood up straight at the vague answer.

"Fine. That's fine, when you figure out the reason why you can't offer ME such a gift, you let me know. I might still be available to explore with you." The woman then turned and strode back up the stairs.

"Grammy, I don't know what to do." Taylor said, as she went into her grandmother's arms, and sobbed.

"Come on child, let's you and I go have a talk."

Meanwhile, Alex was cursing her bad luck. At first she was willing to stay until tomorrow, but she felt like she was going to say something that she would regret, which would be completely out of character for her. She jumped up and packed her bag. Taking out her digital phone, she called for her driver to come from the small town back out to the house and take her back to the airport in the larger city.

"Little one, I know you love her. I know you're overwhelmed by all of the feelings you have for her. I know you're confused as to why or how you came to fall in love with a woman. I know you do want to give yourself to her, but there is something within you that holds you back from admitting that to her. What is it?"

"Grammy you're right about all of it."

"Then why would you think she wouldn't expect such a thing?"

"Grammy...I think I'm jealous."

"Aww child, of what? What could you possibly be jealous of? You've just started this relationship."

"That I will be the only one who is able to give such a gift." Taylor said frankly.

"Hahaha, OHHH...Baby girl...Oh...my sweet little girl, hahahaha. I'm sorry child, but what makes you think she isn't one?"

"Grammy?! How could she be? I mean look at her. She's a powerful, beautiful, successful, world traveled, and world renowned woman, how could she possibly be untouched?"

"Little one, I've never known you to judge anyone, especially someone you claim to love. You never judged your friends as harshly as you're judging her, and you're supposed to be closer to her than to a friend. Besides, when did it become your job to judge anyone? She loves you. She has given you a gift just as precious and as fragile as the gift you would be giving to her. Do you realize how hard it is for someone like her to even THINK about getting seriously involved with anyone. Let alone, someone who is not as sophisticated as she is. She's someone who could have any person she chooses, yet she chose you. She opened her heart completely to you and you turned your back on it and her. She is hurting and you are the cause, and there is no excuse you can give to justify your behavior. You were wrong. I love you little one, but if you really want to try this relationship or any other with her, or someone else, then you need to go and apologize and accept the gift that she has given you. And when you feel ready, give her the gift of you."

"Grammy, I'm so confused. I know you don't really like this, and I don't know why you're helping me with it, when you obviously are against it."

"It's true. I am against it. At the same time, I want you to be happy, although I'm hoping you will change your mind about this relationship. I just hope it doesn't develop too much before I pass from this life."

"Grammy, are you sick?!"

"No child, but you never know when the Lord will call you home." She then patted Taylor's cheek and turned to go get some more logs for the fire.

The girl stood there thinking about what her Grammy had just told her.

"She's right. This isn't like me." Taylor turned and ran back inside the main house to go and talk to Alex despite her serious reservations about how much her grandmother really didn't approve of the relationship. Just as she was about to go up the stairs, she heard a car pulling away. "Oh My God! No! Please, don't let it be her leaving!"

Taylor ran to the door and swung it open in time to see the car turning out of the driveway. Her heart seemed to stop just as the car disappeared out of sight.

"What's going on?" Came a voice from behind the girl. Taylor whipped around with tears in her eyes, and saw HER standing on the stairs.

"Thank Goodness!! You didn't leave!!" She said, running into Alex's arms and wrapping her arms tightly around her neck. She kissed her over, and over, and over again. Telling the woman between kisses, how much she meant to her, and how she was wrong and how she would never judge her or anyone else again. She begged the woman to forgive her, to allow her to make it up to her.

Alex pushed back from her gently, putting her at arm's length, and held her there as she bored into Taylor's moisture filled eyes.

"Do you really mean what you're saying, or are you just relieved that I didn't leave?"

"BOTH! I am so relieved that you didn't leave because then I wouldn't be able to tell you what I just did. I was completely wrong. There is no excuse for it, so I will not try to come up with one. You offered me your heart. I realize now that it is one of the most precious gifts anyone could give. At the time, I was being selfish; thinking that my virginity was more precious than anything you could offer me. I thought about it and realized that both of these gifts have something very important in common. You can only give them whole-heartedly once. After they have been broken, you can never get them back. You can only be a virgin once, and if your heart is broken, you will never recover all the way. I am so sorry! If you can trust me with it again, I promise I will not make the same mistake. I will cater to your heart's every need, want, and desire. Please forgive me for being so thoughtless." Taylor's eyes were brimming with tears, as she all but begged Alex for another chance.

Alex stood holding her at arm's length as she searched Taylor's eyes.

"I will forgive you on one condition." She now said as she let go of the girl's arm and stood to her full height.

"Anything."

"Take me up on my suggestion?"

"Deal!!" Taylor said, without hesitation.

"Then I forgive you." Alex said simply, and the girl flew into her arms and once again hugged her tightly.

Alex lifted her chin up using her fingers, and then gazing into Taylor's light brown eyes, they both smiled. Alex narrowed her gaze and bent down as Taylor closed her eyes and waited for the woman to kiss her. She did not keep the girl waiting long. She was claiming with her kiss, and Taylor was consumed by it. The grandmother was concerned by it.

The rest of the stay was filled with learning. Especially for Alex, to Taylor's chagrin. Taylor's grandmother had told the girl to not go somewhere and she went anyway, and spoiled a surprise that had been planned for her. So as a punishment, the pictures of her as a child were placed in front of Alex, all fourteen photo albums.

"You don't really want to look at those do you?" Taylor whimpered at the woman. Alex glanced down at her. Taylor had been sitting on the floor, originally tending to the fire, but was now trying to talk the woman out of looking at her early days.

"Let me answer that in a way that there will be no doubt in your mind what my intentions are." The woman proceeded to pick up one of the photo albums.

"Alex wouldn't you rather...do something else??" Taylor asked, with a seductive tone in her voice.

"Careful Taylor, tease me and you may end up in a position quite exhausting, to say the least." Alex shot back at the flirting young woman.

Taylor instantly caught Alex's meaning, especially with the gaze that was leveled on her, it was like a predator waiting for its prey to show itself with one... faint... move. Taylor instantly changed her demeanor. And Alex waggled one of her brows at her and a smirk showed on the woman's face.

"Aww, come on now." Taylor now whimpered.

"No, not another word."

"Oh..."

"Ah." The woman said, with a raise of her hand to silence the girl.

Taylor turned around and sat on her behind and began poking at the fireplace again as she pouted. Alex chuckled and then settled back against the sofa and began to look through the girl's life. She even saw the pictures of her parents. Taylor looked just like her mother. Alex went through album after album with Taylor groaning whenever Alex would laugh at one of the pictures. By the time Alex finished, Taylor was glaring at her from across the room. It was more of a pout than a glare, but she knew what the girl was doing. The grandmother decided to leave to go to bed, not wanting to know what was going to happen.

"Come here." Alex said.

Taylor turned her head away, and the woman bit the inside of her cheeks to prevent herself from laughing at her behavior.

"Please come here?"

The girl looked over at her, trying to maintain her resolve, but with the look the woman was giving her, she found herself caving in. She sulked her way over to where Alex sat still biting the inside of her cheeks to keep from laughing.

"What?" Taylor said, with her arms crossed under her chest.

Alex caught her around the thighs and held her there while she spoke to her.

"You were and are so...adorable."

"You think so?"

"I know so, remember I am a model. So I think I know what adorable looks like."

Taylor smiled in spite of herself and Alex pulled her down until Taylor had to catch the back of the sofa to keep from falling on her.

"Give me a kiss." Alex said.

"But what about Grammy?"

"What about her?"

"I don't want her to..."

"She's gone to bed."

"But."

"What?"

"Nothing."

"Then give me my kiss."

"You know you're a little on the manipulative side?" Taylor said, and was answered with a swat to her thigh. "OWW! Why did you do that?"

"Because you're keeping me waiting."

"You're pushy too." She said in a rush.

"You want another one?"

"No." She said quickly, as she leaned down to place a sweet kiss on Alex's lips.

When it was time to go, Alex gave the older woman a hug and told her how grateful she was for what she had done for them. She would take care not to hurt Taylor and she also told her that she understood her reservations about the relationship.

"Remember what I said."

"Thank you. I will take care of her. And if you ever need anything, just pick up the phone and call."

"You'd better be careful Alex, my granddaughter may have opened up a flood gate. If you're not careful, those companies you take over may think they can actually win against you, now that you're "IN LOVE". It's shining all over you child. You better find a way to cover it in business, but I don't really think I needed to tell you that, did I?"

"No Ma'am, you didn't, but thanks for making sure. We'll call when we get back."

"Alright, I had a great time." The elderly woman said, as she hugged Taylor, and then gave her a bit of advice about how to handle the woman. "Child, listen to her, allow her to teach you, and protect you. She shines the brightest when she sees that you are safe and happy. And just because I haven't been verbal about what I think about this, remember what I told you about my hope."

"I will Grammy. You take care of yourself, and don't let George get too fresh."

"Ha, he couldn't do a thing for me even if he managed to get it where it needs to be." She said, shocking Taylor with her language.

"Grammy, we're going to have to talk about your language. I love you. I'll talk to you soon."

"Okay dear. Be safe you two."

The two women then got into the waiting car and waved as they were driven to the airport, where they caught their plane to go home.

CHAPTER 9

When the two arrived home, they immediately went to go and unpack their things. Both women stopped at the top of the stairs. They looked at each other, and then at the direction of each of their rooms.

"Your call. Separate, or together, whichever way you will be more comfortable. If we sleep in the same bed nothing will happen that you don't want. So, what do we do?" Alex said, as she leaned back against the rail and crossed her arms, waiting for Taylor to make up her mind.

"Um...I think this is a good time to tell you something?"

"What?"

"Let's go down to the kitchen, where we can talk."

"Okay, after you." The woman said, as she made a sweeping gesture with her hand.

The girl gave a nervous glance at the woman, and then led the way to the kitchen.

"Okay, what is it?"

"I don't want you to think this is about you or me in any way, but I..."

"What?"

"I have been looking at..."

"At?"

"Homes." Taylor said quickly, and then sat down waiting for the woman to blow.

"Why?"

"Huh? I mean, because I didn't want you to think of me as the guest who never left. I mean now that everything is over with and I'm safe once again, I didn't want to make you feel uncomfortable about having to ask me to leave. Or just not being able to out of concern that I would be hurt or feel rejected or something."

"First of all, you should know by now that if I wanted to tell you anything, I have no problem letting my thoughts be known. If I wanted you out, I would have told you that I think it's time for you to move out. I would have given you a deadline as to when you should be out. So, if that's the only reason you're looking for another place to live, then it is not an issue with me. But, if you are moving because you're scared about living here, with me that's different. If you're worried about my temper, impatience, or this new development between us, then I can tell you that along with those things, I am considerate, loving, and more patient and tolerant with you than anyone. My temper shows when someone doesn't listen to me, and then something bad happens. You know I love you, right?"

"Then are you asking me to stay?"

"Are you offering to stay?"

"I asked you first."

"Doesn't matter, I'm bigger. I can make you answer."

"No you can't." They bickered back and forth as they headed back to the stairs and went up, where they once again stopped.

"Yes I can."

"Do it."

"Okay. I will. Tell me what will we do about the sleeping arrangements?"

Taylor's mouth dropped open, she looked at the woman and her mouth snapped shut. A smirk came to her mouth when she saw the, "I told you so" look on Alex's face. The girl then took on a smug look of her own.

"Okay, I'll let you know." She said, then turned and headed down the hallway to her room. She didn't even look back, although she felt the woman's eyes boring into her. She kept herself from laughing, until she made it to her room and went inside. She closed the door and then lost it, but she covered her mouth just in case. Alex stood looking at the receding figure of Taylor in complete surprise. Then a wicked gleam came to her eyes.

"Okay, you want to try to play with me." She went to her room, washed up, and changed into a very...interesting outfit.

Taylor had changed and had gone to the den where she was reading a new book she had seen displayed at a few bookstores. She had picked it up but never got a chance to sit down to read it, with everything that had happened. It was called "Corporate Raider". A story about a powerful business executive, who uses senior executives to infiltrate other company's upper management positions. They're hired in those positions, and after working in those companies for a while and acquiring the information needed for a takeover, they give the information to The Raider, who then begins proceedings that would lead to her acquiring those companies, via takeover. The agents then disappear after the takeover is complete, and after a few years, they return having had plastic surgery, for which they are paid very well. They use their new identity to go into the next company, so as to do the same thing, without fear of someone from one of the prior companies recognizing them.

Taylor had just finished the prologue and was about to get into the reading, when she saw something over the top of the leather-bound book she was holding. Her eyes fell on long legs that seemed to go on forever. Shapely and muscular, they looked as though they had silk stockings covering them, but when she put out her hand and touched one of them, she was awed by the fact that there was no stocking on it. She didn't think about what she was doing, she was just captivated by what she was seeing. Her eyes slowly moved up until she finally came to some clothing. It was a pair of shorts and they were just that, short. She could see part of the curve of the round behind peeking out and she blushed as a result. Her eyes moved up and over the round hips, and then to the bare midriff, where she was amazed by the tone. The outlines of the muscles were visible under the skin. Taylor swallowed hard and her breathing seemed to be increasing as she continued her curious surveying. Her eyes moved up and her mouth fell open at the sight of most of Alex's breasts practically showing, except for her nipples, and the surrounding contrasting and coloring. Taylor fell back on the sofa as she blinked to break her gaze. She finally managed to continue upwards with her gaze until she got to the long sleek neck, and on to the chiseled chin. Her eyes carried her to the curved full lips that were turned up at the corners in a dubious sort of way. Her eyes slowly made their way to their ultimate destination. They locked on Alex's as if they had been caught and held by some physical means. Taylor's heart was beating out of her chest, her hands were shaking, and she didn't know if she was still breathing or not.

"So...what are you reading?" Alex asked, as she glided down onto the armrest of the sofa. The smell of jasmine delighted the girl's senses as she sat staring at the woman. Unable to speak.

The woman smiled a smile that caused Taylor to lose her balance, even while leaning back on the sofa. Alex was thoroughly enjoying her reaction, so much so that she decided to tease the girl unmercifully, until she was told what she wanted to hear. She reached out and lifted Taylor's hand that was holding the book, as if to read the title. Then she lowered it back down and ran her hand slowly up from the girl's hand, onto her arm. She watched the gooseflesh trail after her provocative touch.

"Is it a good book?"

Taylor was on overload. She had all sorts of feelings racing through her, none of which she had been familiar with until the first time the woman kissed her. Alex knew she was not going to answer her questions, but she wanted it to look like she expected her too.

"I love the feel of your hair." Alex said, as she ran her fingers through the dark tresses.

She then ran her fingers up and down the girl's neck and lingered over her pulse point to feel her heartbeat. A broad smile came to Alex's face as a result. Taylor moaned and gasped at different times whenever an impulse jolted her. The woman then leaned down and whispered in her ear.

"It'll be fun to explore, but only in my bed." She then flicked her tongue at the girl's ear and Taylor felt as though she had been physically pushed over. She jolted over and to the side until she was lying on the sofa. Alex glided down off of the side and slid over her, without touching her body to the girl's. Taylor saw the woman's breasts out the corner of her eyes and she once again trembled. She crawled along the length of the sofa and the woman mirrored her. Taylor came to the other end and found herself trapped, she rolled onto her back and the woman was gazing down at her.

"You're so...beautiful." Alex purred, as she leaned down and claimed the lips under hers.

Taylor was completely dazed and breathless, and all she could do was try to find something to hold onto so as not to be completely consumed. Alex still had not touched the girl's body with her own. When she finally allowed the girl to breathe, they both inhaled deep gulps of air. Taylor was shaking inside and out, and when Alex saw how turned on she was, it ignited her own passions more. She leaned in again, and this time kissed Taylor's neck, which caused the girl to whimper and throw her arms out in an attempt to steady herself. She slid off of the sofa and onto the floor. Alex remained where she was as she watched Taylor struggle to her feet and then stagger out of the room. Alex meanwhile, eased herself down on the sofa onto her belly, and brought her feet up and crossed them at the ankles behind her as she rocked them in satisfaction at the response from the girl.

"Hmmm...that was just too wonderful." She said, as she laid her head down on her folded arms on the sofa. She closed her eyes and let herself drift off with thoughts of Taylor playing through her mind.

When she awoke, she found the girl had not come back and she got a little worried that maybe she might have scared her away. Just as she sat up she saw a note fall to the floor. She leaned over and picked it up to read what it said.

"Wow! Please don't be mad at me? I've never felt such a wonderful, scary sensation before. It rang through me and I didn't know what to do. I didn't even know if I was breathing. But I guess I was. I can only imagine what it will be like when we do consummate this relationship, my goodness, I can't stop blushing, goodness, you are incredible, and I'm so glad you are in my life, I love you. Sweet dreams. I'll see you in the morning. I don't think I can sleep with you next to me, hahaha. I'm sure I sound like a child to you, but I hope you understand? I will tell you, I was really tempted to go to your bed and wait for you. I'm going to take another shower to cool off. I love you so very much, it fills my heart to think about you. Goodnight."

Alex smiled with satisfaction and then, folding the scented note, she rose up off of the sofa and headed for her bed. When she was in it, she laid awake for hours thinking about Taylor and the note, which she re-read a number of times. She thought about what she would do to entice the girl to her bed. She had no intentions of deflowering her yet, she decided she would wait for the girl. But in the meantime, she would find creative ways to get her to come to her bed.

The next day, the two dressed and when they came out of their rooms, Alex was already in the kitchen with cereal, fruit and orange juice sitting on the table for them. When Taylor arrived in the kitchen, Alex looked over at her and the girl immediately blushed.

"Good morning. Did you sleep well?" Alex asked, leveling her gaze on Taylor.

"Good morning. Fine...once I managed to go to sleep." She said under her breath, then spoke up again. "Thank you. How about yourself?"

"It took me a while to drift off, with all of the thoughts running through my mind. But when I finally did, I slept almost like a baby. I could have slept better if I had had some company, but we'll see what we can do about that." She said meaningfully.

Taylor continued blushing, and her hands once again trembled as she reached for her juice.

Alex sat back in her chair and regarded her as she tried to eat her breakfast. While she was putting the dirty dishes in the dishwasher, Alex came up behind her and pinned her between the counter and herself. She kissed Taylor's neck, and spoke to her between kisses.

"You know you haven't even greeted me good morning properly yet? Do you plan on correcting that? Or are you planning on always greeting me with just a simple good morning?" She whispered along Taylor's neck and in her ear.

"Ahh..." Was all the girl could manage. Alex took that as her cue and whipped her around to plant a heated kiss on her.

Taylor's hands found the counter and she gripped it as she tried to hold herself up. Alex had a firm hold on her waist so she was actually safe from falling. When the woman finally broke the embrace, the girl's head was reeling. They both sucked in a large amount of air as the woman continued to lean over the girl slightly, while licking her own lips seductively.

"That's how I expect to be greeted, clear?"

"Yes!" She gasped, as Alex then kissed her nose and backed off of her.

"Let's go to work. Oh, and remember what I said about keeping work and our personal lives separate. I'm very serious about that. I will still reprimand you if you mess up."

Taylor stood where she was, still trying to steady herself, but she managed to nod her head in response.

"Good. Now, can you walk?"

"Yes, just a little weak feeling in my legs, but I'm fine."

"Hmm...just weak, huh? Well, I'll have to do something about that tonight after work, meanwhile, I'll help you to the car."

Are you trying to drive me insane?" Taylor asked with a curious tone and a look of uncertainty as to whether she was going to be able to handle the woman's passion.

"Only insane with passion." Alex purred.

"Are you driving this morning?" Taylor gasped, changing the subject before Alex decided to do anything else.

"No, I thought I would let the driver worry about the road, while I focused on YOU."

"But I thought you said you wanted to keep work and private lives separated?"

"I do, but the car is neutral. Once we step out of the car for business, that's all it will be about, you understand?"

"Yes." They walked out to the car and once they were inside, the woman raised the privacy window and turned her attention to the girl.

"You're not going to get me all worked up again are you? I mean I'll be blushing every moment of the day."

"Is that so bad? I mean, it's not like I'm not as worked up. I find it quite erotic to see you blushing at my every glance."

Taylor didn't let her down with that statement, her cheeks developed the nice undertone that indicated her state.

"Hmmm...we're going to have so much fun in our lives together. I will do my best to make you happy, and keep the relationship exciting."

"I'm already having fun, despite the way it seems, and I'm happier than I've ever been now that you are in my life. As far as excitement, well...I know you won't have any problems there, if last night and this morning are any indications!"

"I'm pleased to hear that."

"I'll do what ever I have to, to make sure you're just as well taken care of."

"I know you will. Come over here."

"Why?" Taylor asked, with a tease in her voice, and a raising of her brow.

"Because I said so, and because I want to hold you."

The girl smiled, then moved over to Alex's open arms and was enclosed from behind in them. Alex laid her back against her and moved Taylor's hair out of the way so that she could get to her neck. At first Taylor didn't realize that's why she had done it, not until she felt the mouth on her neck, and the light sucking as well. She moaned, and tried to ease away, but Alex held her firmly and, in fact, increased her efforts on the neck. Taylor whimpered and Alex moaned as a result. She lifted her mouth off of the soft flesh only long enough to tell Taylor something.

"I could just hold you like this forever and listen to those sounds, especially that little whimper of yours." She saw the shiver that ran through the girl and returned her mouth to the same spot she had just left. Taylor once again moaned and whimpered as she tried to get loose. When the driver said they would be at the building in less than a minute, Alex took that as her cue. She let go of the girl's neck and laid her across her lap. It wasn't a problem seeing how weak Taylor was from the affection put on her neck. The sudden position change caused her eyes to open and she saw Alex grinning down at her.

"Wh...what?"

The woman didn't answer, she just opened one button of the girl's suit jacket. She moved the blouse back a little. Just enough to expose a little more of the breast. Alex then leaned in and Taylor's eyes went wide at the sensations she felt. The woman had sucked some of the soft flesh into her mouth and kissed it hard, then she let go. The girl's breathing had increased and her blushing skin was evident as well.

"There." Alex said, as she ran her fingers over the area of the breast that she had just marked.

Taylor tried to see what she was looking at and caressing, but Alex simply fixed her blouse and refastened the button. Planting a final kiss on the already dazed girl she sat her up and straightened her hair and clothing back up. Taylor's hand went to the area of her breast, although it was over her clothes, and she wondered what the woman had done. But her mind was brought back to the there and now, when she heard Alex talking to her.

"Alright, it's all about work."

Taylor shook her head to clear the rest of the fog away, and then smiling, she stepped out of the car and went to where Alex was waiting for her at the turnstile door. She looked at the woman and Alex raised a brow. The girl caught the hint and turned to wait for the next opening of the door.

CHAPTER 10

They arrived at the office at 6 am. They had spent an hour at breakfast, and although it was a stimulating one. By the time they arrived, people were already coming in. The two walked in together, but Taylor excused herself and went to go and get the morning mail. Alex headed to her top floor office suite.

"Good morning Ma'am, did you have a nice vacation?" Salina said in greeting.

"Morning, and yes. Are there any changes in my appointments today?"

"Yes, just one. The 10 o'clock had to cancel, his wife went into labor just a few minutes ago."

"Did he reschedule?"

"No Ma'am, he said he would be in touch with you in the next few days."

"Hmm...alright. Well, send my first appointment in when she gets here. Also have Shearer report to me with updates on what's been going on within the next hour."

"Yes Ma'am. Ma'am?"

"Yes?"

"May I ask you something?"

"What is it Salina?" Alex asked, as she went into her office and Salina followed in after her.

"Did you and Ms. Young go on vacation together?"

Alex didn't even look back at the woman. She continued what she was doing as if the question did not phase her, but she did answer the young woman.

"Since when did I say it was alright for you to ask me any personal type questions?" She now said, as she turned to level a steady gaze on Salina. "You have overstepped your place in asking me anything dealing with my personal life. I know you continuously try to flirt with me, and probably are feeling like that makes us close or something, but it doesn't. Don't ever presume with me again or you'll end up getting your feelings hurt. Now get to work." She said, as she dismissed the nosey Admin.

"Yes Ma'am." Salina said, as she left the office feeling like a complete fool for asking such a question.

A few minutes later, Taylor arrived on the floor. She sorted through the mail as she headed for the office.

"Well, well, well, you made it back. Wonder what you did on YOUR hiatus?"

"Have you always been so spiteful?" Taylor asked.

"You know why I don't like you?"

"Well, I assume it's because of my position. I told you I had nothing to do with it, so I would suggest you get over it. As far as my hiatus goes, I made a new friend. Now, please call Mr. Hairsten and tell him that Alex wants that proxy list by noon today." She then went back sorting through the mail and headed into the office where Alex was sitting smirking at her.

"Close the door."

"Yes Ma'am." She said respectfully, and closed the door. She handed the woman half of the mail including the red envelope with the white stripe on top.

"Hmm...good, you remembered." Alex praised, and instantly put the other mail down to open the red one.

After which she picked up the phone and called the investor. She spoke to him for a moment as Taylor took the letter and read over it. Then she listened to the conversation that went on as a result of it. The woman hung up the phone and the girl handed the letter back to her.

"So, you have to call him every time you get this type of letter, or else you lose money, right?"

"I can lose money."

"But why do you need to call your stockbroker, when he's the broker, I would think that's what you're paying him for. He should already know to sell, or buy."

"He does, it's just that when we're talking about millions of dollars and it's my money, I feel more comfortable with the final decision. Besides, this isn't the every day trading, that's something entirely different."

"Oh, okay. I think I understand."

"Good." Alex said, letting it drop there.

Taylor smirked, and said under her breath, "I know I owe you a few million."

The woman looked up over the letter she had in her hand and raised a brow at the nonchalant matter Taylor was presenting after having made such a statement.

"Do you really believe that?" She asked, as she went back to reading the mail, while at the same time listening for the answer.

"Yes." Taylor said, as she picked up the phone to make a phone call.

"Hang up the phone." Alex said in a serious, yet still conversational tone.

She hung up the phone and the woman spared a glance at her, and then went back to her mail. Taylor followed her lead and put the one letter she had to reply to on the desk while she went back to the other mail.

"I can't believe you actually think that?"

"Why wouldn't I? I mean, that's a lot of money no matter how rich a person is."

"Yes it is a lot of money, I would be lying if I said it wasn't, but you do not owe me anything."

"But?"

"But nothing. Did I ever say you owed me?"

"No, but?"

Alex slammed her stack of the mail on the table, not as hard as she normally would have, but the point was the same, and then she glared at Taylor. The girl started at the action and her eyes immediately went to the woman's, unfortunately for her.

"I'm only going to say this once more and then I don't ever want to hear about it again. Am I making myself clear?"

"Yes." Taylor said in a rush.

"You do not owe me any money. I don't want or need your money, and I don't want to have to have this conversation with you again, got it?"

"Yes."

"Good. Make your phone call." Taylor picked up the phone and the woman glanced at her over her mail intermittently, until she started speaking to the other person on the phone.

The first two meetings were held in the office, with one of those being Mr. Shearer. The third meeting of the day was the weekly meeting with the upper management.

"Mr. Thomas, go." Alex said, as she picked the people in random order for them to make their presentations.

"Yes, Ma'am. The Corporate Research department has been looking into a little company that, while small, has grown over the last year by almost 50%. Stocks are trading at 110 a share. It's a very hot company that was started by one person and now has subsidiaries overseas in some of the major markets. There are a lot of companies watching this one, but I think we have the upper hand because we already have stock in it. We think that if we can get hold of some others who may be willing to sell their stock, then we can be put in a good position to take it over within the year."

"Hmm...First of all, what makes you think anyone would be foolish enough to sell stock that has increased in value by almost 50% in a year? And what is the product? Which major markets are we talking about, and do they match up in product and market?" Alex questioned, her eyes never leaving the man's. Alex already knew the answers to her questions, she just wanted to see if the man had the answers.

He was nervous, but he knew he had to answer her.

"Well, we have thought about the stock issue, and we figured we could give them stock in one of the companies you already own. That way, it would be more of a swap than anything, and for those who didn't want to trade with us, we could make them an offer. But, we didn't think there would be anyone out there foolish enough to not want to have stock in one of your companies versus a small one. Your holdings have made many people financially well off. The product is clothing, and the markets are Milan, Paris, those markets."

"Okay, next time tell me those things first. You should know that. Go ahead with the preliminary and get back to me when you think you have all the information I will need to begin the takeover. Talk with Johnson in the Cost Analysis department."

"Yes Ma'am."

"Petersen, you're up, go." Alex said, as she went through each of the department heads, praising some, penalizing others. Finally the meeting ended and Alex left with Taylor walking beside her. "What's next?" She asked the girl.

"A business lunch, with Mr. D'Angelo Marazzda of Technology Incorporated." Taylor said, with a grin.

Alex raised a brow at her, and then said in a factual tone. "For me, yes, for you...no. I want you to go and enter those reports about the Kingston's Group takeover in my computer for the meeting later today."

"But why can't Salina do that?"

"Because I told you to." She said pointedly.

"Alright, no need to get testy. This is really going to be interesting." Taylor said under her breath, as she started to turn and head for the elevator.

Alex caught her by the shoulder and turned her back around.

"What does that mean?"

"What?"

"What do you mean what?! What you just said?"

"Oh, nothing. I was just talking to myself." She said nervously, due to the tone the woman was using.

"Well, talk to me. What did you mean?"

"Nothing." Taylor insisted.

Alex abruptly let go of the girl, realizing she was getting upset. Instead of yelling at Taylor and making a scene, she simply took a deep breath and then looked at the frightened girl.

"It's alright, we'll talk about it when we get home. Go do what I told you to do." She said without a second thought.

"It was nothing."

"What did I just say?"

Taylor looked at her, then turned, and with some concern she headed off to do what she had been told to do. The woman, in the meantime, watched the girl and wondered what she meant. She went to her business lunch and met the man she had once thought seriously about dating.

"Ah...there you are. I was beginning to wonder if you had stood me up, my dear Alex?"

"D'Angelo...now why would I do that?" She asked, as he greeted her with a kiss. "Alright D'Angelo, it's not like that between us anymore so just cool your heels."

He smiled mischievously and then spoke to her in Italian. She replied back in the same fashion. They were led to their table, where he pulled out her chair for her and she smirked at him, then sat down. He sat down across from her.

"So, what has my Rose been up to these last few years besides becoming the most powerful woman known in the business world?"

"Well if I'm only known as the most powerful business WOMAN, then obviously, I am not doing what I'm supposed to be doing. You know I want to be THE most powerful business PERSON ever!" The woman said, slightly baring her teeth.

He leaned back in his chair to regard the woman he had been, and still was, very much in love with.

"Actually my dear, you are known as that, but I didn't want to give you a swelled head."

"I take it all in stride, trust me."

"I know you do. So, what else is new in your life?"

"How about I ask you that. I mean, you did fly all this way under the premise that you wanted to talk to me about business."

"I did, but why not combine the visit?"

"Because things are different now. Anyway, tell me about this company you think I will be interested in and why you aren't going after it."

"It's a wonderful company, but I really don't have the finances to go after it. There are a lot of other companies that are looking at trying to acquire this little gem. But I thought of you when I realized I couldn't get it."

"Hmm...go on." Alex said, as she took a moment to order and he did the same.

"Well, It's an international company that started here and has grown over 50% in the last year."

"Really? That sounds pretty interesting, what's the product?" She asked, already knowing the possible company he was speaking of.

"Fashion."

"Hmm...what are the markets?"

"The fashion hubs of course. So what do you think? I know there are other companies trying to position themselves to get this little hot dish, but I think if you move within the next month...it can be yours by the end of the year. Huge tax write-off as well. What do you say?"

"You're practically drooling D'Angelo."

"I know, because I know you won't. But of course, I'm drooling for more than one reason. He said, as he took her hand.

"I think we should eat." She said, as she took her hand back and picked up her fork and knife.

"You still haven't told me what you think of it."

"I don't know yet. I have to think about it."

"Well that's fine, I'm in town for a while. I'll stop by the house this evening and we can talk about it there, and whatever else comes up."

The woman raised a brow at him and a curious smile came to her face.

"Fine. Well, I have to go. I'll see you this evening. It should be interesting." She stood up and D'Angelo came to his feet and they walked out of the restaurant.

Alex arrived back in her office 15 minutes later. Where's my PA?"

"I don't know Ma'am, but she said she would be right back." Salina said, only telling the woman half the story.

"Hmm...when she gets back tell her I want to see her."

"Yes Ma'am." The Admin said with a smile of satisfaction, assuming that Taylor was in trouble.

A few minutes later, Taylor arrived and Salina was more than happy to tell her that she was wanted in the office.

The girl's eyes narrowed slightly, then she looked into the office and saw Alex on the phone walking back and forth, apparently upset about something. She swallowed hard, but then looking at Salina and seeing her delighting in her discomfort, she turned and headed for the office.

"I don't care what you thought. I told you to do something and that is exactly what I expected for you to do. Now, you get it done and then go to personnel and have them put you in a more suitable position, since you can't seem to handle a simple closing deal."

Click!

The woman slammed the phone down and then turned around.

"Where's my report?"

"Oh, here, I put it in your computer like you said to." Taylor said, as she walked over to the desk. She bent over slightly facing the woman, her chest at the woman's eye level. Alex looked up at her, then back down her blouse, and raised a brow in appreciation. Especially seeing the nice mark she had made earlier.

"Here it is."

"Hmmm...nice." Alex said, without looking at the screen.

"You haven't even looked at it."

"I wasn't talking about it." The woman hinted.

Taylor blushed and then stood up straight, moving her hair back as she went and sat down on a chair on the other side of the desk. The woman smirked, then turned her attention to the screen and began reading the report. Taylor sat quietly waiting for her to finish and tell her if things were the way she wanted.

"Excellent job, as always. I'm very pleased."

Taylor smiled brightly at Alex, who sat back and regarded her for a few minutes.

"So...how was your business luncheon?"

"Fine. We're going to have a guest over this evening."

"Oh? For dinner?"

"Maybe. We'll see."

"Hmm...well, should I make dinner, or have the cook come in and do it?"

"You do it.

"Okay, what would you like?"

"Surprise me. But make sure it's something that will keep over conversation."

"No problem."

"Good, thank you." Alex said, showing a bit of her soft side with the girl.

"You're welcome." Taylor returned, and then pulled out her appointment book.

"You have a two o'clock with Ms. Overton of International Banks."

"Alright, I think I will hold that one in the smaller conference room, as she'll probably bring along a few of her loans and investment people."

"Alright. Are you taking out a loan with her bank?"

"No, she's coming to ask me if they can borrow from me."

"Hahahaha, now that's ironic." Taylor said, amused by the irony of the situation.

"Yes, I guess it is." Alex returned, with the same amusement in her eyes, yet the constantly thoughtful gaze also showing within.

At the end of the day, the two left the building heading for the waiting car. Once inside, the woman leaned back against the seat and stretched her long legs out in front of her and crossed them at the ankles. Taylor watched her discretely she thought, but Alex always seemed to know when she was looking at her. She looked up to catch Taylor's eyes on her legs.

"What are you thinking about right now?"

"Um...how do you do that?! The girl finally blurted out, embarrassed at being caught again.

"What?"

"Seem to know when I'm looking in your direction?"

"I feel your gaze on me."

"Really?"

"Yes."

"Well, how come I can't seem to do that?"

"Because you get to flustered at the thought of me watching you, although I do it all of the time."

"Really??" Taylor said again in amazement.

"Yes. I watch the way you move, the way you play with your clothing or your hands when you get nervous. I see the way your eyes fill with moisture when you think I'm upset with you about something that you know I have the right to be upset about. I watch how you fluctuate between being embarrassed and being angry with Salina. I see how relaxed you have become around me when we're alone. I see how you have grown in your confidence in dealing with clients, yet you still seem to balance things. You're still as kind and gentle, naive yet very intelligent, and you have a strong sense of what is right. But sometimes you don't seem to understand that just because something is right, doesn't always mean it is the best for a person. I see all of that in you and a lot more. I've watched you from that very first day you came to the floor. You're a beautiful young lady whom I am pleased to have in my life."

Taylor smiled, as tears ran down her face.

"I absolutely love when you're like this." She said, as she went into Alex's arms and laid against her.

The woman did not intend to get into all of what she did, but once it started and she saw how adorable Taylor was she just couldn't seem to stop the words from coming out.

"That's because you're just a softie." She teased, as she kissed Taylor's forehead.

When they arrived home, they went inside and headed upstairs to get cleaned up. When they got to the top of the stairs, they stopped once again. This time Alex turned to Taylor and said in a matter-of-fact tone of voice.

"This is going to change." She then turned and walked to her room, leaving Taylor standing on the stairs with her mouth open.

After the two had cleaned up, they went into the kitchen and the girl began taking out the things she would need to make the dinner that she had in mind.

"I like your choices." Alex complimented, as she walked around to the other side of the counter and stood next to the girl. She leaned one hand on the counter and looked at Taylor.

"What?"

"You still owe me an explanation, and I'm just waiting for it."

"I don't know what you mean?"

"About the statement you made when I told you to go and do the report."

"Oh! It was nothing." Taylor said, assuming that the woman would let it drop.

Alex continued to study the girl until Taylor looked up and saw annoyance in Alex's eyes.

"You're not getting upset about it are you? I mean it really was nothing."

"Upset about it...no, at you for not answering me...yes." The woman said, as she stood to her full height and walked around to the other side of the counter to look straight at the girl. Taylor's hands trembled slightly, and the woman saw them.

"If it's nothing, then why are you trembling?"

"Because you're upset."

"Then tell me, and maybe I won't be." The woman suggested, although it came out more as an order.

"Fine." Taylor finally said, as she stopped what she was doing and looked over at Alex. "I only meant that it was going to be interesting to see how things worked with you treating me one way at home and another at work. I mean, I know you said you don't mix the two, but there has got to be a middle ground where I am concerned."

"Why?"

"Because, it can get confusing. I mean, what if I did something major at work and you got upset about it? How do you rectify within yourself that you still want to hold me or be near me, when you were only hours before pissed off with me about something that happened at work? How can you do that?"

"Simple, I know me. I am without a doubt able to reprimand you at work and then get home and want to do nothing more than just love you."

Taylor seemed to deflate with the last part of her statement. And she chewed her lips as she thoughtfully chopped up some green onions. Alex waited for her to say something else as she knew she probably would. Finally she looked up at the woman, more understanding.

"Okay, I guess I have to add that to the things that you are good at?"

"I guess so."

Taylor smiled at the sincerity in her tone, and then she went back to chopping with purpose as another thought came to her mind.

"What if I can't?"

"What? Separate the two?"

"Yes."

"Then I will help you learn how."

"How?"

"By constantly reminding you that it is never anything personal when I reprimand you, it is always just about doing your job and doing it right the first time. If you mess up and you admit it to me before I find out about it, I'm usually not as hard, but you've seen that?"

"Yes. Alright. I'll try to remember that."

"Good." Alex said, and then walked back and turned her around and planted a passionate kiss on her.

She only intended to kiss the girl as a thank you for understanding. But that soon changed when she heard her moaning and felt her leaning back and sliding down the counter. Her passion for Taylor ignited. She followed the girl down the counter as she tried to find something to hold on to. The whimpering began and the woman moaned as a result. She broke the kiss and saw Taylor's heavily lidded eyes.

"Ahh...you are so...beautiful." Alex sighed, as she claimed the gasping girl's lips again. She laid her on the floor with her own body raised up in a pushup type position so as not to worry the girl.

Taylor was once again dazzled by the passion of the woman and she began scooting out from under her. Alex let her go and went into a catlike position, poised to pounce.

The girl went to stand up, but when she saw the woman's position and the gaze, her legs went limp and she went to her knees, eyes caught by Alex's hypnotic sapphires that were sparkling with desire. Taylor whimpered as the woman now took on a predatory stance and began crawling towards her in that same catlike, stalking fashion, her eyes never letting the girl's leave hers. Taylor was trembling more noticeably as Alex neared her, her breathing labored and shallow, her body and face colored the blush of passion and fear.

"I want you in my bed tonight." Alex said, as she slowly purred her desires to the girl.

"I want to hold you, caress you, and when you're ready, make love completely to you." Her voice was seductive, and silky to Taylor's sensitive ears. Despite the woman still being a distance away.

Taylor could only whimper as her mind was completely blank except for what was being whispered to her.

"When I get to you, I'm going to burn you with my passion."

The girl's eyes started to close, and Alex's mouth curled with anticipation as she saw Taylor giving in to the idea of being burned. Her movement toward the girl increased slightly, but then...the doorbell rang and Taylor seemed to come out of her trance. Her eyes wide with both fear and relief, she focused on Alex, who was still flushed with passion. A slow smirk came to the girl's lips, and she steadied herself. Alex had stopped her advance towards Taylor for a moment when she saw the expression. Taylor suddenly jumped to her feet, staggered slightly, but was able to steady herself and said with a wry grin.

"Oops...door, I better go get it." She turned and ran out of the kitchen with the woman right on her heels. Telling her the door be damned.

"Don't open that door!" She demanded. But Taylor just looked at her and said in an innocent tone of voice.

"What kind of hostesses would we be if we didn't?"

"Two very satisfied ones, I can assure you." Alex said, as she walked slowly towards her with the intention of pulling her away from the door and continuing in their previous activity.

CHAPTER 11

Taylor watched her come nearer and nearer. She cocked her head at the woman intrigued at the idea that Alex actually believed she could get to her before she opened the door. Just when the woman thought she could grab the girl, Taylor opened the door, right in the middle of Alex reaching for her. The woman's hand suddenly retreated to her own hair, where she made it appear as if she was just straightening it.

"D'Angelo?!" She greeted, in a high pitched, somewhat off guard tone.

"It took you long enough."

"Please come in Mr. Marazzda." Taylor invited, and then looked back at Alex as she closed the door.

"Thank you." He said, as he gave a curious look back to Alex.

"D'Angelo, this is Ms. Taylor Young, my friend and Personal Assistant. Taylor, this is Mr. D'Angelo Marazzda."

"How do you do?" She said, as she shook his hand.

"Fine thank you. Aren't you a little beauty? Careful Alex, you may have some competition when it comes to the men's attention."

Taylor blushed and looked over at the woman who raised a brow at her. Alex gave her a look that she recognized as meaning for her to be careful, if she didn't want to upset her.

"umm, I need to get back to the kitchen, and finish making dinner. I got a little distracted, but I think I will be able to FINISH it now."

"Well it was nice meeting you."

"You too, Mr. Marazzda."

"D'Angelo, please?"

"D'Angelo." She said with a polite smile, and then another glance back at the woman who still had not taken her eyes off of her.

"Um...yeah, okay, I'll just go then?"

"You do that, we'll talk later, you can be sure."

"Of course." Taylor said, somewhat nervous as she turned and walked back out of the foyer area leaving the two alone for the moment.

Alex watched her go but the girl heard D'Angelo's final comment to the woman.

"You know your cheeks are flushed?"

"Oh, I didn't realize it. Anyway, come on in. You can go to the living room and make us all a drink. Wine for me and the same for her. I'll be there in just a few minutes. I need to go and check on something in the kitchen."

"I would think so, considering you have your friend in there cooking in that massive kitchen of yours. I'm surprised she's not getting completely lost."

"Right. Anyway, we'll be there in a few minutes."

"Alright, this way right?"

"Yes, down the hall and turn left." The woman instructed.

"Okay, I got it. I remember now." He said, as he turned and headed down the hallway.

Alex turned and with quick strides she went back to the kitchen. The door flew open and Taylor started at first, and then gave an innocent, wide-eyed, gaze at the woman.

"No. It's not going to work. I want to know what you call yourself doing out there?" The woman asked, as she went around the counter to stand in front of Taylor.

"What?"

"That blushing!" Alex said sharply.

"I...I...he just caught me off guard, that's all."

"I don't want to see that again."

"It wasn't like I planned it."

"You should not be reacting that way to anyone else, or to anything they say in such a way. It leads me to believe that they are saying something more special to you than I am. Is that what you're trying to tell me?"

"No, of course not. I'll remember. Okay?"

"Alright. Now, I owe you for opening the door."

"I had to open it, you invited him?"

The woman didn't say anything else, she just lifted Taylor's chin and kissed her sweetly, then said as she turned to leave.

"I'll pay you back for opening it. If you think what was happening before he came was overwhelming, Ha! Have I got a surprise for you. Hurry out." Alex then left the kitchen, leaving the girl staring in amazement at the very idea of what she could possibly have planned for her.

Taylor finished up the preparations of the meal and now it was just a matter of everything cooking. Dinner would take about an hour and a half with the temperature that she put everything on. She washed and dried her hands, then headed back into the living room.

"So, is your friend living here with you, or just visiting from out of town, or just trying to find a place to live, and staying here with you until she does?"

"She's staying here."

"Aha...got tired of rattling around in this big place all by yourself, huh?"

"Something like that." She said dubiously, and took a sip of her wine.

Taylor came into the room and the man stood up in a respectful fashion. She smiled shyly and moved to sit on the sofa where Alex sat.

"So, how long have you two known each other?" He asked the girl.

"Months."

"Months? Hmm, now that's interesting."

"Why?" The girl asked with curiosity showing its head.

"Well, I remember when Alex and I were dating, I made that same suggestion, only our situation was different. We were in a relationship, but she turned me down flat. Hmm...interesting indeed."

Taylor's eyes looked at the man in confusion. She looked over at Alex and then asked the man, while she continued to look at the woman.

"You two dated?"

The woman simply cocked her head, and took a drink of her wine as she looked at Taylor, undisturbed by the revelation.

"Yes, I would have thought my Rose would have told her friend?"

"Your...R.o.s.e.?" The girl repeated as she looked at the man.

"Yes, it's just a pet name I used to call her when we were together. She IS quite a woman."

"Yes, she is, and just full of surprises." Taylor said, as she stood up to go back to the kitchen.

"Where are you going?"

"To check on dinner." She answered somewhat curtly.

Alex's ears rang with the tone and she caught Taylor's wrist.

"No, the dinner is fine, you just came out of there. Now sit down and behave." The woman said matter-of-factly.

Taylor looked at her with a pout on her lips and the woman simply raised a brow that told her she meant it. The girl swallowed hard and turned to go back to where she was sitting. Alex watched her retake her seat, and the man watched with wonder at the interaction.

"So...anyway, when I asked my Rose why we couldn't move in together, she told me she was not ready to take our relationship to that level yet." The man went on with his previous conversation.

"Why?" Taylor asked of the woman.

"Because I was not interested in taking our relationship to that level, there were too many things I wanted to do to be distracted by a relationship."

"So how long have you known Alex?"

"Quite a few years. I met her in Europe when she was taking over a company there. Things were really vicious, and it was more of a man's genre, but then this brilliant woman comes along. The men who thought they were vicious thought they would be able to walk all over Alex. I remember sitting in this one meeting with some other corporate heads. We were all looking to take the company and the CEO of that company we were all looking to either takeover, or partner with decided to call a meeting of all the interested parties. It was a sight to behold."

"I can imagine." Taylor said, looking over at Alex, who seemed uninterested in the man's praise.

"No, you can't even begin to imagine. The woman you work with today is so much more easy going than she used to be."

"Really??" The girl gasped, completely astonished at that thought.

"Yes, she was...extraordinary. She not only showed how ferocious she could be, but she turned that meeting into a bidding war. The only thing was, we were all making offers to her, rather than the CEO who we thought still owned his company. She had already taken it over as far as the bank and the investors were concerned. She had the loan called in with one phone call and within the hour the Ex-CEO was signing his company over to Alex so that he would at least make a little profit. From that point on, there was no stopping her, and it was that same event that led to her moniker, "The Raider". She became a whirlwind in the business community. She not only gained the respect of every business man and woman, but also intimidated all of them as well."

"What about you? You don't seem to be intimidated by her."

"Oh, I assure you, I was, right along with the rest of the business community, but the only difference was, I showed no fear. I was actually quite intrigued by her. I mean, she was not only fierce in business, but drop dead gorgeous. She was the youngest CEO ever. She was exciting. I had never wanted a woman so badly as I wanted her. I still want her, and I'm hoping that if things work out tonight, I'll have my chance again?" He said, ending with a question directed at the woman.

"Well, at least you're being honest. What do you say to that Alex?" Taylor asked, once again coming to her feet, but this time she walked around the long way to keep Alex from stopping her.

Alex watched her but said nothing except to let her know they would talk later.

"I'm sure we will. Excuse me, I need to go check on dinner." Taylor then walked out of the living room.

"Hmm...she's a little different from the types of friends you usually associate with. How did you two meet?"

"She came to my attention when she tried to save my life." The woman said matter-of-factly."

"Really? Someone tried to kill you?"

"Yes."

"And she saved you?"

"Not directly, but she had the intention to try."

"Well, to be honest, I'm not really surprised by the attempt on you, but I am a little curious as to how that led to you allowing her to move in here with you?"

"I saved her life in return, and this was a safe place for her to stay at that time."

"Someone was out to hurt her?"

"Yes. He actually raped her, but he wasn't able to complete it...if you know what I mean?"

"Oh...I'm sorry to hear something like that happened to her. But it seems you've been able to help her get past that."

"Yes, and in the process, things changed."

"Changed?"

"Ye..."

"Excuse me, but dinner is ready Alex." Taylor chimed in.

"Come here Taylor." Alex called, as she came to her feet.

"Yes?" She said, as she walked over to where the woman stood watching her.

Alex lifted her chin more and looked into her eyes as she asked pointedly.

"Are you jealous?"

"Alex don't." Taylor said, now embarrassed by the statement.

"Jealous??" The man said with knitted brows, as he looked at the two women.

"No need to be." Alex said, as she lowered her head and kissed the now nervous and embarrassed, yet relieved girl.

The man's jaw dropped open.

Alex leaned back from Taylor and gave her a knowing look.

"Are you okay now?"

"Yes." The girl said blushing.

"I would have thought you trusted me by now, after everything." The woman said honestly.

"You're right. I'm sorry. I just thought..."

"I know what you thought, anyway, we'll talk about it later. Let's go eat."

"Okay."

"D'Angelo."

"Oh...right." He said, snapping out of his shock, and then walking towards the door to head for the dining room.

They arrived in the dining room and the maid served the meal. The man complimented the smell and look of the food. Taylor blushed slightly, but she gave a shy glance at the woman sitting at the other end of the table. D'Angelo sat in the middle. Alex took a bite of her food, which allowed for the man to proceed with eating. He took a bite of the delightful looking plate of food and then sighed at how delicious the taste was in his mouth.

"You're a wonderful cook!" He said, taking another bite and closing his eyes for a moment to let the flavors hit all of his taste buds. "Wonderful."

"Thank you." Taylor said with a smile as she looked at the woman who gave a wink to her. The smile brightened more and they all continued eating.

After a bit of just eating, the man finally went back into their conversation of earlier.

"Well, this is a bit of a surprise, but I guess with you? It doesn't matter if it's a man or a woman, as long as you're happy?"

"That's right."

"Well, I'm happy for you...both. I guess that ends any thoughts I may have had about us."

"Yes, it does." Alex said with a smirk.

"Okay then, I guess we should talk about business?"

"That's fine."

"I think I will go and check on dessert, if you'll excuse me?" Taylor said, more to Alex than to the man.

"Go ahead." She agreed. The man stood up to see her off from the table, then sat back down and continued the conversation.

"I think that company is a gold mine, and if you don't take advantage of it, then you're not the same person I met in Italy."

"I'm the same, and I think it is an excellent investment option."

"D'Angelo, what's the name of this company?" Taylor asked, coming back into the dining room with a tray of desserts. She served them to the two people and then took her own. She sat down waiting for D'Angelo to tell her the name of the company, seeing how she still had not heard it.

"It's called Zadria's fashions."

"What?! Is this the company you're thinking about taking over?" Taylor asked, shocked by the news.

"Yes." Alex answered, as she took a sip of her wine, but watched the girl over the rim of the glass.

"You can't take over her business!"

"I can and I will."

"No, she's my friend, you know that!" Taylor stated adamantly. She stood up to leave the table.

"Calm down and sit back down." Alex said, undisturbed by her behavior, at least that's the way it appeared to D'Angelo.

"I didn't mean to cause a problem." He said, apologizing for upsetting Taylor.

"It's not a problem D'Angelo, it's just business. And the sooner my ASSISTANT realizes that, the better." Alex said, directing her statement more to Taylor than the man, as she put her glass on the table.

"This is not just about business." Taylor said, as she continued to stand.

Alex didn't answer the girl, but simply gave her a look that told her to sit down. Taylor inhaled, and then sat back down.

"That's better. Now, as far as this not being about business specifically. That is exactly what it's about. This is what I do, I take over other companies. There is nothing new about that. I realize she is a friend of yours, but as a businessperson she realizes, I'm sure, that these are the risks of owning your own company. There is always someone out there waiting for you to peek your head out so they can come in and take it."

"So you're saying you're a vulture."

Alex flinched at that statement, and then her brows furrowed, as her eyes narrowed at Taylor.

"This is not about anything but business! D'Angelo, I will be in touch with you about this in the next few days." Alex said, summarily ending the evening so that she could talk to the girl alone.

"I understand. I'll talk to you later. It was nice to have met you." He said, kissing Taylor's hand.

"Thank you. It was nice to have met you too." She said, as Alex stood to see the man out.

Taylor went about clearing the table and taking the dishes to the kitchen, where Alex came storming through, after seeing the man out.

"What was that?!" She shouted.

"What?"

"Don't give me what! You know what I'm talking about!"

"I'm sorry for my comment. I didn't mean it. I was just caught off guard by the news."

Taylor said, placing the dirty dishes in the dishwasher, as she looked at the woman.

"Well, don't ever do that to me again! I would never insult you like that, and I don't expect for you to do it to me either. Especially over some business deal. I take those type of comments from you personally."

"It won't happen again. I am sorry for it, and I regret that I said it." Taylor said contritely.

Alex studied the now thoughtful girl, and then decided to let her off the hook.

"Alright, I forgive you. Just don't let it happen again."

"It won't." Taylor said, as she looked at the woman, a sincere gaze lighting her eyes. Alex raised a brow at her and smirked.

"Come here."

The girl walked around to the other side of the counter and the woman took her in her arms, wrapping one arm around her waist, and the other came up to caress the girl's face as she leaned down and kissed Taylor. This time Taylor wrapped her arms around Alex's neck, which caused her to smile to herself at the action.

"Hmm...very nice." She purred, as she began kissing the girl's cheek, then moving down to her neck, which caused Taylor to giggle as she hit a ticklish spot.

"I want to talk to you about your take-over plans?"

"I really don't feel like talking about business. I sort of have personal things on my mind right now, if you know what I mean?" Alex said, as she took a bit of the girl's soft neck in her mouth.

Taylor moaned as a result and began feeling lightheaded.

"Please...?" She asked weakly, her resolve fading, due to the sensations that were washing over her.

Alex raised her head and gave her a somewhat frustrated gaze. She let go of Taylor and walked to the kitchen table to sit down. She waited for the girl to collect herself, which took a few moments.

"Thank you, it's just that it's hard to think with you...well you know?"

"Hmm...yes, I know." The woman said knowingly.

"I just want to talk to you about your plans to take over my friend's company."

"I told you I don't like mixing business with our personal lives."

"But this IS personal to me, she's a friend of mine." Taylor said, defending her argument.

"I know she's a friend of yours, but that has absolutely no relevance. This is business."

"So you're saying. I can't talk you into bypassing this ONE Company?"

"No. And it's not a matter of me bypassing, it's just that if I don't take it, then someone else will. It's a dynamic company that is growing by leaps and bounds, and I would be a fool to just sit back and not look at this company. All of those other companies out there who are looking at Zadria's company, are looking at it for the same reasons I am. But they may actually divide up the company and outsource many of the divisions. Who knows...they may even have economically deprived countries make the garments for a lot less, thereby being able to keep more of the profits, and getting rid of a lot of the higher paid designers. Is that what you want?

"No, of course not, but I know when you take over a company you tend to get rid of all of the upper management. I know it makes sense when you're looking to acquire a company and cut a lot of the excess expense. I understand that, but this is different..."

"Why?"

"Because it's a friend of mine. You're talking about taking a company that she has worked hard to build up and the minute she does, what happens? Everyone wants to take it from her, and why? For no other reason than money. You don't need another company. If you stopped right now and never took over another company, you would have enough money to live on for 5 generations. How much more money do you need?"

"It's not that I NEED more money. This is not about anything other than I find it exhilarating, it gives me a rush, that's why I got into business. This business in particular."

"But can't you pass on this ONE Company and look at some other one?"

"So you would rather let some other company takeover your friend's company and put them all out of business?"

"No, but..."

"But what? I'll make a deal with you."

"What?"

"When I take over the company, I will not let her go, and I won't outsource any of the divisions."

"I don't want you to take it over!" Taylor said somewhat sharply.

Alex pinched her lips together, then glared at her.

"Fine. You know what?! If you don't want me to take over this company, then you come up with another way for me to get my hands on it where I will still be pleased. Then present it to me and the other department heads!" Alex said, annoyed, as she stood up to get more water out of the refrigerator.

"Me?"

"Yes you!! You don't want me to take over the company, so you give me another way, and if I like it, then I will consider it. But, if I don't like it, or there are too many holes in it, I am not going to be easy on you. Then I'll have those departments that need to be involved take over and get the company for me. I will keep Zadria as one of the management, but I will cut all of the other upper management personnel, is that clear?"

"Yes. But you want me to present this?"

"Yes. You will handle every aspect of it. The researching, the budgeting, the planning, the pros and cons, of both plans, and everything else. If you're able to convince me that it is a prudent alternative, then I'll not only be very proud of you, but I'll allow you to make more such presentations."

"And if I'm not?"

"Then I will still be proud of you for trying, but Zadria's upper managers will be out of a job." The woman said impassively.

"And I can use any of the resources of the company?"

"Of course, I would not expect for you to actually try to do all of the budgeting and analysis by yourself. It will be up to you to bring all of them together in a cohesive matter."

"Oh, okay, and you won't try to take over before I can make my presentation to you?"

"Why would I do that to you? Of course I won't. I told you to make a presentation to me and that's what I expect. But like I said, I will not treat you any differently in that meeting. Although, I will not make the sarcastic remarks as I normally would, if I thought there were too many holes in the presentation." She said with a smirk.

Taylor looked at her with both thoughtfulness and concern.

"Does it scare you? The thought of making a presentation to me in front of others?"

"No, it scares me to just make a presentation to you. I know how hard you can be."

"Then you know you have to have a nearly perfect presentation. Are you having second thoughts? You know you don't have to, you can always just let me do what I do and look at this as just another takeover." Alex suggested, with a studied sidelong gaze at Taylor who now was sitting across from her.

"No! No, I'm going to do this. I don't want anyone taking over my friend's company, especially the woman whom I'm in love with. It will make her think that I condone it, and that would hurt her, I'm sure."

Alex leaned back in her chair and nodded her head thoughtfully at Taylor. The woman then smiled. She pushed her chair out and then crooked her finger and beckoned to the girl to come over to her. Taylor smiled back with both confusion and happiness shining in her eyes. She moved out of her chair and headed over to Alex's. The woman raised her hands to her hips, and held her on each as she looked up into the eyes she loved.

"You know I hope you succeed in this, right?"

Taylor smiled, and answered with her heart.

"Yes."

Alex reached one of her hands up to the girl's cheek and guided her head down to her so that she could place a kiss on her lips. She then pulled Taylor onto her lap just as their lips met. Taylor wrapped her arms around her neck as she tried to return the passion that was flowing through her. Eventually, she was moaning into the woman's mouth as she became overwhelmed by that passion. Finally their embrace ended and Taylor swayed while they both took in the needed air their lungs desired. Alex began kissing her on the neck while Taylor squirmed and commented on how much it tickled. The woman then switched between kissing her neck and kissing her lips.

"So...are you...going to share with me tonight?" Alex asked, between kisses.

"I...I...don't think I should just yet, especially with the project that you've assigned me."

"Wait..." The woman said, stopping her activity to look at Taylor. "That project is not to affect our personal lives. If you think you can't keep it out of this part of our lives, then I will just take the company over and forget about it, is that clear?"

"Yes, but there will be times when some of it will spill over just a little. I won't let it affect our personal relationship too much."

"You're already letting it by not coming to my bed because of it." Alex pointed out.

"I didn't mean for it to sound like I didn't want to share your bed with you. I just meant that you make it hard for me to concentrate on anything else when you touch me. I know that when I do come to your bed, I don't want to have this on my mind. I'm not able to clear my mind of things like you're able to."

"Well, I understand that, but I will not allow you to let it interfere with us." Alex said, giving her a knowing look.

"I understand."

"Good, now let's go change into our nightclothes, and then we can relax in the den for a while."

"Okay." Taylor said as she stood up. Alex came to her feet and wrapped her arm around the girl's shoulder and the two of them went to change into their nightclothes.

After they had changed, they went into the den and lit a fire in the fireplace. Alex began caressing Taylor's arm as she laid on her side and the girl on her back.

"What are you thinking about?" She asked, noticing the intermittent knitting of the girl's brows.

"Oh, I was just thinking about how I was going to handle my duties as your PA and have the time to do the research for the project."

"What about it?"

Taylor shifted her eyes over to look up at Alex and saw she had a brow slightly raised.

"That's alright, I shouldn't have brought it up right now." Taylor said quickly, to avoid upsetting the woman.

"No, it's alright. It's a legitimate concern. So, what do you propose?" Alex asked, as her fingers moved to the girl's buttoned top, which she began to unfasten the buttons one at a time. Taylor's mind fluctuated between trying to think of how to resolve her Personal Assistant dilemma, and that of her rising desire and fear at where things were heading at the moment with Alex unfastening her top. The woman saw Taylor's uncertainty but she already knew what she would do, so she continued to unfasten the buttons as she waited for the girl to think of how to resolve her problem. Alex saw the mark she had put on Taylor's breast and a smile curled her lips.

"Ma...may...maybe you can have Salina take over for a while, until I finish with this other project?"

"Hmm...do you think that is a good idea? I mean, you know she wants this position. And with you almost handing it to her on a silver plate, how could she not want to keep it even when you're done with your project?"

"Well, I guess I will leave it up to you to decide whether she deserves to keep the position."

"I created the position for you. I let you remain in it because you're good and I TRUST you. I don't trust her."

"Then why keep her around?"

"She's good at her job, and she likes to flirt with me."

"What?" Taylor said, rolling to balance on one elbow, so as to face the woman.

"Yes, Actually it was quite entertaining."

"Does she still flirt with you?"

"Yes, all the time."

"And what do you tell her these days when she does that?"

"Nothing. She doesn't need to know my business outside of those things that are specific to work."

"But, she probably thinks you're interested in her."

"Why would she think that? I have made no moves to encourage her into thinking that. In fact, she already believes I'm involved with some man, but she doesn't care. Do you know why she tries to entice me?"

"Because she likes you, or wants you?"

"Wants me, yes, lusts after me, yes, likes me, no. But she also sees it as a way to get a recommendation into the Junior Executive Program."

"Oh, so she's trying to get a leg up, excuse the pun, by getting involved with the boss?"

"Right."

"But you're the founder of that program, you can put anyone in it you choose without them having to work for you, and she has to know that it wouldn't have much of an effect with you in business because of how you so adamantly keep business and personal separate."

"True, but she thinks that if she can seduce me, then maybe I will change my stance on that."

"So you've spoken to her about her behavior?"

"Actually, she brought it up. She wanted to know what I had planned for after work one day and I asked her why?"

"What did she say?"

"She wanted to know if I wanted to go and have a few drinks with her."

"And did you?"

"No, of course not. I told her I had a business dinner."

"Was she disappointed?"

"Of course. She had plans, and I sort of blew those plans out of the water."

"With your business dinner?"

"Right." Alex said, not letting on that she really had no business dinner, she just didn't want to go out with the woman.

"Hmm...does she still try?"

"Yes, in fact just recently she asked me if we went on vacation together. Of course, I told her that what I do in my personal life is none of her business. I also believe, if I make her my Personal Assistant then she will think that I am interested in her advances, not to mention how she will have to be around me most of the time."

"I'm glad to hear you told her that. So you really think she will think that?"

"Yes, wouldn't you if you were her? Which, by the way, I'm ecstatic that you're not her, and you have nothing in common with her."

"I guess I would. Well, what do you suggest?"

"No, what do you suggest?"

"Put the position on hold until I return to it and just continue to use Salina as your assistant?"

"Hmm...but I've really come to depend on you to handle a lot of things now." Alex said as she unfastened another button, thereby exposing Taylor's cleavage more.

"I know, but maybe I can still help with the mail and those calls?"

"That would help."

"Okay, then I'll continue to help with the mail. Also, I don't know if you're going to agree with this or not, but I hope you will."

"What is it?" The woman now said, as she was down to the last few buttons and Taylor's top and her breasts were now becoming more open and exposed.

"What do you think about me having my own..."

"I don't think I'm going to like what comes after that."

"Well...it'll only be for a short time...maybe?"

"What will?" Alex asked pointedly, just as the girl's top dropped open exposing the already excited breast and its peak. The woman's breathing shallowed as she admired the sight while still listening to the now rapidly breathing girl.

Swallowing with some difficulty, Taylor continued to talk, although her mind was slowly being drained of coherent thought.

"I...I...th...thought maybe I could have my...my own office?"

Alex cocked her head, while raising a brow at her. She then gave a light push to the girl so that she was laying on her back with her top open.

"What do you think my answer will be?" She asked, as she slowly lowered her head down, while at the same time looking into the girl's eyes.

Taylor's breathing was now faster and her heart was trying to beat out of her chest once again. Her body showing the blush as well as her face.

"I don't know...Yes?"

"Think again."

"Aww...but I need somewhere to make the private phone call and things like that."

"Then I will make a space for you in MY office." Alex said, as she flicked her tongue over one of the already taut peaks.

"AHH! Ohhh..." Taylor shivered as her mind went blank to whatever the last thing the woman had said.

Alex shivered in response to Taylor. She repeated the action and again, the girl shivered and let out a gasp of air as her fingers dug into the carpet-covered floor. The woman focused on the art of persuasion. She wanted the girl to come to her bed. She ran her tongue over the peak and Taylor shuddered, as a result, and jerked involuntarily out from under the woman's stimulating actions. Alex rested her head on her hand as she balanced herself on her elbow, her eyes watched the girl. Taylor was completely unnerved, struggling to catch her breath and compose herself.

"Do I disturb you that much?" Alex asked her.

"I...I...I...goodness! "

"Do you want to be my lover?"

"Yes." The girl managed to gasp out.

"Then you're going to have to stop running from me. Come back over here, I'm not going to bite...not unless you want me to?" She said seductively.

Taylor almost choked as a result of the woman's provocative words. She moved back over to where Alex was, although she was holding her top closed subconsciously. Alex looked at her hand, and then back up into her eyes.

"Okay, maybe I moved a little fast with that. How about if I slow it down a bit? I'll just caress them for a while. Is that okay?"

"I...I..."

"Good, here, lay back down."

"I...I..."

"Come on." She coaxed, as she patted the area right in front of her.

Taylor was flushed from the excitement and fear of not knowing how to handle the sensations she was feeling. She eased back over and laid back down.

"Okay, you have to move your hand."

Taylor hesitated at first.

"Look, I am quite worked up right now, and I'm trying to take this slow enough for you to handle, but you're not working with me on this. I just want to love all of the young woman I am in love with, not just your intellect." Alex said sincerely, as she gently moved Taylor's hand away from the top.

The top hung open, but the breasts were still covered enough to where the peaks were not seen. The woman brought her hand up to Taylor's cheek and she lowered her lips to the girl's and once again kissed her. Taylor wrapped her arms around the woman's neck and pulled her closer. Alex heard her begin to moan and slowly let her hand glide down her neck onto her chest. She slipped her fingers under the blouse, and slipped it off of Taylor's shoulder. The girl trembled, unsure whether it was from the change in temperature, or from being exposed in such a way, she couldn't tell. The woman continued to kiss her as her hand moved back to the girl's neck, and then slowly back down to her bare breast. She lifted her lips away from Taylor's and whispered in a velvety voice.

"Don't jump, just let your body enjoy the feel of my touch, as much as I enjoy the feel of your body. Relax, I would never hurt you. You know that, right?" She moved lightly over one of the girl's warm breasts.

"Ye...yes." Taylor stammered.

The touch was electric and she shivered as a result, but she did not jerk away. Instead, her breathing became slightly labored as she tried to relax. Alex's hand started out being exploratory but soon it began to be firmer as she kneaded the soft flesh in her hand.

Taylor moaned louder and Alex's own breathing was now becoming more rapid. She covered the girl's lips once again, this time the kiss was more intense. Taylor moaned and began whimpering as Alex's hand kneaded it's way up to her peak. At first she just glided over it, but then she felt the girl's body jump impulsively, and her chest arched into the touch. Alex captured the peak between her fingers and rolled, squeezed, pinched, and pulled at it as she felt the tightening of it in her fingers. She moaned and lifted her mouth from Taylor's once again. She moved her mouth to whisper in her ear, and in a husky, velvety voice, she said to Taylor.

"I'd like to feel this in my mouth."

"Yes." Taylor managed to reply.

Alex kissed her again, hard and passionately, then moved to take the requested peak into her mouth. She licked around it for a few minutes and Taylor was gripping whatever her hands touched, in this case it was the carpet once again. She squirmed with each touch of the tongue on her, and Alex felt Taylor's trembling.

"Ahh!!" Was all she could manage when Alex sucked the peak into her mouth and began feasting on the large, delectable tip.

Suddenly Taylor's back arched and her mouth opened as if to speak, but nothing came out except a strangled sound. Her body went rigid and Alex heard her breath catch in her throat. The woman was so excited by the fact that Taylor had reached ecstasy from her touches, that she removed her mouth from the peak, and moved once more to cover the girl's mouth with her own. Alex's body also reacted to what was happening, and out of pure excitement, her own body sang along with the younger woman's and she too, experienced the rapture. Both women were flooded by blissful ecstasies that neither of them had ever experienced before. When Taylor's finally ended, she fell limply back to the carpeted floor. Her breathing labored. Meanwhile, Alex's was just ending and once it did, she laid heavily on top of the girl. Taylor had tears rolling down between her closed lashes, and Alex happened to lift her head enough to be able to see them. Her own eyes misted and she rolled to her back bringing the girl with her. She held her and whispered words of love and devotion to her. Taylor hugged tightly to the woman and eventually, after her breathing returned to normal, she drifted off. The woman smiled, and then she too, drifted off.

CHAPTER 12

Alex woke the next morning still holding Taylor in her arms. They had slept in the den on the floor the whole night. She smiled to herself, and then she kissed the girl on the forehead and hugged her closer. Taylor eventually roused from her ecstasy-induced sleep and stretched to get the kinks out of her body. She felt a light weight around her waist. Eventually her eyes opened, she yawned and then realized that she was in Alex's arms and she became nervous about that.

"Good morning." Alex purred in her sensitive ear.

She trembled as a result of the sound and the feel of the woman's warm breath on her ear.

"Good morning. How did you sleep?" Taylor asked, trying to be conversational, although there was a slight tremble in her voice.

"Hmm...very well. Quite a way to be lulled to sleep, don't you think?" Alex asked, as she kissed Taylor's cheek and neck.

Taylor squirmed and gave a squeeze to the woman's arm. She was trying to show Alex that she enjoyed last night, despite her reservations about what was going to happen in their relationship, now that they both had experienced the feeling of what it meant to reach ecstasy. Of course, Taylor believed Alex was familiar with the sensation from past experiences in her life, especially with the passion that Alex seemed to have for something that was supposedly unfamiliar to her. The woman squeezed the girl to her when she felt Taylor hugging her wrapped arms and again kissed her on the neck.

"I think we need to get up and get ready for work, especially if you want me to have a decent proposal for you." Taylor suggested, not sure what would happen if they laid there any longer.

Alex answered her as she slipped her hand into the open blouse and began caressing one of Taylor's breasts. The girl blushed at the touch and her breathing started to increase as her heart began beating faster and faster. The woman began kissing on the girl's neck with intent and purpose and Taylor realized that Alex was once again getting aroused. When the woman's fingers touched her nipple, she jumped. She immediately realized what she had done, but she needed to get out of the woman's arms before she was once again drawn in.

"I think I need to get cleaned up." Taylor said breathlessly as she rolled to her feet and turned to look at Alex.

She raised an inquisitive brow at Taylor, but allowed her to stand, as she also came to her feet and walked up to the girl.

"Alright, but we have a few things to talk about ."

"Of...of course." Taylor said, as she turned and headed for the stairs, nervously playing with her hair as she went.

Alex followed her up the stairs, then they split and went to their own rooms. After they had dressed, they skipped breakfast and their workout and headed straight for the office. In the car, Taylor asked the woman what she planned to do about the position.

"I think it would be best if I just put it on hold until you finish with this other project. You know my business party is coming up, and I expect for you to have all of this done and presented, so that you will be back in your position and up to date on everything, and every person coming. Is that clear?"

"Yes, but..."

"No buts, if you don't think you can have all of it done before then, I will not allow you to get involved in it, friend or not. I have companies to run, and I can't let my right hand get bogged down with one small venture if it will affect my larger assets." Alex leveled her gaze on Taylor's wide eyes. The girl nodded her head "yes" to the nonverbal question.

"Good. Now what's on my schedule?"

By the time they arrived at the office, Taylor had gone over Alex's schedule with her. Before they got out of the car, the woman pulled the girl to her, and said in a silky voice.

"You still have not given me a good morning kiss."

"Oh..." Taylor uttered, then leaned in and the two kissed for long moments, until the girl brought her hand to the woman's chest.

Alex allowed her to lean back, which the girl did, unsteadily. They both allowed their breathing to return to normal, and then Alex unlocked the door and the chauffeur opened the door for the two women. They went into the building and Taylor excused herself to go get the mail. They had decided that she would still help with the mail, in addition to working on her project. When Alex arrived in the office, she was a little surprised to find Salina already there.

"Good morning Ma'am."

"Morning. You're here early." The woman said casually.

"Yes Ma'am, I thought I would come in and start on those letters you wanted done by this evening."

"I see. Well, fine, carry on." Alex said, as she started for her office.

Then she stopped and called over her shoulder. "By the way, I will need you to prepare for an increase in your workload for a while."

"Yes Ma'am." Salina replied, as Alex continued on inside her office.

Taylor arrived an hour later and the Admin Assistant's mood changed.

"Good morning Salina. You're here early." The girl said observantly.

"Morning. Well it looks like you're not the only one who Alex needs things from."

"I didn't..."

"In fact, she just told me that she was going to give me more things to do, which means that somebody must obviously be failing in her assigned duties." Salina sneered as she returned to her typing, completely ignoring the girl.

Taylor shook her head in disbelief at the young woman's behavior. She then went into the office and closed the door behind her.

"Here you go." She said, offering half of the mail to Alex.

"Thank you. What took you so long?" The woman asked, conversing as she shifted through the mail in her hand. She took the one she wanted to start with out, and putting the rest on the table, and began opening it.

"Oh, I filled out a requisition for a desk and chair and supplies. I hope you don't mind?"

"No, I don't mind, but what type of desk did you get?"

"Just a plain one. It looks somewhat like a high school teacher's desk. Here, here's a catalog picture of the set."

Alex stopped what she was doing, and looked at Taylor over her brows. She took the offered catalog and looking over it her nose crinkled in distaste.

"What? It looks like a teacher's..."

"No, I heard what you said, and I see it also, I just find it hard to believe. When is it supposed to be here?"

"Why? It's a nice practical desk. I was told that it would be here in a few days?"

"Yes, that's true, but so is my desk."

"Yes! But yours is huge, and it's expensive. This whole office cost more than my old townhouse, and it's furnishings, plus my car and everything I own, and STILL it would be nowhere near what this office cost to decorate."

Alex chuckled at her unintended joke.

"True, but I can't allow some...well for lack of a better word, gaudy furniture to be placed in here."

"Well you can always give me my own office." Taylor said, with a raise of her brow.

"I don't think so. I like seeing you. Besides, I don't think I would want to hold a meeting in your office if that desk is any indication as to how it would be decorated."

"Are you saying I don't have any taste?"

"No, not at all, I know you do. I've seen your decorating abilities. Your town house was very nice, that's why I don't understand why you would order such a...conservative style desk?"

"Because it's not my money, it's yours, and I didn't want to be wasteful of something that is not mine."

"Well, I appreciate that, but you can't have that desk."

"Well, what do you suggest?" Taylor asked as she picked up one of the phones on the desk and made a phone call, regarding one of the pieces of mail she was working on.

"I'll think about it." Alex said, as she went back to working on her pile of mail and the packages.

After they had finished with the mail, Taylor wanted to get started on her project.

"Do you mind if I go and start on my research?"

"No, when will you be back?"

"I'm not sure, depends on what all I have to do."

"Well, I guess I will see you later, good luck." Alex said with a smile.

Taylor smiled back brightly and turned to leave, but just as she reached the door, the woman called to her.

"Oh, don't forget, we have some things to talk about this evening."

"Oh, right, okay, I will see you later." Taylor replied, without turning around to face the woman.

"See you later then." Alex said, allowing her to go.

"Okay, bye." She opened the door and left.

Alex watched Taylor get on the elevator and once the doors closed, she picked up the phone and made a phone call.

Meanwhile, Taylor had gone to talk with her friend Marcus, VP in Acquisitions, about some things she would need his help with.

"Mr. Shearer?"

"Yes?"

"Ms. Madison's Personal Assistant wishes to speak with you for a moment. Shall I send her in?"

"Oh, yes, definitely."

The woman then showed Taylor in and closed the door behind her as she left.

"Marcus, how are you?"

"Fine, how about yourself?"

"Fine." She answered.

"Come over here." He said, as he pulled her into his arms and gave her a big hug. "It's been forever since we've gotten together to just talk as friends. I've missed that."

"I have also, but I have to tell you, this visit is business."

"Oh, what sort?"

"Well..." She started, as she sat down in one of the chairs and motioned for him to do the same. "I know you're working on the Zadria deal."

"Yes, Alex wants to take it over and I've started gathering the information that is needed to make it happen."

"Good, I thought you would."

"Why?"

"Well because I'm taking over the project. Alex has put me completely in charge of this particular deal."

"Why would she do that? She knew I was working on it."

"Oh, well she didn't tell me that, but Zadria is a close friend of mine and I didn't want the company taken over."

"Oh, I bet that went over well with Alex." He said, with an amused gaze.

"No, she didn't like it at all. As a matter of fact, she really doesn't want me to get involved with this one."

"So why did she let you? Usually when she says "no", that's it. The conversation ends with those words and any others will lead to embarrassment for the person who continues." The man said, knowing from experience.

"Well, let's just say it's a test." Taylor replied vaguely, not wanting the man to know of her relationship with Alex outside of work. She knew he was a devout Christian.

"Okay, so she's letting you handle everything with this one?"

"Yes, and I hope I can count on your support and help?"

"Of course, but what is it you want to do?"

"Well I'm not sure yet. That's why I've come to talk to you. I know you've probably already done a lot of the financial research, with the help of the accounting and the budget departments, right?"

"Right."

"Great, so, can you give me what you have? Whatever you haven't covered yet, I will take up and do the research on it. I still want your input because you know what Alex likes, especially when it comes to a presentation. Do you mind being on my team?"

"I would love to work with you. It's going to be great working with one of my dear friends!" He exclaimed. "Let me get you the files."

Taylor grinned at the response from her friend and knew that they would make a good team.

She spent a few hours with Marcus, and then left to go and speak with some of the others she wanted on her team. By the time she had met with all of them personally, most of the day was gone. It was nearing quitting time for most people, so she headed back to Alex's office to organize the files she had gathered on the Zadria deal. When she made it back to the office after stopping by the mailroom to collect mail, she saw Salina slamming folders on her desk.

"What's going on?" She asked cautiously.

"Oh, so, the little bedwarmer has returned?" Salina sneered.

Taylor was stunned by the statement.

"I...I don't know what you're talking about."

"Liar!! I knew you had to be sleeping with her for her to have made you her Personal Assistant!" The woman accused, as she stormed over to the girl.

"I am not lying! You don't know what you're talking about!" Taylor shot back as she headed for the door of the inner office. But Salina cut her off and stood in front of the door.

"Then how do you explain it?"

"Explain what?"

"Everything, including this latest thing?"

"She and I have already told you what was happening, and why she made me her Personal Assistant. And what latest thing?"

"Oh, right, like you don't know." Salina said, as she threw open the door to the inner office and stormed inside. With raging eyes she glared at the girl, then looked off to the right and scowled.

Taylor walked in cautiously as she watched the woman. She kept her eyes on the young woman as she spared a glance around the office. What she saw caused her to gasp. Her eyes quickly raked over the area of the office that now had a desk just like Alex's, only smaller, and without some of the amenities of hers. The desk also had all of the needed things like a multi-line phone with video capability, a computer with all the amenities just like Alex's, pens, note pads, staplers, and all of the other things necessary to be efficient. Taylor stared, looking back and forth in complete disbelief at the setup. Finally the silence was broken.

"Oh...don't act like you're surprised. I know you had to know about this. I also know you're sleeping with her! But let me tell you something right now, and I suggest you take me seriously, you either get out of whatever is happening between the two of you, or I will tell all of your dear friends about your relationship with her, as well as this whole company. And I don't care if it's true or not, I'll make it believable. I'll also let the church you go to know about it. I want to get into that Executive Program and you're in my way, so you'd better do something to get out of my way before you get burned." Salina sneered as she then stormed past Taylor, bumping her out of the way as she went out the door.

Taylor steadied herself, and then heard the door of the office slam shut and she quickly looked back at it. Shock ran through her mind, along with fear. Now she was even more confused. She didn't know whether her relationship with Alex was worth all of the possible trouble. Especially considering how her own grandmother felt, not really happy with the relationship in the first place. For her friends to find out about her and a woman being in a relationship; her fear of being shunned was a little overwhelming for her. But when she looked at the desk and everything upon it, her heart filled with the love she felt for Alex, and she really wondered whether she could walk away from that. Salina had gone back to her desk and was now angrily flipping through some of the files she had taken out. Taylor turned and hit the automatic blind closure button and was left to react without prying eyes. She walked over to the desk and looked it over once again in awe. She then put the mail and her files down on it, reached out to touch the table tentatively. Once her hand had touched it, she glided both hands over it and sighed. Then she went around to the large leather chair and did the same thing, as she put her face against it. She slid into the chair and melted into it as if she were a baby in her mother's arms.

"Awww...wow." Taylor slipped her shoes off and curled her feet up in the chair. She leaned back easily. "Mmmm..." sighing again, as she closed her eyes and just let herself forget everything for that moment. She relaxed and drifted off in the chair.

"Well...what do we have here?" Came a soft voice right next to Taylor's ear, which brought her to consciousness once again.

"OH!! I'm sorry, I must have..."

"Fallen asleep?" Alex inserted, as she raised a brow at her and stood up straight.

"I'm sorry, it's just that I came back to organize some things I thought I would get done before it was too late." Taylor looked down at her watch and saw that she had only been asleep for 15 minutes. She let out a sigh of relief. Then she continued. "I got off the elevator and I saw Salina was upset about something. Next thing I know she's yelling at me, and making accusations and things."

Alex's brows furrowed and then she asked tightly.

"What sort of accusations?"

"She was saying that I must be sleeping with you for you to be doing all of the things you have done for me. Speaking of which, I love this!! Thank you!"

Alex smiled, glanced at her watch, and made an executive decision based on the time.

"You're welcome, and I wish Salina was right in her accusation, although progress is being made." She said, with a questioning brow.

"Ye...yes of course." Taylor stammered.

"Hmm...well I'm pleased you like the chair and desk." The woman said, noticing something in the girl's voice and behavior. She went to turn away and head over to her own desk, but Taylor's voice stopped her.

"I..." Taylor started, as she jumped to her feet and went to stand by the woman. Alex turned around and the girl gave a shy smile, then glanced at the windows of the office to make sure they still had privacy. She suddenly wrapped her arms around Alex's neck and in a low whispered voice she said. "I like them very much, but I love you. Thank you." She tilted her head upwards and the woman gazed at her for a moment, then said in a satiny voice.

"Just this one time." As she leaned down and kissed the young girl passionately.

When the kiss finally broke, Taylor leaned heavily against Alex to steady herself, which caused Alex to smirk. She hugged the girl to her and Taylor squeezed her back.

"Okay, we need to get back to work so we can go home...and we'll pick up where we left off." The woman implied.

Taylor leaned out of her embrace and they locked gazes for a few moments. Alex caressed her cheek, then turned and went to sit at her desk. Taylor moved her hair back out of her face and turned and walked pensively back to hers. She picked up half of the mail and handed it to the woman, then she went back over to her own desk and sat down. Alex hit the button to open the blinds and went back to work. Salina had stepped away from her desk before the woman had returned, and she was just returning when the blinds were opened.

CHAPTER 13

Taylor went through her share of the mail and after over two hours, she was finally able to get back to her own work. By then Alex had finished work for the day and was ready to head out.

"Okay, let's go."

"Um...well...I need to stay just for a while longer to get some things sorted out. But I'll be home as soon as I'm finished. I just want to get some of these things filed, organized, and entered in the computer so that I will be able to start right in on them come tomorrow, if that's alright with you?"

Alex studied her for a few moments and then nodded her head.

"Alright, then I'll make dinner and see you when you get home."

"Well..." Taylor started.

Alex turned back and sighed somewhat frustrated.

" What?"

"I don't want you to go to any trouble with dinner for me, I might be pretty late, and I would hate for the food to go to waste. Just make yourself something and I will pick up something on my way home if I get hungry." Taylor said somewhat in a rush.

Alex's eyes narrowed in suspicion as she once again gave a nod of her head.

"I'll wait up for you." She said, testing the girl.

"Um..." Taylor started, but when she saw the woman cock her head and raise a brow at her, she shook off her previous thought. "That's fine! I'll try not to be too late." She said, trying to be convincing that everything was alright.

"Alright, I'll see you later then." Alex turned and went to get her coat and purse. Just before she went out the door, she called back over her shoulder. "Remember what I said, don't let this interfere." She looked over her shoulder and leveled a knowing gaze on the girl.

Taylor chewed her lips, but nodded her understanding. The woman gave an approving nod of her own, then turned and went out the door, closing it behind her. Taylor sat back in her chair and let out the breath she was holding.

"Now what do I do?" She asked herself. After a bit, she let the thought slip to the back of her mind as she went to work on her project. One of the first things she did before getting bogged down with the paperwork was make a phone call to her friend's direct line. The phone rang for a few moments, and then a woman picked it up.

"Hello, Zadria?"

"Yes, oh, hi, how is it going?"

"Okay, how about you?"

"Oh, alright, just some interesting things happening."

"Like what?"

"Well...It's just that there are some other eyes looking at my company, ever since I went International and I may be in for a fight to keep it."

"Well, that's why I'm calling, maybe I can help you."

"How are you going to help me? You're an Admin Assistant."

"Well, actually, I'm now the Personal Assistant to the owner of the company."

"Really?? When did this happen?"

"Just a while ago. It's been so long since we've talked to each other. It's not right that we only see each other a few times a month. I understand with both our busy schedules, but you are one of my best friends, and I would like to help if I can?"

"That's why I love you, you're always there for me and your other friends. But your boss's company is one of those many eyes."

"I know, but if I can come up with a feasible plan to satisfy both of you, I think we can keep your company from being taken."

"I don't know, it's sort of a conflict of interest for you. I mean, I don't know if it's a good idea to mix business with friendships. This could get very ugly and I would hate to lose you over something like this."

"Don't worry, if you work with me, I'm sure we can come up with something."

"Okay, but only because I trust you and you are a dear friend. But you have to promise me you won't let our friendship get in the way of our business dealings. It would really complicate things. Deal?" Zadria asked.

"Deal."

"Great, how about if we meet for dinner and talk about this some more?"

"Okay, when?"

"Tonight, I'll meet you halfway, since you're on one side of town and I'm on the other."

"Okay, where?"

"Jasmine's?"

"Okay, I'll see you around 8:30 or 9:00."

"Okay, see you then. Bye."

"Bye Zadria, see you in a while."

The two hung up. Taylor looked at her watch and saw that it was 6:30p.m., so she immediately went to work on her files for the deal, reading them while she put them in her computer. She got most of them in before she saw that she had to get going to make it by 8:45p.m. Taylor met her friend and they greeted each other with a hug and then were shown to their table. The waitress came over and asked them for their drink orders. When she had left, the two talked about personal things for a bit, but then after a while, they dove into business. By the time they had finished with their dinner meeting, it was almost 1 in the morning. They walked out to their cars and talked for a few minutes more. They hugged each other, then got into their cars and left the restaurant. Taylor headed home to Alex's house. The closer she got, the more nervous she became. She realized how late it was and was worried because she remembered that Alex had said she would wait up for her.

Taylor parked her car and walked to the front door of the residence. She started to open the door, but thought about Alex and how upset she would possibly be at the lateness of the hour. Then another thought came to her. Maybe Alex would be asleep and possibly not hear her. She opened the lock, eased the door open and slipped inside, hoping that the woman was asleep.

Taylor knew she would be in for an earful for coming in so late when she was expected earlier.

The house was dark so she couldn't see much, but she knew where the stairs were by habit. She removed her high heeled shoes and headed for the stairs to go up to her bedroom. She made it to the stairs and looked up them, squinting her eyes to see if Alex was waiting at the top. She headed up, and was startled by the woman's voice from behind her.

"So...you finally made it home."

"OH!!! Goodness!! You startled me. I thought..."

"No. We'll talk tomorrow." Alex said, as she walked past Taylor on the stairs and went on to her own room to go to bed.

The girl stood on the stairs for a few minutes just watching her go, and remembering the look in her eyes as she looked at her. She looked around at the darkened foyer, feeling guilty. Taylor thought about going to Alex's room to apologize, but then she thought better of it. She was really not up to a scolding by Alex tonight, so she walked up the stairs slowly and went to her room. She changed into her nightclothes and climbed into bed. She thought about Alex in the room down the hall and how hurt she looked, behind those angry eyes. Eventually she drifted off.

Taylor woke up a few hours later, completely awake, and her mind immediately went to the confrontation that was in store for her when the woman woke up. She immediately decided she didn't want to be there. She went into her bathroom and cleaned up. Then she dressed and eased out the door. Putting her car in neutral, she backed it out and then once she was a little distance from the residence, she put it in drive and headed into the office. Taylor arrived at the office and went to get the mail. She then went up to the office and sorted 3/4's of it for herself and the other 1/4 for Alex to work on. She went to her desk and took out the rest of her files from the night before and began putting them in her computer. She finished it after about an hour and the sun was just starting to come up. Looking at her watch she saw that it was five thirty. She saved all of her information in the computer and picked up the files and her part of Alex's mail. She straightened her desk up and left. Taylor went to Marcus Shearer's office where she used his computer to pull up her information, and began dealing with the mail.

Alex arrived at the office in a foul mood, and everyone who saw her got and stayed out of her way. She got on the elevator and everyone who was waiting continued to wait. She arrived on her floor and stormed towards her office with the intent of laying into Taylor for sneaking off without telling her where she was and causing her to worry about her. When she went into the office and saw the lights were off, she began to wonder if the girl had come in to the office. Once again, her concern for Taylor came to the forefront. She walked into her office and finding it unlocked, her heartbeat slowed a bit. When she saw the mail in the holders, it slowed to its normal rate.

"Okay, now I know you're here and safe, all I have to do is wait." Alex sat down behind her desk and went to work on her mail. Salina arrived a few minutes later and was immediately put to work.

The two of them worked throughout the morning on different things. Alex held meetings with several people in different places throughout the morning. She had not seen or heard from Taylor, and now she was sure of what was happening; the girl was avoiding her.

"Well, you have good reason to, because I have an earful for you." She thought to herself when she realized that's what the girl was doing.

Alex would glance over at the empty desk from time to time when she was alone working, thinking about where the girl was. She looked at her watch and realized that no matter how much Taylor wanted to avoid her, she wouldn't be able to. She still had to bring the mail, which was due within the next few minutes. Sure enough, Taylor, after much hesitation, realized she had no choice but to take the mail to Alex, especially since there was a red envelope in the pile.

She stepped into the elevator and hit the express button. During the minute it took the elevator to get to the top, Taylor went through all sorts of fear.

"Okay, just take a few breaths, get a grip and go in. Take your chewing out, you deserve it, you were wrong all the way around. All she wants is to love you and you act like a confused schoolgirl. Man! This is going to be so hard to face her. But then again, Salina isn't making this any easier. I hope she's not there." Taylor said wistfully, at the end of scolding herself for her appalling behavior towards Alex.

The elevator came to a stop on the top floor, and when the doors opened, she stepped out and walked slowly towards the office. Salina saw her coming and she leveled a surly gaze on her. Taylor knitted her brows at the young woman, but went past her to the door of the office. After a few moments to calm down as much as she could, she opened the door and walked in. Alex looked up from her writing, and leaning back in her chair to watch her, saying nothing. Taylor's eyes were locked on the woman's and she was unable to break the contact due to Alex's sheer will.

"I...I..." Taylor tried to come up with something to say that would explain her behavior, but she could not, because there was no excuse. Alex simply cocked her head as she brought her fist to her chin and rested her elbow on the armrest of the chair and just waited.

"I have the mail. There's a red envelope with it."

Taylor finally managed, as she handed half of the mail to the woman along with the red piece. Alex didn't change her position except to hold up her other hand for Taylor to put the specific envelope in her hand. The girl walked up to the desk and with a shaking hand, placed it in her hand. Taylor then put the rest of the mail on the table and stepped back. Alex continued to command the girl's eyes for a long moment, then she broke it and casually looked down at the red envelope.

She leaned forward, picked up the letter opener and, with an efficient swipe of it, she pulled out the letter. She picked up the phone and hit the speed dial.

"I...I think I'll go..." Taylor suggested, before the woman started to speak to the person on the other end of the phone.

"You'll leave when I say you can leave." Alex stated sternly, as she glared at her. Taylor swallowed hard, but stood where she was and waited for the woman to handle the phone call.

After a few minutes she hung up the phone and went about dealing with her other mail, as if the girl was not standing there trembling. Taylor was waiting to be dismissed, reprimanded, yelled at, or whatever Alex felt like doing.

Alex kept her standing there for over an hour without speaking to her, only glaring at her from time to time. Finally, she spoke to the teary eyed girl.

"Get to work! There!" Alex ordered, as she pointed to the other desk.

Taylor moved to the desk quickly and eased into the chair. She looked back over at Alex, then lowered her eyes, distressed at the look she was receiving. The girl bought her hands to her head to give the appearance of moving her hair out of her face, but ended up turning her chair around and crying quietly. Alex listened to her as she went about dealing with the mail. Finally she tired of hearing the girl crying.

"Are you going to do any work today, or not?!" She inquired angrily.

Taylor sniffed a few times, then turned back around and not lifting her eyes up to look at the woman, she picked up an envelope, and diligently opened it as she chewed on her lips. Her brows showed her distress, but she finished all of her paperwork after a few hours. Her phone rang, and it was one of Zadria's Senior VPs wanting to talk to her about a few things. He wanted to meet her for a business dinner.

"What time?"

"7:30pm?"

"7:30, um...that...can you hold on for a moment?" Taylor said, and then put the man on hold as she picked up her planner to see if she had any other meetings for dinner.

"Who are you meeting with?" Alex asked, startling her with the harsh tone.

"I...just someone I'm dealing with on the Zadria deal."

"I thought we would talk this evening. We have a lot to discuss." She said, reminding the girl.

"I...I know, and you're right, but I know you will be very disappointed with me if I presented a sloppy report." Taylor tried to lighten the mood, but Alex only scowled more, as her eyes narrowed. "Okay, I won't go. I'll set it up for another day?" The girl said, submitting to the woman's indirect wishes.

She went to hit the hold button to tell the man her answer, but Alex stopped her.

"No. Go to your meeting. I'll see you when you get home."

"I won't be late."

"Make sure you're not. Otherwise, I'm going to be a royal bitch." Alex warned, and gave her a hard look.

"I won't." Taylor took the man off hold and told him she would meet with him.

She left the office a few times to go and meet, or talk with members of her team, but she always went back to the office where she organized her thoughts and papers. When 6:30 came, Alex stood up and stretched her long limbs.

"Well, I'm calling it an evening, I'll see you at home BEFORE 11."

"Yes Ma'am."

"Alright, have a nice dinner."

"I'll bring you something back if you like?."

"No, just bring yourself back before 11." Alex warned. She then picked up her things and headed out the door. Taylor watched her go, then picked up the phone to call her grandmother.

"Grammy."

"Yes child, what is it?"

"Nothing, I'm just a little confused. Well, actually, I'm even more confused about some things, and I'm scared."

"Scared, of what?"

"I..." Taylor went into the whole story of what was happening with her. She swore her grandmother to secrecy that she would not tell Alex anything about the conversation, or about Salina's threats to her.

Taylor's grandmother tried to talk her into telling the woman, but she was adamant that Alex not find out about it. She told her grandmother that she was handling it for the time being, but if things got too much for her, then she would tell Alex herself. The grandmother reluctantly agreed.

After the girl hung up the phone, she cleaned her desk up and then headed out the office to go and meet with the V.P from Zadria's company. She arrived at the meeting place and they talked for a while about what things Zadria was looking to keep, and what she was willing to compromise on. Taylor and Mr. Turrell's meeting looked as though it was going to go past the 11 o'clock time that Alex had asked her to arrive home by, so that they could talk.

The girl looked at her watch and the man asked her if she had to go. He was hoping not, due to having many other things to talk about.

"Um...excuse me for a moment Frederick, I need to go make a phone call, but I will be right back, just something I have to check on."

"Certainly, shall I order you something else to drink?"

"Hmm...yes tea please."

"Okay."

Taylor stood and left the table, going to one of the private rooms to make her phone call. She could either just use the phone itself, the speakerphone, or the video, and not have to worry about anyone interrupting. She locked the door, sat down on the sofa bench and dialed the number to the house.

"Hello." Came the smooth voice of Alex.

"Hello, Alex it's me."

"Are you on your way?" Alex asked, casually.

"Well...umm...That's what I'm calling about...it's seems like my meeting will be going longer than I thought. I didn't want you to worry or anything, I think I will be able to make it around 1 or at the latest two..." She paused for a moment due to Alex not having said anything so far. "Alex?"

"I'm here. Are you through?" She asked calmly.

"Ye...yes."

"Are you calling from a phone with a video?"

"Yes."

"Turn on the video phone." Alex said nonchalantly, as she put the phone she had in her hand down, and hit the video of her phone as well.

Taylor took a few deep breaths, then set the phone she had in her hand down on the stand and hit the video button.

When the picture came up she was sitting with her hands in her lap, nervously playing with her blouse. Alex was sitting in her study, in her large leather chair with her long legs crossed leaning back.

"Taylor, I told you we needed to talk. I don't appreciate being ignored or put off. I have absolutely NO tolerance for it!"

"Alex, I know we need to talk, and we will. It's just that..."

"Be quiet. I'm only going to say this once. Either you are here at 11 SHARP, or I will come there to talk to you."

"Alex?"

"Eleven! One minute after, and I will be on my way there." Alex then hit the button, and hung up the phone.

Taylor hit the button on her end, then just sat in the room just trying to compose herself enough to go back out to face the man who was waiting for her. She eventually did compose herself and headed back out to tell the man.

"Frederick, I'm sorry, I really have to leave."

"But?"

"I will call tomorrow to set up another meeting with you. There's something I have to do tonight, and I can't miss it, otherwise, there will be all kinds of problems."

"Well, if you can't miss it, then I guess I will have to wait."

"I apologize. If I could do anything about it, I would, but I can't. I'll call your office tomorrow." Taylor looked at her watch and saw that it was 10:15p.m. The house was around forty minutes away, if there was no traffic.

"Alright, well I'll talk to you tomorrow then." He said, standing to walk out with the girl.

"Oh, no, you stay and finish eating, I'll be alright." She picked up her purse and coat, and rapidly left the restaurant. She jumped in her car, drove out of the parking lot and was on her way to the house at 10:20pm. She watched the time tick away as she drove. She was lucky to be able to catch a lot of the lights. She checked her watch at the lights that caught her, and by the time she drove into the driveway, it was one minute to eleven. Taylor jumped out of the car, quickly walked to the door and put her key in to open it, but it was pulled open by the woman.

"You do like living dangerously. I think I told you that once before."

"Yes, you have." Taylor answered, as she walked inside.

Alex licked her lips as she watched the girl remove her coat and purse and place them in the visitor's closet. She closed the door and then, giving Taylor a final glance, turned and headed to the den. The girl followed after her and they both went to sit down. After a few minutes of uncomfortable silence, and the girl fidgeting with her clothing, Alex finally let her off the hook with the silent treatment.

"What's going on with you?"

"What do you mean?"

"Don't give me that, it's obvious that something is bothering you, and I want to know what it is."

"It's nothing, I just have a lot on my mind."

"Then tell me."

"It's nothing, really."

"Don't tell me it's nothing. I can see there is something. How do you expect for us to have any type of relationship with you holding back on me?"

"Please Alex, I really don't want to talk about this right now." Taylor said, putting her head in her hands and sighing with frustration, confusion, and guilt.

"So when do you want to talk about this?! I want to know what's going on with you. Are you having second thoughts about us? Did I do something? Did I not do something? What is it?! Did you meet a man you prefer to be with? What?!"

"Alex...it's nothing. I'm just tired. I just have to get used to the longer hours. I'll be fine." Taylor said as she glanced up at Alex, who was watching her.

"So that's it, huh? There's nothing going on? You're telling me that you've been acting like this because you're tired? Is that what you want me to believe?"

Taylor gave a slight shrug of her shoulders when she tried to answer, but found she couldn't actually bring herself to lie. Alex let her gaze look away for a moment as she thought about the girl and her behavior, and the lame excuse she had given her. Finally, she decided to just give Taylor the proverbial rope and see what she did with it. She would just watch her for the next week or so to see what happened. She wouldn't say anything, just watch.

"Fine, since you don't want to tell me what's going on, and you actually believe I am going to buy the "you're tired" excuse, then I will just not say anything else about it. I'm going to bed. Good night Taylor." Alex stood up and walked out of the den, leaving the girl to her thoughts, and her guilt about how she been behaving towards the woman.

"I'm sorry Alex." She whispered, after the woman left the room. She had seen the hurt in the woman's eyes despite her stoic behavior.

CHAPTER 14

Taylor stood up and headed for her bedroom. The next morning, she got up early and made breakfast for the woman, but she didn't eat herself, she just headed to the office. When Alex arrived downstairs, she found the breakfast, and a note from the girl. She warmed up the breakfast and took it to the table. She sat down with it and the note and flipping open the note she read it.

"Alex, I went in early to get some things done before I start in on the other project. I hope you enjoy the breakfast. I'll see you at work. I've already called for the driver. Taylor."

Alex laid the note on the table, then ate the breakfast the girl had prepared for her. She began the extending of the rope with that note from Taylor. She picked up her briefcase and headed out the door. When she arrived at the office she found Taylor gone, and the only clue that showed she had been there was the 1/4 of mail that was on the desk. She had noticed that the girl was doing more of the correspondence lately. Salina arrived an hour later, and they went about taking care of Alex's schedule and setting up meetings.

"Ma'am?"

"Yes Salina?"

"I was just noticing that I haven't seen much of Miss Young lately?"

"She's working on something."

"Oh? You mind if I ask what?"

She looked up from one of the reports she was reading over and then said evenly.

"She's working on a presentation about the Zadria take over project.

"Oh, she's going to give a presentation?"

"Yes. Now I would like to get back to work. How are the plans coming along for the business party?"

"Very well Ma'am. She had many of the things already done, but there were still some things that needed to be worked out with the planner. I think you will be pleased with the way it goes. Will

Ms. Young still be attending it with you as your Personal Assistant?"

Alex gave a thoughtful gaze at the report she was looking at, without showing it to the nosy Admin, then she answered casually.

"Yes." Then she went back to reading, made a few phone calls, and held conference calls with some of the executives from her foreign companies.

Meanwhile, Taylor had left the building to meet with Zadria. Over the next three weeks, she spent little time at the house, and more time at the office. Only going to Alex's office when she had to bring the mail. Alex was beyond irritation with the girl's evasive and avoiding behavior towards her. Finally, the day came for Taylor to present her proposal. Mr. Shearer and the other members from her team were all there, as there were a few proposals from other executives that were also going to be presented doing the meeting.

"Alright people, I expect concise, detailed and near perfect presentations. Johnson you're up, go." Alex ordered.

Johnson gave his proposal, then waited for the woman to tell him whether she liked it or not.

"Good, make sure you keep me updated on the progress."

"Yes Ma'am." He said, as he beamed and took his seat, relieved to be out of Alex's spotlight.

"Carlson, go." She called everyone who had a presentation to give, and finally Taylor was the last one. So far everyone had received her approval.

"Ms. Young, Go." She ordered indifferently.

"Yes Ma'am."

Taylor stood and went to the end of the table where the others had presented their proposals. She and her team quickly setup. After a nervous glance around the large conference room, then at the woman who had a very impatient look leveled on her, the girl became even more nervous. She started her presentation using a videodisc graphics as her visual.

"Th...The Zadria Company is one of the fastest up and coming fashion houses in this country. Now it's making a name internationally, and its stocks have continued to grow. The increase from just the last few months to this point today, as you can see has continued to climb steadily without any fluctuating losses and gains from then to now..."

"I thought you were supposed to be presenting me with an alternative to a takeover. It seems to me that you're only making a case for me to take it over." Alex stated, without any tenderness or compassion in her voice.

Taylor felt and heard the anger, and lowered her eyes for a moment as she recollected her thoughts and tried to steady her nerves against Alex's steady, piercing gaze. She turned away for a moment due to the tension and guilt of everything she had done. Her eyes started to cloud, but she continued to try and maintain her composure so she could continue.

Marcus Shearer stood up and walked down to where the girl was standing, now trembling slightly from the stress.

"Taylor, are you okay?"

"Ye...yes."

"Would you like for me to continue for you?"

Taylor looked up at the man with appreciation in her eyes. He smiled, and gave a squeeze to her shoulder, then turned around to face everyone, along with the girl.

"Ma'am, if it is alright with you, I would like to take over the presentation?"

"No. Now sit down Mr. Shearer."

"But..." The man started, but seeing the woman's glare, he went quiet and then looked back at the girl.

Taylor looked at Alex who was now glaring at her, and resigned herself to the fact that she would have to finish the presentation. She looked at Salina who had just walked in the meeting and went to whisper something to Alex, and was told to take a seat. Salina pulled it up next to where the woman sat, and Taylor looked at the smug look the Admin had on her face. She decided she was going to make the presentation.

"Mr. Shearer, thank you, I think I can go on now." She said, letting her friend off the hook with the woman. "Ma'am, if I may continue?"

"Do it."

"Thank you. Now, I realize that so far, my presentation does appear to be reasons to take the company over, but as you will see, while these are definite pro's for the takeover, I will also show the contradictions for such actions. Over the last few weeks, my team and I have been meeting with members from the Zadria Company. I, myself, have been meeting with Zadria herself. During these meetings and after much research between all of us, I believe I have come up with a plausible and feasible plan for a compromise to the actual takeover. I mentioned earlier that some of the pros were the increase in stock prices, as well as the continuous and steady growth. I will also add that another pro is the fact that you would own the company outright, and could do whatever you wanted, including the elimination of the employees you chose, but...there are drawbacks to a complete takeover also. I'm sure you are aware of them, but just for the record, I will point them out anyway. One...while you make money as long as the company makes money, you also will lose money when the company loses. Along with that, you will not only lose money with that one company, but also with all of your others, due to the connection between all of your holdings. Two...you will have to reassign members from some of your other companies to go in and learn the fashion business, whereas if you allow the company to remain under the control of Zadria, then you not only will NOT have to be responsible for keeping track of all of the nuances of the company, but you also will still be able to reap the benefits of a profitable company. Basically, what I'm saying is, I have gotten Ms. Zadria to agree to a split."

"Meaning?"

"Meaning a fifty one to forty nine split, with Zadria holding the controlling interest."

"Why would I be interested in such a thing?"

"Because it would allow you to have some say in how things are run, while she keeps the staff that has made the company such a prize in the first place. Therefore ensuring the continuation of that success. You also don't have to worry about the day to day operations of the company, as well as the headaches of benefits and all of those things. Another reason is, you will have the company that all of the other companies want, under your umbrella of protection. No one would dare try to take a company that you are involved with. I see a win, win situation all the way around. Ms. Zadria is able to keep her company and continue to run it as she sees fit in order to keep it profitable for both you and her. You win because you will have the company, and will be a silent partner for the most part. She has agreed that if you see some changes that need to be made if the company starts to lose money, then she will be more than happy to accept your suggestions." Taylor lowered her arms and waited for the woman to say something.

All eyes went to Alex after the girl had finished, and although they thought it was a very solid presentation, they didn't say anything. Instead they waited for the woman to say something. Alex leveled her gaze on Taylor, who was shifting nervously from foot to foot, as her anxiety level increased with every silent moment that passed. Finally the girl couldn't wait any longer and had to ask.

"Well...?"

"Well, I'll let you know. I need to think about it." She said sarcastically.

"Think about it? What's to think about?"

Alex's eyes narrowed at the girl's questioning of her, and Taylor went silent as her arms came to cross in front of her and she rocked on her heels. She tried to avoid looking at the angry gaze of the woman.

"Alright." She conceded as she spared a glance at Alex, who had not taken her eyes off of her.

"Of course it is." Alex stood, and looking along the lines of men and women she called an end to the meeting. "Ladies, Gentlemen, this meeting is over." She turned and headed out of the room with Salina following right behind her.

After the woman was gone, the men and women all turned to Taylor and told her that they thought her presentation was excellent, and that it was a good plan. After they all left, Shearer walked up to his friend who had a look of defeat on her face as her eyes were starting to tear up.

"Taylor you did a wonderful job, you are a natural at this. Alex would be a fool not to implement your plans."

"She didn't like them."

"That's not so! She didn't say she didn't like them, and you can't assume that. You just have to have faith that your proposal was worthy, and stick to your guns about it."

"Thank you. I appreciate that." Taylor hugged her friend. Then after gathering her things, she headed to go and get the mail.

She arrived in the office 30 minutes later and found Salina laughing and talking up a breeze with someone on the phone. The Admin saw her coming, but she continued her conversation.

"I know it's great! I'm going to be attending the party with Ms. Madison instead of her Personal Assistant!" The Admin exclaimed, as she eyed the girl's reaction.

Taylor's eyes went wide with the news, and she looked at Salina with both a confused, and a disbelieving gaze. She walked rapidly past the Admin's desk and into the office, closing the door behind her. Alex was on the phone and the girl stood waiting for her to get off. The woman gazed up at Taylor, and knitting her brows, she studied the girl while she talked on the phone. Finally she hung up.

"What is it? I have a lot to do."

"Why is Salina attending your business party with you and not me? I thought I was to be there with you?"

"You've been so busy, I needed to make sure I had an assistant with me." Alex said matter-of-factly.

"But I was going to be there. I thought that's how we planned it. After I finished with the Zadria project I was to attend it with you."

"Well, things had to change. It's too close, and you have not even had time to look over the guest list and learn about the guests. Salina has not only learned about them, she has made sure that the caterer has at least one of each of their favorite foods or drinks. Her research on each of them has been thorough, to say the least, and she has gone with me to meet some of those same people. You have been so tied up with The Zadria deal that you let everything else fall on the backburner. I will not allow anyone who is unprepared attend such an important engagement as this with me."

Taylor had tears in her eyes, but she kept her voice from shaking despite what she was feeling.

"So have you made HER your Personal Assistant?"

Alex gave the girl an indifferent gaze, and then said impassively.

"Yes, she has been doing the job very well."

"So what, you're going to demote me back to just the mailroom?" Taylor asked, holding up the mail and then placing all of it on the woman's desk.

"No, you don't deserve to be demoted. You will go to work with Mr. Shearer as his new Admin Assistant."

The tears now rolled down her cheeks.

"What? I thought you and he were good friends?" Alex asked, somewhat put off by the girl's reaction.

"You're just being mean." Taylor accused.

"Mean?! What are you talking about?!"

"You know what I'm talking about, you're just mad at me! I know I've been horrible, but I didn't do anything to be mean. But fine, I'll go to work with Mr. Shearer. All I want to know is, what, if anything, have you decided about my ideas for the Zadria Company?"

"I haven't." Alex said flatly.

"Do you hate me Alex?" The girl asked quietly.

"No." Alex answered simply.

Taylor lowered her eyes in relief, and then she raised them to find the woman watching her.

"Will you let me know when you have?"

"We'll see."

Taylor felt the anger the woman had towards her, so all she could do was just raise her hand in resignation to her fate within the company and with the woman.

"Fine, fine." She turned and walked out the office shaking her head. She closed the door behind her and to her chagrin Salina was there to rub her face in it.

"So...how does it feel to be stepped over, after everything you've done? Did you really think you could just walk over me and I wouldn't do anything about it? Well, now you know not to mess with me. Oh, and I'm glad you took my advice about staying away from her, it really made a difference." The Admin grinned, then turned and walked away from the girl to go and refill her coffee cup.

Taylor looked hurt by Salina's taunts, and not because it was Salina, but because some of what she said was true. She had allowed things to turn out the way they did because of her fear of Salina going public about her relationship with the woman. Despite the fact that she knew Salina had no proof, appearances would have made people draw the conclusion that was put out there.

Alex watched the interaction between the two, and then saw how Taylor once again shook her head and walked out of the office. The girl's stress grew by leaps and bounds over the next week. Alex wouldn't even speak to her at home, which was hard enough, but it became too much for the girl when it started at work.

CHAPTER 15

Taylor saw her heading out of the building with some men and women, and Salina, as she happened to be coming in. And seeing how she had not heard anything about Alex's decision on the Zadria deal, she decided to try to ask her in the setting of business.

"Excuse me Ms. Madison, may I speak to you for a moment?"

"I don't have time right now, I have to go, maybe later." Alex said.

She had not missed a stride, and only spared a glance at Taylor initially, then she refocused her attention on those with her. She went back to talking with them and calling out things to Salina. Salina grinned evilly as she took the notes and they all left Taylor standing in the middle of the lobby.

Over the next few days, no matter where or when the girl tried to talk to Alex, she was either put off by the woman herself, or blocked by Salina. Taylor went to get the mail for the woman as she had not been told anything differently. She thought getting the mail would give her the opportunity to talk to the woman, but she was surprised. She retrieved the mail from the mail center and went to take it to Alex. When she stepped off of the elevator and went into the outer office, Salina at first tried to stop her, but Taylor told her that she had not been told anything differently. And she had not been picking it up for the last week or so because she had to orient to her position with Shearer.

She was allowed to take the mail in to the woman to the new Personal Assistant's dismay, because she didn't want Alex to turn her anger on her, so she let the girl deliver the mail. She had a plan to eliminate any further needs of the girl. Taylor knocked on the door and saw the woman was on the phone with her back to the door. She heard Alex call to come in, so she stepped in and closed the door behind her. The girl stepped up to the desk and waited for the woman to turn around and get off of the phone. Alex heard the person come in and she could see in the reflection of the window that it was Taylor and she was just standing waiting for her. She turned while still talking on the phone.

"What is it?"

"I have the mail."

Alex put her hand out for it and the girl went to give her half of it.

"No, all of it."

"But...yes Ma'am." Taylor said, as she handed the rest of it to the woman, and then was ready to continue to wait for the woman.

"Leave." Alex said simply, as she gave the girl a certain gaze, then turned her chair to go back to talking to the person on the phone.

Taylor sighed, and after a moment more of just looking at the back of the woman's chair, she turned and left the office. Finally one morning, Taylor couldn't take it any longer and she decided enough was enough. She was going to tell Alex that morning at the house what she had decided to do, but the woman had already gone to the office. So after Taylor dressed, she got in her car and drove to the office with only one thing on her mind...to talk to Alex. She went to get the mail and discovered that Salina had already picked it up.

"Salina?" She asked Mr. Olsen.

"Yes Ma'am, I was also told that you were not to pick up the mail anymore, and that the Personal Assistant would be responsible for it. I'm sorry."

Taylor was hurt beyond words. Alex had now successfully eliminated any excuse for contact with her. She felt completely shunned by the woman.

"Fine!" She shouted to no one in particular, although Mr. Olsen was still standing near her. She turned and headed out of the mail center with the intention of taking lunch, but once she stepped into the elevator, rather than hitting the button for the first floor, she hit the express to go up to the top floor. When she arrived at the top she walked out and went inside the outer office where Salina confronted her.

"What are you doing here? You don't have an appointment!"

"Is someone in there with her?"

"No, but that's not the point."

"Yes it is!" Taylor said, stepping around the new Personal Assistant.

"Wait a minute! You can't go in there!" Salina said, as she went to stop the girl from opening the door, but Taylor simply opened it and walked in and left the door open for Salina to follow.

"What are you doing?!" Alex asked angrily at Taylor's intrusion.

"I came to talk to you, and since you seem to have eliminated all avenues to you, this was the only way I could think of. And since this is about business, then I didn't see any conflict."

"What is it?!" The woman asked impatiently.

"Well I'll get right to the point, since you're so impatient. I've decided since you either don't want to, or had no intentions to come and tell me what your decision is in regards to my proposal on the Zadria deal, I will let you off the hook about it. You can do whatever you want to do with it. I don't care. It is not important to me anymore. The only thing that is important to me is how you have been so... mean to me. I can't keep on like this and I refuse to continue in this painful situation. I was going to talk to you outside of your Personal Assistant's hearing, but then I thought WHY? She would love what I have to say. I quit!" Taylor then turned to leave the office, but was stopped by the woman's voice.

"You can't quit. You signed a binding contract." Alex sneered.

"Sue me! I can't continue like this, and I won't. If it will make you feel better though, I will tell you I have NO intentions of going to work for any other company. I'm going back home to live with my grandmother and help her with things.

"What about school?"

"What about it? I don't plan on working in this field anymore. What reason is there? For all I care, the world of business no longer exists for me. Salina, you got your wish! You've made it. You're on your way to everything you ever wanted, and I laid it in your lap. I was the fool. Oh well, it's all water under the bridge now." Taylor said, with contempt in her voice at the assistant, and disbelief at the drastic change between herself and the woman she loved. She turned her attention back to Alex. "Thank you for all of your help, in everything. I still think you're a great woman, and I know everything that has happened is my fault. If you don't believe anything else, I want you to know...what I did, I never did with the purpose of being mean. There were, and are, many reasons for my actions. Anyway, it was wonderful to have worked with you." Taylor's eyes held Alex's gaze for a moment, and then she turned, and with a derisive glance at Salina, she walked out the door. Her head up, but tears rolling down her face.

She went and stood to wait for the elevator, and once it came, she stepped on, but did not turn around. She kept her back to the door. The doors closed, and Taylor vanished from the woman's sight. Alex, in the meantime brought her hands to her head and ran them through her thick tresses as she contemplated the girl's words.

"I'm terribly sorry Ma'am about her intrusion, she got past me."

"It's fine, leave me and close the door, I have to make some calls."

"Yes Ma'am." Salina turned and left the office, closing the door and leaving the woman to make her calls.

Alex picked up the phone and hit the speed dial, then turned her chair so she was looking out over the skyline of the city. It was the beginning of fall, and the colors of it were everywhere.

"Kiara I want you to keep an eye on Taylor until I tell you differently."

"Where can I find her?"

"You'll find her at my place. Wherever she goes, I expect for either you or one of your detectives to be there also. Is that clear Kiara?"

"Yes Ma'am, very."

"Good, I want reports about where she is and what's going on with her."

"Alright, I'll get right on it. Would you like hourly or daily, or..."

"Monthly."

"Oh, alright. I'll be in touch."

"Oh, and send them attention to me only."

"Alright I'll be in touch."

"Fine." Alex hung up the phone and sat back in her chair, she thought about how hurt and disappointed she was by what had happened to her and Taylor. She was mostly angry at how the girl had lied to her.

Taylor had gone home and packed up a few clothes and things. She left all of her designer clothes, and she left the key to the house in Alex's bedroom. She then left the house and jumping in her car, she headed to her grandmother's place. It would take her 3 days to get there by car. She didn't even say goodbye to her friends Yasmeia and Marcus, but she did feel as though she at least owed a call to Zadria to tell her the change in things. It was a hard call for her, and she was emotional about it, but Zadria understood and put business on the backburner to show her concern for her friend.

After Taylor hung up the speakerphone in her car, she thought throughout the day as she drove. She drove all day, not stopping until she was ready to stop for the night. She pulled into a hotel, went inside and after getting a room and going to it, she ordered room service. By the time she changed into her nightclothes, her food arrived. Taylor sat down on the bed, turned on the t.v., and ate while she watched the news of the day.

While she was watching, there was a little blurb that came on about "The Raider" and her annual spring party. Alex called it a business party, but the news called it the party for "Who's Who in the Business World". There were going to be senators and The Attorney General, as well as other political people attending. But the surprise to the story was that the President of the United States and her husband were mentioned as possible attendees. It was not a secret that the President was a big fan of "The Raider". She credited a lot of the success she had had in her own life as a result of reading and having attended a speaking engagement a few years back where Alex was the guest speaker. She spoke on how focused and determined she was to do what she wanted and how it didn't matter whether anyone liked her, as long as they respected her work. The President remembered how young the woman was at that time, and how that speech changed her own direction, because it was as a result of that speech that she began her preparations to run for the presidency. The President had never told that to anyone until 2 years into her successful presidency. It was on a one on one with an award winning newswoman, in which the president was asked how she had come to decide to run for office. It was mentioned that she evaded the question when she was running for it, and she continued to avoid the question after her first busy year. The President had finally decided to tell how it came about and it was a large story, despite all of the other things that were happening in and around the country. For some reason, the media found it intriguing that the president would be giving credit for her success to a businesswoman.

After the story about the woman's party that was almost 5 months away, Taylor turned off the t.v., more depressed than she already was. The next morning, she got an early start on her drive to her grandmother's house and she arrived within the three days. She was greeted by her grandmother with both happiness and surprise.

"What are you doing here child? Why didn't you call me and tell me you were coming, and where is Ms. Madison?"

"I'm here to stay. I needed to get away for a while, and she's probably at work."

"Wait child, what happened? I thought the two of you were getting close?"

"Grammy, I really don't want to talk about it. I'm tired from the drive and I just want to go to my room and go to sleep for a while."

"Alright child, but I'd like to know what happened that brought you back here."

"Maybe later Grammy."

"Alright child. You go on up and climb into bed. I will see you in the morning."

"Thanks Grammy." Taylor hugged her grandmother and then turned and headed for the stairs to go to her old room.

Over the next few months she cried on her grandmother's shoulder, but eventually told the woman the whole story behind why she had left Alex and given up her career in business. The grandmother was sympathetic to her pain, but in a way she was relieved that things didn't work out. She heard the tremendous pain in Taylor's voice and felt anger towards the Personal Assistant who basically blackmailed the girl into pulling away from Alex. Salina had no way of knowing that the girl was already feeling extremely conflicted by the relationship as it was. Taylor loved Alex, but she didn't realize just how much. She also didn't believe herself to be strong enough to handle such a relationship, and she didn't want her grandmother to be disappointed with her choice. So Salina caught her at the right time in her life to be able to push her out of Alex's.

As time went by Taylor took a job in town at her grandmother's urging working in one of her grandmother's friend's gift shop as a cashier. Just to give her something to do. Her mind was never far off from thinking about the woman, whether directly or indirectly. Those times when she wasn't thinking about Alex, something would come up about her. There would be articles in the paper about what she was up to and her grandmother would make sure to bring up subjects about the stock market and how her investments were doing. Sometimes she would read about the companies that were being taken over by Alex and how the stock prices would soar after she had acquired the company. Taylor would tell her grandmother she didn't want to hear about it, and the woman would tell her that she was being selfish, and that at the least, the girl should be happy that the woman was still succeeding in her life. Of course then Taylor would quickly tell her grandmother she was happy that Alex's life was going well. It just hurt to see it going so well without her. Then she would always find an excuse to leave for a while. There were some men who stopped by to visit with her grandmother and they would tell her about something on Alex that they had heard about or saw on some show or news event.

Taylor noticed that in most of the conversations, or news reports, Salina was mentioned as the Personal Assistant. She couldn't seem to get away from either woman, despite the distance.

"Salina bring the Yost file and your planner."

"Yes Ma'am. Here you go, and would you like me to go over your schedule?"

Alex gave her a look of irritation and then answered tightly.

"Why do you think I told you to bring it? Now go!"

Salina was embarrassed by the biting question and she nervously activated her digital calendar and began going through it with the woman. The relationship between The Raider and Salina had changed slightly in the fact that Alex no longer let her mistrust of Salina hinder either one of them getting their work done.

Over the next few months, Alex was involved in attending speaking engagements, parties and other such business things and the name D'Angelo was now a constant connection with The Raider.

One morning after Alex had held her weekly meeting with the senior executives of the company, she found Ms. Yasmeia Sains waiting to speak with her.

"Ms. Madison, may I speak to you a moment please?"

"Can it wait?"

"It can, maybe you will join me for lunch later and we could talk then?"

Alex looked at her for a moment, and then asked, "Is this about work or is it personal?"

"Both." Yasmeia answered promptly.

She studied Yasmeia for long moments, and then gave a slight nod of her head.

"Two o'clock in my private dining room." Alex turned and walked away.

When two came around, Yasmeia met her at the restaurant and the two of them went through the main dining area and into the private one. After they placed their orders, the women turned to business matters.

"Okay Yasmeia, what is this about?"

"I was talking to Mr. Shearer the other day, and I asked him how things were going with the Zadria deal. He said he thought it was dead."

"Actually, I have not thought about it over the last few months. I would think there are other companies positioned to take it by now."

"So you're just going to let it be taken by some other company?"

"Why not?"

"Ms. Madison, I have known you for a while, and I've been with this company for many years. Not once in all that time have I known you to just let such a jewel pass by you without going after it. So far you've had a near perfect record, and the few you let go were by your choice, so I don't understand, why the change?"

"Maybe it's not for you to understand." Alex said flatly, as she gave the woman a sidelong glance.

"Alex..." Yasmeia said, addressing the woman informally. Which caused the woman to cock her head at her. "Why aren't you going after it?"

"Because it holds no interest for me."

"But it used to. You even made Taylor go through a whole presentation about it so as to talk you out of taking the company outright."

"Is that what this is about? Ms. Young?"

"Ms. Young? You make it sound as if she were just some employee or something, as if you have or had no feelings for her outside those of professional."

"Ms. Sains, I have NO intentions of getting into a conversation with you or anyone else about Ms. Young. If that's what this was all about, then I will end it right now." Alex stated, as she stood to leave.

"So you're telling me that you're just going to let something that that child worked on for months be erased because she quit? I think you're wrong, and I know Taylor will be hurt to know that you've just dismissed her as if she never existed. I had my suspicions about the two of you, and your relationship being more than just employee and employer. I saw how you looked at her during that mess with the rape. And I saw how she looked to you for her strength and support. I saw the love in both of your eyes for each other. I'll admit, at first, I thought you were just using her for your own purposes, but I saw how she went into your arms after that first day of the trial. It was as if she saw and felt security in those arms, love, but...if you want to just discount her from your mind, then Ms. Madison, it is definitely your choice. I guess with months gone past, you were able to forget about her. Well, I guess if one is capable of doing that, then she should; it would hurt less. Ms. Madison, you don't have to leave, I will! Have a nice lunch." Yasmeia then stood and left the dining room.

Alex stood looking after the woman, and then with an irritated sneer, she half sat on the corner of the table with her arms crossed over her chest. Her mind now sent into actively thinking about Taylor.

"Thanks Yasmeia!" She called angrily, as she stood and stormed out of the restaurant.

CHAPTER 16

As the Christmas season approached, Alex had pulled out the Zadria file quite a few times, but she never did anything about it. She would look at it, and read over Taylor's ideas and think about the day she gave the presentation. Alex made a few phone calls to gauge how things were going, and whether or not any other company had made a move to take it over. Other than those types of checks, she did not pay much attention to it. It hurt too much to think about Taylor and the file reminded Alex of her. Two months before Christmas, the building was buzzing with all the talk of the annual Christmas party. In the midst of it all, Alex was not paying the holiday time any attention. Salina was nagging her about recommending her for the Young Executives Program and it was getting on her nerves.

"Ma'am, I was just wondering if you have thought about the program?"

"Salina, sit down and let me tell you something right now before I end up getting really pissed off with you. I don't like being nagged about ANYTHING!! When I am ready to make a decision about this, I will let you know. Is that clear?"

"Yes Ma'am."

"Good. Now get to work on that report."

"Yes Ma'am." Salina went out to her desk where she served as both Admin and PA to the woman. She was upset with Alex, but didn't want to show it just in case the woman would withhold other things from her.

Meanwhile, down in the lobby, Mr. Wellington came into the building and headed straight for the elevator. He hit the button to the top floor, but didn't hit the express button because he wanted to make sure he had what he wanted to say to Alex straight in his head. When the elevator stopped on the top floor, he stormed out of it and into the outer office.

"Mr. Wellington? May I help you?" Salina asked, as she came to her feet to speak to the angry looking man.

"NO! I want to talk to Her!"

"But sir she's in a meeting."

"Well now she'll be in another!" He stormed past the young woman and swung the door open to Alex's office. This caused the two men in the office to startle, and the woman to stop what she was saying in mid-sentence

"Charles? What can I do for you?" Alex asked calmly, as she gave an annoyed look at her PA.

"You can stop trying to take over my company for a start! I know you are behind the recent threats to shareholders, and I know you are buying up the stock, but I will stop you. You aren't going to get your claws on my company,"

"Charles, can we talk about this later?"

"NO! I won't let you just walk in and take my company! I worked damn hard to build it up, only to have a vulture like you swoop down to see if there's a dead carcass to ravage yet! Well I'm here to tell you, ME and MY Company are very much alive and I will do whatever I have to, to stop you!" The man then turned and stormed out of the office. He took the stairs to leave, rather than riding the elevator.

Alex watched the man go, and with anger in her own voice she turned to the men who still sat in her office, and hissed at them. " Get out! We'll continue this later, right now I need to talk to my PA."

"Yes Ma'am!!" Both men said as they came to their feet and exited the office. Leaving Salina standing in the doorway looking after the rapidly disappearing men.

"GET IN HERE!" The woman ordered.

Salina's head immediately jerked around to look back at her. Then swallowing hard, she stepped into the office and closed the door. The next few minutes were the hardest of Salina's life. By the time the woman allowed the young PA to leave her office, Salina was nearly hysterical. Alex had told her that she was completely dissatisfied with her handling of the man, as well as not calling security in a timely manner. Furthermore, she would not be recommending her anytime soon to the Executive's Program. Salina ran out of the office and down the hall to the bathroom where she cried bitterly.

Meanwhile, Alex stood up and pulled the file on Wellington's company. She looked through it for a moment and then decided to go and talk with the executive who had been handling the deal.

Salina, in the interim, had composed herself somewhat. She thought of what she could do to get back at Alex, and then remembered the man.

"Okay, I'll make my own fortune without your help." She ran out of the bathroom and down the stairs to see if she could catch the man.

"Mr. Wellington? Mr. Wellington, I need to talk to you!" Salina called when she saw the man still in the stairwell.

"Who are you? Oh, it's you! What do you want?!" He asked harshly.

"I want to know if you wanted to get her back?"

"What are you talking about?!"

"Well, I figure that you're having a problem holding on to your company because of money right?"

"What about it?"

"Well...how would you like to make the money you need to fight her, with her help?"

What are you talking about?"

"Information."

"Are you suggesting insider trading type information?" The man now whispered, both in concern as well as intrigue.

"Well I guess that would be the technical term, but I would rather look at it as helping a friend? What do you say? Friend."

"I say you're crazy! You know, if we're caught we could be sent to jail for years? Plus, I would truly lose my company then. No one will want to invest in a company where the CEO has been convicted of insider trading."

"But we won't be caught. We can meet outside of here, somewhere private if you like?"

"At first yes, but if we're going to make any money on this, then we will have to find a way to let it leak out so others will buy the stock AFTER we've bought as much as we can. Then we'll sell our shares and make a killing! I like it. But where will you get the information? And it has to be a company that is about to be taken over, or one that "The Raider" has some interest in. In every company she takes over, the investors make millions."

"Okay, I'll be in touch in a few days with something. I have an idea what company, but I'll let you know."

"Well, this has turned out to be a very...interesting day MS...?"

"Salina Lacy, I'll be in touch."

"Talk to you soon, I hope, Ms. Lacy. I'd better get going."

"Alright, bye." Salina turned and headed back up the stairwell, while the man went down.

The plan would have been near perfect if not for one problem, the two conspirators didn't count on someone overhearing their conversation. When they split up, the listener stepped out of the stairwell on the floor one flight down and caught the elevator up to the top to go and talk to Alex. When the woman made it to the top, Alex was still gone. She heard the PA coming into the outer office, so rather than risk questions as to why she was in the woman's office without an appointment, the person stepped into a cramped storage closet. She figured the girl had no reason to check it. Salina came into the office and called for Alex a few times. After a few moments of not getting an answer, she decided to look for the file she had in mind, as well as the one on Mr. Wellington's company. She thought about pulling it up in the computer, but she knew Alex would have a code on those particular files. So she looked for it in the drawers and cabinets.

"Okay, where did she put that Zadria file?" She looked in the desk parts that were unlocked, then moved on to the file cabinet. Finally, she found what she was looking for, and opened it, scanned over it to make sure it was still active, then ran out of the woman's office. She immediately copied the file and put it back in the cabinet. Then she looked for the Wellington file, and, as luck would have it, she found it on the desk that she had just been searching inside of. Salina chuckled to herself as she scanned through it for a moment. She saw a smaller folder within it that said "Confidential" on it. When she opened it and saw that it was a list of anonymous shareholders, she grinned to herself, and once again took the file, copied it, and then put it back where she had found it.

"Well Mr. Wellington, it looks like we're going to get rich off of the back of both Alex and her ex-bedwarmer, it couldn't be more perfect. And now I have the information about what Alex had going on with your company." The conspirator purred to herself, then went out of the office and took the elevator down.

The listener came out of the storage closet and easing around to look out the door to make sure the young woman was gone, then headed for the desk. She went and made copies of the same file, and then pulled the Zadria file out of the same cabinet that Salina had gotten it out of and made a copy of it as well. She put everything back in its place and headed for the elevator. Just as one came up, she moved to take it down, but Alex stepped off.

"OH, Ms. Madison, I'm glad I caught you, I need to talk to you."

"NO! I've had enough of your talking Ms. Sains."

"Ms. Madison, I know I over stepped boundaries earlier, but this is very important."

"I said NO, Ms. Sains. Now I have a lot to do, and I'm sure you do as well." Alex said, as she walked away from Yasmeia.

Alex went into her office and once she was inside, cursed at the fact that once again Yasmeia had reminded her of Taylor despite having said nothing about her. The woman went to sit in her chair and after a few minutes she picked up the phone to make a phone call. After she hung up, she turned her chair back around and logged onto her computer to pull up the Zadria file. She had it on disc, paper file, and in her personal file cabinet. Over the next week Alex began thinking more and more about the Zadria deal. She picked up the phone and called her friend D'Angelo. He ended up inviting himself to her home once again since he was planning on visiting the states again for more business and pleasure. He would arrive in the middle of next month.

Meanwhile, Salina called Mr. Wellington and they met at the EnCarte restaurant at 7p.m.

"Mr. Wellington, I'm glad you could make it, I think we are going to get very rich, and you will be able to keep your company in the process."

"So what do you have?" The man asked, nervous but excited.

"I have a confidential list of anonymous shareholders in your company. These people each own a minimum of 10,000 shares. I'm sure we could persuade them to sell to us, by offering them more than the market price. We have to acquire 51% of the stock in order for you to be able to keep your company, right?"

"Yes, but that won't be a problem. I already own quite a lot myself, and with this list we'll be able to buy up what we need. Since these are all major stockholders, we can get a lot more shares fairly quickly. When we get close to 51%, we'll put out a "buy" order on the open market. We will get some people who will sell, but it will also cause people to start looking at the stock. When they see we are offering above market price, they will think something is about to happen, and they will buy also. This is what will cause the price and value to go up. That will make Alex's takeover plans null and void because it will be too expensive to pursue. There won't be any profit in it for her. Once we get the 51% we need, I will buy you out and I'll own my company free and clear."

"Okay, that sounds great! But I have more news, there's a company that Alex is looking at taking over as well, called the Zadria Company."

"Aha...Yes, I've heard of that company, I actually had thought about that myself, until I discovered Alex breathing down my neck. So what do you want to do about it? Save it?"

"NO! The way this deal was supposed to go down was The Madison companies were supposed to become an umbrella for the Zadria Company. That would keep other companies from trying to take it over, and at the same time Alex's company still makes money as a silent partner."

"Okay....so where do we fit into this?"

"We redraw up the plans tonight, and at first light we have the papers sent to the Zadria Company. At the same time we buy stock in that company and once we have what we want, we leak it to the news that the takeover will happen, and you know the Media..."

"Yes, they'll take it and run like wildfire with the story we want, which will be that "The Raider" has decided to take over that company."

"Right, and as a result, the stock prices rise more, and then we sell, take our money and run with it."

"Right, but you know what will happen?" Salina gave a puzzled look, and the man went on to explain.

"The Zadria stock will plummet as a result of our huge sell off. Others will see it and figure something has happened to cause such a large volume of stocks to be sold. They will try to sell theirs, and stock prices will bottom out. It could wind up bankrupting the company, unless someone comes to the company's rescue."

"And your point would be?"

"Well, I'm just wondering why you want to do this so badly when we already have a plan?"

"Let's just say, it's payback to a FRIEND for coming between me and my goals."

"Okay, but we have to come up with a dummy corporation so we can buy these stocks and not get caught."

"We can use my mother's maiden name, Baker."

"Okay, we'll start the buy up first thing in the morning. In the meantime, I need to go to my legal department and get the paperwork to redraw the Zadria deal."

"Actually, I brought the paperwork with the Madison Company's logo on it, that way everything stays consistent."

"Excellent, let me see it, and I will rework it so that it becomes a takeover bid, rather than a partnership one." Salina handed the forms to the man and for the next few hours they worked on them.

Eventually they finished and with a final grin for each other they shook hands and walked out to their cars. Alex also finished her work and finally went home. She was exhausted, but at the same time pumped up. Over the next month and a half, Salina and Wellington made contact with the shareholders. Many were eager to sell their shares, while a few wanted to think it over. They also had put in a buy order to a broker for any of the Zadria stock that came on the market. They were lucky that the broker was able to find stock on the market when news leaked that "The Raider" was about to take over the company. The stock that Wellington already had in Zadria's company, would be used to buy Salina out for his own company. The profit that the two would make from the stocks of Zadria's company would be enormous, and they would sell them while the prices were high of course.

D'Angelo arrived in town, and after getting settled at the hotel, he went to meet Alex at her home. The maid opened the door, and showed the man to the study where the woman sat reading over some files.

"Well Rose, what are you so deep in thought about?"

"D'Angelo, I didn't hear you come in."

"Obviously, what's going on?"

"D'Angelo, tell me where the Zadria company stands as far as takeover bids?"

"You're asking me? I'm a little surprised, usually you're right on top of companies that you have an interest in, what's going on?"

"Just answer me, have there been many bids?"

"Plenty, but that Zadria is very feisty. She's using her resources to fight off any and all. I also saw in the paper that the stock price for that company is higher.

"Well she's young and she wants to keep her company. I saw that as well." Alex stated, as she thought about the meaning of those higher numbers. Then she turned back to her desk and picked up the phone.

"I'd like to speak with Ms Zadria." The man's eyes raised in surprise, then he decided to pull up a chair and listen. She hit the speaker so as to free her hands to read over the file and refer to it when and if she needed to.

"May I ask who's calling?" A woman asked of the caller.

"Tell her a friend of Taylor Young."

"Yes Ma'am."

After a few moments another woman's voice sounded on the other end.

"Hello this is Zadria, who am I speaking with?"

"This is Alexandra Madison, of the Madison Company."

"OH! Yes, I know who you are Ms. Madison! You have some nerve to call yourself a friend of Taylor's! With friends like you, who the hell needs enemies. What do you want, like I don't already know?"

"Well despite your opinion, I'm calling about business. Taylor had presented a proposal to me, and I was thinking about it."

"I don't care what you were thinking about! I know you made Taylor quit, and I also know you're behind the massive buy up of my stock!"

"I don't know what you're talking about, I haven't made any further moves on your company since Taylor made her presentation months ago."

"I don't believe you! All I know is many of the other companies that were trying to get my company backed off when they heard you were getting in to take it completely over. I've received the paper's drafted by your company for the takeover, sent by your attorney, and then the next thing I know, my stocks are being grabbed up left and right, because of you."

"Well I'm calling to offer you a deal."

"NO! I will fight you with everything I have, even if I have to file bankruptcy to do it. You will not have MY Company Ms. Madison! Especially after what you did to Taylor, and all the hard work she did to come up with a feasible option to your trying to take my company. I told her that you would do this, but no, she said you were interested in a good deal. She believed the partnership was a good deal. She believed and trusted in you, I knew she was being foolish, but she didn't. Well seems like she was wrong, and I was right! She was so pleased with everything, and what did you do? Slapped her in the face and then made her quit! Some Friend!" The woman finished, with contempt in her voice, then slammed the phone down.

CLICK!!

Alex hit the button on her phone to hang it up also. She now had frustration and anger showing in her eyes.

"Wow! Alex was she talking about the young girl who use to stay here with you?"

"Yes."

"Aha...so that's why you look so angry, that's why I haven't seen her around, or you mention her name, and why you're so angry. She must have done something horrible to have you this angry?"

"This isn't even about her."

"Then why the look of vengeance?"

The woman turned her chair to look the man in the eyes, then said through her teeth.

"B.e.c.a.u.s.e...someone is messing with my company, and I plan on finding out who they are."

"Well...I would hate to be the person on the receiving end. What do you plan on doing?"

"Make a few calls." She stated, then picked up the phone and called the Securities and Exchange Commission. I would like to speak to Thomas Rouse...She knew him as one of her agents like Dosman was; an infiltrator into other companies. Rouse moved into a position with the SEC after returning from his three year "vacation", as they called it. Because Alex needed to make sure her company was always clean, and not being maligned or setup without her knowing it. She thought it was a perfect place for one of her spies to be, so that he could watch out for her. What he didn't realize was he himself was being watched as well, by another spy that she had in that same company as well. Rouse had undergone plastic surgery while he was on...vacation...he no longer had blonde hair, his eyebrows were colored as well, his nose decreased in size, as well as having his lips made fuller and cheek implants. He wore brown contact lens.

"This is Mr. Rouse."

"Thomas, this is Alexandra, I'm calling to see if there's anything going on with my company?"

"Actually, I was just getting ready to call you, it seems that there may be an investigation of your company, for Insider Trading, coming up within the next few months, if not sooner. If some type of proof isn't sent here for us to review."

"Well you know I have never engaged in any such dealings, and I will find out who is using my company's name. When I do, I want full charges brought against the person's who have tried to do this."

"I know Ms. Madison. It seems there are many here who feel that there is some reason for what's going on and that maybe you didn't know anything about it. We still will have to investigate if we don't receive any information to the contrary."

"I understand. How long?"

"Three months. Before the investigation becomes public. You lucked out, they usually only give you a month to come up with anything. They've extended it for you by two to just come up with any opposing information."

"Well I appreciate that. Can you tell me the name that is being used to buy the stock?"

"No. We don't have any names yet."

"Alright, well keep watching it, I'll be in touch soon." Alex said, as she hung up the phone.

"Wow, so someone is buying up stock using your company's name as cover, and it's the Zadria Company they're doing it to. What's your next move?"

"I'm not sure yet, but I do know it has to be someone within my company who is doing it, or helping someone do it to me. And their ASS is mine when I find them."

"Hmm...well this should be a hell of a show, anything I can do?"

"I'll let you know."

The two left the study and went to talk over a meal out by the pool. Alex had her detectives working on discovering who it was that was using her company. Yasmeia in the meantime had called Taylor to talk to her about things, and the conversation came up about the company.

"Yasmeia, my Grandmother has been telling me some rumors that Zadria's company is now being actively pursued by Alex. Is that true? She's taking it, rather than going in on a partnership with her?"

"No, it's not true, I mean the company appears to be taking over Zadria's company, but it's not Alex doing it."

"Yasmeia, how do you know it's not her?"

"I know, and it's not her, it's Salina."

"Salina? Yasmeia what are you saying?"

"I'm saying Salina has gone into insider trading with someone."

"Can you prove that?"

"Not yet, I have to figure out a way to put the pieces together, maybe you can help me? I mean if it's not too painful for you to have anything to do with helping Alex?"

"No, I don't want anything to happen to her or her companies. What can I do?"

"There's that heart I knew would always shine through. I just need you to help me research some things."

"Okay, then do you want me to send whatever I find to you?"

"No, aren't you coming up here to visit me?"

"Oh, actually, I was going to call you to tell you I wouldn't be able to, my grandmother has not been feeling well the last few days."

"Is she alright?"

"The doctors don't know, and Grammy won't stay in the hospital. She says she's just tired, and if it is time for her to go, then she's ready, because she's had a good and blessed life. Yasmeia I don't know what I would do if anything happened to her."

"Well I'll come there if you don't mind a visit? Have you talked to your mother's family about your grandmother's health?"

"Of course I don't mind, that would be wonderful, and yes I have, but they don't care, they don't even call. Grammy told me not to waste my time telling them anything, but I thought they should know that she wasn't feeling well. Maybe they should come to the house to visit, just in case, but they just told me that if she goes, she goes, she's old. They make me so mad, they always want, but never want to give anything, they're just users."

"Well your grandmother's lucky to have you in her life. I'll be there by tomorrow okay?"

"Okay, thanks Yasmeia."

"Anytime Taylor. See you tomorrow."

"Okay, bye."

Yasmeia hung up the phone and thought about calling Alex to tell her about the girl's grandmother, but then decided to see for herself how ill her grandmother was first. Yasmeia had planned to take a few days that month anyway, so she decided to put in for the 3 days off tomorrow. Yasmeia arrived in town and was driven to the grandmother's house. The car pulled up at the house a few hours later and Taylor met her friend at the door.

"Yasmeia, oh, I've missed seeing you. Come on in, Grammy's upstairs lying down. I have the intercom on, although there is an aide with her right now just in case she needs something."

"How is she?"

"There's been no change really, I mean one minute it seems as though she is getting better, but then she begins to wheeze and things. We just have to keep an eye on her.

Anyway, you must be tired, let me show you where you can get cleaned up and where your room is. That way you can rest."

"Actually, I do want to get cleaned up, but I'm not tired. I want to get to work on what's going on at the company, if you don't mind?"

"No, of course not." Taylor led the woman to her room and showed her the guest bathroom, then left her to get changed. Yasmeia came down a short while later and Taylor met her in the family room.

"Feel better Yasmeia?"

"Yes, much. Thank you."

"You're welcome. Here's some tea for you. Now, have a seat and tell me what's going on?"

"Actually , I'm a little curious?"

"About what?"

"What type of relationship you and Alex had?"

"Yasmeia, we were just friends." Taylor said, trying to be convincing."

"Friends? Hmm...that's not what I saw."

"What are you talking about?"

"I told Alex what I thought, and she didn't deny it. Tell me honestly, were you two lovers?"

The light caramel toned, young woman blushed, but lucky for her Yasmeia was focused on her eyes.

"Well?"

Taylor licked her lips, and then gave a look of uncertainty, as her friend answered for her.

"I thought so. I saw how the two of you looked at each other." Yasmeia said knowingly.

"Yasmeia, she didn't put me in those positions because of that relationship. She did that because she was making sure I didn't slip back out of her view, and because she wanted my position to match my abilities. We didn't go into a relationship until afterwards, I give you my word."

"I believe you Taylor, so what happened to cause you to quit?"

"It was ALL my fault for the most part, the other bit was because of Salina."

"I'm sure Alex must have had some part in it?"

"Only after I pulled away from her without telling her the reason. I started avoiding her and I came up with excuses to avoid being intimate with her, only because of my insecurities about such a relationship. I used the excuse of needing to work late or go in early to the office because there she told me we were to be about business only. So I felt I wouldn't have to deal with our private life."

"You mean between two women?"

"Yes, I was raised to believe love is love, but also that, that love was supposed to be between the opposite sexes. I couldn't handle the idea of people looking at me as being strange or something. You know I'm a very...well..."

"Shy?"

Taylor smiled timidly, and then nodded her head as she watched Yasmeia's reaction.

"Taylor did you love her?"

"Yes, very much, I still do." She admitted, as tears formed in her eyes at the thought of just how much.

"And I can see that."

"Yes. But she won't even talk to me. I treated her so...badly, and she hadn't done ANYTHING wrong, she just wanted to love me. I hurt her, and I won't ever forgive myself for that, she didn't deserve it." Taylor said through her tears, as she buried her head in her hands and cried.

Yasmeia moved over to where the girl sat on the sofa, wrapped her arms around her friend's shoulders and hugged her to herself.

"It will be alright, I'm sure we can figure something out."

"No!" Taylor said, as she pulled out of Yasmeia's arms.

"What do you mean?"

"Yasmeia, she won't talk to me, that's why I quit, she was giving back to me what I did to her, in spades. She wouldn't talk to me about the Zadria deal and she made sure I couldn't get to her, by having Salina screen all calls and visits from me. When I saw her at the house, she avoided me or told me straight out that she didn't want to talk to me. She said there was nothing to say. I had shown her all she needed to see."

"She was hurting, so she was being cold and distant with you."

"I know, and that's what hurt. I did it because Salina was blackmailing me. She did it because she was angry."

"Maybe partly, but I would say it was mainly because she was hurting. A woman like Alexandra isn't used to giving her heart, and when she does, she doesn't expect for it to be thrown back in her face." Yasmeia stated as a fact.

Taylor flinched at the truth in Yasmeia's words.

"I know, but she was still wrong to be mean about it, she's just pouting." Taylor said, with a pout of her own.

"Taylor, you and Alex are a lot alike. Neither one of you wanted to admit the relationship, albeit for different reasons, and yet you both love each other so very much. Hmm...if I were you, I would go and tell Alexandra Madison about her behavior. But that's only me. Anyway, let's talk about Salina and what I know.

Yasmeia began filling her in on what was happening and the girl quickly filed Yasmeia's suggestion away to think about later, as she now switched her thoughts to those of what she was now being told about Alex's company. Taylor made the logical assumption that the SEC would soon be getting involved if they suspected Insider Trading. She knew that could be costly to Alex's companies and it's stocks, therefore it was unacceptable to her despite what they were just talking about.

"So Salina and Mr. Wellington were heard by you, telling each other that they were going to save his company? And make their money off of Zadria's?"

"Yes, and that they both wanted to get Alex back, and you, what better way?"

"Yes, you're right. What better way than to have the SEC breathing down your neck, while the perpetrators make off scot-free. Well, it's not going to happen. Come on, my grandmother has a computer. We can look up some information on the market, mainly the two stocks to see if either have gone public yet, or if just Zadria's is still being bought up. We can also see if there are any similarities in the way they are being bought, if both are on the open market."

They sat down at the computer and Taylor pulled up the stock reports. After scanning to find the stock reports she wanted, she and Yasmeia printed out the reports and then looked over them. They saw Zadria's stock prices had risen, but The Wellington Company's Stocks were pretty much unchanged from what they had been, if anything they were slowly decreasing in value.

"Well Yasmeia, if Salina and Mr. Wellington are doing anything with his company stock, it must be by way of the shareholders."

"Yes, that makes sense. If they haven't gone public with the announcement to buy stocks, then they're probably using the anonymous list of shareholders to get large blocks of stock first."

"Right, to get as close to the 51% that they would need to save his company from takeover.

"Hmm...so right now we have to figure out a way to find out if they have contacted any of the shareholders with offers to buy their stocks. If they have, I would think they probably would sell all too fast, especially with the loss of value of the stock." Taylor reasoned.

"Right, because it's obviously not public knowledge yet that "The Raider" is taking over his company?"

"Exactly, and that would explain why the stock prices on his company have not gone up yet. That would also explain the purpose of the list of shareholders being used to get as much stock as possible in a short amount of time. By the time they have to go public, they will have most of the 51% of shares they need, and therefore with an open bid for shares, the prices go up. Wellington causes the prices to be so high that Alex will not want to take it over, due to the expense, so he not only saves his company by keeping Alex from wanting it, but also by obtaining the shares needed to save it as well."

"Exactly, and with the Zadria Company they had to go public with open bids to buy, because there was no anonymous list to use. All they want to do is try to get as much stock bought up before everyone else figures this out and jumps in to start buying as well. Then the price goes up, and with Salina and Mr. Wellington having a lot of stock in the company, they sell what they have for a huge profit. Once people realize again that there's been a change, they will now sell because of the sell-off that they see happening, thereby insuring that Salina and Mr. Wellington get rich. Zadria's company goes belly up, and Alex's company goes through an investigation that Wellington and Salina caused, but Alex pays. It's a good plan, but there is only one problem..."

"What's that?" Yasmeia asked, impressed by Taylor's reasoning.

"They weren't counting on someone having overheard, and us coming up with a plan to stop them, and turn it around on them."

"Hahaha, you're absolutely right, and you know what's even better than that?"

"What?"

"The fact that Alex is going to find out that a certain shy ex-lover will have been instrumental in fixing things. I would think she would have to be pretty...grateful for such help?" Yasmeia said with a wry smirk.

"She'll be thankful, but that will be about it." Taylor said somberly.

"Okay, so what do we do now?"

"Let me call Marcus. He may be able to help us."

"Okay."

Taylor picked up the phone and called Marcus Shearer's office.

"Hello, may I speak with Mr. Shearer? This is Taylor Young."

"Oh, hold on Taylor."

"Okay."

A few minutes later Marcus picked up the phone.

"Taylor! How are you doing, I really miss you being here with us, especially coming by with that sweet smile and your kind words." Marcus gushed, as he felt the joy of hearing his friend's voice again after so many months.

"I miss you too Marcus, but I think you miss me because you don't have me to do your reports for you anymore?" Taylor teased. Marcus laughed.

"It is good to hear your voice. What can I do for you? Or is this purely a social call?"

"It's business, I need your help."

"What can I do?"

Taylor went into what she and Yasmeia were doing and what they needed. She told him about the list of names, going through them until she got to a Mrs. N. Funchess. She was known as a very dynamic woman who seemed to have great foresight into the needs of people around her. Especially for children who was being warehoused in hospitals just waiting to die from whatever their illnesses were. She took these infants in and provided the love they needed. To the amazement of even the doctors, the children were now thriving, and in school and learning, just because of the love that was provided to them.

"Wait...I know her, she's a friend of mine." Marcus said, stopping the girl. "I can make a call to her to see if she's been approached by anyone offering to buy her stock in The Wellington Company."

"Great! Give her a call and let me know what you find out. That will tell me if what I suspect is happening."

"Okay, I'll call you as soon as I talk to her. Give me the number to your grandmother's again so I can call you right back."

Taylor gave the number, then hung up the phone and told Yasmeia what was happening. The two then waited for Marcus to call them back. Marcus, in the meantime, pulled up his phone list and dialed the woman's number.

"Hello?" Came a woman's voice on the other end.

"Ms.Funchess? It's me, Marcus Shearer."

"Oh, yes Marcus, how are you doing?"

"Fine, thank you for asking."

"So Mr. Shearer, what can I do for you?"

"Well first of all, do you still hold shares in The Wellington Company?"

"Yes, why?"

"Well I have a client who is interested in acquiring stock, and I told her I would look around to see if anyone had any they wanted to sell."

"Marcus, you know you're the second person to call me asking me about my stock and if I was interested in selling?"

"Really, who else called you?"

"Some woman from a company name Baker. She wanted to buy all of my stock in that company. She even offered me 10% above market price."

"And..."

"And of course my red flags went up. So...tell me why all the sudden interest in that stock, is your boss going after it?"

"I haven't heard anything like that. A friend just asked me to find stock for her, so I told her I would make some calls. I take it you haven't sold your shares to that other person?"

"Right, and I think I will hold on to it for the time being, just to see what develops."

"Well that's fine, I don't have a problem with that, but thanks for the conversation, tell your family I said hello".

"I will Marcus, talk to you later."

"So long." Marcus then hung up the phone and nodded his head in satisfaction. He picked up the phone again and dialed Taylor at her grandmother's.

"Hello?"

"Taylor?"

"Yes, Marcus! What did you find out?"

"Well it seems that some woman from a company going by the name of Baker, called Mrs. Funchess, offering to buy her shares at a higher price then what the current market is. So I would have to say that it is Salina and Mr. Wellington, and they are indeed buying up the shares from the shareholders first before they go public with their offer to buy."

"Yes, that's it. Thanks Marcus, I'll be in touch okay? And Marcus, please don't say anything to anyone about this, especially Ms. Madison. it could mess everything up?"

"Now Taylor, I'm surprised you even had to say that."

"I know I didn't, I was just making sure it still went?"

"It does, we're friends, and I'm always here for you."

"Thank you Marcus. I'll talk to you soon."

"Okay, and I will let you know if I hear anything around here, mainly from your FRIEND."

"Great! And don't insult yourself by calling her a friend of mine. That reflects on all of you as my friends, and diminishes the quality of my true friends." Taylor said, with lightness in her tone.

"Alright Taylor." The man said, catching the hint.

Taylor laughed, and once again thanked her friend, before saying goodbye to him and hanging up. Then she turned to Yasmeia.

"Okay, it's what we were thinking. They are buying up the stocks from the shareholders on the list. Now we just have to keep getting more proof, but maybe you can talk to Alex?"

"I don't know, she doesn't want to talk to me either."

"Why is that Yasmeia?"

"Because I told her what I thought about the two of you. From that point on she has not so much as spoken to me except to tell me that she didn't have time, and she's had enough of my talking."

"Hmm...well I can't imagine why she wouldn't won't to hear this?" But she is excellent at shutting out people isn't she?"

"I'm sure she would, but right now she's hurting and anything, coming from anyone, that knows you, they are put out, and yes, she is very good at shutting people out when she chooses to do that."

"Okay, well we'll have to think of something else." The two stayed up late two nights in a row trying to figure out how to get to Alex, without being intercepted by Salina. They even tried calling

Alex, but Salina picked up and when Yasmeia asked to speak to the woman, she was told that she was in a meeting and could not be disturbed. So they decided they would have to try something else.

"Okay, since we can't reach her by phone, maybe we should go and talk to her in person?"

"Do you really want to be on the receiving end of her temper, if we basically give her the bum's rush?"

"No, I guess not. We will have to try to get the information into the right hands.

Besides, it may be better not to talk to her about this."

"Taylor?"

"No, I mean, if Alex knew that Salina was messing with her companies, she would probably wipe the floor with her...literally?"

"Hmm...you're right. Who knows what power she has and how she would use it against someone messing with her company's good name?"

"Okay, so, what shall we do?"

"I'm not sure." Yasmeia admitted.

"Hmmm...I know!! Why don't we just contact the SEC ourselves and give them the information that we have. That way maybe they can start an investigation."

"Investigation? Taylor I thought we were trying to stop an investigation?" Yasmeia asked with concern at the suggestion.

"We are."

"Then I'm lost."

"Okay, here's what I'm thinking. We will tell the SEC what we have, and tell them that Alex had nothing to do with this, that two people are trying to get revenge against her for her trying to takeover Mr. Wellington's company, and Salina is just doing it out of greed and spitefulness."

"Okay..."

"Then they will launch an investigation of Salina and Mr. Wellington, without them knowing about it. Also, the SEC will not have to release Alex's company's name to the media, because it will no longer be a business that is dealing in insider trading, but two private citizens who happen to be in the business community."

"OH!! Alright. Right, the SEC can only keep the name of the company confidential for so long. With this information, Alex's companies are no longer the focus. In fact, Mr. Wellington's company becomes the focus, because he is the owner of his company. I love it Taylor! It's brilliant. I always knew you were smart, and I know Alex knows it as well, otherwise she would have not kept you as her Personal Assistant, no matter how cute you are." Yasmeia said with a smile.

"Thank you."

"For what?"

"Being my friend and Alex's."

"She's my boss. I like my job, plus I get excellent benefits." Yasmeia finished with a humorous smirk.

"Oh, so you do like her?"

"I admire her success...and yes, I do like her. I've known her for a while, but I never really saw the other side of her, until you happened into her life. Then I saw a soft, caring side that really suits her."

"I think so too." Taylor said, with a longing tone in her voice.

"I know it's hard to think about someone you love, but not be able to be there with them. But...look at it this way, this may be a way to get her attention. You don't think you have the courage to face her in person, which I'm not criticizing, I know first hand how intimidating she is, and I know it's worse for someone like you who isn't used to it. Although I would think you are a little more used to it now?"

"Maybe a little. Anyway, it's late. Let's get something to eat and then I can go check on my grandmother, before I turn in for the night.

CHAPTER 17

On the final day of Yasmeia's stay, Taylor went through her routine of checking on her grandmother and taking care of some things around the house and then they sat down at her grandmother's computer. Using the copy part of her fax machine, they copied the information they had, then Taylor called the SEC.

"Hello, may I speak with someone regarding information on possible insider trading?"

"Hold a moment, I will get Mr. Rouse."

A moment or so passed and a man's voice came on the other end.

"Hello. This is Thomas Rouse."

"Yes, Mr. Rouse. My name is Taylor Young. I worked with Ms. Madison as her PA for a while and it has recently come to my attention that of Ms. Madison's companies may be about to undergo investigation regarding inappropriate actions?"

"How do you know this?"

"I told you, I used to work with Ms. Madison, but that's irrelevant now. The point is, you and I both know that Ms. Madison has never, and could never be involved in any misbehavior, or anything that appears to be illegal."

"I take it you have something that would help to prove that?"

"Yes, and I will send it to you via fax, if you will agree to one thing?"

"What's that?"

"If you will give me your word that you will not tell Ms. Madison about what I am sending you. I believe it could be detrimental to your investigation of the two people that the information is about, if Ms. Madison were to find out that they are the one's who are messing with her companies."

"I understand. Alright, we won't let Ms. Madison know about who we're investigating, for now."

"Good, because one of the people is Ms. Madison's new Personal Assistant."

"OH!!! Okay, then send me the information, and we will start our investigation immediately."

"How long will you take to conclude it?"

"Well it depends on the information you have. It could take years, months, weeks, or days."

"Well, if you follow your instincts when you see the information, I think you can have it concluded within a few weeks, or before the holiday at the most. Please let me know how things are going. Also when you do decide that you have enough evidence to prosecute, please don't do it in a way that will embarrass Ms. Madison. I'm sure you can be discreet."

"Yes, don't worry, we can do this without Ms. Madison ever knowing if we choose."

"Well that won't be necessary. Oh, by the way, I'm sending the fax to you right now. Let me know what your initial reaction is to it. If you find it to be enough, which I'm sure you will, but if you do, it would mean that Ms. Madison's companies will not be mentioned as being under investigation by the SEC right? Because you know that it is like a death sentence for a company to have that mentioned about it.

"We realize that, and depending on what I see, Ms. Madison's companies are safe. Ah, hold a moment, the fax just arrived..." The man said, then he picked it up and took a moment to scan over the information. "Hmmm...well now. Hello?"

"Yes, I'm here."

"Just from the quick scanning I did, it seems like this will be a pretty quick investigation. I'll have to read everything first, but right now I can tell you if the rest of the information is like this, Ms. Madison has nothing to worry about when it comes to her companies."

"Really?"

"Yes. I believe Ms. Madison would appreciate knowing who helped her."

"Well, we'll see how things go. First you have to do your investigation."

"Very well, I will be in touch. and if you come across any further information please call me directly." The man suggested, and then gave her the number.

"Okay, thank you."

"Thank you."

The two hung up and Taylor turned to Yasmeia, who was giving her an approving nod of her head, seeing how she had listened to the whole thing.

"Excellent, well it looks like Salina and Mr. Wellington will be getting theirs, and Alex's companies are safe." Yasmeia said, praising Taylor's handling of the SEC.

"Well I just hope this is resolved soon. It would be a shame to go into the holidays with this hanging over her head."

The rest of the day the two spent helping Taylor's grandmother. Alex, in the meantime, already had her detectives working on finding the person, or persons involved.

"D'Angelo, I know I'm missing something obvious, but for the life of me, I just can't seem to see it."

"Well Rose, I know you will, but right now I think your mind is divided between other things. The holidays are coming up, and then a few months later your annual Business Party."

"Who can think about the holidays with the SEC possibly looking at investigating my companies for some illegal activity!" She said bitterly.

"Well, hopefully all of this will be resolved before the holidays get here."

"Well, I'm not one for waiting for things to happen, you know that."

"I know, but you can't do any more than you already are."

"Maybe not, but I am not in the holiday spirit right now."

Over the next month, Alex was able to give some information to the SEC. Her contact inside told her that they had gotten some information that indicated it was not necessary for her to worry about her company being investigated."

"What have you discovered?"

"Well Ms. Madison, I can't tell you that at this moment, because the investigation still taking place."

"But my company is in the clear?"

"Yes, but it is someone in your company that we are investigating, so I would suggest you not let on that you know."

"Who?!"

"Ms. Madison, I can hear in your voice that if I tell you, then you will most likely do something to the peoples."

"There's more than one?!"

"Only one in your company, and one outside of your company."

"How long before you wrap up your investigation?"

"We thought we would have it done before the holidays, but it looks like it will go on until around February."

"Damn it! I didn't want to have to think about this over the holidays! Well at least my companies are in the clear." She said.

"Right. I apologize that this will go on through the holidays and get so close to your annual spring Business Party, but the two that we are investigating seem to be planning on other endeavors."

"With my company as their shield?!" Alex said through her teeth.

"They assume." Thomas Rouse replied.

"You're learning Mr. Rouse. You're learning."

"I learned from the best Ms. Madison." The man said, giving credit to his mentor, although the SEC didn't know that.

"True. Well keep me updated, and I still want to know who it is in my company. I will find out one way or another. Talk to you later."

Click.

Alex went back to reading over the reports from her own investigators. Yasmeia and Taylor continued to work behind the scenes, with Taylor putting more and more together. At the same time, Taylor was hurting from the information that Yasmeia had tried not to talk about. She had seen in the papers or heard around the office about Alex and D'Angelo being seen around town together at different events more and more. Taylor began feeling anxious every time she spoke to Yasmeia. She had opened a can of worms about what Alex was up to, and the man escorting her around town, by begging Yasmeia to tell her what she knew. Yasmeia tried to play down all that she had heard and read, but finally decided it was best to tell the truth. She hoped that maybe Taylor would get over Alex, but instead it only fed her desire for the woman.

One morning Taylor stayed home from work due to her grandmother seemingly doing worse. She was very worried about her, especially when she saw her grandmother's attorney over at the house. When Taylor had asked what was going on, she was told that her grandmother just wanted to go over her will. That was very disconcerting to the girl, but her grandmother seemed to be doing better at that time, so she just filed the memory in the back of her mind.

Just when Taylor thought her grandmother was doing better, she took a turn for the worse. Taylor was stressed over everything that was happening within her life, her grandmother's illness, the company and Alex, and what was happening between Alex and D'Angelo. The holidays were in the next few days, and it appeared to Taylor that her grandmother may not see them. It made her heart heavy at the thought, and she stayed by her grandmother's bedside, only leaving to go to the restroom or to get something to help make her grandmother as comfortable as possible.

On the 23rd of December, Alex had her annual employee Holiday party, for all of her companies. She and D'Angelo attended a few of them that were in state, and she called those out of state, or sent faxes to all of the others to wish them a happy holiday. When the festivities were over, D'Angelo and Alex returned to her place around 3 in the morning. The man began kissing and fondling her, but Alex never let it go any further with D'Angelo, despite how close she felt to him. While they were involved, the phone rang, but Alex didn't answer it due to D'Angelo telling her to let it ring. Since he wasn't going to be able to make love to her, he at least wanted to enjoy what he was allowed to do. The answering machine picked up the call.

"Hello, Ms. Madison, this is Yasmeia..."

Alex heard the voice and name and actually turned her head to look at the machine. She couldn't believe Yasmeia would be calling her, let alone at 4 in the morning.

"If you're there, please pick up, I'd rather not say what I have to say...um...to an answering machine." Yasmeia's voice cracked, and Alex heard it, and concern crossed her face.

"Stop D'Angelo, I want to hear this, something's wrong!" The woman chided due to his continuous attempts at distracting her.

"I guess you're not there, well..."

Alex's heart started racing and it wasn't because of D'Angelo. There was something about Yasmeia's voice, the tone, the stress in it that made the woman focus all of her attention on the phone.

"It's about Taylor..."

The woman now practically knocked D'Angelo off the sofa trying to sit up. Her heart racing, her breathing appearing to have stopped for that moment in time, as she thought something horrible had happened to Taylor. She was tempted to pick up the phone, but she couldn't bring herself to lift the phone. So she just waited. Fear showed all over her face.

"Her grandmother just passed away at 1 this morning and Taylor's not taking it very well. They took her grandmother's body to the mortuary and Taylor refuses to leave. I'm calling from the place now. I flew in when Mr. Daniels called me and told me what had happened. He said the community is worried about Taylor, and I know I don't have to tell you, of all people, how much she loved and depended on her grandmother. I'm heartbroken for her and I don't know how to...comfort her...I don't believe anyone can, except maybe...Well anyway, she knows I am here, but she keeps talking to her grandmother telling her that she's all alone, and there is no meaning for her anymore. I'm scared for her...please...I know you've moved on with your life, but I didn't know who else to call...I'm sorry to have to leave this message on your machine, especially on this day. The funeral will take place on the 28th and she will be laid to rest at Wright's Cemetery, at 3 PM. Again, I'm sorry for the way you're hearing about this." Yasmeia then hung up.

D'Angelo noticed that Alex was trying to control her breathing so as not to let on to what was really happening with her.

"Rose?"

"Please leave D'Angelo, I need to be by myself for a while. I'll call you at the hotel sometime tomorrow." She managed to say without her voice cracking.

"Alright Rose, but if you need me, just call and I'll be right here. I love you, and I'm sorry for your friend's loss."

"Thank you." She said, without looking back at the man as he put his shirt on. D'Angelo put his shoes on and left the woman alone.

After he had gone out the door, she lay on the sofa and let her tears roll freely as she thought about Yasmeia's message. Alex knew how much pain Taylor was going through at the loss. She also felt the pain of losing such a kindred spirit. The next day Alex went to the office to check on some things and then went back home. When she got home there was a message from Thomas Rouse at the SEC. He was calling to tell her that bids had been placed on the open market to buy any Wellington stock that became available. The investigation was winding down and arrests were expected in the near future. She shook her head in anger and frustration at having that back at the front of her mind along with trying to decide whether or not she should go to the funeral. She thought about that and other things for the next few days, and finally, the day of the funeral, at 10AM, she had her driver take her to the airport where she got on her private jet and flew into the larger city just outside where Taylor was. She had a car waiting for her when she arrived. She told the driver to take her to Wright Cemetery.

Meanwhile, Taylor and all of the many people who came to the funeral to offer condolences and support to her arrived at the cemetery. Taylor was standing, still crying and holding herself, despite Yasmeia also holding her. The minister stepped up to the head of the open area, where the casket was. He opened his bible and began to quote a scripture. Taylor kept her eyes lowered on the casket and just let her tears fall. When the minister had finished, he signaled for the casket to be lowered. The girl's eyes widened and her trembling was now apparent. She stood watching the casket until it was within the grave and then fell to her knees and called for her grandmother. The sight tore at everyone's heart, and the elderly women whispered to each other as they, themselves went and stood around the girl. They all rallied to soothe their adopted grandchild, but Taylor was inconsolable.

Yasmeia thanked everyone for coming out and for their love and support of Taylor and her grandmother. The people eventually left, still wanting to stay and help in whatever way they could, but realizing that she needed to be alone, so they allowed her privacy. Yasmeia went back over to where Taylor sat on the ground on her heels and now rocking with her arms crossed in a hugging type fashion.

"Taylor...I'm so sorry." Was all Yasmeia could manage before she lost her own composure.

After a bit, Yasmeia looked up and when her eyes glanced around the cemetery, she noticed that there were no other people around. It was starting to get late, so she told Taylor they had to go. At first Taylor didn't want to budge, but then, she lifted her eyes to let Yasmeia see that she had no intentions of leaving. In the distance she saw a figure, just standing tall and regal, watching everything. Taylor stood up and Yasmeia followed her. She too, turned her head to look at whatever it was that had the girl's attention and had caused her to quiet.

"She came." Yasmeia said, more to herself than Taylor, but Taylor heard it and spared a glance at Yasmeia. A faint attempt at a smile tried to make its way to the girl's mouth, and then she saw the woman in the distance cock her head as if in wonder. Taylor took a step in her direction, and Alex seemed to snap out of whatever trance she was in. She turned, and the driver opened the door of the black limo, and she stepped inside. Taylor's heart seemed to stop and she gave an audible gasp as if she had been struck, she brought her hand to chest and watched the limo drive away.

The tears rolled once again, this time at the profound loneliness she felt due to the indifference she felt from the woman. Yasmeia felt it as well, but she recognized it for what it really was. Alex was just showing her respect for Taylor's grandmother. She still had not forgiven Taylor for what she did to her, and how she just left. Therefore, she did not want to get into anything unpleasant with the girl on such a solemn occasion.

Alex flew out that same day and returned to her home. Taylor, in the meantime, had returned to her grandmother's home, where she appeared lost. Yasmeia stayed with her until after the New Year, but then had to return home. She tried to get Taylor to return with her for a while, until she felt better, but was unable to convince Taylor to leave with her. Yasmeia arranged for some of the women of the community to stop by and check on the girl just to make sure she was all right. Yasmeia returned to work the following day after arriving back in town.

CHAPTER 18

The first few weeks of work were spent on getting back into things and catching up, but she called Taylor every night to check on her. Meanwhile, Alex appeared to be going on with her life. She and D'Angelo, once again, were seen about town and overseas, on business trips or just social events. Yasmeia watched them whenever they happened to make an appearance together. One day Yasmeia happened to have a need to go to the top floor because her Admin had gone on another errand for her, and some analysis needed to be taken to Alex's office. Yasmeia arrived on the top floor and headed into the office. She expected to see Salina, and to just be able to give the reports to her, but Salina had also gone on an errand. The only person there was Alex. She saw Yasmeia get off the elevator and come into the outer office with a folder in her hands. Yasmeia knocked on the door of the inner office and Alex looked up at her and beckoned for her to come in.

"Ms. Sains, what is it?" She asked flatly. Sounding like the Raider of old.

Yasmeia raised a brow at the formal recognition and knew what it meant.

"Don't worry Ms. Madison, I just came to drop these analyses off. I would have left them with your PA, but she wasn't in, so here you go. If you have any problems, which I doubt, but one never knows, anyway, you know where to find me, not that you would. Have a nice day Ms. Madison." Yasmeia turned to leave, and Alex watched her until she made it to the door of her office, then she spoke.

"How is she?"

Yasmeia stopped and thought about whether she should say anything, then she decided she would. She turned to face Alex.

"Not good, but between myself and those who care about her, we're looking out for her."

"And you think I don't care about her?"

"Oh, I didn't say that. By the way, I'm glad you could pull yourself away for a moment to pay your respects to her grandmother. I know Ms. Young appreciated it. Well, I have to get back to work. Is there anything else Ms. Madison?"

Alex's eyes narrowed and her nostrils flared.

"No that's not all! Close the door and sit down Ms. Sains!" She ordered.

Yasmeia turned and casually closed the door, although her heart was racing due to the anger she was seeing and hearing in Alex's eyes and voice. She walked over to one of the chairs, sat down and leveled her gaze on the woman.

"Now you listen Ms. Sains, I don't appreciate your attitude, and I won't tolerate it."

"Ms. Madison, I have worked at this company for many years, and while I enjoy what I do, I have no concern about being fired, demoted or whatever you decide to do to be vindictive. My only concern is how you have treated Taylor, and for that Ms. Madison, I cannot and will not pretend that I have respect for you. You have treated that child horribly, and she doesn't deserve such treatment."

"You don't know what you're talking about!"

"Oh, I know, Taylor told me about your relationship, months ago. She hurts at the loss of you, at your cold shoulder treatment towards her, and at your relationship with D'Angelo, and everything else that has anything to do with you."

"She'll get over it." Alex said flatly.

"No, she'll never get over it! You know that! You know her! Her rape was not as painful or scarring to her as the way you have behaved towards her. You're wrong, and if Taylor hadn't asked me not to quit, I would have done so a long time ago. That child loves you, but she sees that you're moving on with your life and she doesn't want to be in your way. I've told her she needed to move on with her own life, and you know what she told me just recently?"

Alex cocked her head and leaned back in her chair with a sneer on her face, waiting for the answer.

"She told me and I quote, 'My Grammy and Alex were my life. I now have neither, and it's my own fault. If I hadn't let Salina blackmail me, I would at least have Alex in my life.'"

"Blackmail?!!"

"Yes Ms. Madison, it seems your new PA has been very busy interfering in your life. She told Taylor that if she didn't back away from you, then she would tell all of Taylor's friends and the people in her church that Taylor was in a relationship with another woman. We both know how uncomfortable Taylor was about that; it actually scared her. You know she is very timid and for something like that to be told about her and then the consequences of that revelation with people looking at her as if she were strange, was a very heavy load for such narrow shoulders as that child has. You knew when you went into the relationship that she was scared and inexperienced in such a relationship. Her grandmother's concern about the relationship was also a factor, but it was Salina who pushed her back. Ms. Madison I will tell you this, IT HURT that child to pull away from you, it hurt her deeply, but she thought she would be able to handle it, as long as you didn't hate her. But when you stopped talking to her and acted as if she were invisible to you, the hurt was profound." Yasmeia stood up and walked up to the desk.

"Alex, I know you still care for Taylor, and I would even venture to guess you still love her. The only reason you are out and about with your friend is because you're just trying not to have time to think about her. You're selfish! There was no one in this whole building, except for myself, who cared anything about you, and then this warm, adorably shy, young girl comes to my office and tells me she was told to report to me, and that she was my new Admin. She used to ask me about you, just out of curiosity. She would tell me that she had everything there was written about you. She used to say that you and her grandmother were the inspirations for her to get into business. But she always said she would die if you ever walked into our office. She had both admiration and fear for and of you. Alex, Taylor has done so much for you, and you don't even realize it, but a lot of people in this company do, including your little PA. Taylor would have continued to try to get past her insecurities with the relationship because she loved you. But Salina was too much for her. I'm sorry I laid all of this on you, but you asked. Alex, I don't hate you or anything near that, I just feel bad for you and Taylor. I know the two of you would have made a wonderful team together, both in public life and private."

Alex studied the woman for long silent moments and then she finally spoke again.

"First of all Ms. Sains, I do care for D'Angelo, and with the way things are going he has ideas about something more permanent."

"Well Alex, if that's your choice, then I truly do hope you will be happy with it."

Yasmeia turned to leave, figuring there was nothing further to be said.

"Yasmeia sit down."

Yasmeia turned and looked at the woman. After a moment she returned to her seat.

"Okay."

"Yasmeia, I do still love Taylor, very much, but I can't trust her."

"What do you mean you can't trust her?? She is the most trustworthy person there is!"

"Not in a relationship she's not. I didn't want to get into this with you, but I won't allow you or anyone else to make assumptions about me, my motives, or my handling of Taylor. I will admit I am shocked to learn about the blackmail, and I will deal with Salina appropriately for interfering in my life. But looking past that, Taylor wronged me twice before I ever thought about moving on, and what's worse is, she just up and left."

"Alex, how could she stay? You weren't talking to her, you were barely speaking to me, or anyone else who spoke about Taylor."

"Why should I have spoken to her?!! She wasn't telling me anything. She didn't trust me enough to come to me and tell me what was happening!! I gave her every chance to tell me, I asked, I pleaded, and I scolded...nothing worked. I decided to just sit and watch her, and try to give her the time she needed. I thought she would realize that I had been there for her through everything else and, the odds were, I would be there for her in whatever it was that was bothering her. But instead of realizing I was waiting for her to come to me, she chose to use that to pull further away, and Yasmeia...it hurt! So despite how badly I feel about Taylor's loss of her Grandmother, it changes nothing. Taylor and I are history. I hope she is able to move on, but if she's not, then I am sorry for that, but I did not create this situation. I never hurt her. All I wanted to do was to love and take care of her, but she didn't want that, or couldn't handle it. I know it's as a result of her insecurities about our relationship, and you know, it may actually be better that things didn't work out, because now I see that she could never be in a relationship with any woman, including me."

Yasmeia leaned back in her chair, then shaking her head, she stood up, looked Alex in the eyes and spoke sincerely to her.

"You have every right to be upset with her. But I will make a suggestion to you, and it is up to you to do what you want to do."

"What?"

"If she ever comes to you, at least grant her a moment of your time?"

"I'll think about it."

"Fair enough. " Yasmeia turned to leave, but she stopped at the door and turned back around. "Alex...I'm sorry you're both hurting. I hope one day it will stop." Yasmeia then turned back around and left the office, closing the door behind her.

Yasmeia felt both relieved and frustrated at the conversation. Alex, in the interim, sat back in her chair and turned it to look out over the skyline of the city as tears rolled down her face.

The next few weeks of that month ended somewhat quietly, except for the call that the SEC was going to make an arrest in the insider-trading scam come March. It made Alex uncomfortable with it being so close to the date of her Business party.

"Well D'Angelo, I can't do anything about when they move, I'm just happy that they're about to arrest the people involved."

"Yes, well, I understand. Let me change the subject a little. What about Salina, is she still going to be at the party acting as your PA, or what?"

"I have my plans, and yes, she will still be here. Oh, by the way, did I tell you?"

"What?"

"I made a royal fortune in the sale of my stocks in The Wellington Company, and off of the stocks I have in the Zadria Company."

"You sold your Zadria stock?!"

"Of course not. If I did that, it would look as though I was a part of the insider trading. No, I just held on to my stock."

"Oh, okay. You had me worried there for a moment."

"No, I've been distracted, but not to that point."

"Well I'm happy to hear that Rose."

D'Angelo then laid a kiss on Alex. She pulled him in and turned it around on him so that by the time she allowed him to breathe he was gasping for air.

"Wow Rose! What was that for?"

"Hmm...no reason, I just didn't want you to think you were in control of anything." She said casually, as she stood and walked over to the fireplace, and straightened a photograph.

"Always have to be the dominant one, huh?"

"Always, and you lose points with me when you question me." She said with a serious tone.

The man chuckled and then said in the same tone.

"I don't mind allowing you to have the power."

"Allowing?" Alex said, turning around to look at the man, with knitted brows in surprise.

"Yes Rose, allow, do you think you really are superior to me?"

"Ha! It's not that I think it, because I KNOW IT, it's how others see us, and I am considered to be the superior one even to them."

"Okay Rose, I think we'd better change the subject?"

"Oh...why, are you afraid of the truth D'Angelo?" The woman said, challenging him.

"Rose?"

"D'Angelo?"

"Okay Rose, I'm going to leave before we get into it about who's who in the relationship."

He stood and walked over to place a kiss on the woman's lips. Then he turned and called over his shoulder as he went out the door.

"I'll see you tomorrow Rose."

Alex stood watching the man leave and then once he was gone, she walked thoughtfully towards the sofa chair and sat down. She thought about D'Angelo's words, and how he felt he actually believed he was the dominant one in the relationship.

"Hmm...I'm going to have to watch you D'Angelo."

Meanwhile back at Taylor's grandmother's, Taylor had received a call that her grandmother's attorney wanted to see her, so she went to see what she wanted.

"Ahh...Taylor, come in. We have a lot to discuss."

"Ms. Leta, is it possible to do this later? I'm really not up to this right now."

"I know Taylor, but it's important, and I know your grandmother would be very put out by us if we were derelict in our duties. We've put this off for as long as we could, but we have to settle her estate."

"Okay, but where's the rest of the family?"

"Oh, we've already dealt with them, this is now just about you."

"Oh...alright." She said apprehensively.

"Great! Come on in the boardroom, I want to introduce you to everyone."

Taylor allowed the woman to lead her into the large room where several men and women in business attire sat. She was dressed in a business suit also.

"Nice suit." One woman complimented, as the girl was led to her seat.

"Thank you."

They smiled at her once she was seated and Ms. Leta, the primary attorney, began the introductions.

"Ms. Taylor Young, this is Mr. Payne, he was your grandmother's broker, and this is Ms. Temens, she was your grandmother's accountant. This is Mrs. Olin, your grandmother's business partner years ago. This is Mr. Lev, your grandmother's investment attorney, and this is his partner Mr. Reese. And of course, you know me, I am your grandmother's personal attorney, and I will be doing the majority of talking, they are all here just in case you have questions about anything, okay?"

"Okay." Taylor said, still in the dark.

"Alright, let's get down to it. First of all, I assume you know your grandmother had invested in the stock market?"

"Yes. I helped her with the stocks I thought would be good investments."

"Right, she said that, but did she ever tell you about how well or poorly they were doing?"

"No, except to say they were good choices, and then we would drop it there."

Everyone began smiling, and Taylor's brows knitted at all of the curious reactions.

"Ms. Leta, I don't mean to sound impatient, but I really do want to get back to my grandmother's house."

"No, actually, you want to get back to your house. Your grandmother left it for you in her will."

"Really?" She asked quietly, as tears ran down her face at the love she felt for her departed grandmother. "Well thank you all for letting me know, I appreciate that."

"That's not all Taylor. She left you everything within the house, everything on the land, and all that made up the home."

Taylor smiled slightly in an appreciative way, but then lowered her eyes out of sadness.

"We realize this is hard, but it was out of love that your grandmother took the time to make sure her final wishes were carried out to the letter. She loved you, and I will honor her memory by doing my job."

"I understand."

"Thank you. This next thing basically says she left all of her worldly belongings to you, the cars and everything. Any questions so far?"

"No."

"Okay, now...we come to the 2nd to the last thing." The woman passed a folder down to her. "The folder that is coming to you contains a list of all of the stocks, bonds and other municipals that she held, as well as her checking and saving's accounts that she used for daily things. The checkbook is in there also, with her insurance policies, social security, IRA accounts, and all of those things.

Taylor took the folder, opened it and saw list after list of stocks that her grandmother had owned.

"She owned all of these?"

"Yes, she used to, now you own them."

"Me??"

"Yes, and I must say, it's a pleasure to tell you that you are now a multi-millionaire."

"Mill...million??"

"Yes, with those stocks and things alone, your grandmother was worth millions. And now it's all yours."

The people in the room smiled warmly at her. She, however, sat in shock. But after a few minutes to take it all in, she said in an unsure voice.

"If Grammy left me all of this, what did the other family members get?"

"Ten thousand dollars each and tuition money for their children's educations. They've signed a waiver against any further desires from the estate. It was pocket change to what massive amount that your grandmother had accumulated over the 80 years, plus, the inheritance her own mother and father left her."

"If I may ask..."

"60 million give or take a few thousand."

"60??!!" Oh my goodness gracious. Lord have mercy on me. I never knew! I mean, I figured she had a few million, but nowhere near 60...wow! So...what do I do now?"

"Well, the first thing you need to do is determine who you want to handle your finances. You need to get attorneys and other such people to handle things."

"Well, I think the smart thing to do is find out if all of you would be willing to stay on as my new attorneys, accountants and all the rest?"

"YES!!" Came the combined voices of all at the table.

Taylor smiled slightly at the response, then she told the woman she had a lot of thinking to do, and would be in touch with her very soon. Taylor was about to stand to leave, but the attorney once again stopped her.

"Wait! One more thing."

"Oh? What?"

"This envelope, it's for a Ms. Madison, the note on it says that you know who she is?"

"Ye...yes."

"Good, this is for her." The woman then passed the large envelope down to Taylor, who took it, and her hand trembled slightly as a result.

The next week Taylor gave thanks for her grandmother's love. One day Yasmeia called her to tell her that she had a conversation with Alex a while back, and Yasmeia purposely added words to the woman's own.

"She said she will never forgive you for not apologizing for walking out of her life. Her coming to your grandmother's funeral was simply her way of showing her respect for a woman she respected because of her honesty."

"Yasmeia, I apologized to her, she didn't accept it!"

"Well, you know her, she expected for you to stick around and give her a chance to calm down, but instead you just left. At least that's how she feels about it."

"Really?! Well, we'll just see about that."

"What are you talking about Taylor?" Yasmeia asked, feigning innocence.

"I'm planning on coming there to talk to her...she'll probably eat me alive and then spit out my bones, but at least I'll know I've tried."

"You ARE still in love with her, aren't you?!"

"Yes, I can't help how I feel. I tried to put her and anything that reminded me of her out of my mind, because it hurt too much to think about how badly I screwed up. I was only able to bury them superficially. When I saw her standing across that cemetery, all of the feelings I had for her came flooding over me. Yasmeia, I do love her, and I know I am being a foolish young woman, for still having such strong feelings for her. But I would just die if I didn't try, and she ended up marrying D'Angelo...Gods Yasmeia, I can't lose her."

"But Taylor, her party is going to be taking place in the next few days. With that and the SEC thing looming, she will more than likely not be in the talking mood, plus, what reason will you give her for just showing up?"

"I have a few gifts for her."

"Gifts?"

"Yes, I bought her a birthday gift and card, and a Christmas gift, and a Valentine's day gift, it's the most special, because of the meaning behind it."

"Taylor, you bought her gifts, even though you two were no longer together?"

"Yes. I still care, and even if they never got to her, at least I would have the memory." She said sadly.

"Well I think it's a great idea, and I think you should catch her either the day before the party, or of the party."

"Yes, I can go to the house, the maid will remember me and let me in, and then I can talk to her."

"During the party?"

"Hmmm...I don't know yet, but I know if I do go on that day I had better dress the part to fit in."

"No, that would only tell her that you had been talking to me, and she may not appreciate the fact that I told you."

"Okay, then I will dress normally."

"Okay, well I have to go Taylor, but I will talk to you later."

"Okay Yasmeia, thanks for calling and checking on me."

"You're my friend and you were hurting."

"Thank you, I'll talk to you later."

"Alright Taylor, bye."

"Bye Yasmeia."

The two hung up and Taylor picked up the paper that was lying near the phone and looked at the picture of Alex and D'Angelo. Above the picture it read, "The CEO of Madison Inc., will be giving her annual Business Social. She will be escorted by her long time friend and companion D'Angelo Marazzda". Taylor balled the paper up and threw it to the floor. She picked the telephone back up and called her new attorney.

"Hello, this is Ms. Leta's office, may I help you?"

"Yes, I would like to speak with Ms. Leta, tell her it's Taylor."

"Yes Ma'am."

After a few minutes, Leta got on the phone.

"Taylor, what can I do for you?"

"I need a three million dollar cashier's check, within three days."

"May I ask why?"

"I owe it to someone, and I told her if I ever struck it rich, then I would pay her back. Well...it's happened, and I plan on paying her every cent I owe her."

"How is it that you could afford to even borrow that amount? If you don't mind my asking?"

"I didn't borrow it. I used to work for this person and she had told me specifically about something and what the results of my not following through could mean. Well, I didn't follow through one day, although it was an accident. Anyway, she lost 3 three million dollars that day. Of course she told me I didn't have to pay her back, she was adamant about that, but I have to pay her back, especially now that I am able to."

"But she said you didn't owe her."

"That's not the point! This is a woman who is moving on with her life, and I don't want her to have to waste her time thinking about me. Especially seeing how she wants to move on. So please have it made and sent to me."

"Alright Ms. Young, it'll be sent out to you tomorrow."

"Thank you Ms. Leta, and I will be leaving town for a while. One of my grandmother's friends will be staying here."

"You're welcome Ms. Young."

Taylor hung up the phone and ran upstairs to pack a few clothes. The next day the cashier's check arrived and she got in her car and drove to the airport. She arrived back in the town where her life would forever change, one way or the other. She rented a car and drove to one of the hotels that was near Alex's home. After she settled in, she called Yasmeia and told her she was in town and where she was staying. Yasmeia told her that the party was going to take place tomorrow, and asked if she was going there today or tomorrow.

"I don't know, now that I'm here, I think either way is foolish. I mean, just showing up out of nowhere and going to her party to try and talk to her is really, now that I think about it, way out there."

"Don't back out now Taylor. You're going to have to face her sooner or later. If it's later, you will always wonder if she would have forgiven you and if you two would have been together. You need to tell her everything." Yasmeia stressed.

"Yasmeia, I feel like I'm going to be sick. I feel the same way I did that first day she told me to bring those reports to her personally. I don't know if I can do it. I'm feeling extremely...well, scared!"

"I know, but you'll be fine."

"Okay, I think I am going to get some rest, but I'll talk to you after tomorrow."

"Okay Taylor. I'll talk to you later. Maybe I'll stop by the hotel tomorrow. Good luck."

Taylor hung around her hotel room for the day, listening to the news about Alex's party, and who would be attending. Meanwhile, Alex was talking with agents who had come out to the house to secure the area. She had given them a list of all of the guests who were scheduled to arrive along with their escorts. She also gave them a list of all of the servants and staff that would be there. All care was being taken to assure the safety of not only the special guest, but also those overseas businessmen and women who had come into town specifically to attend this business function.

"Is that all you need?" Alex asked of the head agent.

"Yes Ma'am, the security sweep has been done and the place is secure. There will be agents left here from tonight up until the event ends, so as to be assured security is maintained."

"Fine."

"Everyone's ID badges will be given to them once their identification is verified upon arrival, and then they will be required to wear it at all times. No one will be allowed in who is not on this list."

"I understand. I will send over the servants for you to go over what will be expected of them."

"Thank you ma'am, and thank you for your cooperation Ms Madison. It really does make it easier to do our jobs when we have people working with us."

"I understand the need for the added security."

She turned and gestured to the head servant to gather all of the other servants and go over and listen to what the agent had to say about what was going to take place.

The whole day was spent on getting final things done for the party that was going to start at 2 p.m. and go long into the night. Everyone who had come for the last minute instructions, mainly those who would be serving, greeting or cooking, were required to be there. The residence was decorated in spring fashion. The sliding doors that made up the wall of the living room on one side were now open to reveal a very large ballroom area.

That night when the woman went to bed, D'Angelo stayed over with her. He slept in one of the guest bedrooms. The next morning Alex woke up somewhat anxious, and for the life of her she couldn't figure out why. She knew it wasn't because of the party later, she had been giving this same party every year since she took over her first international company.

"What is it Rose?"

"Nothing, I'm just a little off balance at the moment, I'll be fine after I work out." She headed for the gym.

"Good morning Ma'am." One of the agents called to her as she passed.

"Morning." The woman returned, as she continued to her gym.

Once there, she stretched and then called up her trainer. She worked out for over an hour, then went to go and get cleaned up. She found that the feeling was still with her.

"Damn it! What's going on?" She cursed to herself, not liking the feeling at all.

She finished dressing and went to have breakfast with D'Angelo.

"Well, morning again. Do you feel better?"

"No!" She growled, as she made herself a plate from the food that had been spread out on the table.

"Wow! You're in a bear of a mood this morning."

"If you have a problem with it D'Angelo, you can leave." Alex said sarcastically.

"I know that tone. I guess I'm going to have to walk on eggshells around you today, as will everyone else."

"They're too noisy when they're stepped on." She said teasingly.

D'Angelo heard it and a smile curled the corners of his mouth as he proceeded to eat. Alex glanced up at him over her brows, then lowered her own eyes to her plate as she thought about the two of them.

As the day went on, Taylor woke up anxious and feeling nauseous. She ran to the bathroom and proceeded to get sick. She cleaned up and then got dressed.

At first she was going to go to the restaurant to eat breakfast, but since she was feeling extremely anxious and shaky, she decided to order room service. She sat down on the chair at the small desk and tried to calm her nerves.

She's going to be so angry, and she has the right to be."

Taylor covered her face with her hands and let her tears soothe her. After calming down, she wiped her eyes and then she picked up a little jewelry box out of a box that held a few other gifts, and opened it to look at it for the umpteenth time. It was a gold chain with a silver and gold, heart shaped, pendant hanging from it.

The pendant had two silver and gold clasps on the back of it and they were in the open position. It made the pendant look like it was an accordion. She had seen it at a jewelry store and the woman behind the counter told her it could represent many things, but most people used it to represent the loss of love ones, hence the broken heart. Taylor, on the other hand, saw a different meaning behind it, and it brought tears to her eyes just to think about that meaning. By the time the party came around, she was nauseated again. Taylor decided she couldn't face Alex at that moment, so instead she lay down on the bed in her hotel room and fell asleep, hoping the nausea would pass. Meanwhile Alex was in her element, despite the feeling she still had.

CHAPTER 19

"Ms. Madison, it's a wonderful party, as always."

"I know Mr. Henderson." The woman said with a smirk, as she gave a slight tilt of her head and walked away from the man.

"So, any plans for a takeover coming up that you would like to share with us Alex?" A CEO of one of the rival companies asked, hoping to find out a little information. He knew not to expect any, but he didn't think it would hurt to ask.

"Yes, but who knows what company? Maybe it's yours Grayson?" Alex said with a devilish glance at the man, who nearly dropped his glass. "Careful Grayson, or you'll owe me a new floor." She said, as she gave a wicked grin, then excused herself from the flustered man.

"Alex, you are something! You have a wicked sense of humor."

"You think so Julia?" She asked out of curiosity.

"Oh yes, definitely, no one ever knows when you're serious or kidding."

"Just the way I like it Julia. By the way, I see that your company's stock has gained a few points more over the last few months, and they even split??"

"Um...yes, but not enough to really make an impact." The woman quickly added, when Alex turning to face her squarely, with apparent interest in what was going on with her company.

The woman noticed the look in Alex's eyes and she became uncomfortable.

"Um...where's your PA?"

"Hmm...she's around." Alex said with a knowing smirk, enjoying the obvious discomfort the CEO of Technology Data Security's was experiencing.

"Ahh...well, I would love to meet her."

"Certainly, I'll make sure you do. Enjoy yourself Julia. I'll be watching." Alex purred, as she walked away to speak with other guests.

Salina was making her rounds, talking to different people, gaining information for Alex, but also for herself and her partner. Alex saw Salina make her way over to Mr. Wellington, who was standing off to one side, making conversation with some of the others. She noticed how Wellington excused himself from other CEO's and VP's to go and talk with Salina. She found that very inappropriate and strange, so she watched the two discreetly as she made her way around, talking to the different guests.

D'Angelo joined her around 6 that evening as he had been forced to take care of some business with his own company overseas. He had used the phone in Alex's study to make his calls.

"D'Angelo, so...you finally made it. I was beginning to wonder if you had been shot or something by the Secret Service?"

"I know, I'm sorry it took so long. Has she arrived yet?"

"Who?"

"Who?? What do you mean who, Alex? The President of the U.S.A."

"No, and why are you so excited? It's not like she's your President or anything. Matter of fact, she's only an adopted one of mine. If she shows up fine, if not, fine, it's her loss. All the business men and women who have any clout are already here." She smirked, as she took two glasses of champagne off of a tray that one of the servants was passing around.

"And I would bet that they're all concerned when you show the least little interest in any of their companies."

"Well, it is nice to be feared." She said, flashing a bright smile at the man.

The two went around together for most of the evening, but there came a point when Alex went to greet The President who had arrived at nine, with her husband. They spoke for a bit, and then Alex introduced the President to some of her admirers, while she went back to talk to one of the agents at the front door. When she finished talking, she stood near the door in view of the window from outside. She was talking to some people who had filtered out of the other room to be able to talk quietly to one another about some business or another.

Meanwhile Taylor had finally decided to go and talk to Alex. She had slept up until 6:30, but she didn't decide until 9:30p.m.

Taylor drove her rental car to Alex's resident, and up the driveway, where she observed the agents standing either on the stairs or off around the side of the house. Taylor slowly got out of her car. At first she thought about bringing her small box of gifts with her, but looking at the faces of the agents it made her a bit nervous to even think about reaching for it, so she left it for the time being. She walked up the stairs and just as she arrived at the top, one of the agents stepped up to her.

"May I help you Ma'am?"

"Oh, I'm here to see Ms. Alexandra Madison."

"Is she expecting you?"

"No, but I need to speak with her for just a moment."

"I'm sorry Ma'am, we cannot allow you to go in. I'm sorry, but you will have to leave."

"But I just want to talk to Ms. Madison, it's very important."

"I'm afraid we can't allow you to go inside."

"Okay, well...can you ask her to step out here for a moment?"

"No, we can't."

"But she's right there! Please, just ask her to step out here for a moment?" Taylor was trying to tamp down her rising anxiety.

She had come this far, she knew if she didn't do it now, then she would never be able to do it.

"I'm sorry Ma'am, it's for security reasons that we can't allow you inside."

"I understand that, that's why I'm asking you to ask her if she would step out here? I have something for her. It's in my car. It's a box with a few gifts inside."

"Check it out." The lead agent ordered one of the others.

The agent brought the box back to the landing of the stairs and walked it over to where a machine was set up. He put it inside and it read the contents of the box, as well as gave a visual. The man picked the box up and handed it to Taylor.

"We had to check to make sure."

"I understand. Now may I talk with Ms. Madison?"

"I'm afraid not Ma'am, maybe you can come back tomorrow?" The man said more compassionately, when he saw how upset she was becoming.

Taylor was near tears, but she kept them in check. She looked back in the window, and saw Alex looking out at her. She saw the look of confusion cross the woman's face, but yet she made no move to come to the door. She simply watched her and saw how Taylor lowered her eyes to look at the box. Her heart was once again shattering, the tears fell, and she lifted her eyes to see Alex still looking at her, until one of the guests pulled her out of the view of the window, with conversation. The girl swallowed hard, and hurt was written all over her face, to where even the agents felt for her, even though they didn't know the reason why she was so hurt.

"I'm sorry Ma'am."

Taylor lifted her eyes to the man, and with a failing attempt at a smile, she turned and headed down the stairs. Once she had reached the bottom stairs and had walked halfway back to her car, the front door opened and Alex stepped out to speak to the agents for a moment before she spoke to Taylor.

"Ms. Young."

Taylor stopped in her tracks and slowly turned around to see Alex standing on the landing with her arms crossed over her chest.

"Alex? I mean...Ms. Madison." She said, not sure of how to address the woman.

"What did you want?" Alex said, getting right to the point.

"Oh! I came by hoping I could talk to you."

"No, I'm right in the middle of a function. It's just not a good time." She answered pointedly.

"Well, can I talk to you later?"

"When? Tonight? After this?" Alex asked in a 'you've got to be kidding' tone of voice.

"Tonight, tomorrow, the day after, whenever you say, I'll be there."

"What if I said never, then what?"

Taylor literally flinched at the harsh words. She tried to think of something to say to that, but she had not actually considered that the woman would say such a thing. It wasn't completely unexpected, but she didn't think Alex hated her enough to tell her to stay away. She lifted her eyes back up to the woman on the landing and all she could manage was a weak shrug of her shoulders. She looked back down at the box, and thinking about all that was inside of it, she decided to give them to the woman anyway. After all, she had bought them specifically for her. Taylor walked back to the stairs and walked up them slowly, as she watched the woman, not sure of what to expect from her.

"I know you're angry with me Alex." She said, as she came to a stop on the step just below where Alex stood, which made her look that much more dominating.

"Really? I didn't know it was a secret Ms. Young?"

Taylor's eyes instantly watered as she took Alex's biting sarcasm.

"You have the right to be, I was completely wrong...once again, and you were right, as usual. I should have been stronger. If I had been, then I would not have lost...well the point is, I wasn't strong enough, and therefore I allowed for things to turn out the way they have."

"Are you trying to tell me that someone else made you do all the things you did?"

"Yes. I mean no. Not all of it, as a matter of fact, as I think about it, it wasn't anyone's fault but my own. I chose to pull away out of my own fear and insecurities. The other person only gave me a reason to use to justify it."

"So you're admitting that you willingly chose to pull away?"

"That's such a harsh way to look at it. I know hindsight is 20/20, but I didn't think I had any other choices. I'm not as strong as you are! I will never be. I admit I was wrong not to come and talk to you about what was going on with me. I admit it Alex! But I swear to you, I NEVER wanted to hurt you! I know how hard it was for you to trust anyone with your heart, and here you were entrusting it to me. So what did I do...I screwed up! I will offer no excuses because it would only insult and diminish the feelings. I will say this, and I mean it from my heart Alex, I am so...sorry, if I could take the pain away, and take it on myself, I would. If I could take that look of anger and resentment out of your gaze, and replace it with honest, forthright love once again, I would give anything. Alex I do love you. I have loved you and I will always love you. I want you back in my life, but from the look in your eyes, I can see it's not going to happen. It's...well, anyway, thank you for coming out and listening to me, it means a lot. I'll leave you alone, but I have a few things for you."

"What?"

"Just gifts, your birthday, Christmas, and this one, a Valentine's gift." Taylor handed the open box to the woman after taking out the necklace container. Alex took the small box of gifts and handed it to the agent who was standing nearby. He walked over and took it and walked back away so as to give the two a semblance of privacy.

"Why a Valentine's gift?" She asked with wonder.

"Because of what the necklace represents."

Alex knitted her brows at the statement, and then took the gift and slowly opened the box to look at what was inside. She lifted the necklace out of the box and held it up looking at it with knitted brows. She saw that it was supposed to be a heart, but she couldn't quite put her finger on the meaning. She had an idea that it was probably a symbol of loss, so that's what she said.

"It's supposed to represent the loss?" She asked, as she now looked back at Taylor.

"No, it represents the number of times I've broken your heart, albeit always unintentionally, but nonetheless I did."

"So why give me such a gift?! Why would I want to remember such a thing Taylor??!" She said, now getting angry at the very thought.

"No...not so you would remember the broken heart." Taylor said, stepping up on the landing and taking the pendant part of the necklace in her hands, while the woman held the chain part. Taylor closed the heart's clasps, thereby making it look like a whole heart. Alex's eyes lit with understanding, but then she said in an even tone.

"But the breaks are still there."

"Yes, but over time, I would hope you would forget that they were there, and just see the wholeness. Alex, if you give me another chance, I promise you I will make this up to you."

Alex studied her for a very long and uncomfortable moment for Taylor, and then she said evenly once again.

"Is that all? I need to get back inside with my guests."

"Um...yes, except for two envelopes inside of the box, one is from me, and the other is from Grammy. She left it for you in her will."

"Really?"

"Yes, I think it's a letter of some sort."

"Hmm...well, thank you for bringing it. It wasn't necessary, you could have mailed it."

"No, it was necessary. At least I got to see you one last time. I hope you and D'Angelo will be happy. You deserve it Alex. You're a wonderful woman. Well, I'll let you get back in to your guests. Take care." Taylor turned and then headed down the stairs, slowly at first, and then as her anxiety rose, she then ran down the stairs to her car.

"Taylor!! Don't you dare!!" Alex shouted at her, noticing the same behavior Taylor displayed when she was driving like a madwoman in the heart of the city sometime ago.

Taylor stopped in her tracks once again and looked back at the woman who was now glaring at her. Taylor understood what Alex was saying, so she simply nodded her head and turned back around and walked the rest of the way to her car. She got in but didn't start it. Instead she sat in it, crossed her arms and with the stress of how she was feeling, she then cried. Alex took in a deep, relieved breath, then turned and walked over to the agent. She picked up the box and spoke to him.

"Make sure she does not leave here until she has either composed herself, or one of you drive her back to wherever she is staying. I don't want her to leave here as upset as she is. She has a tendency to drive recklessly and that could be even more dangerous up here, especially with the winding roads."

"No problem. We'll make sure she's alright before she leaves here, otherwise I'll have someone drive her home."

"Thank you." Alex then turned back around to look at the girl who was now leaning on the steering wheel crying. She pinched her lips, and then turned and walked back inside to attend her party.

Taylor sat in the car for over an hour just crying and trying to calm down enough to drive herself back to the hotel. The agents stood watching her making sure she didn't leave until she was okay. Finally, she composed herself. The moment she put the key in the ignition and turned in on, the head agent went out to the car to the driver's side.

"Are you okay?"

She looked up at the man, and with tears still rolling down her face, she simply nodded.

"Okay, I had to ask, you were so upset. You're sure you're okay to drive this road?"

"Yes, thank you." She said, then put her car in gear and pulled slowly away from the place. The man, still worried, decided to have one of his agents follow her just to make sure. So Taylor drove back to the hotel without knowing that she was being followed.

Meanwhile, Alex had intermittently checked to see if the girl had left yet. The final time she checked, she saw the agent talking to Taylor and then she pulled off. A few moments later she saw one of the agents pull out and follow after Taylor. Alex went back to her party and D'Angelo was by her side. Salina would come over to the two and talk to them for a moment about things she had found out. Alex would watch and listen to Salina with suspicion, and anger. She didn't allow her contempt to show outwardly, but it was there.

The party continued throughout the night, into the early morning. Alex's time was taken up mostly by the President, the Senators, and other political people. They were, of course, trying to garner support for their upcoming elections, but Alex played the game and talked around any guarantees to any of them. She loved the conversation and the challenge that they offered her. When the event finally ended and everyone had gone, Alex and D'Angelo went upstairs and talked for a bit before they turned in.

"So...great party Rose."

"Yes, it turned out the way it was supposed to." She said, distracted.

"Made a lot of contacts." D'Angelo said, noticing she was distracted by the box that was sitting on the dresser.

"Yeah, perfect environment."

"Okay Alex, it's obvious to me that you're not going to bring it up, so I will." D'Angelo said with frustration at being ignored.

"What are you talking about?"

"That box, and who gave it to you!"

"What about it?" The woman said flatly.

"I know you want to look inside and see what all is in there, so fine!" He jumped off of the bed, got the box, and set it down on the bed next to Alex.

She looked at him like he had lost his mind. She felt like he was challenging her. Then she lowered her gaze to the box. After a moment, she picked it up and opened it. She took out the two other gifts and the cards that went along with them. Opening the card to the birthday gift first, she read it and then read the hand written part of it.

"Although we are apart, you will always be in my heart. I hope this day will be full of joy for you. The thought of your happiness brings a smile to my face and fills my heart. Happy Birthday Alexandra." Alex noticed that the girl obviously couldn't decide on how to sign it, so she ended it by writing "Taylor", after crossing out the "L", and the "your" that she had started signing it with.

Alex put the card down and opened the smaller box that held the gift. She discovered that it was a crystal, tulip-shaped vase. She admired the small token, then D'Angelo reached for it to look at it while the woman knitted her brows at the gesture by him. She gave it to him and picked up the other gift that was in the box. Again, she read the card and the hand written part of it first, before reaching for the Christmas gift.

"I saw this and I thought of us, as I'm always doing. Grammy thinks that I should go back there to talk to you and see if we can work things out, but I told her I didn't think there was any chance of it working out. She asked me why I would be buying you gifts if I didn't have some hope and I could only tell her, "for the memories". If you never receive any of these, I'll always remember the love I felt for you when I bought them. I hope you have a blessed and Merry Christmas Alexandra...God Bless you in all you do. Taylor Young." Again Alex picked up the Christmas wrapped box. She opened it and pulled out a figurine of two women. One was taller than the other and both were standing within arms reach of each other, facing one another. The taller figure was holding her hands with the palms facing up with the smaller woman's hands resting on top of them. Both figures were looking into each other's eyes. Alex held the figurine up for a while, just looking at it and then thinking about the meaning of it.

"Alex!" D'Angelo called, nearly shouting, making it obvious that he had called her a couple of times.

"What?!" She shouted back, as she looked over at him.

"I was just saying how it's obvious that your friend still has a thing for you."

"So...she's no different than anyone else, mainly you! That's why you're here, isn't it?" Alex stated matter-of-factly.

"Yes, but I want you to marry me. She's only offering you sex."

"D'Angelo?! That's not true at all, and I thought you liked her?"

"I did when she was not competing for your affections. She had you, and lost you. Now it's my turn and I don't plan on losing you to her, or anyone else." D'Angelo said, as he laid a passion filled kiss on the woman.

After breaking the kiss, she smirked and said in a wry tone.

"If I didn't know better, I'd think you were jealous of a woman."

"Jealous? I have no reason to be jealous of your little friend. You're with me now."

"Am I now? When exactly did I ever tell you that you and I were together?" Alex asked, as she turned to face the now surprised man sitting on her bed next to her.

"What are you saying Rose?"

"I'm not saying anything that I have not said before D'Angelo. I'm just trying to get answers. Look D'Angelo, I love your company. You're funny, challenging, smart and intelligent. While I am flattered that you want me in your life forever, I don't think I'm ready for that right now. Then again, who knows? I may take you up on your offer of marriage, but not now. There are just too many things happening in my life right now."

"The girl?"

"One of which is her. I admit it, there are a LOT of unresolved issues between us, and I cannot and will not make any decisions until everything is resolved, one way or the other."

"Rose?"

"D'Angelo, that's my decision. If you don't want to accept it, then you are free to leave." Alex said, with sincerity and compassion.

D'Angelo heard the compassion and he had to smile as a result of it.

"What?"

"What do you mean what?"

"Why the smile D'Angelo?"

"Oh, that. Because out of all the years we've known each other and have done business with each other, for the first time I can see a change in you. There's a compassion that you never had or showed before. I was just wondering if I was the one who helped bring that out in you?" He said, in a hopeful tone.

Alex raised a brow at him, then turned her attention back to the box while at the same time letting a smirk play at her lips. The man sat waiting for her to answer the question, and she knew that's what he was waiting for.

"Well?"

"Well what D'Angelo?" She asked, as she lifted out the envelope from Taylor and the one from her grandmother. She put the one from the grandmother down as she opened the other one.

D'Angelo was looking at the woman with frustration and in the midst of it, he asked her the question again. Instead of getting the answer he expected, he got one directed somewhere else.

"Damn it!! I can't believe this!!" The woman hissed, as she jumped up off of the bed and immediately went to changing back into street clothes. She threw on a pair of jeans and a tee shirt with tennis shoes.

"Rose?! What's going on? Where are you going?"

"I'll be back after I wring someone's little neck." The woman sneered, as she snatched up the envelope and her keys and flew out the door. She stopped for a moment at the bottom of the stairs to make a call.

"Yasmeia!"

"Ms. Madison, it's 4:30 in the morning! Is something wrong?"

"Where is Taylor staying?"

"At the hotel right down the road from your place. Why? Is everything alright? I mean, you sound a little tense?"

"Well, I'm a little tired. What room?" Alex said, not wanting Yasmeia to call Taylor before she got there.

"5120."

C.L.I.C.K!!

The woman hung up the phone and raced out of the house to her car. She put it in gear and sped out of the estate, down the winding road, to the hotel that was nearby. She parked her car and walked, focused on getting to the girl.

CHAPTER 20

Alex took the elevator to the fifth floor, where she stormed off of it and headed down and around the hallway to where Taylor's room was located. Alex banged on the door loudly! The girl was inside asleep, and when the banging rang through her hotel room, she was startled awake. She jumped out of the bed, and eased towards the door that was still being banged on intermittently. In a shaking voice, she called out to the person on the other side.

"Wh...who is it?"

"OPEN THE DOOR!!" Came Alex's authoritative voice.

"Alex??" Taylor said to herself, surprised by the visit. She peeked out the peephole and then opened the door slightly.

The woman stood glaring at her and Taylor stood holding her robe closed.

"Alex? What's wrong?"

Alex pushed the door all the way open and stormed inside. She went half way in, then turned around to see the girl was still standing at the open door.

"WHAT THE HELL IS THIS?!!" She shouted at the girl.

Taylor jumped, but she closed the door so as not to disturb any of the other guests in the hotel. Then she walked slowly turned towards Alex and looked at the envelope the woman was holding up.

"Oh...that's just the money I owed you." Taylor said, slightly relieved.

"First of all, did I or did I not say you didn't owe me anything, as long as you didn't make the same mistake?"

"Yes, but I had it, so it was the right thing to do. Is that what you're so upset about? The fact that I paid you back??"

Alex was now baring her teeth, and as a result she began speaking through them.

"Secondly...where did you get 3 million dollars?"

"It sort of...fell in my lap." Taylor answered sincerely, but Alex didn't hear it that way, she only heard an evasive response.

"Fell into your lap, huh? From where?" Alex asked, now leaning forward slightly to look deeper into the flinching girl's eyes.

"Alex, what does it matter? The point is I paid you back!"

Alex leaned back up straight and her eyes narrowed. She then hissed through her teeth at the girl.

"Why are you being so evasive Taylor?"

"I'm not. Why are you acting like I've done something terrible?"

Alex crossed her arms over her chest and rested back on one heel as the other foot was tapping the floor impatiently.

"You've heard, I'm sure, that my companies are about to be investigated by the SEC right?"

"Yes, I heard...WAIT! Alex!! You don't think..." Taylor was now in shock, and couldn't believe what the woman was accusing her of. Alex saw the moment Taylor realized what she was saying.

"Tell me where you got the 3 million." Alex said evenly.

"I can't believe you actually think I could do something like that to you?! Goodness! I knew you didn't trust me, but..."

"Where did you get it?"

"I never thought you could ever think I would do something like that??"

"Never mind all of that, just tell me where you got the money!"

"No! And I think you'd better leave Alex." Taylor said, hurt and angry by the accusation.

Alex brought her arms down to an akimbo position as she now looked at the girl with ironic amusement.

"No...No?"

"That's what I said." Taylor said, standing up to the woman from a distance.

"Well aren't you just the one? What are you going to do if I don't leave, Taylor?" Alex asked sarcastically, with a dangerous tone ringing through her voice.

Taylor wanted to stand up to the woman, but she knew Alex could break her in half if it came to a physical confrontation. So she did the next best thing.

"Fine! Then I'll leave!" Taylor said, turning to head for the door. Alex made it there before her and backed her away from it by just moving towards her.

"Oh...no Taylor, we're going to finish this, you're GOING to tell me where you got this money. I'm not leaving until you tell me where you got 3 million dollars!"

Taylor knew the woman was determined and she saw the rage in her eyes. She felt trapped and tears began to roll down her face from hurt, frustration and fear. She looked for any escape, and seeing none, she realized the bathroom would have to do.

"Fine!" She shouted, then darted into the bathroom and locked the door just as Alex reached it.

"Taylor come out of there!!"

"No!"

Alex huffed at the response, then hit the door while at the same time calling to her.

"OPEN THIS DOOR TAYLOR!!"

"NO!! I can't believe you think that about me!!"

"Taylor I'm starting to get pissed! Open the door!!"

"No!" Taylor shouted back through the door.

Alex hit the door again, this time out of frustration.

"Open this damn door Taylor!!"

"No." Taylor said more quietly. She didn't want to add to Alex's anger by yelling at her.

The woman let a volley of colorful expletives fly from her mouth towards the door and the girl behind it. Taylor covered her ears and sat down on the closed toilet as the tears rolled down her face. Suddenly there was a knock at the door of the room. Alex smirked and then knocked on the door of the bathroom very gently.

"Taylor?"

"What?"

"Someone is at the door to the room."

"Who?"

"I really don't know." Alex said, in a deceptively sweet voice.

"Well open it."

"No, this isn't my room. You have to open your own door...hmmmm...you better do it soon, they seem a little anxious." Alex said, now leaning against one side of the door jam of the bathroom door. Waiting for Taylor to come out.

"Will you please see who it is?" Taylor asked kindly.

Alex walked over to the door, looked out the peephole, then casually walked back to the bathroom door and waited for the girl to say something else.

"Well are you going to see who it is Alex?"

"It's Yasmeia."

"Yasmeia? Well let her in!"

"No."

"Please let her in?"

"No, I'm perfectly satisfied to keep this between you and me. Who knows? There's no telling what I may have to do."

Taylor swallowed hard at the indirect threat.

"Why are you doing this Alex?!!" Taylor asked with frustration.

"Open the door and I will tell you why." Alex stated evenly.

"Taylor?!! Open the door!" Yasmeia called fearfully.

"Hmm...you know if you don't open the door soon, Yasmeia is going to think you're hurt. She will worry and then she'll have to go and get help as a result. In the interim, I may just make such a thing happen Taylor Young, if YOU DON'T OPEN THIS DAMN DOOR NOW!!!" The woman's voice rose to a crescendo.

She once again began banging on the door of the bathroom and this time her strength was showing. The door shook with every blow against it. She continued yelling at the girl to open the door and what would happen if she didn't. Taylor was yelling back for Alex to stop and to calm down.

Meanwhile, Yasmeia had caught one of the housekeepers on the floor getting ready to use her master swiper to go into one of the recently vacated rooms.

"Excuse me, can you open this door for me? I think my friend has her t.v. up too loud and therefore she can't hear me at the door."

"Oh, okay." The two women walked back over to the door and the housekeeper heard the loud voices and assumed that it was the t.v.. "You're right, it is up loud." She swiped the key lock and the door clicked. Yasmeia thanked the woman. Then she waited for her to go back to the previous room, and then she turned and opened the door to Taylor's room.

When the door opened, Yasmeia was stunned to see Alex banging on the door and cursing at Taylor to open it, and Taylor refusing. Yasmeia immediately closed the door of the room and walked nearer to the scene.

"Ms. Madison??"

"Yasmeia." Alex said, irritated by the intrusion.

"What's going on?"

"Ask Taylor, she's locked herself in the bathroom and won't come out."

"Well I can see why she wouldn't! It's a bit scary for me to see you banging on the door like you were a moment ago. I can only imagine that the child is scared to death to come out. I know I wouldn't come out."

"Well she had better come out, otherwise I'll be going in." Alex said tightly.

"Well go over there and I'll try to get her to come out."

"Fine." The woman said as she stormed over to the bed. She crossed her arms as she waited for Taylor.

"Taylor it's me, Yasmeia. Please come out?"

"Yasmeia?! She wants to hurt me, and I didn't even do anything! I'm not coming out."

"No Taylor, she doesn't want to hurt you. She's just upset, but she would never strike you...right Ms. Madison?"

Alex glared at Yasmeia, but seeing the request for an answer, she complied.

"Right, whatever! Just get out here Taylor!" The woman shouted.

"See Taylor? Please come out. I'm here now anyway, and she won't hurt you with me around." Yasmeia hoped, but looking at Alex she wasn't sure.

Alex stood, casting a gaze at Yasmeia as if to say, don't bet on it. Taylor, meanwhile, thought about Yasmeia's logic and after a moment, she eased the door open. Alex went to move near, but Yasmeia's hand went up to tell her to stay where she was. Alex glared and then sighed with frustration. She turned and walked back over towards the bed. Taylor eased out the door, all the while watching the angry woman pace and cast evil glances at her.

"Yasmeia!" Taylor cried, as she went into her friend's arms and sobbed bitterly.

"Taylor it's alright. I'm sure things can be worked out. Most likely it's just a misunderstanding."

"No! Alex has been cruel and mean and hurtful!" She said, lifting her head to look at Yasmeia and then looking back at Alex.

"What's going on?" Yasmeia asked, not wanting to take anyone's side.

"Tell her Taylor."

"Tell her what?!"

"Tell her about the 3 million dollars."

"Three million dollars? What about it?"

Alex waited to see if Taylor was going to tell her, but then realized she wasn't.

"Fine, I'll tell her. It seems that Taylor was able to pay me 3 million dollars, paid via cashier's check."

"You gave her 3 million dollars??"

"Yes, I owed it to her."

"So what's the problem Alex?"

"Ask her where she got 3 million dollars cash to pay me! As if I didn't know!"

"See! There you go again, accusing me! I told you I could never do such a thing, and I don't know why you would even think it!" Taylor cried, as she shouted back as much as her tightening throat would allow.

"Then tell me where you got it from!"

"NO!"

"Taylor TELL ME!!!"

"No! I won't! It's none of your business!! You're not the boss of me anymore! And I mean that literally!" Taylor shouted.

"See! See why I'm pissed? She won't even answer a simple ass question!"

Yasmeia understood both women's points at the moment. Taylor not wanting to tell Alex because of Alex's anger, and Alex taking Taylor's silence about the money as an evasive response.

"Alex, does it really make that much of a difference where she got the money?"

"Yes!" Alex said sharply.

"Okay...Taylor why don't you just tell Alex where you got the money from, and then this can all be over?"

"NO! Not after what she accused me of!!"

"Accused you of?"

"Yes!"

"Alex? What is she talking about?"

Alex sneered at the questioning, and after a moment of glaring at Taylor, she turned her focus on Yasmeia, and raised a brow at the thought that came to her mind at that very moment.

"Interesting."

"What?"

"Yasmeia, have you heard that there's an investigation going on of a person inside of my company and someone outside of it, for insider trading?" She asked, as she cocked her head at the woman standing near her.

Yasmeia gave a confused look and then she answered.

"Yes, but what has that got to do with any of this?"

"It's sort of convenient to suddenly have 3 million dollars, wouldn't you think?"

Yasmeia's brows knitted at first, but then Taylor spoke out again.

"I didn't do anything!!"

"Then tell me where you got it from!!" Alex shouted at her.

"No!" Taylor said, and Alex moved to get to her, but Taylor ran back into the bathroom and barely had time to lock it before Alex was on it.

"Taylor open this damn door!!"

"No! Not until you apologize."

Alex literally flinched at the statement.

"Ha! You've got to be kidding! What have I got to apologize for? I'm not the one who suddenly ended up with 3 million dollars!"

Suddenly Yasmeia put it together and she couldn't speak quickly enough.

"ALEX?!! You can not honestly believe what I think you're thinking?!"

"Why can't I?!"

"Alex...no. You are sooo...wrong, I...I'm shocked that you could even think that that child would EVER do anything like that to hurt you. It's a malicious and vindictive act, and I cannot believe, no! I won't believe that you think that child, or myself, could EVER be a part of Insider Trading? Alex that child could no more have anything to do with that than you yourself. I know you don't believe Taylor to be such a wicked person. I know you don't!"

Alex inhaled deeply, and looked at the closed bathroom door. She turned away from it and faced Yasmeia.

"What am I supposed to think when she won't tell me otherwise? What am I supposed to do? Alex said, moving back towards the bed.

Suddenly Taylor came out of the door.

"Think about who you're accusing. Trust in the knowledge that I would never do something like that!" Taylor blurted out, and then went back into the bathroom and locked it.

Alex initially started to move back towards her, but Taylor finished and ducked back inside the bathroom. When both Alex and Yasmeia figured Taylor was through and that she was not going to come back out, Yasmeia started to answer Alex's questions also.

"I..."

Taylor then made another sudden appearance from the bathroom.

"And another thing, I don't appreciate having you question my integrity!" Taylor once again ducked back inside the bathroom.

Yasmeia and Alex both waited for Taylor to come out again and finish, but after a few minutes and not a sound from Taylor, they once again returned their attention to each other.

"Look Alex, you are so wrong. If you knew the truth, you would be ashamed and embarrassed by your behavior toward this child." Yasmeia said, with both respect and honesty.

"Yeah!! You would be VERY ashamed of yourself!" Taylor inserted once again with her random appearances.

"Taylor, either you're going to come out of there or stay in! But do one or the other!" Alex demanded.

"I'll do what I want to do. We're not together anymore! Why don't you just go back and be with D'Angelo? I just gave you your money and it's up to you to take it or leave it." Taylor said from within the bathroom.

Alex finally got fed up and she growled out her anger and frustration.

"Fine Taylor! Keep your ASS in there!! But let me make something perfectly clear to you little girl. I don't want you calling me, coming anywhere near me, or asking about me. I'll make sure to make you invisible the way you wanted to be. I refuse to deal with all of this drama and pain. Have a great life Taylor Young!!" She then turned and stormed for the door.

Yasmeia looked at the closed door and then at the departing woman. She knew if she didn't do something to stop Alex, then Taylor would beat herself up about hurting Alex yet again, and Alex would possibly hate Taylor.

"Alex Wait! Please?!" Yasmeia called to the woman.

"Yasmeia there's nothing else to say. Taylor refuses to tell me where she got this money."

"Taylor, please come out. You know you don't really want Alex to leave. Especially after all the courage it took you to come back here and talk to her. Please come out now, otherwise you will regret this day for the rest of your life."

Taylor opened the door after a few moments and stepped out into the main part of the room. She on one side and Alex on the other, still facing the door to leave.

"Taylor please tell her where you got the money?"

"Why should I? She thinks...I'm a thief, and a malicious vindictive person..." Taylor cried through her statement.

Although Yasmeia had asked the question, her focus was squarely on Alex, her voice one of a plea, and of demand.

Alex heard the girl's pain and she felt it as well as her own. She turned and stared at Taylor for a moment. Then she slowly walked back over to where Taylor stood. Taylor obviously debating whether to run back into the bathroom or stand where she was. She decided to stand still, although she was trembling at the very thought of what Alex was going to do to her. Finally, Alex was right upon her and Taylor kept her eyes looking straight ahead, fearing that if she looked up at the woman directly in front of her, she would just pass out from the fear.

"Taylor, I'm only going to ask you one last time and you can either answer me or not. I don't want to hear anything else but the answer to my question. If you answer any way other than the way I expect and want, then I will turn around and walk out of here and forget you ever existed." Tears rolled down Alex's face with those words, but she didn't seem to notice.

Taylor had her own tears rolling to match. "If you do answer my question, and I find that I was wrong, I will offer my profound apology and hope that over time you will forgive me for my mistrust and questioning of your integrity. Now please, tell me where you got the money."

Taylor and Alex both stood within inches of each other, both just looking straight ahead. Alex was looking straight over Taylor's head and Taylor looking at the woman's long neck, but neither really seeing. Yasmeia stood away from the two just waiting and hoping that Taylor would answer Alex.

Finally, after Taylor thought about what it would mean, she took a deep breath and lowered her head for just a moment to allow herself a moment to clear her throat. Then she raised her head back up to look at the woman's neck.

"My Grandmother left it to me in her will."

CHAPTER 21

Alex didn't move. She continued to stand where she was, still not convinced.

"She just happened to leave you 3 million dollars? Maybe a little more? I mean, I can't imagine that you would give me 3 million dollars if that's all she left you?"

"No, it was a little more. And you're right, I wouldn't give you all of it. But I would give you half of it, and then once I made the other half again, I would give you the rest."

Alex glanced down at the girl out of disbelief, but Taylor didn't know it.

"So how much more Taylor?"

"57 and some change."

Both Alex and Yasmeia's brows knitted. Then they both caught on at the same time.

"57 MILLION?!!" They both said in unison.

Taylor heard the shock and the surprise in their voices and a small curl came to the corners of her mouth. She found the courage to finally look up into Alex's eyes that were now staring at her.

"Yes. Grammy left me everything except a few million that she gave to her other kids and their children."

"She had 60 plus million dollars Taylor?" Alex asked shocked.

"Yes. Her attorney told me that she had been investing in aggressive stocks since she was a little girl and that it was her parents who first invested for her. She just recently converted to less risky stocks. After she retired from her business, she was living off of the interest. Plus the money she was left by her parents when they passed on."

Alex now felt the shame that Yasmeia said she would. She lifted her head upwards and rolled her eyes at her own mistake. Then she took a deep breath and looked back down at Taylor.

"I'm sorry. I didn't want to believe you would do anything like that to me, but when you wouldn't tell me, my mind and my blind anger ran away with me. I can never find the words to tell you how sorry I am for scaring you the way I did. If it helps to know, I would have never hit you, I might have shaken you a bit, but I would not have struck you. Taylor, I hope you will accept my apology and one day forgive me for my temper." Taylor looked into Alex's eyes, and made her own deal.

"I'll forgive you, if you will forgive me for the pain I've caused you?"

Alex smirked at the deal, but then with a smile, she said in a gentle voice.

"You have a deal Taylor Young. We were both wrong and made fools of ourselves."

"I agree, only you're scary about it." Taylor said, with a mild tease in her tone.

Alex chuckled slightly and then brought her hand up to shake Taylor's hand. Taylor just stood looking at it, and then she thought of a better way. She looked up into Alex's eyes and saw the inquisitive look. Taylor knew that her next move would be a bold one and completely unexpected by Alex, and she was taking a chance of being rejected, but she had to risk it. Taylor brought her hand to Alex's cheek and with uncertainty, but resolve, she pulled Alex down to her and kissed her fully. At first Alex stiffened, but then she slowly relaxed and before she knew it, she had her arms around Taylor's waist pulling her close. Taylor moaned as she felt both relief and excitement at the response her body was having to Alex's embrace.

Alex felt herself being pulled in, but she couldn't allow herself to, not without finally clearing up some things first. So she suddenly broke the embrace.

"No Taylor. I can't go there with you."

"But?"

"Taylor I'm sorry, but I can't go there with you without knowing."

"Knowing what? What Alex, I'll tell you anything you ask!" Taylor cried, scared that Alex was going to turn away from her.

"I need to know if you can handle this relationship. You have to be honest with yourself. That's the only way you can be honest with me. I can't and I won't go through the rejection again."

"I still have my fears, but not like they used to be. I admit, I will most likely still be shy about certain things, but knowing that it's you I'm sharing with will alleviate those times of shyness."

"Trust me, I only want to love you. As far as your shyness, I can deal with it. I actually find it quite adorable. It's the pulling away that I can't deal with."

"I trust you Alex, and I won't ever pull away from you like this again. My biggest fear about our relationship is the thought of...losing you out of my life. I will endure anything if you're with me."

"Then Taylor Young, you'll never be alone." Alex said with a smirk.

Taylor didn't know whether to laugh, cry, or just jump up and down, so she did all of them. Taylor wrapped her arms around Alex's neck and planted a kiss on the woman that caused her to stumble backwards onto the bed, bringing Taylor with her.

"I love you, I love you, I love you so much Alex, I won't ever hurt you again I promise." Taylor exclaimed through the kisses.

"I love you Taylor Young." Alex managed to say between Taylor's kisses. Taylor actually was taken aback by the sincerity that she heard in it. Taylor stopped her show of affection at hearing the tone. She looked into Alex's eyes, and all the emotions, stress, pain, and joy she had felt over the year, came out in her tears. She lay down on Alex gently and just cried as she hugged and bathed in Alex's embracing arms. A deep sigh slid from Taylor's throat and Alex heard it and understood.

"Well...I think I will just leave the two of you alone. It seems there's a lot to be expressed, besides...I think I left my stove on." Yasmeia said, recognizing where things were heading and knowing that the two had obviously forgotten about her.

"Yasmeia?"

"Yes?."

"Thank you." Alex said, with sincere appreciation in her voice.

"Thank you for not leaving."

Alex smiled and then said as she hugged Taylor to her.

"Thank you for believing in us."

"You're welcome." Yasmeia then turned and left the two alone.

Taylor continued to lie on Alex, only now they were more comfortably on the bed. Taylor continued to sob until she finally fell asleep. Alex had caressed Taylor's hair and back until Taylor had fallen asleep and then she too drifted off.

CHAPTER 22

The next morning Alex and Taylor woke up still in each other's arms, although it was the middle of the day. This was not all that bad, considering the two had argued from 4:45 that morning until 7a.m. that same morning.

"Well sleepy head, are you ready to get up?"

"That would mean I would have to be out of your arms wouldn't it?"

"Yes Taylor, it would. I think it would be hard to dress or do anything if I couldn't use both arms. Well not anything, but most things." Alex said, correcting herself as she rolled over onto her side so that she was now leaning over Taylor, who was looking up at her.

"Well you don't have to get dressed, so that eliminates one excuse." Taylor said with a coy smile.

"True, but it would be a little hard to drive, although I could manage." Alex said as she leaned down and captured Taylor's lips in a love filled kiss, then leaned back away for a moment.

"I thought we were going to get up?" Taylor asked breathless.

"We are, but I want to enjoy you for a bit before we go and see D'Angelo, so you can tell him I'm not going to marry him."

"What?! Me?!! Alex I can't tell that man that you're not going to be with him. You have to do that." Taylor gasped in shock.

"No, you have to tell him. If you don't, then he will continue to pursue me, and then what?"

"You tell him it's over, and you're involved with someone that you're planning on spending the rest of your life with...HAPPILY." Taylor emphasized.

Alex laughed, and then said with a tease. "If I didn't know better my little sweetling, I'd think you were jealous."

"No, I just plan on holding on to you from now on and...sweetling??

Alex smiled at the sudden change of Taylor's train of thought.

"Yes, that's what I've been seeing you as, but you never gave me a chance to try it out. I like the way it sounds, and the look it's caused in your eyes. Hopefully I'll always see that gaze."

"You will, I can promise you that. I love you, and I never thought I could feel closer to you, but I do."

Alex kissed Taylor once again, acknowledging she heard and was willing to accept her at her word. Taylor moaned at the feelings and the contact. Then when they broke their embrace, Taylor took a moment to catch her breath and said in a sweet voice.

"I am completely in love with my boss."

"Well, the feeling is mutual, only I'm in love with one of my employees. You know, in the military, this would be like fraternization. I would be an Officer and you would be like an enlisted, and we could both be court-martialed?"

"Well Ma'am...I'm willing to take the risk."

"I'm glad to hear that."

"Meaning?"

"Meaning, my little sweetling, that you have a lot of making up to do."

"I thought we were even?"

"We are as far as your major transgressions, but it's the little ones you still owe me for."

"I think you're taking advantage Alex!"

"Really? And what are you going to do about it?"

"Well...I haven't thought of anything yet, but I will."

"Well in the meantime, I think we should go and talk to D'Angelo." Alex said with a smirk, then jumped up off of the bed lifting Taylor along with her. Taylor yelped as a result, and Alex let her down easily onto the floor, as if it were no big deal.

"Now?!!" Taylor asked, after she calmed down from the abrupt position change.

"Yes sweetling, we go now." Alex said, as she kissed Taylor once more before she turned to straighten her hair and her tee shirt and tuck it back into her jeans. Taylor changed her clothes and dressed in casual wear. Alex told her to put a top on that had buttons down the front, and finished the statement with a wry smile. Taylor's hand came to her cheek to cover the blush that suddenly glowed under her naturally caramel skin tone. The two kissed again for long, passionate moments and just before they walked out the door, Alex stopped in the middle of the doorway and looked back at Taylor.

"What is it?"

"I was just thinking."

"What?"

"How much I love kissing you."

"Really??" Taylor asked with a coy grin.

"Yes." Alex responded and then turned completely around in the doorway to face Taylor. "From now on, I want us to always greet or say goodbye to each other with a kiss, no matter what."

"I think I can do that. But, what about at your company when I come to visit?"

"Well, there we'll have to keep it professional for right now and...Visit?? What do you mean visit? You're not leaving are you??" Alex asked, shocked at the very thought!

"Well Alex I don't have a job or a place to live. That won't be a problem now that I have money, though. I don't even need a job, and I will just take a few weeks off before I think about looking for one. In the meantime, I can just enjoy being back with you. Anyway, outside of that, I could find a place here in town I'm sure."

"Hmm...well if that's the only problem, then it's not a problem." Alex said, now relaxing.

"What do you mean?"

"It's not a problem. You'll move back in with me and when you're ready to return to work, you will return as my PA." Alex stated as a fact, but then had a moment of doubt about whether Taylor even wanted to live with her again. "That's if you want to?"

Taylor smiled at the thoughtfulness, and then smirked as a result of the thought that came into her mind at that moment. She walked past Alex without so much as a backward glance.

"Taylor?"

"Yes Alex?" Taylor responded, as she continued walking to the elevator, to where Alex had to walk rapidly to catch up with her.

"Well?"

"Well what, Alex?"

"What are you going to do?" Alex was now standing next to Taylor looking hard at her.

Taylor smiled again, and the elevator sounded as the door opened. She stepped casually inside and pushed the button for the first floor, then turned to see Alex still standing outside of the elevator just looking at her.

"Aren't you going to get in?"

"I don't know." Alex stated evenly.

"Well my dear Alex, the doors are going to close in a moment."

"Fine, but I want an answer."

Taylor looked up at the woman as Alex stepped inside still facing her, only now she had her arms crossed.

"I love you."

"Uh-huh. Now answer my question."

"I will, but...oops, can't right now, the door, we have to get off," Taylor said, as she nearly jumped out of the elevator.

"Taylor?!" Alex called as she walked to the middle of the lobby and stopped.

"Come on Alex, I know you want to get over to your house to tell D'Angelo that you won't be marrying him."

"Taylor, please answer my question."

Taylor stopped walking at the sound of Alex's voice. She turned around and the smile she previously had on her face left when she saw the look in Alex's eyes, and the deeply knitted brows. Alex was standing there with her hands at her side looking very vulnerable.

Taylor's heart felt as though it constricted. She quickly walked back over to where Alex stood, and their eyes locked. Taylor saw the glistening in Alex's eyes and her heart stopped.

"Alex? Please tell me you know I was just playing with you? I'm so sorry if you were worried." Taylor wrapped her arms around Alex's neck and hugged her close. "Alex, of course I will move back in with you. I love you. I was hoping you would ask me. Alex I'm sorry, I was just playing with you, honestly, you know, like the bedroom thing, remember? Taylor whispered to Alex in the middle of the lobby. People cast gazes over towards the two women but none stopped as they passed them.

Alex buried her head in Taylor's mass of hair, then raising her head she said in a quiet voice.

"I was worried, but I see you were only playing. Usually I can pick it up when you do that."

"Don't worry about it. You have a lot on your mind and weren't focused on me playing around. You asked me a serious question and I shouldn't have played about it. I'm sorry." Taylor said, leaning back to look in Alex's eyes.

"It's okay, I forgive you, and I should have known you were playing, it's as much my fault as it is yours. I guess I'm just sensitive."

Taylor smiled, lifted up and kissed Alex, while the two of them stood in the middle of the lobby of the hotel. After they broke their embrace, Alex turned around and guided Taylor towards the doors. As they went out, Alex looked down at her and said with a bright smile that made Taylor's heart skip all sorts of beats.

"You know, you did something very brave back there."

"Brave? What are you talking about?" Taylor asked, as they made it to Alex's car. After hitting the remote alarm and automatic door unlock, Taylor opened the door and sat down inside on the passenger side of the sports car and waited for Alex to get in and answer her.

Alex got in and put the key in the ignition and turned the car on, then answered Taylor's question.

"The fact that you kissed me back there in the middle of the lobby with all of those people walking past and watching us, yet you didn't seem to notice, or care."

Taylor blushed fiercely, then covered her face in both surprise and embarrassment. Alex laughed out loud and said in an amused tone.

"I see, you didn't notice...hahahaha, aww my poor sweetling, she was more concerned about her love than she was about what others would think. She simply reacted to comfort that love." Alex cooed in the third person.

"That's good, right?" Taylor asked, thinking it was good but wanting Alex to say it.

"Very, and I am so touched by that simple act. Thank you. It showed me a lot."

"You're welcome, but I did it because I don't ever want you to wonder about my feelings for you again. I love you and I want you to always know and feel that in your heart. Besides, I have to make you forget that those breaks are there, right?"

Alex smiled as she lifted the necklace from within her tee shirt and let it dangle by the chain from her fingers.

"You're wearing it?!"

"Yes, I put it on when I returned back inside the house during the party."

"Really Alex?"

"Yes."

Taylor gazed at Alex for a moment, then smiled as she looked straight ahead and let the emotion wash over her. Alex put the car in gear and headed to her home to talk with D'Angelo. As they drove, something occurred to Taylor and she had to find out.

"Alex?"

"Yes?"

"Does D'Angelo live with you?"

"No, but he spends a lot of time over at the house."

"Have you two been intimate?"

"Wow! That was straightforward. I'm impressed Taylor."

"Well, I just want to show you that I won't hold back from you when something bothers me. I'll ask you or tell you what's bothering me."

"Well I'm happy to hear that. Anyway, we've done some petting, but nothing major."

"So...you two didn't...well you know?"

"Hmm...can't say it, huh? It's alright, I suppose it will take you sometime to be able to ask that straight out. But in answer to your question, no, we didn't."

Taylor grinned brightly at the revelation and then subconsciously nodded her head in approval. Alex cut her eyes over to watch intermittently as she drove the winding road. They arrived back at Alex's and got out of the car. Alex and Taylor walked up the stairs together to the front door and opened it to go inside. Taylor became nervous once again.

"Alex you're going to tell him right?"

"Yes Taylor, I was just playing with you. It's my place to tell him. Don't worry about it. Go make some tea for all of us and bring it into the den, alright?"

"Alright. I love you."

"I love you too, sweetling."

Taylor's fears disappeared at those simple words, and Alex saw when they did.

"There's that gaze." She whispered, then leaned down to kiss Taylor, who returned the feeling in kind as her hands came up to hold Alex's face between them. Alex sighed and pulled away slightly. Taylor's hands were still holding her cheeks. Breathing hard, she gazed lovingly up into Alex's matching gaze.

"Now go." Alex said, shooing her towards the kitchen.

"Okay."

"And Taylor?"

"Yes?"

"Hurry up and join us."

"Okay." Taylor said beaming, and then turned and headed in the direction of the kitchen.

Alex watched Taylor go and a quick thought flashed in her head, which brought a smirk to her face. Once Taylor had disappeared around the curve, Alex turned and headed for the den, where she heard D'Angelo on the phone.

"Mizani, I will call you back, go ahead and take care of those documents. Right, I'll call later." D'Angelo hung up the phone as Alex came to sit down in her recliner chair, although she did not recline it.

"So...you finally made it back Rose. Are you okay?"

"Why wouldn't I be okay D'Angelo?"

"Why? Because of the way you went out of here. I hope you didn't hurt her...too much?"

Alex raised a brow at the man and leaned forward in her chair. She rested an elbow on one armrest and her chin on her hand.

"D'Angelo, I did go over there with the intention of verbally laying her out because of what I thought she had done. I discovered that I was wrong, terribly wrong. She not only didn't do what I thought, she could never have done such a thing to me."

"What did you think she did?"

"I thought she and Ms. Sains were the one's doing the insider trading, but I found out it's not them."

"Why would you think that?"

"Because she gave me a cashier's check for a very large amount of money, which I knew she could not have had, or earned, at least legally."

"So what changed your mind, did you find out who the insider trader's are?"

"Her Grandmother left her a large amount of money, and no, I haven't found out yet."

"Okay, so now the two of you are on speaking terms again, that's fine."

Alex leaned back in her chair and tossed her hair back behind her head as she studied D'Angelo for a moment.

"Rose? Is something else on your mind?"

"Yes D'Angelo, and this is not easy for me. I wanted to tell you how much I care for you. We have gotten closer to one another and I do honestly care about you."

"Rose, are you about to tell me that you're breaking things off?"

"Yes."

"Did I do something?"

"No."

"Did I not do something?"

"D'Angelo, you did nothing that brought this about. It's just that Taylor and I were able to straighten a lot of things out, and I find myself still very much in love with her, and she with me."

"So...so you're breaking up with ME for HER?!"

"D'Angelo, I know this has got to hurt, but I am not going to allow you to assume that I did this on purpose. I didn't, so anything you have to say, just remember that." Alex stated in warning, not willing to sit and hear D'Angelo or anyone else lambaste her inappropriately.

"Alexandra, I love you, and I want to marry you! I thought you were thinking about us coming together in the same way. Yes Rose, I am very hurt, I don't want to lose you. It took too many years to get back together, and when we did, I thought it would be forever. Everyone expects to see us together. We've been everywhere with each other over this last year. But then when she shows up, you're suddenly willing to just drop me like a hot potato and run off with her, despite all the pain she has caused you! I never caused you any pain, and I never would, but she has, and she's done it twice. I think you're being foolish."

"D'Angelo, I know you love me. I see that. But I told you when we first started spending more time with each other that I still had a lot of unresolved issues about Taylor. I told you I couldn't promise that things would work out between you and I, at least not until those things were resolved. I never misled you about that. I was always straight with you. I even told you to be careful about your feelings getting away from you because of those unresolved issues. D'Angelo, I didn't plan this. In fact, I went to bless Taylor out and then I was going to return here and focus all of my time and energy on seeing what could develop between you and I."

"Then what happened?"

"We were able to resolve all of those issues that were unresolved. D'Angelo, Taylor makes me feel complete, and I intend to spend my life with her."

"But Rose, you said yourself that you had never been hurt the way Taylor hurt you!"

"Exactly D'Angelo. No one could hurt me the way she did, because I was never in love with anyone the way I am with her."

"Does that include me Rose?"

"D'Angelo the first time we were together, I was very much in love with you. But I was more focused on my career than I was on us. That's why when you told me that I had to choose, the only choice for me at that time was my career. You know how much fire I had in me, and the rush I got from work. D'Angelo, no matter how much I loved you, at that time I actually loved my work more, the time for us was not right. After that, I never got involved in another serious relationship, just companions or escorts, but not anyone I wanted to love. Then Taylor came along, and I saw in her a spirit that just calmed me. A spirit that touched my very soul, and I was drawn to her. Mostly out of curiosity at first, but as time went by, I saw how brilliant she was. She's introverted and kind, loving and loyal, and as naive about the world as a newborn. She's beautiful both inside and out, and my heart sings when we're together. D'Angelo, I am sorry that this hurts you, but I was really on the rebound and I can't and I won't apologize for my feelings. I'm only sorry that you're hurting, and if you decide that we cannot continue as friends, I will understand."

"And there's nothing I can say or do to change your mind?"

"No."

"Then...I guess I have no choice. I'll have to accept your decision. I am hurt, but I will admit that I knew you were on the rebound, and I should have known better than to try to gain your affections when there was so much going on with you. I should have been your friend rather than trying to be your lover, so, in a way, it's my own fault."

"So, where do we go from here? Do I still have a friend, or not?"

"Alex, you are blunt, if nothing else."

"Well?"

"Yes Rose, you still have a friend for as long as you want. I can't say I won't be hoping things don't work out between the two of you. That way I get another chance."

"D'Angelo?! Are you saying you're hoping my relationship with Taylor fails?" Alex asked, amused by the statement, and the fact that she was able to maintain a longtime friendship.

"Well, there's got to be some hope, right?"

"Well...I guess. Although it's going to be an eternal type hope." Alex said with a wry smile.

"Well as long as there's hope." D'Angelo grinned.

Taylor walked into the room with the tray of tea and cups. She looked over at Alex to see if things were alright, especially when D'Angelo looked at her and then back at Alex with a questioning gaze.

"Come over here Taylor." Alex said, motioning for her to come and sit on the sofa next to the recliner, where there was a table to put the tray of tea down on between them. Taylor moved to where Alex asked, set the tray down and then greeted D'Angelo.

"Hello D'Angelo."

"Ms. Young." D'Angelo greeted flatly. Taylor heard the tone and glanced over at Alex.

"I told D'Angelo what the situation was and he understands. He's not happy about it, but he understands."

"I'm sorry that you're hurting D'Angelo. I know how Alex is capable of drawing people to her and making them fall in love with her, whether on purpose or inadvertently. It does hurt to lose her, and I can only imagine to lose her twice is a little much."

"Yes it is, and it does hurt, especially to know that I lost her to such a young one as yourself. But I can see why she loves you. You have a compassionate heart, and you're obviously good at business, otherwise I don't think she would want you around."

"Thank you."

"For what?"

"For not making her feel any worse than she already does about having to hurt you."

D'Angelo chuckled and nodded his head at her statement, which indeed proved what Alex had just told him about Taylor.

"I wanted to hate you, but I can't. You're just too adorable. I hope you and Alex will be happy together. I do plan on being around as a friend, but if you screw up like you did this last time, I'm going to try to win her affections. So don't screw up!"

"Trust me, YOU won't ever have a chance at Alex again. She knows that I don't make the same mistake twice."

"Then it is truly my loss and your gain."

"Okay you two, that's enough! Taylor, are you going to pour me some tea?"

"Oh, yes. Would you like some D'Angelo?"

"Yes, thank you."

Taylor poured the tea and the three sat and talked for the better part of the day. Then D'Angelo said he was going to go to one of his state side offices and check on some things. He kissed Alex goodbye and gave Taylor a kiss on the cheek that made her blush, and she covered her cheek as a result. After D'Angelo left, Alex turned to Taylor and with a raised brow she leveled an inquisitive gaze on her.

"He caught me off guard! I wasn't expecting him to do that, especially with everything that's happened." Taylor explained.

"Uh-huh, well, I'll let it go this time, but I don't want to see that again."

"Alex I can't control it."

Alex didn't say anything. She just looked at Taylor with the one brow still raised.

"Okay, okay, I'll try."

Alex still didn't say anything.

"Okay."

"Alright, now I'm hungry. What do you want to do about dinner, go out, stay in, you cook, I cook, we both cook? What?"

"We cook, therefore, we will stay in. By the way, when do you want me to move back in?"

"You already have."

"How is that, I don't have any clothes here?"

"Oh, but you do, right where you left them."

"You mean you didn't throw them out?"

"Taylor, those clothes are way too expensive to throw in the trash, besides...I was hoping things would work out between us and we would get back together." Alex said with a gentle tone, as she raised a hand to caress Taylor's cheek.

Taylor caught her hand and held it to her cheek as she smiled up at Alex.

"Okay, so, what do you want to make for dinner?" Taylor asked, as she gave a quick kiss to Alex's hand, then stood and turned and headed for the kitchen.

"You mean us, and I thought it should be something special. A celebration of our reunion?"

"I like it! You're such a closet romantic Alex. You know if people knew this side of you, it would shatter all their perceived images of you?" Taylor said, as she and Alex entered the kitchen and headed over to get what they thought would be a good celebration meal.

"Well, that's one thing that they don't need to know, my little sweetling." Alex said, as she put her items on the counter and walked around to wrap her arms around Taylor's waist from behind. Taylor wrapped her arms over Alex's arms and squeezed them slightly. Alex then began kissing Taylor's neck, causing her to squirm from the tickling sensation. Suddenly Alex felt a deja vu feeling, as if they had been there before. Then she remembered they had, it was just before D'Angelo came to the house sometime ago and met Taylor for the first time. A wicked smile came to her lips as she proceeded to repeat those actions again. She turned Taylor around and kept her between herself and the counter. There was such a look of desire in her eyes that Taylor was taken aback by it.

"Alex? I...I thought we were going to cook?"

"Oh...my dear sweetling...we are, of that you can be sure." Alex's voice was so low, smooth, and silky that it made Taylor's ears ring.

Alex brought their lips together once again, and although the kiss started out slow and tender, it soon increased to a more needing passion. Taylor moaned as a result, and Alex sighed as a result of that, and soon Alex was once again following Taylor down the side of the counter to the floor. They ended up with Taylor on her back slightly pushing at Alex's chest so as to be allowed to catch her breath. Alex allowed it and the moment they broke the kiss, both she and Taylor took in large gulps of air. Alex watched Taylor catch her breath and saw how her skin tone had the red undertone that showed her that the girl was blushing fiercely. When Taylor opened her lidded eyes, she saw the gaze of desire in Alex's eyes was even more apparent.

"Good, you see what I'm feeling. Now all I have to do, sweetling, is show you." Alex purred, as she lowered her head once again to kiss Taylor.

Taylor began squirming to move out from under Alex's upheld body. Alex was supporting her weight with her hands and had not touched Taylor's body with her own. Taylor scooted out from under her and Alex allowed her to, watching Taylor repeat the same behavior as before, only this time, there would be no one coming by to stop them. That thought made Alex grin, baring her teeth at the thought that Taylor was playing right into her hands. Taylor, in the meantime, had made it a little distance away from Alex and had managed to make it to her knees. Alex was once again crouched in a catlike position, looking as if she were ready to pounce. Taylor looked over at her and saw the look in her eyes. She now felt like she had been there before, in that same position. She tried to look away, but Alex held her gaze with her own. Taylor's breathing, which was already increased from the feelings and sensations running through her, now had Alex's gaze to contend with, and it made her unsteady.

"Alex...Alex, we...we have to..." Taylor tried to speak, but she found it getting harder and harder with every provocative move Alex made towards her. She began swaying as a result, and Alex's gleaming teeth bared even more.

"Taylor ,my sweetling, I want you. I've wanted you for a long time, and I'm going to have you. You understand?" Alex's voice was low and sensual, adding to the hypnotic effect she already had on Taylor.

"Al...Was all Taylor managed, as she swayed more and more. Alex increased her catlike stalking towards Taylor and the girl's breathing increased and became slightly labored.

Alex's own breathing had increased at the thought of her and Taylor. Although she had all the intentions in the world of taking the two of them to the full pinnacle of ecstasy, she decided she didn't want that to happen in the kitchen. She wanted it to be in her bed. But, in the meantime, a few preludes would not be a bad start.

So, after a few more feet, she raised herself up off of her hands just enough to level their gazes. Alex brought her face to within inches of Taylor's, looking deep into her lidded eyes.

"Kiss me." Alex ordered in a loving tone.

Taylor gasped, but leaned forward and closed her eyes as she brought their lips together. Alex increased their contact. Taylor attempted to stay with her, but lost in a big way as she was once again overwhelmed and slowly lowered onto her back. Alex's hand guided her, and once Taylor was on her back again, Alex began unfastening her blouse. She would fluctuate between kissing Taylor's lips to kissing on Taylor's neck. Once Taylor's blouse and bra were open, Alex brought one of her hands to Taylor's exposed breast. She kneaded the flesh in her hand and both women flushed as a result. Alex purposely avoided touching Taylor's taut nipple, despite Taylor's chest subconsciously rising for that very purpose.

Finally, after a bit, Alex allowed her hand to graze over one and Taylor's breath caught for a moment, as a result. Alex lifted her mouth off of Taylor's neck and brought her head back up, just enough to look Taylor in the eyes, and speaking in a husky voice she said to Taylor.

"So...responsive to my touch aren't you, sweetling?"

"Yes!!" The girl managed to gasp out.

Alex grinned through her highly aroused state and once again laid a kiss filled with passion on the girl as Taylor whimpered and moaned. She also trembled at the possible end result of everything, and both excitement and fear took hold of her. She brought her hands up to Alex's tee shirt and began lifting it. When it was out of the way, she unfastened Alex's bra, which allowed her breasts to pop out. Taylor placed a shaky hand on one and after a moment to get used to the feel of another woman's breast in her hand, she found she liked the feel of Alex's, and began copying her actions. Alex now moaned and they each slowly discovered the other's upper body. Alex lowered her head to Taylor's breast and then went on to her areola. Taylor's body tightened and after a few minutes of Alex loving her breast, the girl's back flexed up. Alex was once again so amazed at her ability to please Taylor in this way, along with what Taylor was doing to Alex's breast, that they both fell over into the ecstasy. Taylor was gripping hard on Alex's breast as her body locked in ecstasy. Alex's body was also stiff as a result of her own. Her mouth was still holding onto the firm tip, sucking on it as Taylor's moan's vibrated from deep in her throat as the sensations washed over her.

When it ended, both she and Alex collapsed, their breathing labored and shallow. They both drifted off right there on the kitchen floor for a brief nap. When they woke up, Alex kissed Taylor who stretched her way back to wakefulness, then yawned.

"Wow!!" she said, through a yawn. "That is such a wonderful, absorbing feeling. I love you so very much Alex."

"I know, it is, isn't it? And I love you Taylor Young."

Taylor lifted up off of the floor, wrapped her arms around Alex and hugged her tightly. The two embraced for long moments, right there on the floor. After a bit, they finally made it to their feet, and once again, tried to go and make the dinner that they were now starving for. When the evening was winding down, the two of them decided to go and turn in. Taylor didn't have to go to work in the morning but she still had things she had to get wrapped up back at her late grandmother's home. They headed up the stairs, and as if it were yesterday, the two stopped at the top of the stairs, and once again Alex felt that feeling of deja vu..

"So..."

"So...what? Taylor asked with a wry smile.

"What will it be?"

"Well, let me ask you this; no matter what I decide, you won't get mad or feel hurt or anything, right?"

"Well, I can tell you I won't get mad, but I will feel disappointed with a certain decision."

"That's fine, as long as you realize that it's just a matter of me getting used to being back here with you, okay?"

Alex gave a small understanding smile, then said in a tender yet longing tone.

"Okay."

Taylor smiled and stepped over to where Alex leaned against the rail. She wrapped her arms around Alex and kissed her with all the love she felt for her. Then she stepped back, and with a gentle smile for Alex and her feelings, she gave her answer.

"I just need a little time, okay?"

"Alright, see you later?"

"Yes." Taylor responded, as Alex walked up the remaining stairs and headed down to her room. Taylor watched her go, and a warm smile came to her face at Alex's complete understanding of her feelings. She knew then that things were going to be fine.

She walked up the remaining stairs and headed down the hall in the opposite direction. She went into her room and after pulling out a nightgown that she had left there, she went and got herself cleaned up as did Alex in her room. Afterwards, when they were both in their nightclothes, Alex climbed into bed and laid down. After about a half-hour of thinking, she closed her eyes with the intention of going to sleep.

Within a few minutes, there came a knock on her bedroom door.

"Come in." Alex called, to Taylor. Taylor opened the door and stood in doorway. "Taylor, is something wrong?"

"Yes."

"What? What is it?"

"I was feeling...restless, and I had this anxious feeling was running through me."

Alex listened to what she was saying, and at first she had a concerned look on her face. Then she thought about Taylor's words and saw the slow smile curving the girl's lips. Alex cocked her head and Taylor smiled fully and walked over to the bed and crawled in under the covers. She lay down on her side, facing towards Alex, who was now looking down at her. Taylor had not only crawled into bed with her, but had taken hold of Alex's hand with her own and had closed her eyes. She whispered, "I love you. Sweet dreams." And she drifted off to sleep.

Alex didn't know what to do. She wanted to laugh, to cry, to grab the girl up in her arms and squeeze her so tight that her eyes would feel like they were going to pop out of her head. At the same time, she wanted to just lay down and let the love that was filling her wash over her. Her heart smiled, and that feeling made its way to her face and mouth, and she smiled. She decided to lay down and allow the feelings to wash over her, and so she scooted down under the covers. She brought her other hand over top of

Taylor's waist and put her head next to the girl's. She whispered her own words of love to Taylor and then contently drifted off to sleep.

The next morning Alex awoke and found Taylor laying on her belly with her head turned in the woman's direction. Alex smiled again, and just gazed at the peacefully sleeping young woman. Alex stayed in the bed just watching her sleep, until Taylor finally woke up. She was disoriented at first, but everything came back to her quickly when she saw Alex smiling down at her.

"Good morning sweetling."

Taylor stretched out the kinks of the night and then, after yawning, responded back.

"Good morning. How did you sleep?"

"Like a baby, thanks to you." Alex said, with a grin lighting her face.

"Why thanks to me?" Taylor asked, still not moving from her position. Alex sat up, pursed her lips at Taylor's question, and then started to answer her.

"Because I got in bed last night trying not to be as disappointed as I was feeling. I understood your reasoning, but I had hoped you would come to my room and be willing to make it your room as well. Then when you walked in and told me that you in essence missed me, I thought I was hearing things. But when you crawled into the bed, I just knew I must have fallen asleep and been dreaming. Taylor, you don't realize how much it means to me, the trust you displayed by coming to my bed. I was able to drift off completely at peace. Thank you."

Taylor raised up to a sitting position and turned to look Alex in the eyes as she spoke from her heart.

"You've never given me a reason to not trust you. All the things you have done for me have been to help me in one way or another, and again, I am so sorry for my behavior towards you. You only showed me love and I... well, just know that it will never happen again."

"Taylor, that's all behind us. This is the first day of the rest of our lives together, and I look forward to it."

"So do I." Taylor said as she turned to give Alex a hug. They embraced for a bit before Alex said with reluctance.

"Alright, I need to get up and get to the office."

"Okay, I need to get up also."

The two went to their respective rooms to shower. After they had dressed, they both went down to grab something to eat before leaving the house.

"Are you going to join me for lunch this afternoon, sweetling?"

"I love when you call me that." Taylor said as an aside, and then answered Alex's question. "Anyway, not today. Actually I am going to go back to my Grammy's house to get things settled there."

"What are you going to do with the house?"

"I thought I would allow Mrs. Jackson's daughter to stay there. She's entering the university on a four-year scholarship. She doesn't want to live on campus, but she doesn't want to stay at her mother's home either, as her mother is a little overbearing at times. I thought that it might be a good idea for her daughter to move into the house, and that would take care of two problems at once. I get someone to look after the house and the grounds, and it allows her a place to concentrate on her studies, rather than having to worry about her mother looking over a shoulder, as well as getting distracted by campus living."

"I think it's a great idea Taylor, and a very kind gesture." Alex said, caressing Taylor's cheek.

"Thank you, but it's a little selfish on my part. I just can't stand the idea of the place standing empty. There was too much love there not to pass that on." Taylor said, with a thoughtful gaze in her eyes.

Alex let a supportive gaze come in her eyes, then leaned over and kissed Taylor. Taylor couldn't help moaning, and Alex only increased the pressure of their embrace. Finally, they broke their embrace to catch their breath. They were both aroused, but realized that if they didn't get going, they would not make it out of the house. They leaned back from the kiss, and smiled a mutual smile that told each other that they both understood.

"You mind if I escort you to the airport?" Alex asked, as they headed for the door of the house to leave.

"If you have time, I would really like that."

"I'll always make time for you."

Taylor wrapped her arm around Alex's waist and gave a squeeze as Alex put her arm over Taylor's shoulder and gave a squeeze to her in return. They got in the waiting car, and the driver closed the door and then walked around and got in the driver's seat. He headed for the airport, after being told they were going there.

CHAPTER 23

The two talked about a few things and Taylor asked how the party went. She was awed by the fact that the President herself, had come to the party. When they arrived at the airport, the chauffeur got out, walked around to the other side and opened the door for the two of them to exit the car. Alex and Taylor headed for the terminal without stopping to purchase a ticket since Taylor had an open ticket. She had purchased it when she first came back to the city, not knowing how things would turn out.

She hadn't wanted to get stranded just in case things didn't work out. When they arrived at the terminal, Taylor presented her ticket to the attendant at the desk just to make sure there were no problems with it. They went and took a seat while they waited for the boarding call, and resumed their conversation.

"Taylor, I was just thinking about something."

"What?"

"I found out that Salina was blackmailing you and that it was because of her that you felt you had to pull away from me."

"Yes, partly. The other reasons were because of my own insecurities."

"Because of your grandmother, and your religious convictions?"

"Right. I'm sorry."

"It's in the past. I didn't bring this up to open that up, I brought it up because of what Salina did. I plan on causing her some real pain when I get to the office, but I wanted to let you know that I had found out about what she did."

"So what are you going to do?"

"Hurt her."

"We will now begin boarding flight 439 to Atlanta, Georgia, all first class Gold Flyers may board at their convenience."

"Oh, that's my flight Alex."

"Oh, okay. Well I'll see you in a week or so?" Alex said, as they both came to their feet to face each other.

"Yes."

"Well I expect to hear from you every evening, 8:30 p.m. sharp, alright?"

Taylor grinned coyly, then said in a whisper.

"Okay, I'll call every night that I am there."

"Good. Well you better get going."

"Oh, okay, I love you." Taylor said, as Alex smiled and then leaned down and placed a kiss on her cheek. Taylor kissed her in return in the same fashion and they embraced each other.

"I'll see you soon, sweetling."

"Yes, but you'll hear from me every night."

The two headed off towards the boarding gate and Taylor handed her ticket to the attendant, then took the other part back. She started for the door, but then stopped.

"Alex, by the way, don't do anything to your PA."

"What? Why not?"

"I'll tell you later. Right now, just promise me you won't let on to her that you know, okay?"

"Taylor?"

"Ma'am I really need you to board?"

"No problem. Alex just promise me okay?"

"I won't do anything today, but when I talk to you tonight, I expect for you to tell me why I shouldn't let on."

"I'll talk to you soon. Love you, bye."

"I love you, talk to you later."

Taylor turned and headed into the catwalk to the plane, looking back at times to see Alex still standing there just watching her go. She waved, and Alex gave a brief wave as well. As soon as Taylor turned the corner, Alex took a deep breath, then turned and with a final glance at the plane, she headed back to the pickup zone where her driver and car would meet her. Alex arrived back at the office an hour later. When she arrived, she saw Salina on the phone. Salina, upon seeing Alex, hung up the phone immediately.

"Hello Ma'am."

"Ms. Lacy, bring your schedule book in and go over my schedule for today. Call Mr. Shearer and have him come to my office with all reports and updates. Also call Ms. Sains and have her follow sometime after Mr. Shearer's appointment."

"Yes Ma'am." Salina said, as she turned back to her desk and collected the schedule, then picked up the phone and made the two calls.

Alex watched the young woman as she went and sat down in her office chair and turned on her computer to log on. Salina came in the office a few minutes later, sat down and booted up her schedule log.

"Ms. Madison, the party was a huge success. There have been all sorts of reports about it." Salina said, making small talk.

"I know, I've seen and heard most of them." Alex said evenly as she looked at Salina over her brows, while picking up a stack of mail that was laying on the desk.

"Uh, I'm ready to go over your schedule for the day, whenever you are."

"Fine, go." Alex said as she turned her chair to look out over the city. She both listened to Salina and read her mail for the day. She commented at various times during Salina's listing.

After Salina finished with Alex's schedule, she dismissed her to go and finish whatever work she had been doing and instructed her to send Shearer in when he arrived.

After meeting with Marcus Shearer and being updated on all that had occurred at the company, Alex had three meetings before Yasmeia arrived to see her.

"Ms. Madison is in a meeting, but she will be done anytime now. You can have a seat and I will let her know you're here, Ms. Sains."

"Fine Ms. Lacy." Yasmeia said somewhat curtly.

Salina called into the inner office and informed Alex that her next appointment was there to see her. After receiving her instructions, she directed her next statement to Yasmeia.

"Ms. Sains, Ms. Madison will be with you in five minutes."

"Thank you."

After a few minutes of waiting, the person Alex had been meeting with came out of the office and Salina told Ms. Sains she could go in. Yasmeia went inside and closed the door behind her.

"Ms. Sains, have a seat." Alex said flatly.

"Thank you."

"So Ms. Sains, how is everything going with you?"

"Fine, Ms. Madison." Yasmeia replied in the same formal fashion.

"Good." Alex said as she put down a folder she had been holding in her hand.

"Ms. Madison is something wrong?"

"Wrong? Why would you think that?"

"Just the way you're acting."

Alex studied the woman for a moment, and then she hit the automatic blind closure. Once the blinds were closed she smirked, and Yasmeia was feeling a little uncomfortable at the devilish smirk that played at the woman's mouth.

"Ms. Madison??"

"Yasmeia everything is absolutely wonderful!!! I could not be happier!"

Yasmeia now smiled, cautiously at first, and then when she saw the bright grin on the woman's face, she realized everything was fine.

"Well Ms. Madison, I am very pleased to hear that!"

"Alex." She said, inviting Yasmeia to call her by her first name.

"Alex. So I take it that Taylor is just as happy?"

"Very."

"Wonderful. Where is she?"

"She went back home to take care of some things. She'll be back in a week or two."

"Great. Well if she needs a place to stay until she can find a place of her own, she is always welcome to come and stay with me."

"Thank you Yasmeia, but that's not necessary. She's living with me again."

"Really?? "

"Yes."

"Well, I guess things are working out for the two of you? I'm very happy for the both of you."

"So am I. But Yasmeia, that's not the only reason I called you up here. I wanted to let you know how pleased and how very grateful I am to you for helping get Taylor and me back together."

"I saw how much the two of you were hurting and I knew neither of you would admit it out loud, unless you had some help. So...I played a small part in misleading Taylor into thinking that you believed something about her that wasn't necessarily true."

"Knowing Taylor's desire to not let a misjudgment on my part keep us apart, you knew she would come and try to explain things, if for no other reason than to correct a misjudgment?"

"Yes. Taylor values your opinion of her as much as she did her grandmother's."

"I see that."

"Well then, you understand why I had to do it the way I did to get her back here?"

"Yes, I do understand. I want to show my appreciation to you by promoting you to an upper management position. Then, depending on your performance in that position, I will promote you again."

"Alex, that really isn't necessary. Besides, I would not want to take a position based on what I did to help you and Taylor. That was personal, and it has nothing to do with my professional life. I would want to be promoted or demoted, whichever the case may be, for my work performance."

"I'm glad you said that Yasmeia, it adds validity to my decision. I am not promoting you based on what you did for Taylor and me. I am promoting you because you deserve to be promoted. You allowed Taylor to help Mr. Shearer with his reports and helped her understand them in the beginning. Taylor may have had some natural abilities when she came here, but without you to guide and mentor her during her years here, as well as not demonizing me to her, she would have never come to my attention because she would not have had the inclination to come to this floor to warn me of the danger on that day. So no, Yasmeia, this promotion is not because of your personal involvement with Taylor and me, but it is based on skills that I have seen you instill in Taylor. Her work is always neat and on time. I have not received one of Shearer's reports that I had to tell him to do over. They have been wonderfully prepared, and Taylor has told me that it was you who showed her how to write such reports in the first place. Unless Taylor did all of yours as well?"

"No, I did my own. Sometimes, if I had other reports to do, I would ask Taylor to do them, but it was rare."

"Good, so you understand WHY you're getting this promotion?"

"Yes, and thank you."

"You're welcome. Now I need to make a few calls, will you excuse me?"

"Of course, and thank you again Alex."

Alex gave a nod of her head and Yasmeia stood and headed for the door, leaving the woman to make her calls. Later that day, Taylor arrived back in her hometown and was met at the airport by a car and driver that Alex had obviously set up for her. Taylor first went to see her attorney and her broker. She told them what she wanted to do with the interest off of five of the 60 million. Then she went to her grandmother's home and called Mrs. Jackson.

"Hello, Mrs. Jackson, this is Taylor. How are you doing?"

"Oh, I'm making it. How are you holding up?"

"Good, thank you. I was calling to ask you if Marisal was still going to go to the University in town or not?"

"Yes, that's what she wants to do. She and I have been going at it about where she will live. I don't understand why she doesn't want to live here with her father and me. But you know, her father is right on her side. They think it would be a good experience for her to be on her own. But you know Marisal, she's such a quiet girl. Except for now! We have gotten into many arguments lately, and I just don't know what I'm going to do. She is adamant about not wanting to live on campus, and she doesn't want to live here. She's nervous about living in the city by herself, so I think her only option is to just commute from home. That way she doesn't have to worry about anything."

"I understand, but you know Marisal is very responsible, and she's almost compulsive about living somewhere that is clean. She was such a help to my grandmother when she was alive, and I know Grammy really liked her. She said that Marisal and I were almost twins in that we were both so shy and introverted."

"I would have to agree with her. You two are a lot a like."

"Well Mrs. Jackson, I think I can help with living arrangements if Marisal is willing."

"Oh, how?"

"Well, I am going to be living back in the town where I used to work. I will need someone who I can rely on to look out after the house and land and things while I am away. I don't want to sell it, and I don't want to leave it empty."

"But Taylor, Marisal couldn't afford to pay the monthly mortgage note on that house!"

"That's not a problem. The house is paid off. The only thing she will be responsible for is the electric and gas bills, and such."

"Taylor are you sure? I mean, it will be for at least four years, and that's if she doesn't decide to go on and get her graduate degree."

"The longer the better. I had a renter's contract drawn up by my lawyer. I can have it sent over to you and Marisal and your husband to look over, and if you have any questions just give me a call. I'll be in town for about a week, maybe a little longer."

"What will you do with the place if Marisal doesn't want to live there while she's in school?"

"My lawyer will have a management company send out caretakers to maintain the property."

"Oh, I see. Well I have to admit, it would be the perfect solution, and you're sure about this?"

"Yes Ma'am. She would be able to move in anytime. The place is already furnished, so all she would need would be to bring her own bedroom set if she doesn't want the one that is already in the master bedroom."

"No, she loves the furnishings in the house. She always told me what good taste your grandmother had."

"Thank you. So, you think she will want to?"

"I do! It's perfect. I'll talk to her and her father about it. If you'll send the papers over, we will look them over and get them back to you within a day or so, okay?"

"That's fine."

"Taylor, thank you."

"You're welcome Mrs. Jackson. I'll send those over today via courier."

"Alright. Bye Taylor."

"Bye, oh, and tell Marisal I said hello."

"I will. Goodbye Taylor."

The two hung up, and Taylor looked at her watch and saw that it was getting late in the day. So she picked up the phone and called for the courier. When he arrived, she sent the contract off with him to be delivered to Mrs. Jackson.

Taylor then headed upstairs to go and pack her clothes and her personal items. She also went and got the boxes of her grandmother's personal things like her jewelry, and handmade quilts, and all of those things that made up who her grandmother was to her. Taylor had already cleaned out her grandmother's room of all of those things. She even stripped the sheets off of the bed, washed and packed them away, and went to the store and bought new linen for the bed. Taylor was only halfway done when she saw that it was getting dark outside. She once again looked at her watch and saw that it was 7:30p.m.

"Man! I haven't even cooked anything to eat." She gasped, as she looked at the mess before her. She thought about how she didn't want to leave it for another day, but she couldn't be late calling Alex at 8:30. So she decided to leave the rest until tomorrow and go and cook herself some dinner before she called Alex. She ran downstairs, washed her hands, and pulled out the things she wanted to have for dinner. After she put everything into the oven to cook, she ran back upstairs to get cleaned up for the night.

By the time she had finished it was 8:25. She made her plate and headed into the family room. Taylor set her plate down, hit the speaker button, and dialed Alex's number.

"Hello." Came Alex's voice, light, yet smooth.

"Hi, it's me."

"Hmm...cutting it a little close, huh?"

"Well I had a lot to do! You realize I left a mess upstairs because I had to call you? I hadn't even eaten, and when I looked at my watch it was 7:30. I still had a lot to do, but I had to make something to eat and then go and get cleaned up for the night. So...I'm clean, I have my food right here and I called ON TIME, so be nice." Taylor said, with a hint of a pout to her voice.

Alex grinned at the thought of Taylor pouting.

"Okay now, sweetling, don't pout. I'll be nice...IF you answer one question for me?"

"What?" Taylor asked as she put a bite of meat in her mouth and began chewing it, waiting for Alex to ask her the question.

"Tell me why you asked me not to break Salina in half. It was all I could do to keep from choking the life out of her every time she came near me, or every time I saw her."

"Well, I'm glad you didn't let on to her. I believe that she will get hers. God does not like ugly, and the wickedness she did will come back to bite her harder than she ever could imagine."

"That's all fine and well Taylor, but why should I wait if I can help it along?"

"Trust me Alex, you'll be quite excited about the payback."

"Is that right?"

"Yes."

"Well tell me what it is and I can tell you if I will be or not."

"No, but trust me, you'll absolutely love it."

"Hmm...well Taylor Young, since you believe that I am going to be so...excited about this payback to Salina, how about a little wager?"

"What sort of wager?"

"Well, first tell me that you're willing to wager me, and then I will tell you the wager."

"That's not fair, especially with you! I've seen the results of your wagers."

"Well then, I guess I will just have to have a little...talk with Salina tomorrow."

"Alex?"

"Yes."

Taylor sat quietly for a moment, and Alex knew that Taylor was thinking about it, so she sat quietly, just waiting for her to answer.

"Okay, what is the wager?"

Alex grinned at her victory, and then said in a smooth voice.

"Great. The wager is, if I am not as excited as you say I will be, then you will serve me breakfast in bed for one week..."

Taylor grinned at what she thought was a simple enough bet, and because she was sure Alex would love the payback to Salina.

"Okay, is that it?"

"Yes, except...you have to serve it to me...only wearing an apron."

"NUDE?! Alex? Nude?"

"Yes, I love these wagers."

"So I see." Taylor said, with a pout now obvious in her voice.

Alex chuckled, and then sat back and laid her recliner back.

"Okay, so what do I get if I win?"

"Whatever you want?"

"Okay, I want the same thing, only I want breakfast...and dinner!"

"Deal! I look forward to my meals and my sweetling's blushing body."

Taylor actually blushed at the thought and at the sound of Alex's voice.

"Well, I guess you're going to be disappointed, because I am going to win."

"Hmm...we'll see. So...how was your day? Did you get in touch with Mrs. Jackson?"

"It was very productive. I got a lot done outside of the house, and I did get in touch with Mrs. Jackson. She was telling me how she and Marisal have been going at it over where she was going to live."

"So you think she'll move in?"

"Yes, she'll make a good caretaker for the place. Grammy's men friends will call and see if she needs anything, but I'm sure her father will be over to handle any problems."

"Well, it sounds like this Marisal will be a good house guest."

"She will, I'm sure. So, how was your day, other than the desire to kill Salina?"

"Well outside of that, it was a typical day."

"I miss you already, but it helps to talk to you and hear your voice." Taylor said quietly, as she now settled in on the sofa to talk for a while with Alex.

The two talked way into the night, and around 1 in the morning, Taylor started drifting off, the days events having finally taken it's toll on the young woman. Alex was talking, telling Taylor about some plans she had for remodeling their bedroom now that they were sleeping in the same room, when she heard little mumbling sounds coming from the other end of the phone.

"Taylor? Taylor?" Alex called Taylor a few more times, then she realized the girl had fallen asleep. "My poor sweetling, hm...sweet dreams, baby, I love you." Alex took the phone with her to her bedroom and left the line open, just in case Taylor woke up and remembered the phone.

Taylor slept through the night, and when she was stretching, she heard sounds coming from somewhere. Her eyes popped open and she immediately looked around the family room, slightly disoriented, and confused as to why she was still there. She couldn't see where the noise was coming from, and it started to bother her. She pulled herself up off of the sofa, and began to look around the room with concern.

"T.a.y.l.o.r...are you awake?"

"AH!! GOODNESS!!" Taylor exclaimed, when it suddenly dawned on her what had happened.

She ran over and snatched the phone up off of the holder.

"Alex! I am so...sorry. I can't believe I fell asleep! I'm sorry. Please don't be mad, I didn't mean to fall asleep!"

"Taylor." Alex said calmly. "You're finally awake."

"I'm sorry. I'm so embarrassed."

"Taylor calm down, it's alright. I'll forgive you this time, if I can add something to our little wager?"

"Anything."

"Hmm...careful, you should know better by now than to tell me that. It just leaves so many things open for me."

"I'm so sorry Alex. It's just that I had been busy cleaning up and organizing, and all of that, and I guess I was just more tired than I thought."

"It's okay! You just owe me another week of service, only it'll be breakfast and dinner. I really like your idea, because so many other things can happen."

"Okay, you have a deal."

"Great. Well, I have to get to work, and you need to get that mess upstairs cleaned up. I will talk to you later, and I'll call this time."

"Okay, I'll be in and out today, but I will be here for your call."

"I wish you were here, but as it is, you're not, so I'll have to deal with the phone. The only thing that bothers me about the phone where you are is that I can't see you, or you me."

"Well it's only temporary, and then I'll be back there and you'll see me all of the time. Maybe too much?"

"Never too much. Well I have to get going, but I love you. If you need me, give me a call, okay?"

"Alright, I love you Alex."

Alex smiled to herself and made a kiss type sound, then said bye and the two hung up their phones. Everyday for the next week Taylor made arrangements for the house and land. She also hired a lawn service to maintain the land. She decided it would be better than having the older men coming over to the house with the girl living there by herself. She also suggested that the girl ask one of her friends to move in with her. That way they could watch out for each other. Not that the area was dangerous or anything, but to have a girl living at the house by herself could lead to problems if some of the young men decided to pay her a visit. Neighbors were close enough to see anyone going to the house, but at night it was a different story, and Taylor had her concerns about it.

CHAPTER 24

Taylor was helping the girl get settled in when the phone rang.

"Hello."

"Hello, may I speak with Taylor Young?"

"This is she."

"Aha, great. This is Mr. Rouse."

"Oh, Mr. Rouse, what's going on?"

"I just called to let you know that we will be making an arrest any day now. We have almost all the evidence we need, but I'm calling to ask a favor of you."

"Anything."

"We need for some type of exchange to take place in order to close in."

"Okay, so how can I help?"

"Well, I need the inside person to get shaken up."

"Okay, how?"

"Well, I figured since the insider is out for revenge against you and Ms. Madison, maybe you could come up with something?"

"Hmm, well, I'll think about it. I really don't know what I can do, but I will try to think of something."

"That's fine, but the sooner you think of something, the sooner we can move in and make the arrest. And don't worry about us not being there, we'll be watching, so when you do come up with something, we'll know and be ready."

"Oh, okay, then I will fly back tonight, and that way I can think about it and possibly come up with something."

"That's great."

"Okay, Mr. Rouse. I am a little surprised that you don't already have enough evidence. I mean the stock prices have risen so much and I would think there would be offshore accounts and things where funds are being sent as a holding place until all is said and done?"

"There are, but it's under a dummy corporation, and although we have all of the evidence to link the accounts to the two, we now want to close any loops. We haven't caught them exchanging any information or money on tape."

"What about phone calls?"

"We have those, but never any that led to the passing of information or money."

"Okay, I think I understand. Well, I'll call the airport and head out tonight."

"Thank you. By the way, do you want me to tell Ms. Madison that you were the one who tipped us off?"

"I'll leave that to you. I just want this to all be over."

"I understand."

"Okay, I'll call you and let you know if something comes up."

"That's fine, but we'll know."

"Oh, alright. Thank you for calling."

"You're welcome."

The two hung up and Taylor dialed the airport and made arrangements to leave that night. The car would come to pick her up at 5 that afternoon. Later that day, Marisal was ready to move in. She was able to get one of her friends who was also going to be attending school to move in with her. Taylor knew Kara as well. She was a church going young woman who was responsible, but a little vain about herself

"Okay ladies, you have everything you need. I think you'll be fine. I am going to be leaving, but you know if you have any problems with the property or something, you can call Ms. Levy, or your father, depending on what the problem is. Call me if it's just a simple question."

"Okay Taylor, thank you for letting us live here while we're in school. It takes a lot of concerns away, and we'll take good care of your house."

"I know Marisal, otherwise I would not have made the offer. Well, I have to get upstairs and get my things. I've sent off all of the boxes, along with my clothes. I'm just carrying Grammy's jewels on the plane with me." Taylor hugged each of the girls and then ran up the stairs to get her things.

The two girls talked between themselves about how much Taylor had changed, and how good looking and confident she was, now that she didn't look like an old time librarian.

Taylor heard bits of the comments before she went into her room, and it brought a thoughtful look to her eyes. At five, the driver pulled up and got out of the car. He came to the door, knocked and told Marisal that he was there to pick up Ms. Young to take her to the airport.

"Taylor, the driver's here."

"Okay, I'll be right there." Taylor called from the kitchen. After washing her hands, she came out to find the driver had already taken the small carry-on case to the car and was waiting outside the door of the car, holding it open.

The two girls hugged Taylor again and Taylor turned and took one last look at the house where she grew up into adulthood. Tears came to her eyes but she didn't let them fall, instead, she smiled and turned and walked out the door.

Taylor arrived at the airport, caught her plane and was on her way back to Alex. She arrived in town at around 7:00 or so, and taking another car, she was on her way home. By the time she was within 15 minutes of the house she looked at her watch and saw that it was nearly 8:30.

"Oh, oh, Alex is going to be a little upset." Taylor said to herself, but then she thought it would be alright, especially considering she was back earlier than Alex was expecting her. She didn't expect Taylor for another 3 days, but she had been able to get things done, and Mr. Rouse's call made her see that she was needed back here.

Alex had just turned on the automatic fireplace, to knock some of the coolness of the night out of the air. It had been hot during the morning, but now it had turned somewhat cool, and rather than turning the heat on, she just decided to turn on the fireplace. She went into the kitchen and made herself a fruit snack and some hot tea, then went back into the den and made herself comfortable in her recliner. Picking up the phone, she dialed Taylor's grandmother's house.

"Hello."

"Hello? Who is this?"

"This is Marisal Jackson."

"Oh, Ms. Jackson, I'm calling to speak to Ms. Young."

"Oh, well she's not here."

"Not there? Do you know when she will be back?"

"No, I'm sorry I don't." Marisal answered cryptically, considering the person never said who they were.

"I see, well, I'll call later, thank you."

"Okay, bye."

Alex hung up the phone, her brow raised in concern as to where Taylor was. They always talked at 8:30, and knew to call and leave a message letting the other know if something had come up, or was going on that might interfere with their nightly call. As it was, they had not missed a day.

"Where are you Taylor?"

Suddenly the doorbell rang, snapping Alex out of her thoughts. She got up to answer the door as she had given the maid the rest of the evening off. She walked to the door and looked out, only seeing a figure with her coat drawn around herself, rubbing one arm obviously trying to stay warm.

Alex's brows knitted but she opened the door.

"May I help you?" Alex asked, somewhat put off by the interruption.

"Yes, move. It's cold out here." Taylor said, as she shook the hood from her head and walked inside of the house past the stunned woman.

"Taylor??!" Alex finally said, snapping out of her shock and closing the door. She turned back around to see Taylor hanging up her coat.

"HI!" Taylor said, as she turned with a big grin on her face. "Surprise!!"

"You can say that again! Come here!" Alex said, as she opened her arms to Taylor.

Taylor quickly went into Alex's arms and the two hugged for long moments.

"I've missed you Taylor." Alex purred into Taylor's ear.

A shiver ran down Taylor's spine from the sensual sound.

"I've missed you, but I had to come back."

"Why, other than the fact that is obvious?"

"Because I had finished everything I needed to, and there was no reason for me to stay any longer."

"Well I am so happy you're home! I have a little surprise for you in our bedroom. Something I had done while you were gone."

"Really? What?" Taylor asked, turning to go to the stairs, but Alex caught her and stopped her.

"Oh no you don't. First of all there are a couple of things that are wrong."

"Wh..what?"

"Well, first of all, you're late."

"Late? Alex you weren't expecting me for three more days! I'm early!"

"Yes, but you still were late, since you didn't get my call at 8:30, then you should have been here at that time."

"Alex that's not fair."

"But that's the way it is, so...you owe me."

"What?!?"

"Yes, I've decided that since you made me worry you owe me."

Taylor crossed her arms over her chest as she stood pouting. Alex's eyes narrowed in curiosity as she gazed at the young woman. Then pinching her lips to keep from laughing at the look she had on her face, she waited for Taylor to ask.

"Okay, what do I owe?" Taylor finally asked.

"Another 2 weeks."

"ALEX?!! That's a whole month?!" Taylor gasped.

"I know. Isn't it wonderful?" Alex cooed.

"For you." Taylor said, as she stood with her arms crossed.

"Hmm...maybe. But I can assure you you'll appreciate the results. Now, the other thing is, you still haven't let me greet you properly."

"Okay." Taylor said as she once again went into Alex's arms. Only this time she wrapped her arms around Alex's neck and the two greeted one another with a passionate kiss. After Taylor steadied herself from the kiss, she asked about her surprise.

"So what's the surprise?"

"No, first you go up to your old room and get washed up for the night. Have you eaten?"

"I had something on the plane, so I'm fine."

"Okay, well go ahead and get cleaned up, and then meet me in our room alright?"

"Okay. But at least give me a hint?"

"Alright...you're going to love it."

"Really? What?!"

"Go, I'll be there in a moment."

"Oh...alright, but it's not fair." Taylor said, as she was turned and with a swat to her behind, was sent on her way.

Alex watched her go and a smile seemed to have become fixed on her lips. She watched Taylor disappear up the stairs and her heart beat rhythmically in her chest. She then went to the den to get the food she had taken in there. She took the tea and reheated it. Then, taking the fruit and tea with two cups she went upstairs to her room to wait for Taylor to come in. Taylor arrived a bit later and just as she was about to come in the room, Alex caught her and covered her eyes.

"Okay, here we go." Alex led Taylor to a spot in the room that faced a door. "Okay look." Alex said, as she removed her hands from over Taylor's eyes.

Taylor opened her eyes and it took a moment to focus, and then another moment to get the purpose of her standing in front of a door. Suddenly it struck her.

"Wait a minute, this door wasn't here?! Alex?"

"Open it."

Taylor knitted her brows at the smirking woman, and then turned to look at the new door. She walked up to it and with a final look back at Alex, she opened it. Taylor's mouth dropped open as a result of what she saw.

"Oh...my goodness. Alex! It's...it's...it's beautiful, wow, you did this for me?"

"I wanted you to feel like this was truly your room as well as mine. My home is your home. What better way?"

Taylor turned and walked back over to where Alex stood, with a deep sigh of contentment and love, she wrapped her arms around Alex's waist and hugged her as the tears ran down her face. Alex hugged Taylor close and the two just stood embracing each other. When they finally let each other go, Alex took Taylor's hand and pulled her into the closet so that she could look around.

"Alex, this is huge...I haven't got enough clothes to even come close to filling up this room."

"That's okay, you'll eventually have enough to fill it, and then you'll be wanting a bigger place."

"No, I don't think so. You can put a whole bedroom set in here and still have room for a sitting room." Taylor gushed.

Alex laughed and then began telling Taylor what each compartment was for. Taylor saw that Alex had unpacked her clothes and things, as well as having moved her designer clothes into the closet.

"You've been busy haven't you?' Taylor asked, seeing all the things that had been done.

"No more than you." They walked out of the closet and Taylor crawled up on the bed with Alex following her from the other side.

"Would you like some tea?"

"Yes, thank you."

Alex poured Taylor a cup of tea and handed it to her. She poured herself some and then stretched out her long legs. She sipped on her tea as she watched Taylor do the same.

"So, sweetling, how much did you miss me?" Alex asked, as she looked out of the corner of her eye.

Taylor sipped her tea and looked out the corner of her eye the same way.

"Hmm...I missed you. Did you miss me?"

Alex put her tea on the bedside table and turned to look Taylor fully in the eyes. Taylor was so startled by the action and the intense look in Alex's eyes that her hands trembled. She almost spilled the contents of her cup.

"I'll show you just how much, sweetling." Alex purred as she leaned forward and placed a kiss on Taylor that caused the girl's arms to weaken. Alex's reflexes caught the cup and saucer, and placed it on the table on Taylor's side of the bed, without breaking the embrace.

Alex wrapped her arm around Taylor's waist and pulled her forward, so as to lay her down on the bed. This time Alex allowed her nightshirt covered body to lie against Taylor's. Alex kissed along Taylor's cheek and neck as she brought one of her hands up to Taylor's opposite cheek and caressed her face. Taylor finally managed to find some strength to raise her own hands to Alex's cheeks, and guided her lips back to her own. Alex lowered her hand down along Taylor's neck, downward to her chest, and eventually over Taylor's breasts where she kneaded the breast under the gown cover. She caressed the aroused peaks. Taylor moaned at the love Alex was placing upon her, and she returned the caresses in turn, to Alex's breasts. The two women undressed each other, so that they both were lying nude on the bed, each expressing their pleasure with each other through their moans and sighs. There were frequent sharp intakes of air, at unexpected sensations.

"Taylor?" Alex whispered huskily as Taylor was loving Alex's breast with her hands, lips and mouth, while Alex laid on her back caressing Taylor's back and hips.

"Yes Alex?" Taylor answered back breathlessly.

Alex lifted Taylor's head up and with her hand guided her back up from her chest to where she could look in Taylor's eyes.

"I want to love all of you." Alex whispered as she kissed Taylor's lips, while at the same time looking deep into her eyes.

Taylor's hands, which had stopped shaking, now began to tremble once again.

"I love you Taylor! I just want so badly to love all of the woman I am in love with, just as I am ready to let you do the same with me. I know you love me sweetling, but we have to move further in our relationship. Kitten, I'm not trying to pressure you or anything like that. I told you once before, we would only do what you felt comfortable with, until you were sure it was me you wanted in your life. I meant that then and I still mean it. I will wait for you, but I'm asking that you not make me wait too long."

Taylor raised her hand to Alex's face as she now came to straddle Alex's thighs so that she was in a sitting position, facing her.

"Alex my love, I'm sure it's you I want in my life. I trust you not to hurt me, and I pray I won't ever hurt you again. I know what you're asking me and I have mixed feelings about it."

"Well, if you tell me what they are, maybe I can help you resolve them." Alex offered, as she leaned in and gave a gentle peck to Taylor's lips.

"It's just that...well there is no one else whom I would give my gift to but you. But I just wish..."

"Wish what Taylor?"

"I just wish...well, you know. Anyway, it's silly, and you have already given me so many gifts of yourself, it's wrong of me to ask for anything else from you. I am very much in love with you, and I give all of myself freely to you to love, as I will love whatever you wish to give to me."

"Taylor...you...you have..." Alex tried to express her joy at Taylor's trust and the love that she had just offered her. She pulled Taylor into her arms and the two of them held each other, just letting their hearts renew in each other.

While the two were embracing each other the phone rang. Alex was willing to ignore it as she held Taylor in her arms, both naked against one another, but Taylor thought they should answer it.

CHAPTER 25

"What if something's wrong? I mean, it is rather late for someone to be calling with good news, don't you think?"

"Taylor, I just want to stay right here and make love to you."

"And I you, but please answer it?"

"Oh...alright!!" Alex gritted her teeth, mad at the interruption of what was about to change both of their lives forever. She snatched the phone up and hissed into it.

"WHAT?!!" Taylor covered her mouth to keep from laughing at Alex's obvious irritation.

Taylor decided to play with Alex while she spoke on the phone. So she let her hands lower to Alex's breasts and, leaning forward, she kissed along Alex's neck, which was blushing already from her highly aroused state. Alex's breathing began increasing as she tried to focus on the phone call.

"Hello, Ms. Madison?"

"Yes, this is she. Who is this?"

"This is the police. We just arrested a young man for arson."

"And you're calling me, why?!" Alex asked, completely missing the point of the call due to Taylor's distracting actions.

"He started a fire at one of your companies."

"What?!" Alex exclaimed, which caused Taylor to stop what she was doing and listen to the side of the conversation she could hear.

"What is it?" Taylor asked, lifting off of Alex and moving to sit next to her.

"Yes ma'am."

"How much damage?"

"It doesn't seem to be much. The fire department was able to contain the fire quickly."

"Oh, good. Well, which one?"

The officer told her where, and they hung up. Taylor was waiting for Alex to hang up to tell her what was going on.

"What is it?"

"There was a fire at one of my companies."

"What?! How bad?" Taylor asked, shocked to hear the news.

"The officer didn't think that it was too bad because the firemen were able to get it under control quickly. But I need to go there to see for myself. They said they caught a young man who started the fire."

"Why would he do that?"

"I don't know, maybe he knows someone in the company and wanted to get them or get back at me for something. There are many people out there who would love to get back at me for some perceived wrong that they think I've done them. Anyway, I need to get dressed and get down there." Alex moved to get up and Taylor caught her arm.

"I'll go with you."

"No, you stay here. I don't want anything to happen to you out there at this time of night."

"Alex I'm not going to let you go out there by yourself! Besides, I thought we were supposed to be there for each other?" Taylor said with a gentle smile.

"Okay, but you stay where I can see you."

"Alright."

"Taylor, I'm serious! We have to go through a not so good neighborhood to get there."

"Okay, I understand."

"Alright, get dressed then." Alex said, kissing Taylor's forehead and then turning to go and get cleaned up a bit. She threw on some pants and a shirt.

Taylor did the same thing and they decided to let the chauffeur take them. They arrived at the site of the fire and saw that the building did, indeed, only have minor damage, which would be easily repaired. The two got out of the car and Alex was greeted by the officer in charge and briefed once again as to what was going on. She was taken around the building with the chief fireman also escorting them. Alex and Taylor spent about an hour with the two men.

"Where is the suspect?"

"He's already been taken from the scene. I would think you want full charges brought against him."

"Definitely. Is there anything else that you need from me?"

"No ma'am. If something else comes up, we'll call you."

"Fine. Taylor, let's go."

Taylor and Alex left the scene after only being there for a short period of time, Alex having gone just to see the extent of the damage. After seeing the results, she decided it was not necessary to stay around so they went back to the car and headed back home. On the way, they talked, but eventually Taylor laid her head against Alex's shoulder and soon she was asleep. When they arrived home Alex gently nudged Taylor awake, and they walked into the house. Taylor literally stripped out of her clothes as she entered the bedroom, and by the time she made it to the bed she was only in her underwear. Alex had watched Taylor the whole time and an amused smile lit her eyes. She followed Taylor into the bed, and when she lay back, Taylor rolled over into her arms and within moments of wishing Alex a goodnight, she fell asleep. Alex hugged Taylor to her and drifted off, content with the girl in her arms.

The next morning Alex woke Taylor up.

"Okay sleepy head, time to get up."

"Aww...Alex I don't have to be anywhere today, just let me sleep for a few more hours?"

"No...come on, you have to get used to getting up early again. Besides, when was the last time you worked out?"

"Oh...Alex no...I'll start everything tomorrow; getting up early, exercising, all of that. Just let me sleep for a few more hours. Besides, we didn't get to bed until almost 4 in the morning."

"And your point would be? Now come on! Get up, or I'll make you beg me to let you out of this bed."

Taylor's eyes popped open at the thought of what that meant, and Alex saw what she was thinking.

"You have to go to work, you don't have time to get that involved."

"Are you getting up or not?"

"Hmm... I'll get up in one hour, okay?"

"No. You have five seconds."

"Alex, only three hours of sleep, that's all I get?"

"Times up." Alex jumped astride Taylor's hips in one move and began tickling her unmercifully.

Taylor squealed as she struggled to get free of Alex's unexpected torture.

"Okay, okay, I'll get up, I'll get up! Please stop? Please Alex?!" Taylor begged, between bouts of hysterical laughter.

Alex suddenly stopped and jumped up off the bed onto the floor and waited for Taylor to calm her laughter.

"Okay, I'm waiting."

Taylor continued to giggle as she crawled off of the bed. After she composed herself, she crossed her arms and was about to head over to the dresser to get her workout clothes, but Alex already had them out and waiting. She picked up the clothes and put them on quickly and then headed out of the bedroom, leaving Alex grinning after her. The two did their workout and then went and made breakfast for themselves.

"Are you going to start back working as my PA today?"

"No, I thought I would take a few more days off before I do."

"Oh, okay. Well you are going to join me for lunch everyday until you're back working."

"Are you asking?" Taylor asked, irony ringing in her voice.

"No."

"Oh, well in that case, I guess I don't have a choice, do I?"

"Hmmm...NO."

The two finished eating and got cleaned up in the separate showers. Taylor called for the car for Alex and when she was about to leave for work, she reminded Taylor to not be late for lunch. They agreed she would meet Alex in her office and they would go together from there.

"Okay, I'll see you around 1pm?"

"That's fine. See you then. If you need me, call me Taylor, alright?"

"Alright."

Alex kissed Taylor and after eliciting the sound she was going for, she let her go and headed out to the waiting car and driver. Alex arrived at the company and was met by Kiara.

"Ms. Madison, we need to talk."

"Fine, walk with me. What is it?"

"I've been watching the Zadria stocks along with your attorneys. It had been rising steadily until 2 months ago. Now it's dropping rather rapidly. It looks like the company will go belly up in the next few days or so."

"What is Zadria doing about it?"

"There's not much she can do. She's tried splitting her stocks, but it didn't help. Whoever it was buying the stocks, bought too much of them for it to have any real affect. It looks like she's going to have to file for bankruptcy."

"Hmm. Well hopefully we'll find out who is doing this, and then maybe we can do something about it."

"Well, because you suspect someone in the company you know I've pretty much had all of the phones in the building tapped, except for your office of course."

"And?"

"There are some questionable calls made, but I can't say that any of them are suspicious."

"What about Ms. Lacy? Have you heard or seen anything suspicious?"

"No, not really, but her conversations are usually on her phone in your office, therefore I can't listen in to any of them."

"Well have there been any calls made to any one number consistently over the last months?"

"Not really, all pretty sporadic."

"Hmm!" Alex sighed with frustration.

"We're trying ma'am." Kiara said, somewhat nervous about Alex's possible line of thought.

Alex cut her eyes over at Kiara and with a slight nod of her head, she acknowledged Kiara's words.

"I know."

Kiara relaxed and when Alex stepped onto the elevator she stayed where she was and just said in a cryptic fashion.

"I'll be around if you need me."

Alex nodded her head and glanced at one of the employees who was holding the open button for her to finish her conversation. She nodded at him and he hit the top floor button. Alex thought about the conversation all the way to the top floor. When she arrived, she stepped off the elevator and took a few breaths to rein in her contempt for Salina, then strolled into the office.

"Good morning ma'am."

"Ms. Lacy bring my schedule in, along with the Chi-Tech report."

"Yes ma'am."

"Is my mail on my desk?"

"Yes ma'am."

"Fine." Alex went into her office and after opening her shades to let the light filter in better, she picked up the mail and flipped through it. Salina came in a few minutes later and began going over Alex's schedule for the day. Alex only made one change to her schedule and that was a 1 to 3 meeting. She didn't want anything interfering with her lunch date.

"Okay, buzz me when my first appointment arrives."

"Yes ma'am. Can I get you anything else?"

"Just my tea."

"Oh, yes ma'am. I'll get it right now."

Alex watched the woman go and saw how she looked over her shoulder. Salina had a funny look in her eyes; one that made Alex knit her brows. Salina obviously didn't realize that Alex had seen the look and was bothered by it. When Salina brought in her tea, Alex dismissed her and went back to going through her mail. She saw Salina peek back inside the inner office when Alex brought the cup to her mouth. Alex had no intention of drinking the tea, but she let the young woman think she was. Alex felt that while Salina wouldn't try to poison her or anything, she was capable of adding undesirable flavorings to the tea; one's that would not be seen or smelled. She put the cup down and pretended to swallow, although she had nothing in her mouth. She saw the smirk on the woman's face when she set her cup down.

"Hmm...what are you up to Salina, and why are you being sneaky?" Alex asked herself as she read her mail and watched Salina return to her own work.

CHAPTER 26

Taylor stayed around the house talking to the maid and reading until it was time to go and meet Alex for lunch. When Taylor arrived in the building after being gone for such a long time, she was surprised that so many people remembered her.

"Ms. Young? Welcome back! You are back, aren't you?"

"Hi! No, not yet."

"Oh, are you going to go talk with "The Raider"?"

Taylor smiled to herself, knowing what they were thinking, but she played along.

"Yes, I heard she's mellowed A LOT."

"Well, she hasn't demoted anyone since her spring annual."

"Then she has mellowed. Wonderful! Maybe I do have a chance of getting my job back. Well I'd better get going before something happens to change that mellowness."

"Yeah, that's true. She's so unpredictable. Well, it was nice to see you again, Ms. Young."

"Thank you. Bye." Taylor turned and headed for the elevator and once inside, she hit the express button.

Alex heard the familiar warning, and pushed the panel to turn on the monitor without raising the small screen from within the desk. When she saw Taylor primping in the elevator, a smile and a warmth came over her, due to the fact that Taylor was doing it for her. When the elevator door open and Taylor stepped off, Salina almost choked on her own saliva. She watched in both confusion and horror as Taylor walked off of the elevator headed for the office. Taylor was wearing a white silk, skirt suit that resembled Alex's, except it was a different color, and it was a skirt whereas Alex's was pants. Taylor saw the distressed look in Salina's eyes when she walked up to the desk.

"Hi Salina, how are you?"

"Taylor?! What are you doing here?! I know you don't work here anymore, do you?!"

"No."

Salina visibly relaxed a bit.

"I'm just here to have lunch with Ms. Madison."

"What?! Well you can't, you're not on her appointment list!"

"Oh, well she invited me."

"Well I don't know what's going on with you, but you've obviously forgotten the consequences of being here, or should I remind you?"

"Oh, Salina, that's not necessary. I'm quite comfortable in my relationship with Ms. Madison. Besides, I have to finish working on the Zadria deal. I heard it was having some major problems, and since Zadria is a friend of mine, I figure between Alex and I, we could figure out what happened, and what to do about it. Now, if you'll excuse me, she's waiting for me."

Taylor walked away from the desk and knocked on the door of Alex's office. Alex waved her in and Taylor opened the door and strolled inside, closing the door behind her. Salina stood looking in the window of the office, then turned and tried to take her mind off of the fact that Taylor was back. The thought of Taylor and Alex looking into what was happening with The Zadria company was too much for her to handle, but she had to wait until Alex and Taylor left for lunch before she could do anything about it. Taylor and Alex spoke for a moment before they came out of the office to leave for lunch.

"I'll be back in a while Ms. Lacy."

"Ye...yes ma'am."

Alex turned and she and Taylor walked out of the office and got on the elevator. Salina was so nervous that every time the phone rang, she nearly jumped out of her skin.

Meanwhile, Alex and Taylor had left the building to go to a restaurant around the corner.

"I've been waiting to see you all day." Taylor said to Alex, as she covered her hand with her own hand on top of the table.

Alex smiled and squeezed Taylor's hand.

"I've missed you also, my little sweetling."

Taylor grinned brightly at the sensual tone in Alex's voice.

"So, what did you do today?"

"Nothing really, just hung around the house, and talked to the maid. Then I read for a while, and came here."

"Did you think about me at all doing all of that?"

"Yes, throughout all of it. As a matter of fact, the maid told me some very interesting things about her early days with you. I didn't know she came here with you from overseas."

"Yes she did, but I think I'm going to have to have a talk with her. I don't know if I like the idea of her talking about me to you."

"Why, are you afraid she'll tell me something you don't want me to know?" Taylor said teasing, as she took a bite of her food.

"Yes." Alex answered simply.

Taylor saw the humor in her eyes and she just pinched her lips. She put another fork full of food in her mouth so as not to be drawn in. The two sat, ate, and talked throughout their lunch. Salina, in the interim, had decided to at least go and call Wellington. She left the office, got on the elevator and went down to the lobby area of the building to use the pay phone. Kiara, the detective who had camped out in the security office that day, happened to come across Salina on the elevator and saw her pacing within it. This piqued her curiosity and she watched Salina get off of the elevator and head to the pay phone. Kiara watched her via the cameras that were discreetly hidden. Kiara zoomed in on the pay phone to watch the number that was dialed as the camera recorded both sound and pictures.

"Hello, Charles Wellington please."

"Hello, this is Mr. Wellington."

"Charles it's me."

"Oh, Salina, what is it?"

"I just saw Taylor Young."

"Taylor Young?"

"Yes, Ms. Madison's ex-Personal Assistant and the friend of Zadria."

"Aha, yes, okay, so what's the problem?"

"I'm nervous about her sudden appearance. I think I'm ready to get my money and get out."

"Do you think they're onto us?"

"I don't know. I don't think so, but I don't want to take a chance. I want my money, for the stocks, both the Zadria stock and yours."

"Alright, when do you want to meet?"

"Well Ms. Madison is at lunch right now, so when she returns, I'll leave here."

"Okay, meet me in my office and I'll give you your share of the money. I can't believe we pulled this off. I got to save my company while at the same time making a fortune off of Zadria's Fashions."

"Yeah, I know. The only thing that I'm disappointed about is the fact that "The Raider" was able to make a very nice piece of change from the sale of her stock in your company when she saw it would be too expensive to take over. But, all in all, it worked out. Anyway, I'll be on my way as soon as they return from lunch. I should be there a few minutes after I leave here, since your building is just a few blocks away from here."

"Oh, you're not driving over?"

"No, it might draw attention. I'll walk there. I'll see you in a while. Oh, and make sure you have a cashier's check, and not a personal check."

"What? After all of this, you don't trust me?"

"It's not a matter of trust, I just want to get my money and go. See you soon." Salina then hung up the phone and headed to the elevator to go back up to the office to wait for Alex and Taylor to return from their lunch.

"Oh my goodness." Kiara gasped, as she sat back in her chair, shocked at what she had just heard. After getting over the initial shock, she jumped from the chair and grabbed the disc out of the machine, then turned and raced out the door to the elevator. She arrived on the top floor and saw Salina was sitting at her desk as if nothing was amiss. She went inside and spoke to Salina.

"I'm here to speak with Ms. Madison."

"Oh, do you have an appointment?"

"No, but I would like to wait."

"Okay, she should be back anytime."

"Thank you." Kiara walked over to the water cooler and took a cup and filled it. She watched Salina nervously tap her pen on the desk, looking at the door as if she could will Alex and Taylor back.

"Is something wrong?" Kiara asked Salina, as she walked to one of the chairs to sit down.

"Oh, no, I'm just waiting for Ms. Madison to return so I can go to lunch."

"Hmm...it must be a very important lunch date?"

"Uh...yes, I'm supposed to meet my boyfriend. He's taking me to that new little tearoom that just opened up."

"Aha...really?"

"Yes."

Suddenly Salina heard the elevator, and jumped up out of her chair intending to tell Alex she was going to go to lunch. When Alex and Taylor stepped off of the elevator they went into the office and saw Kiara.

"Ms. Madison, I need to speak with you!"

"Ms. Madison, I'd like to ask you...."

"Wait." Alex said, raising her hand towards both women.

"First I will talk to Ms. Young, and then I will talk to the two of you." Alex went into her office with Taylor beside her. Closing the door she turned to Taylor and smirked.

"What?" Taylor asked, with a perplexed smile on her face.

"What do you think all of that is about?"

"I don't know, but it's obviously something important."

"Yes, maybe. But you know what?"

"What?"

"I've never seen Salina so anxious."

"Really, well evidently there's something bothering her."

"Yeah, well let's see what's going on with her."

Alex hit the intercom button and told Salina to come in.

Salina knocked and Alex sneered but motioned for her to come in.

"Okay Salina, what is it?"

"I was just coming to let you know that I wanted to go to lunch, if it's alright with you?"

"Is that what all of that was about out there?"

"Yes Ma'am, it's very important. I'm meeting someone for lunch."

"Fine." Alex said curtly.

Taylor saw how anxious Salina was, and she thought about what the guy at the SEC had told her.

"Have a good lunch Salina. Taylor said with false sincerity.

"Thank you, it'll be the best I've ever had I think." Salina said sarcastically in response.

Salina turned and closed the door and left. Once she was at the elevator, she pushed the button to go down. Meanwhile, Alex was about to turn her attention back to Taylor, when Kiara literally ran into the office.

"Ms. Madison! I'm sorry to disturb you...hello Ms. Young."

"Hi, is everything alright?" Taylor asked, due to the distress she saw on the woman's face, and the way she ran into the office.

"Oh, I'm fine, I need to speak with Ms. Madison about something in private for a moment, if you don't mind?"

"No, not at all." Taylor said agreeably.

"Thank you."

"No problem, I'll just wait out there." Taylor said, speaking to Alex.

"Alright, I'll be done in a moment."

"Okay." Taylor replied, then turned and went out into the outer office closing the door behind her. She saw Salina get on the elevator and the doors close. Salina had been wearing a weird looking smile on her face.

"Okay, now what is it?!" Alex asked, angry at the interruption.

"I'd rather show you!" Kiara said breathless due to her racing heart, at what she thought Alex's response would be to her discovery. Kiara put the disc in and they both watched.

Alex's eyes narrowed at the first sight of Salina going to the pay phone.

"What is she doing using that phone?"

"She didn't want to take a chance that her conversation would be overheard I would think."

Alex listened to the conversation and as she sat there, her eyes showed the rage that was inside of her. A sneer came to her lips, and when Kiara happened to glance over at the woman, she could have sworn she saw smoke coming off of her.

Normally Alex never allowed her emotions to get away from her when she was at work, but for some reason, she couldn't help it. Suddenly a vase went flying at the image, causing a loud crashing sound to emit from the office. Alex was now on her feet, cursing like a sailor, and throwing things. Kiara had to duck a few times to avoid being hit by flying objects.

Taylor raced back into the office barely missing getting hit by a vase that crashed next to her.

"ALEX?! WHAT'S WRONG?!!" Taylor shouted after getting over the near miss by the vase.

"Where is she now?!" Alex growled at Kiara.

"Heading over there I think." Kiara stated quickly.

Suddenly Alex was on the move! She flew past Taylor and headed for the stairs and raced down them. Kiara and Taylor both stood for a split second looking at each other and watching Alex disappear out of sight. Then they both were on the move, chasing after Alex. Meanwhile, Salina had been stopped from leaving the building. One of her junior executive admirers caught up with her before she made it to the lobby doors.

"Heading off to lunch Ms. Lacy?"

"Yes, and I'm in sort of in a hurry. What do you want?"

"Well since you're going to lunch now, maybe I can join you?"

"I don't think so. You see...my boyfriend may have a problem with that, and he may beat you senseless. So, do you still want to join me for lunch?" Salina asked evilly.

The young man gave a distasteful smile, then turned and headed in the opposite direction.

Salina headed for the door and left. Meanwhile, Taylor was yelling to Kiara.

"What's going on?!"

Kiara was focused on catching Alex, now that the fear was over for her. Taylor kept shouting at Kiara to tell her what was going on, but the only thing Kiara said to her was;

"We have to stop her, otherwise she'll kill her!"

"Kill who?!" Taylor asked, as panic and fear set in. They raced down the stairwell trying to catch up with Alex, who was not even winded by the activity. Taylor looked over the rails to see Alex a few floors ahead of her, and Kiara one floor ahead. Alex made it to the first floor and whipped open the door. She flew out and ran into the lobby, only stopping long enough to see if Salina was still in the building. She ran to the front security desk and asked if they had seen Salina, and was told that she had left about two minutes before. Alex gritted her teeth and then took off for the lobby door. Yasmeia happened to see Alex come out of the stairwell. She saw her talking to the security personnel and then take off running once again. She also saw the anger in Alex's eyes, and she knew something was wrong.

She called to Alex, but Alex didn't hear her, or didn't care. She raced out of the front doors of the building, followed moments later by Kiara, and a moment after her, Taylor. Yasmeia called to Taylor, and Taylor stopped only long enough for Yasmeia to catch up with her.

"What's going on?"

"I don't have time to talk! Come on, I have to catch up with Alex. Something is wrong."

"What?"

"I don't know. But whatever it is, it could lead to someone's death if I don't catch up with her." Taylor ran for the door with Yasmeia following her.

They saw Alex and Kiara racing down the street, and ran after the two. Just as Alex came around the corner three blocks up, where she had seen Salina turn, she saw the woman heading into The Wellington building. Alex cursed to herself as she slowed down and went into a rapid stride. She now realized who the insider was. She arrived at the building and with gritted teeth, walked inside and headed for the elevator. She planned on confronting Wellington and breaking Salina into a few satisfying pieces.

But, just as she was about to hit the elevator button, her hand was caught and held firmly. She was so focused on catching Salina, that her first reaction to having her hand caught so firmly was to quickly free her hand, which she did. She did a twist of her wrist and caught the hand that had held hers.

"Ms. Madison, I'm sorry I startled you." The man said, as he felt like his wrist was about to be broken.

"Oh, it's you, what are you doing here?!"

"Stopping you from spoiling things."

"What are you talking about?"

"Ms. Lacy just arrived here a few moments ago and took the elevator up to Mr. Wellington's office. The arrest is going down as we speak, and if you go up there, you'll spoil everything."

"Arrest?"

"Yes Ma'am, for insider trading. Both the agents from the SEC and the Justice Department are up there. The next time you see Ms. Lacy, she will be in handcuffs."

Alex's breathing was rapid, and mixed emotions went through her at that moment. One was anger that she did not catch Salina before she made it to the building, but also utter excitement and elation at the fact that the whole thing would be over in a matter of moments.

Meanwhile, Kiara ran inside the building, followed only moments later by Taylor and Yasmeia. Taylor saw Alex standing with some man dressed in a dark blue suit and she, Kiara and Yasmeia all headed over to the two.

"Taylor? Are you alright?"

Taylor raised a brow at Alex's question and then said breathlessly,

"Me...oh yeah...great! Do you mind telling me why you went running out of the building like a mad woman possessed?!"

"I wanted to catch up with Salina."

"Salina? Why?"

"Because...she's the one who has been dealing in insider trading in my company, which almost led to my companies being investigated. I just wanted to have a nice little TALK with her."

Alex said through her teeth, as Taylor leaned against the wall of the elevator to catch her breath.

"Oh!! Now I get it. That's what you were talking about moments before?" Taylor said, directing her statement to Kiara.

"Yes."

"Okay, that makes sense, so...why are we waiting down here? Why don't we go up and confront them?"

"Because ma'am, an arrest is taking place at this very moment by the SEC and Justice Department."

"OH!! Great!" Taylor exclaimed.

"May I get all of your names just in case we need to contact any of you for any reason?"

"Of course."

"Wonderful. If you'll step over here to the visitor's desk, I will take your information." Sidney led the group over to the visitor's desk. He began asking each person her name and relationship to Alex. He started with Yasmeia and got all of her information and was about to turn to Kiara, who conveniently made her beeper go off. She excused herself and went to make a pretend phone call. After a moment she came back and said she couldn't stay because she was needed back at the office. Kiara left and the agent looked at Alex to see if she wanted him to pursue it, but Alex gave him a signal that indicated for the agent to leave it alone. The agent gave a slight nod of his head in understanding and then turned to Taylor to take her information.

"Okay, your name?"

"Taylor Young, I..."

"Aha! You're Taylor Young?!"

"You know each other??" Alex asked with a raised brow at the two.

"I...I..."

"Yes Taylor?" Alex asked, looking at Taylor with an inquisitive brow.

"Oh, we don't know each other personally Ms. Madison, I just know of Ms. Taylor through all of the information that she provided to Mr. Rouse. She was instrumental in refocusing the SEC's investigation from your companies to Ms. Lacy and Mr.

Wellington. Congratulations Ms. Young, without your information we would have been going in the wrong direction."

"Thank you." Taylor said, now uncomfortable with the look of shock and amazement being leveled on her by Alex. Yasmeia knew Taylor was now very embarrassed that Alex found out right there that it was Taylor who helped with the investigation.

Taylor's eyes looked over at Alex who was still staring at her in surprise.

"Um...so, how long before they come down?" Taylor said, trying to change the subject as a blush came over her at Alex's continuous and steady gaze.

Meanwhile, upstairs, Salina had made it to Wellington's office. They were just talking for a moment, because there were people meandering around, pretending that they were involved in conversations or some other activity. Salina didn't pay them any mind as she had passed them on her way to the office.

"Okay Charles, here are the stocks to your company, now give me my money so I can leave."

"Okay, it's in my safe. I'll get it."

"Okay, but hurry up, I have this terrible feeling."

"Alright, calm down. You're so jumpy."

"Okay, okay, just hurry up." Salina said, as she paced up and down in the office, waiting for the man to get the money for her.

"Okay people, we move in the moment the exchange takes place." The head SEC agent said to the others who were staked out in different areas of the floor.

"Okay, here you go. It's a lot of money, but I'm sure you can find something to spend it on." Wellington stated in a joking tone.

"Yeah, yeah, yeah, just give it to me, and here, here are my shares." Salina said, anxious just to get her money and go and forget about all the chattering.

Just as the two exchanged papers, Rouse gave the order to move.

"Now!" Suddenly, there were agents coming out of the woodwork, at least that's the way it seemed.

"OH GOD!!" Salina exclaimed in horror as she and Wellington were surrounded.

Rouse walked up to them and looking at both of their hands, he plucked the two items from them. With the aid of a light through the white envelope, he saw the amount of the cashier check and who it was made out to and signed by. He opened the manila envelope that Salina had handed to Wellington and he saw what he was looking for inside.

"Okay, we got it. Salina Lacy, Charles Wellington, you're both under arrest for Insider Trading. You're also being arrested for..." Rouse continued, as he listed the charges against the two. After their rights had been read to them and the cuffs were placed on, the two were then led out of the office. As they walked down the hallway in front of Wellington's employees, the people whispered to one another at the sight of seeing their boss being led out with handcuffs on. They were put in an elevator with Rouse and a few of the agents. Everyone headed down to the first floor to leave through the front entrance of the building. When the elevator bell announced the arrival of the elevator on the first floor, Alex closed her mouth and simply said to Taylor.

"We'll talk about this later." Then turned her attention to the group getting off of the elevator.

Rouse was ahead of the group and he headed towards Alex. Salina and Wellington were both looking at Taylor and the others. Alex stood glaring at both of them, but especially Salina. Finally she took a step towards Salina, but Taylor caught her arm.

"Don't." Was all she said.

Alex inhaled deeply, and broke eye contact with the obviously frightened PA. She glanced at Taylor and, looking into her concerned eyes, Alex sighed again, and with a slight nod of her head, she reassured the girl. Taylor smiled and looked at Salina with disdain and then back at Alex, who now gently removed Taylor's hand from her arm. Alex stepped up to Salina and Wellington, and Salina flinched at what she thought was about to happen to her. Alex surprised Salina by directing her initial comments to Wellington.

"Charles, I'm very disappointed with you. I thought you had more honor in your business dealings. You were losing fair and square and rather than using your business savvy to try to save your company, you resorted to a cliche. Too bad, I was looking forward to seeing what your next move was going to be, before you decided to join up with this nobody. Oh well, now you not only will be going to jail for a while, but by the time you get out, I'll have taken your company and torn it apart with outsourcing. So when you return, only the mailroom will be left...under contract of course."

Alex then looked down at Salina who was standing slightly to the right of her, and spoke to her. "Ms. Lacy, today was your lucky day. When I found out that it was you who had betrayed me, your ass was mine, but...you made it here before I got my hands on you. I had so many plans, but, that's alright. I'm pleased with your arrest, it'll have to do. I hope you enjoy your prison time, from what I understand, it's brutal, but you shouldn't have to many problems. Just be the political slut you are and you'll be the most popular in your cellblock. I can't believe you tried to screw me, you little nobody. Well, now it'll be your turn to get screwed...if you know what I mean, which I'm sure you do." Alex cut her eyes to Rouse. "You better get her out of here before I change my mind."

"Take them out." Rouse ordered, and the other agents moved Wellington and Salina along.

Rouse turned back to look at Taylor who was rubbing Alex's back trying to calm her.

"Ms. Madison, Ms. Young was instrumental in all of this."

"I know Mr. Rouse, and I plan on having a talk with her about it later." Alex said, cutting her eyes over at Taylor, whose hands now went back to her own arms to rub nervously up and down them.

"Well, I thought it was important for you to know that."

"Yes, thank you, and thank you for your work on this. I do appreciate it."

"My pleasure ma'am." Rouse gave a slight tilt of his head to Alex and then the same to Taylor and Yasmeia. Then he left along with the last of the agents.

"Well, what a rather interesting day this turned out to be, wouldn't you say Alexandra?" Yasmeia asked, amused.

"Yes, I would say it has been. Right Taylor?"

"Um...yes, so, anyone as thirsty as I am?"

"No, but I have a lot of questions to ask you." Alex answered.

Taylor swallowed hard, but then a thought came to her.

"Hey, wait a minute, now that you know what was going on at your company, tell me how you feel about it all?"

"I told you." Alex said as she turned and headed for the exit, with Taylor and Yasmeia walking next to her.

"What?"

"I'm pleased."

"Pleased?! That's it, just pleased?!" Taylor said, shocked that Alex wasn't overjoyed.

"Yes, pleased." Alex said with a straight face as they walked back down the street. Yasmeia was laughing at Taylor's animated behavior, and wondering why Taylor was so set on Alex being more than just pleased.

CHAPTER 27

When they arrived back at the building, Alex walked over to the security desk and told one of the people to call for her car.

"Well ladies, I guess I will head back to my new office."

Taylor's brows knitted as she stopped badgering Alex and now focused on Yasmeia.

"What do you mean your new office?"

"Oh, didn't I tell you? It must have been all of the excitement."

"No you didn't. Neither of you." Taylor said with a stern gaze at both women.

"Well, I have a new position."

"Really? What?!"

"VP in charge of operations." Yasmeia said with a smile at Taylor's wide eyes.

"Yasmeia! Congratulations! You truly deserve it. I am so proud of you." Taylor said, as she gave her friend a great big hug.

"Thank you, but it was Alex's idea."

"Hmm...there it is again, that side that makes my heart swell." Taylor said, as she squeezed Alex's hand that she had discreetly taken in her own.

"Hmm, what do I get for it?" Alex teased.

Taylor blushed and then looked back at Yasmeia who just chuckled at Taylor's embarrassment to Alex's direct question.

"Whatever you want! Not that there's that much more left. I already owe you...and speaking of which, how can you not be excited and happy that all of this is over with?"

"Are you back on that?"

"Yes! Because I don't understand it, and until I do, I'm going to keep asking! So...you might as well tell me now, because I know you can't just be pleased."

"Yasmeia, we'll see you later. It seems I need to get Taylor home before she talks my ear off."

"I understand, and I'm very happy that all of this is over and you two are where you belong, together."

"Thank you Yasmeia."

"Yes, thank you my friend, and again, I am so happy for your long overdue promotion. Thanks for helping me with Salina and Wellington."

"You're welcome, anytime." Yasmeia said as she gave Taylor a hug.

"You were involved also??" Alex asked, again surprised.

"Yes, she's the one who overheard the initial conversation between the two."

"Really?? So why didn't you tell me then?" Alex asked, now crossing her arms as she faced Yasmeia.

Yasmeia crossed her own arms and walked up to Alex and stood right in front of her. She looked her straight in the eye and without blinking, told her straight.

"Next time Ms. Madison, you'll listen to me when I say I have something to tell you." Yasmeia gave a knowing look at Alex, then turned and walked away, waving goodbye to the two for the day.

"I guess she told...you." Taylor said with a smirk, as she now turned and walked away from Alex, heading for the waiting car. Alex stood watching for a moment, looking after Yasmeia and then at Taylor. Then, with a thoughtful gaze, she headed for the car with Taylor. Once they were in the car and heading home, Alex turned to Taylor and in a serious tone of voice, she told Taylor what she thought.

"Well my little sweetling, let me tell YOU. I expect my breakfast at 5 sharp, and my dinner at 8 sharp. You know my favorite foods so I won't even go into that. I want them served with a bright smile and the one article of clothing that I told you that you could wear. Of course, it will be the one I choose. Also, you owe me for not telling me that you knew about Salina."

"But I would think you owe me for telling the SEC?"

"Okay, we're even on that one. Actually, as I think about it, I'll give you one week of my serving you. I am so grateful to you, Taylor, for your help in this. Even when we were at odds with each other, you were there for me. Thank you."

Taylor heard the change in Alex's tone and saw the sincerity and emotion in her eyes. She smiled a gentle, loving smile and leaned over to lie against Alex.

"You're welcome, and I would do it again."

Alex smiled and hugged Taylor closer to her, and the two rode the rest of the way home in that way.

CHAPTER 28

When they arrived, they got out of the car, went inside the house, and headed upstairs to get cleaned up. This time, Alex told Taylor to go ahead and use the shower in their room while she went to answer the phone. She had told the maid to have the cook make dinner and then they were dismissed for the rest of the evening. Alex answered the phone as she watched Taylor strip to go and take her shower.

The phone call turned out to be a wrong number so she hung up and thought about Taylor in the shower. It was too much of an image that flooded her thoughts, so she stripped out of her clothes, put on her robe, and went into the bathroom to join Taylor in the shower.

"Alex?"

"You mind if I join you, sweetling?" Alex asked from the other side of the frosted glass shower, only able to see Taylor's outline.

"No, not at all." Taylor replied, as she stepped more to the back of the large shower.

Alex smiled and removed her robe. Opening the sliding glass door, she stepped into the shower. Taylor was trying to maintain her composure, but her heart was racing, and her breathing was betraying her as well. Alex didn't help any with her gaze slowly lowering from Taylor's eyes, to travel down her nude form. Alex's eyes took in all of Taylor's beauty as Taylor stood still, not sure if she could move, considering the way her legs were trembling.

"You're very beautiful, sweetling." Alex said as her eyes came slowly back up to meet Taylor's nervous eyes. I know that this is further than we've gone before, and I will admit I'm a little...well, nervous."

Taylor's brow's knitted and when she spoke, her voice was somewhat unsure, as to whether or not she should ask.

"You...you're nervous? Why?"

"How about if we finish washing up, then we can discuss this in the bedroom."

"Oh, okay." Taylor said, a small smile showing on her face.

"Come here, and I'll wash you up and you can do the same for me."

"Okay." Taylor said, as she moved to stand in front of Alex under the water.

Alex reached for the body soap and the washcloths. She handed one to Taylor and she kept the other. She squeezed out some of the body soap onto each cloth and then she began slowly washing Taylor. Taylor stood, still holding her cloth and Alex knew it was because of fear that Taylor had not moved. So she took Taylor's hand that held the cloth and she placed it on her shoulder, thereby telling her it was okay. Taylor smiled, more out of nervousness than anything, but Alex saw it and once again she began lathering Taylor, as the girl was now lathering her. Alex could see the reddish undertone of Taylor's blushing body and she took the opportunity to turn the washing into a provocative romancing.

Alex took the washcloths and set them down, and moved closer to Taylor's body. She now used her hands to continue to lather Taylor up. Taylor followed Alex's lead and she too continued to lather Alex up using nothing but her hands. Alex leaned in and brought their lips together. In so doing, Taylor was quickly overwhelmed by all of the sensations and she leaned her body back against the wall of the shower without breaking their increasingly passionate kiss.

Alex followed Taylor to the wall, her hands caressing along Taylor's sides and belly, and then over her hips. Alex's hands slipped around to slide upwards slightly to catch Taylor around the waist and hold her tightly to her. Taylor sighed at the caressing touches and she used her hands to caress up Alex's arms, to her chest and then slowly down to her breasts. Taylor and Alex's breathing was rapid and uneven, and when they finally broke their kiss, both were gasping for air. Their eyes, though lidded from their highly aroused state, were locked on each other's. Alex managed to speak, but only in a whisper next to Taylor's ear.

"Turn around."

Taylor let out an audible gasp at the sound of Alex's sensual voice and slowly turned with Alex guiding her. Alex moved against her as she washed Taylor's long, lean back. Taylor nearly swooned at the feel of Alex's slick body against her own. Alex brought her lips to Taylor's ear once again and in that silky smooth, contralto voice she whispered to her.

"I love you." And then she kissed the soft cheek.

They managed to thoroughly wash each other before certain very intimate touches, caused both Taylor and Alex to experience a journey to ecstasy. This caused both of them to lean heavily, Taylor against the wall and Alex against Taylor. Eventually, Alex guided Taylor and herself under the water and let the falling water rinse and cool their bodies. Once they were rinsed, they both stepped out of the shower. Alex lifted a large towel up off of the silver towel rack and patted Taylor dry. Taylor lifted another towel and she used it to do the same to Alex. By the time they headed out to the bedroom, Taylor was breathing rapidly once again, due to some provocative teasing by Alex prior to her being wrapped up in the towel.

Alex guided Taylor to the bed as they kissed. She only stopped long enough to get the scented oil to oil Taylor and herself up. Again, Alex made it into a romancing. She gave Taylor an impromptu massage that covered every bit of Taylor's hot, blushing body. When Alex had finished, Taylor returned the massage. She was not as proficient as Alex was, but she was effective nonetheless. Once both were oiled, Alex pulled Taylor down on top of her and then rolled over, which left Taylor on her back. Alex brought their lips together once again, and this time she was planning on taking things to their conclusion. She moved her head to kiss Taylor's chin, as their hands explored each other's body in earnest and for the intended purpose of consummating their relationship once and for all.

When one of Alex's hands moved down Taylor's belly and slowly towards her womanhood, Alex felt her stiffen.

"It's alright, sweetling, I only want to love all of my heart." Alex said, lifting her head from Taylor's neck to look her in the eyes.

Alex had to smile when she saw the tears balanced, along with the slight nodding of Taylor's head. Alex's heart skipped many beats at that moment. There was a brief moment where she hesitated; it was when Taylor asked her in a small sweet voice.

"Will it hurt?"

Those words touched Alex to where she leaned in and kissed the lips that had asked such innocent words.

"I don't know for sure, but I would think it will, a little."

Taylor was so near delirium, that she almost missed Alex's answer, but somewhere inside her mind, she thought she'd heard wrong. Taylor's eyes now widened slightly, as she looked Alex in the eye.

"You don't know?? How is that possible Alex?" Taylor asked quietly.

Alex smiled, somewhat embarrassed, and Taylor tried to lift up.

"Alex?"

Alex lifted off of Taylor and rolled over onto her side. She was still holding Taylor in her arms, but now they were both balanced on their elbows.

"I don't know if it will hurt Taylor."

"But how is that possible, I mean you had to feel something when you first made love, right?"

Alex licked her lips that had suddenly gone dry. Taylor saw the uncertainty in Alex's eyes, and Alex saw the girl's brows knit in worry. It was the last thing she wanted to happen that night, so she admitted to Taylor why she didn't know whether it would hurt or not.

"Taylor, my little sweetling, I don't know, because...I have never experienced it myself."

"WHAT??!! You...you're a...a virgin?!"

"Yes Taylor. Don't sound so surprised."

"Alex...I...I have to admit, I am. I'm sorry if that is wrong, but I am truly surprised, shocked and struck dumb. I have always assumed that you were experienced! I mean you're so... good at...well you know, making me feel things."

"No, I never met anyone that I wanted to share that part of myself with, at least...not until now. Taylor, I've never given much thought to when it would happen, and I will admit, I never thought it would be another woman. But...I was never one to rule out possibilities, and now...the possibility is a reality. I want to share

ALL of myself with you, as you're willing to share all of yourself with me. I love you."

Taylor inhaled a shaky breath and then leaned forward enough so that she could kiss Alex. Her tears now ran down her face in joy. Alex returned the sentiment. Alex then pulled Taylor into her arms.

" So...now you know, sweetling, I'm all yours." Alex said kissing Taylor's damp cheek.

"Now I understand why you were so upset with me that day at my grandmother's, you were offering yourself to me and I was withholding myself from you, or at least that's how you saw it. Why didn't you tell me back then?"

"Because I didn't think it was important for you to know at that time. You would have found out soon enough."

Taylor lowered her gaze for a moment, to nervously caress Alex's chest with her fingers, and then she looked back up into Alex's loving gaze.

"You're right, it didn't matter. I'm just glad I came to understand that before you left." Taylor said, as she leaned down and began kissing Alex's face.

Alex brought her hand up to catch hold of Taylor's chin, and she guided her lips down to hers. Their kiss started out tender and understanding, but soon developed into a more desirous and needing embrace. Taylor's body laid flat along Alex's long firm body, as Alex's hands soon moved down along Taylor's soft curved form. Taylor moaned at the sensual touches, as Alex's hands slid down her back and used her fingernails to graze gently down and over Taylor's back and behind. Alex kneaded the firm flesh in her hands, while pulling Taylor closer to her body. Soon Taylor began moving down Alex's body so as to take an aroused nipple into her mouth.

Alex now moaned as Taylor's loving mouth feasted on one of her breasts, and her hand kneaded and teased the other. It was Alex's turn to blush fiercely as her body lit up showing her aroused state. Alex's hands slipped up under Taylor's body and found their way to her breasts, where she took each breast in a hand and began caressing and kneading them. Her hands located Taylor's peaks and she rolled them between her fingers. Taylor's breathing was interrupted with gasps at different points as Alex's fingers pulled and twisted the peaks.

Alex's back soon arched, and Taylor's body trembled and then both stiffened as they once again brought each other to ecstasy.

After their rapture had passed for the moment, both women collapsed, with Taylor on top of Alex, their breathing heavy and labored. After a few minutes, Alex's breathing returned to normal and although Taylor's was still somewhat labored, Alex rolled the two of them over and she was now over Taylor.

"Are you ready for this to continue, sweetling?" Alex asked huskily.

"Yes, are you?"

"Oh...YES!" Alex stated emphatically, and brought her lips to Taylor's and hungrily kissed her. Taylor was soon caught back up, and they were both moaning into each other's throats.

Alex's hand soon drifted slowly down Taylor's body as she rolled onto her side and Taylor remained on her back. Alex's hand glided along Taylor's belly and down towards her womanly tresses, as she kissed Taylor intermittently. She felt Taylor's trembling body against her hand, and although Taylor was nervous, and a little scared, she trusted Alex to be gentle. So when Alex's hand put a little pressure upon Taylor's inner thigh, Taylor slowly spread her legs, and Alex smiled down at her. Taylor's hands slowly made their way down Alex's side and around to her belly, where she looked into Alex's eyes, slightly unsure of proceeding. But upon receiving an encouraging smile and a slight nod of Alex's head, Taylor's hand slid down over Alex's tresses as well. Alex closed her eyes as she felt Taylor's tentative touch, but opened them when she felt Taylor's exploring caress, becoming more confident, as she saw Alex's response to her touch. The two gazed deeply into each others loving, yet desire filled eyes.

Alex leaned down, and just before she captured Taylor's lips with her own, she asked with her eyes if she were ready once again. Taylor not only smiled to show she was, but she led the way, and slipped her exploring fingers into the forest of hair. Alex gasped at the entry, but she soon followed, and then the two captured each other's lips and for a while they just explored the different textures of each other's virtuous secrets. When they could no longer wait to experience their full love for one another, both women's bodies damp with perspiration, they wrapped one arm around each other and held each other tightly. They both seemed to be of one mind as they soon were experiencing the pain of their full love. Both gasped at that moment of their deflowering, and Tears filled both their eyes at the love and connection they felt for each other. And then...moments later, with encouragement from each other's touch, the sheer bliss of each other's love came crashing over them in such a powerful way, that both of their bodies shook in a cataclysmic orgasm.

When the body shaking orgasms had passed, and their bodies fell limply back to the bed. Alex was so wiped from the experience she was barely able to roll her and Taylor over, so that Taylor would be lying in her arms. Alex kissed Taylor and before they fell into their bliss induced slumbers, they whispered words of love to one another, and then drifted serenely off to sleep, embraced in each other's arms.

The next morning when Alex awoke, she moved somewhat stiffly as she turned onto her side to look at Taylor. Leaning forward she kissed Taylor on the forehead, and Taylor yawned, and stretched. She too felt stiff.

"Hmm...how do you feel, sweetling?" Alex asked, looking down at the somnolent figure as she caressed Taylor's cheek.

"Sore, but happier than I've been in my life. How about you?"

"Pretty much the same. Some experience last night huh?"

"Yes, it was. All sorts of emotions went through me at that very moment, but the strongest was the love and trust I have for you Alex."

Alex smiled.

"I know the feeling Taylor. I was actually scared for a brief moment, but then...I thought about how much I loved you and trusted you with my heart, and it was easy to trust you with all of me."

Taylor lifted up onto her elbow and, looking into Alex's beautiful eyes, she made an oath to Alex.

"I promise you, Alexandra Madison, you will never regret last night. I will do everything I can to make sure of that. I'm still overwhelmed at the thought that you entrusted ME not only with your heart a second time, but this time you added all that is you.

You left yourself open and vulnerable, and I promise never to cause you to question your choice. I absolutely love you. I get to see a side that NO ONE else has seen, and it causes my heart to swell with such love and admiration for you! I will find ways to show you every hour and moment of the day just how much I love and cherish you."

"And I will do the same. You will never regret last night if I can help it."

"I have no regrets. Now, I think I owe you breakfast in bed My Lady." Taylor said, as she leaned in and gave Alex a quick peck on her cheek. "I'll go get cleaned up and then I'll go make breakfast for you."

"Alright, and the apron is in the top drawer in the kitchen, the one you're to wear."

Taylor blushed and then grinned. She eased out of the bed, and her gait was different, but she made it to the bathroom. She knew she would have a reminder of last night on her thighs, due to it having been the first time for both of them. Taylor got in the shower and cleaned up.

Afterwards she dried off and oiled herself up. With her teeth, face, and body now clean, she put on a robe and went out of the bathroom, heading to the kitchen to make breakfast.

"See you in a bit." Alex said, as she watched Taylor make her way to the door.

After Taylor had gone, Alex started to jump out of the bed, but found she was a little too sore for that, so she too eased out of the bed.

"Hmm...very interesting." Alex said, allowing herself to feel everything as a result of last night. She was imprinting in her mind all of the feelings and sensations related to last night's experience. She would remember all of it, and although Alex would probably never tell Taylor that she did this, she couldn't see herself not doing it. It had been such a soul touching experience for her. That thought brought tears to Alex's eyes, and she inhaled slowly to compose herself. Then she stripped the bed, put clean linen on it, and went to get cleaned up herself.

CHAPTER 29

When Taylor returned, Alex was sitting on top of the freshly made bed in a white silk nightshirt.

"You got up, changed the linen and cleaned up?" Taylor asked, somewhat surprised.

"Yes, it didn't make sense to not do it. Anyway, the food smells wonderful, and YOU look absolutely d.e.l.e.c.t.a.b.l.e." Alex purred, as her eyes raked over Taylor's partially covered body.

The white apron had two straps that ran over the shoulders and fastened in the back on each side. The square cut top, covered Taylor's breasts just enough, but left a little to the imagination. Of course, Alex had no trouble with it. The apron covered all of the rest of Taylor's front, down to her thighs, and it had a strap across the back that held it in place, due to it being completely open.

"Turn around, sweetling." Alex cooed, as she continued to admire the sight of Taylor.

"Alex?" Taylor whimpered.

"Please?" Alex asked, with a voice that made Taylor shiver unexpectedly.

Taylor cocked her head at first, due to the ever so sweet plea coming from Alex. Then she slowly turned around while still holding the tray of food. Alex sighed with contentment, and then said to Taylor just as she came back around to face her.

"Beautiful." Taylor couldn't help blushing as a result of Alex's piercing gaze.

Taylor moved slowly over to the bed without taking her eyes off of Alex's. She bent down slightly to place the tray of food over Alex's lap, after extending the legs of the tray. Alex's gaze lowered just briefly to take in the sight of Taylor's breasts peeking out from within the top of the apron.

"Looks wonderful." Alex complimented. Not necessarily talking about the food.

Taylor caught it and grinned. Alex brought her hand up and guided Taylor's mouth to her own and placed a kiss of devotion on the young woman. Taylor had to hold herself up due to the weakening effect of Alex's kisses. After Alex let her go, Taylor barely was able to stand up straight, but she managed, as she composed herself. Then she looked into Alex's eyes, and she had to ask.

"How do you do that?!" She was still slightly breathless from the kiss.

"What?" Alex replied, as she picked up and broke a piece of toast. Using a fork, she took a bite of the sunny-side up eggs, as she looked up at Taylor.

"Kiss like that."

"Like what Taylor?"

"Like...well you know. It seems like every time you kiss me, I feel like I'm going to fall to the floor. I just can't understand how you're able to make me feel like that?"

"Hmm...I never thought about it. If I had to say something, I would have to say it's because of you still having such a fascination about me, and the fact that you are in love with me. You know how much I love you, and I think all of those things heighten your sensitivity to my touches, which I will admit, I certainly do love." Alex finished, as she raised a teasing brow at Taylor, who was now trying to hold back a grin.

"Okay." Taylor said quickly, due to not knowing if she could say anything more without embarrassing herself.

"Here, sit down and have some." Alex said, offering some of her breakfast to Taylor.

"You know we never ate dinner last night, but all of the food was put away in the refrigerator?" Taylor asked, informing Alex of what they had forgotten about.

"I know. I thought about it, before I came into the shower with you, but I decided I wanted you more than I wanted the food."

"Aha...well, as a result, you're stuck with me." Taylor said, with a different tone than the one she had previously been speaking in. Her hand came up to Alex's cheek to caress it, but this time, Alex caught her hand with her own, and looking Taylor straight in the eyes, she smiled and turned the hand over and kissed the palm. Taylor's eyes now glistened and when Alex let loose of her hand, she leaned in and wrapped her arms around Alex's neck.

"I just love you so much." Taylor said through the tightening in her throat.

Alex wrapped her arms around Taylor and whispered the same to her as they held one another.

"You're such a sensitive soul Taylor Young."

Taylor leaned back and said with a smile.

"And you're a closet romantic Alexandra Madison."

They both laughed at the teasing, and then went back to sharing the food. The two finally decided to get dressed, but Alex was surprised when Taylor dressed in a business suit.

"Where are you going?"

Taylor just smiled and walked over to the dresser, and opening the drawer, she pulled out Alex's appointment book and began going over her schedule for the day. Alex grinned brightly and gave Taylor a big hug as a result, then she settled into Taylor's cadence of her schedule. After Taylor finished and a few changes were made, Alex turned to look at her.

"Welcome back, sweetling, and thank you."

"Happy to be back, and you're welcome."

"By the way Taylor, I need you to do me a favor."

"What do you need?"

"I'd like you to call Zadria when we get to the office. Explain everything that has been happening and ask her if she will meet with us later today or tomorrow. Maybe we can help her save her company, and if she wants to, I want to implement your proposal. I called her once while you were gone, but she read me the riot act and hung up on me. She thought I was behind the buy up of her stock and she was also furious at me for hurting you. I don't think she'll talk to me until you explain it all to her."

Taylor walked over to Alex and said. "I'm sorry she yelled at you Alex."

Alex replied. "Don't be, sweetling. The fact that you evoke such loyalty from your friends shows what a special person you are. I'm just so sorry I treated you and your proposal the way that I did. Never in my life have I let my personal feelings affect work.

You did a superb job on that proposal, and found a way for everyone to benefit. I should have told you how proud I was of your work."

Taylor had tears running down her cheeks as she quietly said. "You just did. I love you Alex."

They embraced for long moments once again. Taylor then turned and picked up the phone and called for the driver. The car arrived and they headed to the office. When the car pulled up to the front entrance, Taylor was amazed by all of the activity that was going on.

"What's all this about?" Taylor asked, somewhat nervous.

"I don't know, but if I had to guess, I'd say it's about the arrest of the CEO of Wellington Inc."

"Oh, so what are they doing here?"

"I don't know, but there's only one way to find out. You up to this?"

"What?!" Taylor asked, now scared.

"Up to being questioned by reporters?"

"No, no, I can't! Alex!" Taylor gasped, now near tears at the very thought.

"It'll be alright. I promise. I'll be right there with you and if any question gets you stumped, I'll answer it, okay?"

Taylor looked into Alex's eyes and saw that she would be fine, and she visibly relaxed as a result.

"Okay, but only because I trust you, not them." Taylor said, making sure Alex understood why she would endure such public acknowledgement.

"Good. I know the first few will be directed at me, but the moment they find out who you are, they will be on you like white on rice. Don't worry, I will be there the whole time."

"Okay."

Alex leaned over and kissed Taylor in a reassuring manner. When she was sure Taylor was ready, she unlocked the door and the driver opened it. Alex stepped out first, wearing a white and black trimmed, double-breasted suit, and the press was all over her.

"Ms. Madison! Ms. Madison! Is it true that it was one of your employees who was involved in the insider trading with the CEO of the Wellington company?!"

"Yes." Alex answered simply, as she was surrounded by the press. Taylor stayed in the car for a few moments to watch Alex deal with the press with grace and sophistication. Her admiration showed in her eyes, and when Alex turned to glance in Taylor's direction, she smiled and then took a deep breath.

Alex smirked at Taylor, although the press thought she was being her usual self. Taylor stepped out of the car, and Alex introduced her after receiving an approving nod of Taylor's head to indicate she was ready.

"This, ladies and gentlemen of the press, is my Personal Assistant, who was instrumental in the discovery of who the insider was."

Suddenly it seemed as though time itself had stopped, when first one, then another, and then finally all of the press were now surrounding Taylor and throwing question after question at her. Taylor was initially flustered. Then Alex came to stand by her, and she looked up into her eyes and with a slight nod from Alex, Taylor took another deep breath and finally spoke.

"Yes it is true." That was all Taylor needed to say, because the press was off and running with question after question. Soon Taylor had gotten comfortable and her confidence showed as she answered some questions and deferred others to Alex.

Finally, they excused themselves from the press and walked inside of the building. At first the two were just walking side by side, but when Alex put her arm around Taylor's shoulder and pulled the girl to her to congratulate her on how she had handled the press, a reporter happened to be watching them, and he took a quick few pictures. That afternoon, the papers all ran a special edition. The headlines said different things, but all had the same theme.

"Personal Assistant Takes Down Wellington, Company and all."

Both Alex and Taylor were on the front cover, but on one of them, it was two pictures, one of the two of them talking to the press and the other of Alex with her arm around Taylor's shoulder, holding her close to her. Underneath the picture was a caption that read.

"Personal Assistant, and obvious companion and friend."

Alex smirked when she saw it, and upon reading the article her eyes widened with both amusement and concern. She glanced at Taylor, and then handed the paper over for her to look at.

"Here, what do you think?"

Taylor took the paper and after reading the caption, she looked up at Alex. Then she looked back down at the paper and read the article.

"Oh my goodness!! They found out all about me, and my inheritance."

"Are you okay with their assumptions and the fact that the world knows about your inheritance? I mean, they are correct, but they don't know that for sure."

"Hmm...actually, I don't know. But it won't change anything between us, I promise you that. I am a little concerned that they found out about my inheritance. There's no telling what creeps will come out of the woodwork."

"That's all I wanted to hear Taylor. I just want you to know that I know this morning was scary for you, as is this, but you trusted me, and it showed in how you handled the press, very impressive. I'm so proud of you. You've come out of your shell a lot since that first time we met. You've grown into a very sophisticated young businesswoman, despite your having left for a while. You haven't lost a step. If anything, it made you stronger. It took a lot of courage to come to me and tell me how you felt. You risked rejection, and my anger, but you had the courage, and you swallowed your pride to come to me, and it paid off. Now, as far as your inheritance, just ask me about any strange requests or opportunities that seem too good to be true. Also, be watchful at what's going on around you, that way no one will take you by surprise. Always, and I can't stress this enough, always tell me where you're going and when you will be back. Leave me a note or something, that way I won't worry about you. Even if you get upset with me about something."

"Okay. But you know I will never leave for any reason again. You know I never make the same mistake. Now, as far as coming to talk to you about things that day, it was so...scary, but not as scary as when you showed up at that hotel I was staying in. I was sure you were going to break me in half if you got your hands on me. Lucky for me, Yasmeia showed up and was able to help explain things. By the way, did I say thank you for the promotion you gave Yasmeia?"

"Yes, but I didn't do it because I owed her anything. I did it because she deserved it."

"I know, but thank you anyway."

"You're welcome."

The rest of the day Alex and Taylor went about their work. Taylor having her own desk and things once again set up in the large office of Alex's. Taylor had set up the meeting with Zadria after explaining everything to her. The meeting had gone well. Zadria apologized to Alex for what she had said, but Alex told her not to worry about it. She was just glad that Taylor had friends who were so loyal to her. The three women had worked out the business aspects after that. Alex's corporation would form an "umbrella" of protection for Zadria as well as pumping much needed capital into the company. Within a week of the information getting to the media, Zadria Fashions was well on the road back to recovery.

Over the next few weeks, things seemed to be going smoothly, as if Alex and Taylor had not been apart.

One morning when Taylor and Alex were working in the office, the phone rang and Taylor picked it up.

"Ms. Madison's office, Ms. Young speaking, may I help you?"

"Taylor, this is your Aunt Dorothy."

"Oh, hi, how are you and the family?" Taylor said somewhat uneasily.

"Fine, just fine. We saw you in the paper sometime back."

"Oh."

"We were so proud of you when we read that you were the key person who brought that man and his company down, along with that woman inside of the company you work for."

"Well, thank you, um...I don't mean to sound impolite or anything Aunt Dorothy, but...why are you calling?"

"Oh, I wanted to get together with you and talk. I mean, we see so little of each other."

"Oh, well, I don't..."

"Oh please don't say no. I'll meet you at mother's house, or better yet, we can meet at the hotel in town."

"There??"

"Yes, you know this area, I don't know that one."

"Oh, well, alright, I'll see you tomorrow at 1pm at the hotel in town?"

"Okay, see you then. Bye Taylor." The woman hung up and Taylor sat shocked that she had agreed to meet her aunt. She hadn't seen much of the family before, and definitely not after her grandmother's death.

"Taylor? Everything alright?" Alex asked having heard Taylor's stressed filled voice.

Taylor looked over at Alex who was watching her with a concerned look on her face.

"Oh, yes, fine. That was my aunt. She wants to see me, so I told her I would see her tomorrow at the hotel."

"What hotel?"

"The one in my home town."

"Oh, well I guess no one could miss it, considering it is the only one in the town close to your grandmother's. When will you be back?"

"Tomorrow night. I have no intention of staying there, away from you."

"Well, I'm happy to hear that. At least I know I'll have my pillows." Alex said with a wry smirk. Taylor blushed.

"You're so bad." Taylor chided playfully.

"I know." Alex said waggling her brows.

Taylor chuckled at Alex's playfulness, then stood up and said she was going to go and get the mail.

"Okay, scaredy-cat." Alex teased.

"Very funny, ha, ha, ha." Taylor said, opening the door to leave.

"I'll call and make arrangements for the jet to take you there and a car to meet you and take you to the hotel. I'll also reserve a room for you just in case you can't make it back, okay?"

"Oh, okay, thank you, but I won't be staying." Taylor said again, assuring Alex that she was just going there to see her aunt and return home.

"Good, but it doesn't hurt to be prepared. Go get the mail and I'll take care of your arrangements."

"Alright, do you want anything from the dining hall while I'm down that way?"

"Hmm...I'll take a slice of cheesecake, a very SMALL piece."

"Okay, I'll be back in a few minutes."

"Alright." Alex picked up the phone and called the airport to have her pilot and the plane prepared. Then she called the operator for the number to the hotel in the town where Taylor was going to be meeting her aunt. Alex gave the operator the information she needed and then the operator gave the number to Alex. She dialed the number and made the arrangements. Then she thought about something that Taylor had once told her about her grandmother's kids. How they seemed to always show up when they wanted something, always taking, but never giving. Alex made another call to Kiara and told her what she wanted. Kiara assured Alex she understood what she wanted, and they hung up. When Taylor returned a while later, Alex made a suggestion to her.

"Taylor, I was just thinking while you were gone. Would you like me to go with you?"

"Oh...Alex that is so sweet of you, and I really am touched by it, but you know, it really isn't necessary. I'm only going for a short time, and I'll be back before it gets late here. Besides, I know we have a lot of meetings planned. At least by you staying, you'll get all the information first hand and you can tell them exactly what you want from them."

"Okay, you made your point, but you know I would leave it to Shearer to handle in a moment if you wanted me to go?"

"I know, and I appreciate it."

"Okay, well here's all the information for your trip tomorrow."

The next day Taylor said goodbye to Alex, and after a love filled kiss, Alex let her go.

Taylor got into the waiting car and was off to the airport. Taylor arrived at the hotel, went inside and was greeted by not only her aunt, but also all of the other aunts and uncles. There were four aunts and two uncles. Taylor was taken aback by the sight of all of them.

"Taylor you made it! I was afraid you'd changed your mind."

"What's going on?"

"Oh, nothing, I just told them that you were coming for a visit and they wanted to see you."

"Oh, well I can't stay long. What is it that you wanted to see me about?"

"Well, rather than talk about this here, why don't we get a room and we can talk there."

"Well, I already have a room." Taylor said, as she turned and walked over to the desk. She asked for her key and then headed for the elevator with her family following her. They all got on and went up to the fourth floor; Alex had gotten a moderately priced room due to what she thought the family was up to. Taylor got off the elevator and led them to the room. After she opened it and went in, they all followed inside. She stood holding the door open for a moment longer, while watching all of them look around the room, and then she closed the door.

"This is nice Taylor, it must be something to be able to afford this suite?"

"It's okay, it's not expensive, and it's not a suite, it's just a room."

"Well, at least you know you could afford an expensive room if you wanted to."

"What do you mean?" Taylor asked, now certain of where the conversation was going, but not wanting to let on just yet.

"Oh, Dorothy, stop beating around the bush! Taylor we know about the 60 million dollars!" Ray, her uncle, stated bitterly.

"Okay, I wasn't trying to hide anything, the whole world knows about it. What's your point?"

"We want our share of it!"

"Excuse me?"

"You heard me!"

"Ray! Calm down. Taylor, it's just that we're her children and that money should be ours."

"Well, obviously Grammy didn't see it that way. Besides, she left all of you a nice bit of money for yourselves and all of your kid's educations."

"Well Mom was wrong."

"How was she wrong? You know Aunt Dorothy, I had a feeling that this is what this meeting was about. I was willing to give you the benefit of the doubt, but...you've proved my first thoughts right! The only time you guys show up is when you want something! Whenever Grammy called for any of you to help with something, well actually it was me who called, because Grammy never wanted to ask any of you for anything, because she knew. I told her that maybe she was just being a little sensitive about all of you. But she said no, you guys were leeches to the 10th power. Think about it! Every time I called and asked any of you to help with something of Grammy's, what did you tell me?" Taylor paused for a moment to give them time to think of what they had said, but when they didn't answer she answered for them. "I'll tell you what you said, 'Sorry Hon, but I just don't have time to come over there and do that.' Or, what about this one, when the roof needed to be reshingled, and she wanted to hire someone to come in and do it. I told her to ask one of you guys to come over and do it, especially seeing how both of my uncles had experience in construction. But did you come? No, instead you told me, 'Have the old woman hire someone to do it, I don't have time.' Or this one, when the ice caused the pipes to break and there was no water for four days...Uncle Larry can you come over and help with repairing the water pipes, they've ruptured and now there is no water. Your answer: 'Sorry darling, it's just too cold to go outside, when it warms up I'll stop by. In the meantime just collect some of the ice from outside and melt it down and you can use that as your water supply. HA!' Then you hung up. But then, whenever you needed anything, any of you, Grammy, though reluctant, which you never knew, gave you help with what you wanted and asked for because I talked her into it. Time and time again, Grammy was there for all of you, but never not once were you there for her.

You only showed up to the funeral so that you could meet the lawyer who would read the will. Well, what Grammy left you is all you will get, and to be honest with you, none of you deserve that! You were horrible children to your own mother, and now when you hear she had a lot of money, oh...all of you come crawling out of the woodwork like bugs. Well I'm the 'Raid' and you might as well just crawl back in, because it will be a cold day in hell when I even THINK about giving you any more than Grammy already left you. I would also venture to guess you guys have already tried to get your way with Ms. Levy. She told you there was nothing you could do legally, because it was a will that a woman in her right mind wrote up and signed. The fact is each of you waived any further claim on Grammy's estate when you got what you thought was all there was to get. Not hearing my name mentioned during that meeting, I'm sure you all thought what a fool I've been assuming Grammy really cared about me. Well, you see she did, just like I adored Grammy. Anyway, I believe that's why you guys asked Aunt Dorothy to call me and see if I would be willing to give you some of the money. Well, now you see, I'm not. So if that's all, I think I will be leaving." Taylor turned to leave, but was stopped by her Uncle Ray's voice.

"Well, it's going to be a shame that Pastor Samuels and the church has to find out about his favorite little missionary. Being involved in a relationship with a WOMAN should be enough to have you thrown out of the church I would think."

Taylor turned slowly around to look at Ray and then looked at the others. She saw they were serious, and they saw her uncertainty.

"You think about it. You have one week, and then it's either you give us all 5 million each, or you get kicked out of the church."

Taylor now had anger and hurt in her eyes and she once again turned to leave, only to hear one of her aunts say in a taunting tone.

"Wow, hell sure froze fast."

Taylor didn't look back, she just gave a derisive "hmpff", and walked out the door. She made it to the lobby before the tears began to roll. She had the concierge call for her car. She paid for the room while she waited, and the woman behind the counter asked her if she was all right.

"Fine." Taylor said as she saw the car pull up. She quickly headed out the doors for it. She jumped inside and was just being driven away when she saw all of her aunts and uncles come out and watch her go.

After Taylor was out of sight, Kiara had one of her investigators pretend to be a reporter wanting a story.

"Excuse me? Hi...Do you all know that woman?"

"Yes, why?"

"I'm doing a story on her."

"Oh, what type of story?"

"Well it's not really her that the story will be about, but those people who know her. I am collecting different comments from friends of hers. I haven't met any of her family yet, but who knows? Maybe I will."

"Is there any money for us if we give you an interview?"

"Yes, but it depends on who you are to the woman."

"Oh, okay, well we are all her aunts and uncles."

"Yeah right, as if her whole family would just happen to be in one place?"

"Well that's who we are! Whether you believe it or not is your choice."

"Okay, fine. Here, here's a hundred dollars for each of you. Now I need to get all of your names and addresses on this, along with your phone numbers and occupations. This is in case I want to get more comments from you later, we need to be able to contact you." The fake reporter handed them a pad and they wrote all the information that was requested, and handed it back to him.

He then proceeded to ask them questions on how they felt about their niece having been the one to discover the insider-trading scam. They gave him answers of how proud they were of her and things like that.

"Well, thank you! I think I have enough to write the article, thank you." The man turned and walked to his rental car and left them all standing there, talking excitedly to each other.

CHAPTER 30

Kiara called Alex and told her about the conversation she had overheard. She said that the family information would arrive soon so she could collect the tax information on all of them.

Later that night Taylor arrived back home and after going inside, she was greeted by Alex, and they talked about other things for a bit. Alex sat waiting for Taylor to tell her about the trip and what had happened, even though she already knew everything. Taylor talked about anything other than her meeting. Alex decided to wait for the girl to bring it up. For the next two days Taylor was quiet and somewhat aloof.

That night when Taylor went to sleep, Alex looked over at the figurine that the girl had bought for her, and in so doing, she remembered a letter from Taylor's grandmother. The one that she had left for Alex in her will, that Alex had yet to read.

She jumped out of bed and went to the dresser. Pulling open the third drawer, she picked the envelope up and closed the drawer with her hip as she turned and headed back to the bed. Alex climbed back in the bed and opened the envelope to read the letter. Alex read the words that brought a smile to her lips. They read... " Ms. Madison, Alex, I know that Taylor has been stressed over the loss of you in her life, and her worry about me. Although I can't do anything about The Lord calling me home, I figure I could leave a loving gift for my granddaughter. I was not excited about the fact that you and my little one were about to get involved in a relationship with each other. But because of my love for Taylor and my great desire to always see her happy, along with the conversations I've overheard between her and Ms. Sains, I see now how much you are a part of her life. I realize she could never be happy with anyone else but you, and because of all of these reasons, I am now willing to admit I may have been wrong. But wrong or right, you and Taylor belong together, and therefore the two of you have my blessing. I hope you will work things out and both be happy. Always TALK! It's the only way for a relationship to work or have any chance of working. Well, I'm a little tired, so I am going to end this and say I send my love to both Taylor and to you. Welcome to our family Alexandra Madison. God Bless."

Alex once again saw where Taylor got her sensitive heart. She also saw the potential for strength in the shy young woman, who had grown in confidence, but still had a ways to go.

The next morning, on the third day after Taylor had returned from seeing her family, Alex planned on confronting Taylor on her behavior if Taylor didn't tell her. Something must have been in the air that morning, because when they arrived at the office and were working on different things, Taylor happened to look up into Alex's distressed eyes. At that moment, Taylor saw what she was doing.

She stood up and walked over to the office door and closed it, then walked over to Alex's desk and hit the blind closure button. She then sat on the edge of the desk next to Alex's chair, Alex watched her, perplexed at what Taylor was doing.

"Alex, I have been holding something back from you because I didn't know how to handle it. Just as I was sitting there, I looked up and even though you weren't looking at me, I saw the distress in your eyes. I knew it wasn't about these reports you were reading over, but about me. Alex, my LOVING family is trying to blackmail me, and I don't know what to do. Will you help me?"

"That's all I wanted to hear Taylor. I knew the first night you came back that something bad had happened, but I was sure you would tell me the next morning. When you didn't, I thought well, she just needs a day to figure out a way for her to handle it herself. When two days came and went and still you hadn't told me, I started to get worried. Then this morning came and you didn't tell me, so I had planned on confronting you. But...you didn't break your word, you didn't repeat the same mistake, and for that I am very thankful. Thank you, sweetling. Sit here." Alex said offering Taylor a seat on her thighs.

Taylor sat down on Alex's lap and wrapped her arms around Alex's neck and they held each other for a few minutes. Then Alex held Taylor back to look her in the eyes. After handing her a Kleenex, she picked up the letter from Taylor's grandmother and handed it to the girl to read.

"This is from your grandmother to me. It's the one you brought to me during my spring party. Read it."

Taylor took the letter and quickly read over it. Tears started running down her face for two reasons; one, that she was able to read her grandmother's last words, and two, because her grandmother left her with a gift that was going to make her happy for the rest of her life.

"Grammy..." Taylor sobbed, and Alex took her in her arms once again and held her, as Taylor let her heart open fully, with no reservations left.

"See, things always work out."

"I see. You're my lucky charm." Taylor said through the tears that were still rolling down her face, but now she had a smile on her face. The stress that she and Alex had was a thing of the past. They both just wiped the tears from each other's cheeks and then hugged once again.

"Okay, now I already have plans for your LOVING family." Alex picked up the phone and asked Taylor for her aunt's number. Taylor gave it to her and she dialed it. She set up a meeting for the next day.

The next day came and she had the meeting set up in her conference room. She knew the aunt would bring the others. This time she had them come to her. Taylor was not there on purpose at Alex's request.

"Now, I understand from a reliable source that you all want five million dollars each of Taylor's money?"

"It's not Taylor's money."

"The law says it is, therefore, it is."

"Well whatever, the point is, it was our mother, and therefore, it belongs to us anyway."

"I heard the whole argument, so let me tell you what the point is, this way, there will be no confusion. I know for a fact that the money that your mother left to Taylor was accumulated mostly from Taylor's direct advice to her grandmother about investments, and between the two of them, her grandmother was able to accumulate the vast amount of her money. But if that's not enough to convince you to back off, then let me tell you this. I have financial information on all of you, and in looking over all of it, I see that all of you have lied numerous times on your 1040's, especially in the deduction column. I'm sure the IRS would love to see why you've received refunds, when in fact, according to your financial statements, you should have been paying. And judging from the number of years that you all have been doing your taxes, you all owe at the minimum, 20 thousand, give or take a few thousand."

"So? I'm sure you padded your taxes as well, so as not to pay capital gains." Taylor's Uncle Ray stated.

"Actually there isn't enough padding in the world where I could get out of paying capital gains. I own too much! Anyway, this isn't about me, but about all of you."

"What do you want?"

"It's simple enough. You stay out of Taylor's life. You have no contact with her and you should be satisfied with the fact that your mother had some feelings for such an ungrateful group of people. She still left you something in her will."

"And if we don't?"

Those words brought out "The Raider's" competitive nature, and her eyes narrowed and a predatory gaze was cast at all at the table. Alex then said, with obvious adrenaline coursing through her veins, "Then I will ruin EACH and EVERY ONE of your lives, and never get my hands dirty. So, what will it be? You have five seconds to decide."

"Okay, you have a deal. We won't bother Taylor again, and you don't give the IRS that information." Dorothy said with a wavering voice.

"Great, now get out. " Alex growled, and motioned for the guards who were standing outside the door to come in and escort the group out.

"Yes ma'am?"

"Show them out." Alex stood and headed for the door, but stopped when she got to it.

"Enjoy your stay for the day, and then I don't ever expect to see any of you again." She then turned to walk out of the room. Just before she walked out the door, she saw Taylor's Uncle Ray looking at her. Alex could tell from the look on his face that he was already trying to think of a way to get even with her. She continued through the doorway while making a mental note to keep a watchful eye on him. If there was any trouble in the future, it was a good bet he would be behind it. She could hear the group cursing as they were escorted out into the elevator.

Later that night, Alex and Taylor were talking. Alex had just told her the highlights of her meeting with the family. Then Taylor said in a contented voice.

"You're just so...good."

That reminded Alex of something that Taylor had asked her once before, and so as she held Taylor she began listing some things.

"I'm not patient. I have no tolerance for a liar or a thief. I'm not good at showing my feelings to anyone other than you. I'm not good at letting others have their way. I'm not good at holding my tongue if I think something needs to be said. I'm not used to showing my emotions, but I am learning. I'm not used to all of the emotions you've elicited from me, and I'm very unsteady as a result. I'm not good at camping and have no interest in it. I'm no good at staying on my side of the bed when you're in it, and I am no good at controlling myself when it comes to my love for you."

"I knew there were things you weren't good at. There had to be." Taylor said, as she yawned and her eyes fluttered, trying to stay open, but finally they just stayed closed. She drifted off right there on the carpet-covered floor in Alex's arms.

"Yes, sweetling, there are. Sweet dreams kitten." Alex said, as she kissed Taylor's forehead, and then laid her head next to Taylor's. They let the warmth of the fireplace flow over them as the rain poured down beating a methodical rhythm against the roof and sides of the house outside.